"*A Taste of Desire* is de... paced. Once I start a Beverley Kendall book, I don't put it down until I'm done."

—Cathy Maxwell, *New York Times* bestselling author

"Sexy and dramatic—*A Taste of Desire* solidifies Beverley Kendall's reputation as a rising Victorian talent."

—Sophia Nash, author of *Secrets of a Scandalous Bride*

SINFUL SURRENDER

"Beverley Kendall is a fresh new voice in historical romance."

—Anna Campbell, author of *My Reckless Surrender*

"*Sinful Surrender* is a delightful and captivating mix of rich characters, heart-warming romance, and heart-pounding sensuality. I loved it! All I could think was, I want James. I want two of him."

—Alissa Johnson, author of *Destined to Last*

"*Sinful Surrender* is a well-written, rich journey filled with intrigue, desire, and heartfelt romance. Don't miss this exciting debut!"

—Jacquie D'Alessandro, *New York Times* bestselling author

"*Sinful Surrender* is a delightful debut! Beverley Kendall writes with wit and passion!"

—Sophie Jordan, *New York Times* bestselling author

"In her fresh and charming debut, Kendall's natural wit and fine voice shine through . . . an en...

—*RomanticTimes Book Reviews*

Also by Beverley Kendall

SINFUL SURRENDER

Published by Kensington Publishing Corp.

A TASTE
OF DESIRE

BEVERLEY KENDALL

ZEBRA BOOKS
KENSINGTON PUBLISHING CORP.
http://www.kensingtonbooks.com

ZEBRA BOOKS are published by

Kensington Publishing Corp.
119 West 40th Street
New York, NY 10018

All Kensington titles, imprints, and distributed lines are available at special quantity discounts for bulk purchases for sales promotion, premiums, fund-raising, educational, or institutional use.

Special book excerpts or customized printings can also be created to fit specific needs. For details, write or phone the office of the Kensington Special Sales Manager: Attn. Special Sales Department. Kensington Publishing Corp., 119 West 40th Street, New York, NY 10018. Phone: 1-800-221-2647.

Zebra and the Z logo Reg. U.S. Pat. & TM Off.

ISBN-13: 978-1-4201-0870-5
ISBN-10: 1-4201-0870-0

First Printing: January 2011

10 9 8 7 6 5 4 3 2 1

Printed in the United States of America

To my mother,
who has always been there for me,
and is always *there for me.*

I love you, Mom.

ACKNOWLEDGMENTS

To Mary-Cannon and Anastasia, as always, your critiques are essential to a good story and clean manuscript. To Barb, the best query critiquer ever. And most of all, to my son, Ryan, who slept early enough to allow me to write this book. I love you, sweetie.

Chapter 1

London, 1856

As Thomas, Viscount Armstrong, digested Harold Bertram's words, he came up straight in his seat, his hands finding the curved arms of the chair. Although the marquess delivered the request with all the gravity of a clergyman officiating a funeral, Thomas *prayed* he hadn't heard him correctly.

"You would like me to do what?" Thomas issued the question in a soft voice and an even calmer tone, but the sound cracked the air like the report of a rifle.

The marquess gave a mirthless laugh and shot a quick glance at the study doors before shifting his regard back to him. "I am asking you to-to take my daughter under your care during my stay in America."

Thomas suffered through the second such insupportable request in as many days—this one even more painful than the last.

Only the prior day, a peer in the House of Lords had presented him with the kind of offer that sent honest men hurtling full-tilt down the unsavory road to perdition. He hadn't thought it could possibly get more unseemly than that.

He was wrong.

What Harry spoke of was not about politics and one-thousand-pound bribes; this was one hundred times worse.

"It would be—er—up until the new year unless I could conclude the negotiations in less time."

Harold Bertram, the Marquess of Bradford, or Harry as he preferred close acquaintances to call him, was not a lack wit—though many might doubt that assertion at the present time. He possessed the sharpest mind in matters of finance and business, and could articulate—when not suffering a brain lapse—with the eloquence of an orator the likes of which Caesar and Henley never saw. However, his nineteen-year-old daughter could fray the nerves of even the most battle-seasoned soldier. Thomas himself could attest to that.

Fixing the marquess—who had fallen conspicuously mute—with an unblinking stare, Thomas cocked his brow. Harry must have indeed taken leave of his senses. The chit had finally driven him to that.

"If this is a joke, I assure you, I do not find it the least bit amusing," Thomas replied, when he finally recovered enough to speak. "I mean, we are speaking about Lady Amelia, are we not? Unless, pray tell, you have yet another daughter hidden away who is *not* a disrespectful termagant?"

A round of uncomfortable clearing of the throat ensued, followed by a weary-to-the-bones exhalation. "Heavens, then tell me what I'm to do with her? If I take her with me, I would have neither the time nor energy to keep her out of her usual mischief, especially in a country where I lack familiarity. At present, you are the only person I trust enough to come to regarding this matter. Perhaps if the trip weren't of such importance, and I could rearrange my schedule. . . ." Harry sent him a silent look of appeal.

At his words, Thomas's conscience received a faint prick, but thankfully, the feeling lasted no more than a few seconds. In his estimation, voyaging to America in the interest of a business endeavor could not compare to subjecting himself to playing taskmaster to Harry's recalcitrant daughter.

Leaning forward, Thomas's fingers curled into the napped fabric of the armrest. "If you requested I take your place at the guillotine or the hangman's noose I would consider that less of an imposition."

Harry's eyebrows met above a straight patrician nose as his mustachioed mouth gave a faint twitch. "I am going to be frank with you. That gir—daughter of mine seems most determined to deliver me to an early grave. She's managed to embroil herself with yet another ne'er-do-well. This time, if my manservant hadn't been so careful, I would be forced to call that worthless Clayborough my son-in-law." He spat the man's name as if a more foul sound could not pass his lips.

"Harry," Thomas said on a long, drawn-out sigh, subsiding back into the chair. "Perhaps it would be best if you permitted her to marry whomever she pleases. Wouldn't it be easier than chasing her across the wilds of every county in England? She *has* reached the age to wed." Let some poor unfortunate bastard take her on. Thomas was certain the man would be crying foul within months of the marriage once he realized the bargain he'd struck.

A dull thud echoed throughout the study as Harry's fisted hand collided vigorously with the glossy veneered finish of his mahogany desk. "No! The last thing I want is that wastrel for a son-in-law. Heavens above, I am well aware my daughter is a considerable handful, but I have a duty as her father to protect her from such men." His voice dropped low. "Her poor mother would turn over in her grave if she knew what has become of her only child."

A poignant sadness dimmed the light in his friend's eyes at the mention of his departed wife, and in that moment, Thomas was ashamed of his unfeeling suggestion that he knowingly allow Harry's daughter to wed a gambler and fortune hunter. But good God, if any woman deserved such a fate, surely Lady Amelia Bertram topped that ignominious list.

To even contemplate Harry's request—which he certainly was not—would be a hairbreadth shy of insanity, but the friend in him felt compelled to justify his refusal. "Just what would you have me do with her in that time? I will assume you wouldn't allow me to put her to *work?*" Though, the thought did bring a rueful smile to his face. It would be nothing less than she deserved. Thomas was certain she didn't even know the meaning of the word, much less participate in any activity more taxing than angling her insolent nose in the air.

Harry's face brightened like a street urchin spying a crown on a sidewalk along the streets of the East End. "Now that is something I never considered. It is really a capital idea, albeit somewhat unorthodox. Yes, it might be just what she needs to acquire a modicum of temperance. This time I am determined she learn her lesson. Mind you, the work itself cannot be menial or anything of that sort." The latter he added more solemnly.

So, Harry would be amenable to putting her to work. Thomas had only intended it as a joke. The notion was absurd. He smiled. But so fitting.

After a moment, the marquess's eyes sparked again. "Perhaps she could act as a companion to your sisters?"

Thomas sobered immediately. The gleam in his friend's blue eyes signified hopes soaring high, something he had to quash before he found her deposited on his front doorstep, trunks and all. "My sisters will be accompanying my mother to America for six weeks this winter." And one of the ten plagues of Egypt would plunge London into utter darkness for three days if he even considered thrusting Lady Amelia upon his family.

Plowing a hand through his hair, Thomas sighed again. "Lord, you've seen us together. I'd have an easier time taming a wild boar. She'd exhaust my patience in the first hour, never mind days, much less weeks on end. What your daughter needs is a guard dog."

Harry compressed his mouth into a straight line.

"Or perhaps you can find her a suitable gentleman who will divert her from her more, er, spirited activities," Thomas corrected more judiciously. He really must remember to whom he spoke. As close as he and Harry were, the poor man *was* the girl's father.

Harry tugged at the brass closures of his navy blue waistcoat as if it had suddenly become too tight. "Well, I cannot say that I particularly blame you, as the two of you did not have an auspicious start."

Ha! That was like saying Waterloo had been a mere spat between neighboring countries. "I'd say that would be phrasing it nicely," Thomas said, his tone arid.

Pushing the chair back, Harry slowly arose. Thomas took his cue and came swiftly to his feet. With resignation sketching his features, the marquess extended his hand across a desk surfeit with plumed pens, elegant black inkwells, and stacks of papers and books. Thomas accepted it with a flash of regret. Not regret for refusing his request, but regret that it had been one he could not in his right mind accept. Had he been feeble of mind, perhaps. Sound of mind, never.

"I bear you no ill will, although I had hoped . . ." Harry offered a faint smile. "It is quite unfortunate that Amelia did not choose to take up with a man more like you."

Thomas's gaze probed his friend's as he disengaged his hand. He had known Harry for six years and was well aware of the man's deep affection for him. But surely Harry hadn't made this proposal with hopes that he and Amelia would . . . ?

He tried to veer away from the thought before it could fully form in his head and take up residence in his mind. Unfortunately, the thought had a life of its own. The utter notion was beyond absurd, but in all likelihood would send Harry into fits of jubilation—were he inclined to such behavior. A union between he and Amelia would not only give the marquess a son-in-law he both admired and respected but more important, someone with mettle enough to control his unruly daughter.

A dark laugh emerged from somewhere deep in Thomas's throat. "That would indeed be a match bound for the fires of perdition."

A wry smile twisted Harry's mouth. "Yes, it appears so."

In silence, both men made their way to the study entrance. While they paused at the door, Harry clapped his hand across the width of Thomas's back, giving his shoulder two solid thumps.

"I still have another month before my departure. If you should reconsider, please let me know."

Thomas admired the man's doggedness, but he'd willingly board a ship of prisoners bound for New South Wales first.

Amelia knew her father was angry.

He'd spoken not one word to her since that loathsome Mr. Ingles had dragged her, quite literally, from the coach not even two miles outside of town. With the crush of conveyances on Piccadilly and Regent Street, she and Lord Clayborough would have been better served if they'd attempted their elopement to Gretna Green on foot.

Thirty minutes gone, her father had requested her presence in the study. Still more than piqued at the unfairness of her three-day confinement to her bedchamber, she'd dawdled, doing absolutely naught before commencing the interminable walk downstairs to meet with her irate parent.

Upon reaching the study, she blithely thrust open the door, only to make jarring contact with a body standing on the other side.

She heard the *thwack* and a low masculine grunt—the sound a mixture of surprise and pain. Instinctively, she took a quick step back, her hand still clutching the knob. Lord, what was her father doing—?

Before she could complete the thought, Lord Armstrong's imposing form stepped into view, tapered fingers rubbing a spot near his right temple. He observed her through narrowed eyes, emerald green and ponderously lashed, pinning her with the type of look meant solely to make a person squirm.

Squirming was not in her nature, but her heart performed an odd lurch and her pulse quickened at the sight of her father's protégé. She was once again unsettled to discover that with each meeting, the golden-haired viscount could elicit such a response in her. But then—she made a surreptitious sweep of his body—he did exude an elegance and raw masculinity she grudgingly conceded might appeal to a less discerning woman—which, thankfully, she was not.

"Pardon me." Amelia kept her tone level and polite. Easing the door open wide enough to allow for the sheer volume of two layers of stiff petticoats beneath her blue, flounced skirt, she entered the room. She immediately blinked against the glare of the sun pouring through large paned windows dominating the eastward-facing walls.

She caught the clean, subtle whiff of bergamot and rosemary. His scent. She'd recognize it blindfolded and spun around. How she'd grown to thoroughly dislike that scent. She loathed the man with whom she'd forever associate it even more. Inhaling a breath deep and slow, she took up a spot on the area rug, a comfortable distance from both men.

"I didn't expect *someone* would place himself so near a closed door," she added in case he'd misconstrued her statement as an apology.

Her father's face seized up as if in the midst of an apoplexy. Lord Armstrong's mouth flattened, his regard narrowing to a squint. Amelia returned his stare placidly. He could stare—or glare, as it were—at her all he wanted. She didn't give a whit, ignoring her heart knocking a frantic beat beneath her breastbone.

"It is also customary to knock before opening a *closed* door," came the viscount's glib reply.

"Might I remind you, my lord, it is *I* who resides in this house." The gall of the man, trying to chastise her. Who told him he should situate himself thus? Hinges on doors were not meant as frivolous ornaments; they *did* have a purpose.

"Amelia is regrettably sorry," her father hastily interjected.

Like hell she is. The bloody woman had probably parked herself outside waiting for the opportunity to bash his head in. Thomas wouldn't put anything past her.

Tamping down his growing irritation, he replied smoothly, "Yes, Harry, I am quite certain she is."

"I do hope I'm not preventing you from leaving. You were on your way out, were you not?" she asked in dulcet tones, a smile curving her lips.

If it had been any other woman, Thomas could have envisioned many other uses for such a mouth, with plump lips the deep pink of a man's erotic dreams. And if one were dealing purely in aesthetics, who could fail to appreciate the dark-haired beauty's jaw-dropping figure, shown to its best advantage in a gown the exact sapphire blue of her eyes, the fitted corsage allowing for the glorious display of creamy skin. But as stunning as she was, he wouldn't have her if she begged him. Not that he would mind the begging part. That he would relish if only to have the pleasure of refusing her.

"Er . . . Thomas, thank you for calling. I expect I shall see you again before my departure."

Thomas issued Harry a curt nod. "Yes, I expect you will." He returned his attention to her. "And as always, Lady Amelia, it was a pleasure," he said, managing to remain quite straight-faced, for surely Judas could not have told a grander lie.

For a brief moment, something sparked in her blue

eyes, breathing life into the flawless, glacial beauty of her countenance and hinting at a slumbering fire. If he gave a damn—which he most assuredly did not—it'd give him cold satisfaction to see her icy hauteur reduced to a puddle on the floor.

"Yes, but as we are both well aware, if I claimed likewise it would be a blatant untruth."

The cheeky little piece!

The sound of Harry's sharp intake bounced off paned glass and dark paneled walls. "Amelia—"

Thomas held up his right hand to forestall Harry's coming reprimand. She must always have the final word. God, he'd sooner strip naked and immerse himself in a vat of leeches than spend a minute in her company, which meant he'd already remained in her presence at least four minutes too long.

"That's quite all right, Harry. I certainly wouldn't want your daughter to lie."

"I'm glad we can agree on that," she said tartly.

Not trusting himself to issue her another word—at least not a civil one—Thomas dipped his head in a shallow bow, giving her one final glance. Lord, what was it about her that always had his control splintering under the weight of her acerbic tongue? And just what was her grievance against him? In dealing with him, she was more than merely cold— as was her reputation. She wore the requisite pointed black hat and rode about perched on a broom like her sisters of the dark craft.

Women, ladies, matrons, the female population as a whole, simply did not despise him on sight.

Lady Amelia had.

Many claimed even children were not immune to his brand of wit and charm.

Lady Amelia most definitely was.

Annoyed at the direction of his thoughts, as if he gave a damn about her opinion, Thomas turned to address Harry. "I

will see myself out. Good day, Harry . . . Lady Amelia." He
then calmly took his leave.

If Amelia was one to indulge in tears, she might have
wept in relief at the sight of the broad back of Lord Armstrong exiting through the doorway. And then whooped in
exhilaration when his long, unhurried strides traversed the
polished hardwood floors of the corridor until he vanished
from view.

Arrogant, insufferable swine.

"You were unconscionably rude to Lord Armstrong," her
father said, disapproval a heavy stamp across his dignified
features.

The clock on the fireplace mantel measured her lack of
response in even strokes. When it became evident none
would be forthcoming, Harold Bertram emitted a sound of
displeasure. Amelia had long grown accustomed to the nu-
ances of that particular sound.

As he raked a hand through his hair, he made his way to
a small circular table in the corner of the room, on which sat
crystal decanters containing some of the most expensive
port in all of England. After loosening his neckcloth with
three sharp tugs and then tossing it on the nearby sofa, he
poured himself a drink. It was ten in the morning.

"Father, you wished to speak with me?"

He moved to stand in front of one of the windows and
tipped the glass to his mouth. For several seconds he appeared to contemplate the yellow azaleas bordering the
garden, his face presented to her in profile. Slowly he
swiveled to face her, his eyes devoid of all perceptible
emotion.

As Amelia regarded him, it struck her that she hadn't
really *looked* at her father since her eventful arrival. She'd
never seen him thus: his waistcoat unbuttoned, his hair
tousled. And his recently discarded neckcloth made his

incessantly adorned neck look barren and out of sorts. One could go so far as to say he appeared elegantly unkempt. For a man who was usually groomed in a manner that would have tailors on Savile Row bending at the waist to concede to his superior taste, this anomaly could push the sordid tale of Lady Grable's affair with her footman off the front page of the gossip sheets.

"How many times do I have to ask you to please not address me in that tone? It wasn't so long ago you called me Papa."

The latter statement he seemed to make to himself. Perhaps a wistful musing? Amelia dismissed the thought with a self-preserving kind of haste before it succeeded in penetrating the walls guarding her heart. The part of her that had once cared what he felt for her was long gone. Hit broadside by a frigate and shredded by its screw propellers.

"I was told you wished to speak with me," she reiterated as if he hadn't spoken.

"Sit down, Amelia." A sweep of his hand encompassed the newly upholstered leather armchairs by the desk, plush brocade side chairs, and a plump sage sofa situated around the fireplace.

Amelia took a cursory look around before returning her gaze to him. "I would much prefer to stand."

The color of his face took on the hue of a ripe beet, and his lips quivered when he spoke. "This last antic of yours has not only caused me needless moments of worry and considerable stress, but countless amounts of money."

Amelia was certain it was the last item that aggrieved him most. Lord forbid she cost him a fraction more than she should. He possessed fortune enough to keep the queen in jewels for life, and his sole purpose in living was to accumulate more. However, any additional funds spent on his only child had him claiming financial woes. Although, she was certain he'd have spent his last sixpence ensuring Thomas Armstrong's financial recovery without batting a lash.

He studied her, his brows drawn. The lines fanning his eyes and the grooves bracketing his mouth made him look every one of his forty-seven years. "You have left me to deal with you the only way I know how." His tone was hard and stern.

The year past, her punishment for running off to marry Mr. Cromwell had been a six-month suspension of her pin money. So what would he do this time, refuse her money for *nine* months? Make her forfeit her next Season? No, it would be a futile endeavor to remove her from the circle of eligible and prominent gentlemen of the peerage—men he hoped to foist her upon so he could wash his hands of her.

"Shall I be locked forever in my bedchamber?" At the coldness of his stare, she masked the flare of pain that commenced in her chest with a bored lift of her eyebrow.

He paused, eyes narrowed and lips pursed. She could tell he was throttling her silly in his mind. When he spoke, it was ominous in its quiet tone, purporting a brewing storm. "I do not believe those scoundrels for whom you regrettably acquire an affinity will think to look for you in a convent."

Chapter 2

Amelia's breath suspended on its journey from her lungs. For a second she feared she'd meet the exquisite Persian rug in a dead swoon.

"But we belong to the Church of England."

"And I believe this is as good a time as any to embrace Catholicism. I've heard nuns have a manner about them conducive to obedience."

Good Lord, he sounded serious. "You are mad!"

Harold Bertram emitted a humorless laugh and polished off his drink. Strolling over to his desk, he dropped the empty glass atop it. "Yes, I must be. But I have reached the end of my tether with what to do with you. Perhaps a year in the sisters' care will succeed where it is obvious I have failed."

A year! She nearly gasped at the enormity of the proposed sentence. He had to be bluffing. "Have you forgotten what happened the last time you sent me away?" Amelia asked, forcing herself to display a calm she didn't feel.

Even as derelict as he'd been in his parental duties, surely he remembered her stay at the boarding school taught predominantly by rigid nunlike creatures had been fraught with nothing but difficulties.

"I believe perhaps some time of quiet religious intro-spection is exactly what is required in this instance. It appears only the Father himself can curb your rebellious streak, and I welcome him to the task."

A deep inhalation did little to quell the panic flaring in the pit of her belly. "What of my Season? I'm to miss it to be cloistered with some overly pious nuns?" She despised the insidious creep of hurt in her voice and the sudden clammy feel of her hands.

"What else would you have me do?" Her father asked the question in a subdued tone as he circled the desk to take a seat in his chair. Over steepled fingers, he fixed her with a grave stare. "My presence is required in America for the next several months. If I leave you here, the moment I am gone you will be gallivanting from Cornwall to Northumberland with God knows who, and I will be met with a *fait accompli* upon my return. Lord only knows which bounder you'll present me with as your husband."

"Why is it so important that he has your stamp of approval? I would imagine it should be enough that you will be rid of me." The words came out more charged and emotional than she would have liked. But that came more from anger than hurt. She didn't care that her father didn't want her. Not anymore. That need in her had been exorcised from her not long after her mother's death.

Amelia paused, unfurled the fingers digging into her palms, and continued in a carefully modulated tone. "I am now a grown woman. Don't I have the right to choose the man who will, in the eyes of the law, own me for the rest of my life? Won't you afford me even that small concession?"

"And have you tied to a man like Clayborough?" Her father did nothing to keep the disdain from his voice. "You would find yourself living the life of genteel poverty in too few years. And who do you think your husband would look to when that occurs?" With only a slight pause in his speech, he continued, "Me, that is who. Even that self-serving Clayborough knows I would never permit my own flesh and blood to live in such a manner. Can you imagine, the daughter of a marquess living in a run-down estate with threadbare carpeting and traveling in equipage long past the hackney stage?" He emitted a sound of disgust. "I expect much more for you than that."

Yes, good heavens, what would society say? The embarrassment, the mortification simply could not be endured by someone of her father's stature. But living in genteel poverty had to be a vast cry better than being locked in a convent. And he must know she would never descend to ask him for one shilling.

However, Amelia hid any response she might have been tempted to give behind a vacant stare. She lacked sufficient interest to rouse herself from the inertia of arguing with her father over her selection in men.

"Twice in one year, you have run off to marry without my consent. Twice I have been forced to hire investigators to bring you home. You are fortunate that I was able to keep your escapades off every nattering tongue in society, for then there would be no hope of finding you a decent match. Can you not see you have left me with no other option?"

Amelia knew her father did not actually expect her to agree. Leaves would cease to turn color during the autumn months before that miracle occurred. However, a real tendril of fear misted over her like the thick London fog and quite literally had her heart beating double time. Her father had a look in his eyes and an uncompromising mien that she'd never witnessed in his dealings with her.

"Have you forgotten what I endured as a child at the hands of those women at that school? Or don't you care what becomes of me?" Amelia had no practice in cajolement. She'd never had any particular need of it. Not when she was a connoisseur in the art of guilt.

Harold Bertram sat back in his chair, his gaze thoughtful. For several seconds he watched her, and she wondered if he too recalled the beating she'd received—one which had left her skin bruised and broken. That had been the punishment she'd received after attempting to run away. Away from women who thought the cane the sole recourse for even the smallest infraction. When her father had learned of the incident, he'd removed her from the school in an act charged with righteous indignation.

She'd returned home under the misguided belief his actions had meant he cared for her. It had been a false assumption. The week following her return to their country estate, he'd left for London and stayed away nearly an entire year. Her thirteenth year. During the one time she'd needed him most.

Upon his return, he'd never once inquired of her well-being, how she'd fared during that period without him. He hadn't cared. That had been about the time he'd taken an interest in the blasted ship-building company. And when that wretched man, Lord High and Mighty Thomas Armstrong, had floated down like the Angel Raphael from up on high to assume a ranking higher than that of a flesh-and-blood daughter—that of his business partner.

"Given the seriousness of your offense, there is only one other option I will consider," he admitted, after a lengthy silence. "Work."

Amelia could not help two rapid blinks and one convulsive swallow. *Work?* It took several long moments for her brain to process the word in its fair context, before it settled with the repugnance of haggis in a bed of potatoes and turnips.

"You expect me to work?" The affront in her voice was neither feigned nor exaggerated. "You mean that I should join a charity of sorts?" Of course. That was the only thing that made one mite of sense.

Harold Bertram lifted his shoulders in a negligent shrug, as if the "what" was of little consequence. "I imagine something clerical in nature. Some bookkeeping and taking dictation perhaps. You needn't fear my dear. It will not be anything so significantly beneath your status."

Anything so significantly beneath her status? Someone of her status did not work! Really, the whole idea was simply beyond the pale. She was not going to a convent, and she refused to be put to work like some unfortunate woman of trade. Had her father forgotten she was a lady?

"Father, this is absolutely ludicrous. Suspend my pin money as you have done in the past. I hardly think there is any reason to go to quite these lengths to prove how exceedingly displeased you are. I can only imagine the scandal it would cause if society ever caught wind that you'd put me to work." The barest hint of a scandal usually sent her father off to his chambers pleading a migraine. "Moreover, I know absolutely nothing of clerical work and the like." And she had no desire to acquire that particular bourgeois knowledge.

"What is ludicrous is your behavior, and not just your last two antics, but the many more you have perpetrated over the last several years." He eyed her grimly. "Naturally, I will ensure the members of society will not hear of this. It will be during the off-Season. Everyone will have returned to the country by then anyhow. I can only thank heavens that unlike most of those simpletons out in society, you're at least a young lady of solid intelligence—if not temperance. You know, a head for numbers is very rare in a female. This will be a singular opportunity for you to put that God-given talent to competent use."

Her father thought her intelligent? Amelia suppressed an unladylike snort. How odd as he currently did not believe she had the sense to choose her own husband.

"It's really quite unfortunate that it has come to this. I promise you this however: you will do one or the other. The choice is yours."

Choosing between two ghastly forms of punishment—one only slightly less heinous than the other—was hardly a choice. But Amelia was not a fool by anyone's standards.

She would play the clerk in some dreary back office in Wiltshire before she would willingly spend even a week with some wretched nuns—something her father was well aware of.

"I am not going to a convent," she said, her jaw clenched tight, her hands fisted at her sides.

To Amelia's fury, his mouth quirked in something akin to amusement, his head dipping in a sage nod. In response, she blindly averted her gaze from the satisfied expression on his countenance.

Harold Bertram flicked his hand in the direction of the door. "Yes, do go. We are finished for now. I will apprise you of the particulars of this 'work' situation once I can secure the position and ensure the man's absolute discretion in the matter."

Amelia quietly quit the room with her head held high, her back ramrod straight, and her dignity lying bruised on the study floor.

At his residence twenty minutes later, Thomas silently made his way down the corridor, divesting himself of the tailored confines of his jacket. As it was too early to commence drinking, he'd instructed his butler to have coffee brought to him in the library.

By the time he slumped onto the sofa in the sitting area, he'd escaped the prison of his cravat and loosened the top three buttons of his linen shirt. In his wake lay the dress protocol of society, draped over one Utrecht plush armchair and discarded on an oversized ottoman.

With his forearms propped on his thighs, he shot a disgruntled glance at the desk at the far end of the room. A reform bill, a stash of receipts from Tattersall's and various documents from Wendel's Shipping awaited his attention. But the plague that was Amelia Bertram, made it all but impossible for him to concentrate on his eminently more important tasks.

He pushed to his feet in a move that marked his impatience. From one wall of book-laden shelves to the other, he prowled the length of the room, finally permitting himself to go back there . . . to his introduction to the current source of his discontent. And the memory came rushing back with the kind of clarity that came with a day passing . . . not an entire year.

Thomas had immediately known who she was as she crossed the threshold of the ballroom at her father's side. Harry Bertram had indicated that his daughter, Amelia, would be accompanying him to Lady Coverly's Season-ending ball.

She had looked stunning in a glittering gold gown, her tall, slender length fashioning it better than any woman present could. She had worn her dark mane upswept, silken tendrils wisping the sides of her face. From that distance, however, he hadn't been able to discern the color of her eyes, just finely arched brows and a slender nose set in an oval face.

Harry met his gaze over the throng of partygoers and then immediately started in his direction. Thomas took in her graceful walk with nothing short of frank male appreciation.

"Thomas," Harry said moments later once he reached his side. With his face wreathed in a smile, the marquess proffered his right hand.

"Nice to see you in attendance, Harry." Thomas clasped his outstretched hand and gave it two firm pumps. He then introduced him to his sister, Missy, who had joined him only minutes before.

After making his acquaintance with Missy, Harry said,

"And this is my daughter, Amelia." He urged her forward with a nudge to her elbow.

Missy performed a graceful curtsey. Thomas bowed, smiled broadly, and said, "Your father speaks most highly of you, Lady Amelia. I'm delighted to finally make your acquaintance."

Lady Amelia treated his sister to a polite smile and then turned to look askance at her father. Harry flushed a crimson red. Like a queen addressing one of her lowly subjects, she turned her attention to Thomas. "Is that so? And I've heard you are considered, at best, a rake about town, and at worst, a debaucher of women and maiden sensibilities. I certainly hope you are not going to ply your trade here this evening."

Thomas heard a sharply indrawn breath and a muffled giggle. He could only stare at the dark-haired beauty utterly stupefied while his brain ordered him to continue the life sustaining process of breathing.

The young debutante stared back at him, her manner supercilious, her visage placid and cold. However, he noted her eyes, the richest royal of all the blues, were replete with satisfaction. That she had enjoyed delivering him that particular set-down was evident.

"Amelia, you will apologize to Lord Armstrong at once." Harry Bertram gave the order in the severest of tones.

She met Thomas's gaze directly. "I do apologize, my lord, that you felt the need to lie to me. My father could never bring himself to speak highly of me, but perhaps that is something you were not aware of, making the lie you just told me quite innocuous. I, however, did not lie, and for that, I do apologize. As I have found, there are certain truths that should never be voiced in polite society."

Missy gave a high-pitched squeak, and Harry made an audible sound in his throat. Thomas dared not move a muscle, for he feared, if he opened his mouth, he would surely annihilate the imperious harridan standing before him. That, or give her the sound thrashing she deserved.

"Father, I believe I have apologized. Are there any other gentlemen you wish to introduce me to?" Lady Amelia asked, her expression deadpan, her tone unruffled.

Harry sent a beseeching look heavenward as if he prayed for deliverance from his own child. Red-faced, he muttered an apology before ushering his daughter off.

As well as making him angry, the little wretch had made him feel every bit the fool, bringing to mind his association with yet another beautiful aristocratic female of a similar age.

At the age of twenty-one he'd been caught up in the euphoria of his first brush with love. But Lady Louisa Pendergrass—so named prior to her marriage to the Duke of Bedford—had cured him of it soon enough. She'd taught him of the treachery and deceitfulness of women, a lesson well learned and one he'd never forget.

Thomas forcibly pushed thoughts of *her* from his mind. Mistakes were better left in the past. And seven years was long in the past. Which left him to brood over Harry's request and his own refusal.

"Sir, your coffee."

Thomas's head snapped to the direction of the door. He'd been so lost in his thoughts he hadn't heard Smith, his footman, arrive.

"Just place it on the desk and I'll tend to it myself."

With an alacrity that bespoke years of service, Smith did as he was instructed before quickly exiting to leave Thomas to his burgeoning feelings of guilt.

He owed Harry a debt of gratitude he could never repay. Thomas had been introduced to Harry at a society ball shortly after he finished his schooling at Cambridge. Harry had been a fountain of information concerning investment opportunities for the aristocracy. With his assistance, Thomas had restored and added immensely to his family's empty coffers by turning a stable of racing and show horses into a profitable stud service operation. And Harry's dealings with Derrick Wendel had prompted Thomas and his boyhood friends, Alex Cartwright and James Rutherford, to buy into what was now the largest ship building company in all of England.

Lord, if Harry had asked anything else of him, he would do it without hesitation. However, assuming responsibility for Lady Amelia was a different matter altogether. She was the kind of female any man in full possession of his faculties should avoid at all costs. So, until he somehow found himself tragically deficient of his and was carted off to Bedlam, that was precisely what he intended to do.

Chapter 3

Amelia brought her flowered, silk fan up to her face and began a gentle flutter. A sweep of her gaze revealed an elaborately decorated ballroom enclosed in a glass dome. Treated in blue and white, it had two massive crystal chandeliers soaring high above a crowd at least five hundred strong.

She searched the sea of faces at Lady Stanton's ball, hoping to spy Miss Crawford returning with her refreshment. Of the many she viewed, her chaperone wasn't among them.

After her former chaperone had abruptly left her post, her father had hired Miss Melinda Crawford as her eminently qualified replacement. This had been all well and good until Amelia discovered the woman regularly apprised her father of her every move like a brigadier reported troop field positions to his generals. If the woman had not slept like night fell but once a year, Amelia would never have managed her last—subsequently doomed—elopement attempt with Lord Clayborough.

But even with the objectionable woman in tow, the opportunity to attend the evening fête had been heaven-sent—one Amelia had pounced upon to fend off the sheer boredom of her own company. After spending the last three days staring at four pink and gray walls when the only books left unread were the dry offerings from various Greek philosophers, spending an evening out had been a rainbow cresting the horizon following forty days and nights of nothing but unremitting rain.

Several young gentlemen, all of them in their evening white tie and tails, lingered close, their regard intent upon her. Amelia quickly yanked her gaze away from the group, uneasy with the heat in their eyes.

"Lady Amelia."

The high feminine voice came from behind her, sounding tentative, almost unsure. Amelia turned in its direction and spotted Miss Dawn Hawkins only feet away, near the back wall beside two other ladies whose faces she vaguely recognized but names she could not recall—if in fact she'd ever had knowledge of them.

Miss Hawkins was a pleasant miss, and much more timid than the standard fare of maidens on the husband hunt. As it appeared Miss Crawford had had to travel to the opposite end of the Continent to fetch the refreshments, she could stand some tame female conversation. It would certainly be more welcome than being measured and weighed by the young bucks entering the marriage mart who were mentally calculating her worth.

"Good evening, Miss Hawkins," Amelia said, reaching her side in a few short steps.

"Oh, please, Miss Hawkins is so formal for people I consider my friends. Do call me Dawn," she said, casting a brief gaze downward.

Amelia smiled. Dawn really was so unaffected. A refreshing change from forced smiles and feigned interest into the status of one's well-being. "Then you can hardly address me as Lady Amelia."

Dawn's countenance fairly glowed at the invitation. Quickly, she turned and introduced Amelia to the two ladies at her side: Miss Catherine Ashford and Lady Jane Fordham.

"We were just conversing about the men we most want to ask us for a dance. Not that any gentlemen will, mind you," Dawn added, her smile and tone self-deprecating.

Amelia's heart gave a forlorn beat at the commiserative look the three women shared at the comment, that silent bit of communication that bespoke a secure and trusting bond. With her only friend, Elizabeth, the Countess of Creswell, whom she'd met during her first Season, currently in confinement in Kent, Amelia had no one with whom to share that sort of intimacy.

Shrugging off her momentary pang, Amelia had to agree with Dawn as much as she wished it wasn't so. She could not remember a single instance when she'd seen the poor girl grace the dance floor. Dawn was plump, moderately plain in the face with a diminutive stature, and had been the only female to befriend her since their introduction earlier that spring.

Her friends also appeared to be suffering a similar fate, perched along the periphery as if the yellow walls they propped up lacked beam support, and the threat of falling hung ominous in the air. The poor women undoubtedly had little in terms of a dowry, the death of any marriage-minded lady not blessed with a comely visage or an enviable figure.

"Naturally, you have no such problems or worries," Dawn continued in her high-pitched little-girl voice. Miss Ashford and Lady Jane added their staunch agreement with vigorous nods.

"I do not dance much at these affairs either," Amelia said, managing an expression she believed must have been something between a grimace and a smile. Most thought that with her looks and dowry she never lacked for male attention. Unfortunately, the majority of the gentlemen who sought her hand in marriage were more suitable to fill the role of her father's son-in-law than that of her husband.

"But that is because you do not care to, not because you lack the opportunity to do so." Dawn gazed up at her with a mixture of envy and admiration.

"Do tell, which of the esteemed gentlemen in attendance tonight had you hoped would beg a dance?" Amelia forced a light laugh, while shifting uncomfortably under the younger woman's regard.

Miss Ashford shot a quick glance about the noisy room teeming with highbrow aristocrats, before lifting a gloved hand to her mouth and leaning in. "I don't believe he is here at the present time—at least we have not seen him enter—but we have all agreed that Lord Armstrong would be our first choice."

Amelia forced herself not to roll her eyes, trying to ignore the disturbing quickening of her pulse as a too vivid image of him came to mind. "Please tell me you have more sense than to be charmed by golden locks and dimpled cheeks?" Amelia raised a brow, endeavoring to look properly chastising. A look her father swore she'd perfected at the knee of her departed grandmother, who had turned expressing displeasure into an art form.

All three ladies exchanged looks of surprise, undoubtedly wondering what umbrage she could have with the young lord frequently likened to the Greek god Apollo. Amelia thought Eros more apropos considering the rumors of all those women.

"Are you speaking of Lord Armstrong?" Dawn whispered the man's name with the same reverence most of the gentry and the aristocracy saved for royalty.

Amelia bit back a pained smile. "The very one and the same."

"Why, I think he is utterly charming," Miss Ashford said, her angular features softening, her cheeks becoming flushed as if the mere thought of the man turned her insides to mush.

"The man's a rake. Would you have a man who believes it is his duty to bed every woman in town? I find him to lack any form of subtlety and his transparency particularly vulgar." Amelia recalled with full clarity, the smile he'd bestowed upon her during their initial introduction. A smile meant to charm, to mesmerize. Her pulse thrummed. Yes indeed, vulgarly transparent.

Dawn pressed two white gloved fingers delicately to her lips, and Lady Jane and Miss Ashford gaped.

"Surely you jest?" Lady Jane whispered on a sharp inhalation.

Really, would she jest about something of this nature? The man *was* a rake. So perhaps he did not think it was his duty to bed *every* woman in town, but who would really quibble over the two dozen or so she had missed in her claim. "You ladies are much too sweet to be taken in by that scalawag." Which was the truth. He was all that and more.

"Are you much acquainted with the viscount?" Dawn asked, her eyes wide and curious.

"Unfortunately, my father and he are well acquainted, and I have been forced to suffer the man's presence—though thankfully only briefly—on several different occasions." Yesterday's encounter had exceeded the usual scope of their verbal exchanges. She could only pray future occurrences proved few and far between.

"How can you fault a gentleman who treats Mr. Foxworth's sister with that kind of magnanimity? Why, ever since Mr. Fox—hmm, I suppose that would be Officer Foxworth now. Well, ever since he joined the navy, it is Lord Armstrong who has been escorting her about town to social events. And if she attends a ball she is not relegated to the wall like some." Miss Ashford paused to share another look of lament with Dawn and Lady Jane. "I think his loyalty to his friend is commendable. Truth to tell, if not for him, Miss Foxworth would otherwise be wasting away the Seasons in some town lacking proper roads and transportation."

Amelia refused to mollify her opinion in the light of his altruism toward Miss Foxworth or his apparent dedication to his friend. However, the circumstances did explain why the thirty-one-year-old spinster had one of the most eligible bachelors squiring her about. Their association giving hope to all whey-faced ladies whose petals drooped on aging stems that *their* princes were not far behind.

"The poor woman is clearly smitten. That is as obvious as the nose on my face." On the two occasions Amelia had seen the two together, Miss Foxworth had stared up at him with starstruck eyes, a splotch of pink lending color to her waxen complexion. If ever she'd witnessed a woman in the grip of lovesick infatuation, Camille Foxworth had surely been her.

"Well, smitten or not, I think it is kind of him to treat her so."

Apparently, Miss Foxworth wasn't the only one smitten, for Miss Ashford defended him with the zeal of a court barrister endeavoring to sway the jury to spare his client's neck.

"Yes," chimed in Lady Jane, "the man could have his pick of the most sought-after ladies of the ton." She then blanched and shot a look of trepidation at Amelia. "Or at least the majority of them," she corrected.

In the strictest definition, that relatively small, revered group did include her. But her offers had tapered since her first Season, when she'd accumulated twelve proposals of marriage. This Season would conclude with no more than five, all from gentlemen quite new to the marriage market.

Since Lady Victoria Spencer, the youngest daughter of the Marquess of Cornwall, had scandalized the ton by marrying Sir George Clifton, Amelia had gained the dubious honor of being dubbed the new *ice maiden*. Though, should they ever discover her association with Mr. Cromwell and Lord Clayborough, she'd go from icicle to strumpet faster than a pickpocket in St. Giles could relieve a nob of his valuables.

"And not only is he kind," Dawn said in her girlish titter,

continuing in his relentless praise, "but he is rumored to be an extraordinary lover."

Amelia's brows climbed to hitherto unscaled heights as she eyed the furiously blushing blonde. And just when she'd equated Dawn Hawkins with a wilting violet. Proper young ladies did not lend themselves to such discourse. She certainly could, but then she'd never endeavored to fit in with the ladies of the peerage, many of whom were just sheep in a herd where titles, connections, and wealth led with uncompromising rigor.

"Posh, surely a rumor Lord Armstrong himself helped to circulate."

Once again, three pairs of eyes, all in varying shades of brown, widened and turned on her as if she had just taken over the pulpit and declared to every Sunday worshipper supplicant in prayer that God was just a myth. Blasphemous!

"Men tend to think very well of themselves when it comes to such matters. I am quite certain one is no more proficient than the other, though invariably it's the handsome ones who like to boast the advantage." And Amelia imagined that the viscount was just such a man.

The women stood mute. Each appeared to be digesting what they'd just heard. Amelia wasn't a stranger to certain male and female intimacies. How could she forget the rather wet kiss Lord Finley had pressed upon her in the garden at the Walsh ball. He had assumed that with a face that could have inspired the phrase *beautiful as sin,* she would welcome his advances. His shins had paid dearly for his presumption. Good looks did not necessarily equate to skillfulness in a lover. They might one day discover those truths and be much wiser for it, though she was certain some poor gentleman would topple from his pedestal in the process.

"Then why do so many women eagerly follow him to his bed?" Lady Jane's face climbed three shades of red, the question emerging hushed in a mixture of reticence and urgent curiosity.

At that moment, the music crested as the piano, violin, coronet, and cello reached a melodious crescendo. With her recent encounter with the man fueling her renewed dislike, Amelia did not allow the intrusion of the noise to cause her to pause for even an instant. Instead, she raised her voice to be heard above the final notes.

"The same reason you would gladly accept his request for a dance. Women are easily charmed by his dimples and handsome visage. Moreover, the man is a viscount and said to be one of the richest peers in all of England. On paper, he is the ideal catch. In reality, the man is no more than a rake. Lord Armstrong is the type of man who is too self-involved to care about the pleasure of others—in any regard. I would stake my dowry he does not come remotely close to his rumored sexual prowess."

The three ladies stared at her wide-eyed and slack-jawed. Their gazes shifted to the area beyond her bare shoulder just as a cacophony of female gasps and low baritone snickers punctured the silence.

A silence that had not existed only moments before.

Amelia spun quickly on the heel of her patent leather shoe to confront a scene only fit for some ghastly tableau.

Coiffed matrons and properly turned-out debutantes wore scandalized looks of disbelief.

Gentlemen hid their smiles behind pristine white-gloved hands.

Not one note of music rent the air to soften words ripe for public reproach.

Dear Lord, when had the music stopped? Her gaze darted about frantically. And when had the guests surrounding her become mutes? She could not even sigh in relief when the harmonious melody of a waltz rang out like a rescuing cavalry arriving fifteen minutes too late to stop the slaughter. Amelia could not recall the last time she'd felt this thoroughly exposed. So stricken and besieged. So completely mortified.

Never.

Then to punctuate the totality of her humiliation, the crowd before her parted as if Moses himself had brought his staff down upon the waters of the Red Sea. Hushed tones could barely contain their glee. And condemnation. Through a sea of bejeweled gowns and black waistcoats strode the tall, commanding form of none other than the man whose prowess she'd just eviscerated in the full hearing of the ton.

Chapter 4

Murder might be a hanging offense, but Thomas could see there were times when the trespass was well worth the consequence. But he'd be damned if he allowed the blasted chit to cause his masculine pride to supplant a level head.

He strode through the crush, his gaze locked on the source of his ire donned in a peach ball gown, her hair a mass of dark, silken curls elaborately arranged atop her head. She stood frozen, her face cherry-blossom pink, her eyes like a deer on the verge of flight. What a pity beauty that blinding hid a heart encased in stone and housed such a virulent tongue.

The crowd watched spellbound. Randolph, Smith, and Granville did little to squelch their amusement, their chuckles reaching his burning ears. And there wasn't a single guest present fooled by the loud and prolonged coughs of Essex and Cartwright.

Lady Camden, Lady Dalton, and Widow Ramsey looked on in mute denial, their expressions stricken—and they should know, they themselves had experienced enormous pleasure at the hands of his alleged sexual shortcomings.

Thomas imagined at least half those attending the ball waited in salacious delight at what they hoped would be a scene from a particularly titillating melodrama.

"Lady Amelia." He managed a pleasant enough tone and a courtly bow. But his mouth strained under the effort of producing a smile.

Cobalt blue eyes stared up at him with such stark horror he was almost moved to laugh. Almost, but not quite. She swallowed, and then like a curtain being drawn, her expression became shuttered.

"Good evening, Lord Armstrong," she replied coolly, her delicate chin tilted high as she performed a modest curtsey. But the quaver in her voice betrayed her nervousness . . . or fright.

She had every right to be scared. He hoped she was quivering in her lacy French drawers.

"Will you do me the honor of a dance?" he asked in cordial tones, extending his hand. Hardly the gesture of a man whose images of wringing her neck had barreled back in his mind with the force of a ferocious storm.

He could *feel* the shock ripple across the guests standing close enough to hear his request. Much like spectators at a pugilist match, this crowd wanted blood, though they'd be loath to admit such a thing. They yearned for something raucous to break up the humdrum of their dreary week.

The air was taut as the collective ton suspended their breaths to await her response. They made no attempt to even feign disinterest in the encounter that he was quite certain would top the list of conversation topics in parlors and drawing rooms all over town.

Amelia thought she must be losing her mind—or at least had rattled her brain. He could not have just asked her for a dance.

Her heart had only just begun to beat again. Now the wretched man stood too close, her senses picking up his distinct scent. Why had she come to this blasted ball? How she now craved those four silken walls. At the moment, she'd welcome Socrates, Plato, or Aristotle. Really, she'd willingly read anything at all.

But there he stood, his jaw firmly set, appearing the height of civility. Yes, this was more his style. Crush her with kindness. Watch her squirm. Make a show of philanthropic compassion. And the moment they took to the dance floor . . . She shivered. She could well imagine the kind of retribution he intended.

But if he expected her to stutter in embarrassment or issue a false apology, he'd wait an eternity. It was clear he intended to weather the incident with the veil of gentlemanly decorum. Well, so could she. Though her father would vehemently protest otherwise, she could act the proper lady when the occasion called for it. At the present, the occasion called out rather loudly.

"Good evening, Lord Armstrong. As much as I would—"

Someone tugged sharply on the tulle bertha of her gown, halting her before she could complete her refusal. A startled glance to her left revealed her chaperone appearing even more dour than the high-necked, brown poplin dress adorning her too-thin figure.

How perfectly splendid. Now she returned. If the blasted woman had returned only minutes before, she would undoubtedly be sipping some sweet drink instead of facing down this wretched man in a ballroom full of the crème de la crème of society.

Miss Crawford shot her a hard look that said, *Refuse him and I'll make you regret the day you were born.* She then gave a shrill laugh, to cover the silence that had befallen their rapt audience. "She would be delighted, my lord."

This she tittered to Lord Armstrong, who wore the same smile Lucifer must have worn when committing the sins that brought about his expulsion to earth.

A low murmur started amongst those surrounding.

"What did she say?" one woman inquired.

"Did she order the Bertram girl to dance with him?" an older gentleman asked of another balding, portly one.

"Move closer, Henry—I cannot hear a thing," the hostess, Lady Stanton, instructed her husband.

Amelia darted a glance around. Eyes alight with almost fiendish anticipation stared back at her. Their expressions said they wanted her to refuse. It was as if the taste of a scandal had bestirred their hunger and her refusal would merely whet their appetite for more.

What choice did she have but to accept? At present, she'd do anything to halt this embarrassing debacle before it grew to such proportions that someone—namely Miss Crawford or perhaps even Lord Armstrong—would apprise her father of her gauche. Lord, he'd have her on the next train to some godforsaken convent to spend a year on bended knees, clutching a cross, and reciting *Hail Marys* and *Our Fathers*.

"I would be delighted." She echoed her chaperone's sentiments, praying her abhorrence wasn't writ plain on her face for all to see. Placing a gloved hand on his proffered arm, the innocuous touch igniting a shower of sensation from her fingertips up the length of her arm, she followed his lead.

They made what seemed like a mile-long walk to the dance floor amid a flurry of movement as onlookers hurried to clear a path for their progress. Amelia wasn't certain which was worse, the intense scrutiny and whispers, or having his hands on her person as he drew her into the circle of his arms. The impulse to jerk from his touch overwhelmed and alarmed her . . . as it did to every one of her nerve endings.

Her instincts told her to run, to go. Then pride tugged her up by the shoulders, lengthening her spine and tipping up her chin. Amelia didn't mind if people called her cold and emotionless, but she'd never give them cause to call her a coward. So instead of bolting, she rested her hands on his shoulders, ignoring the tingling of her flesh in all the places they came in contact: her hands, her waist, the small of her back.

With his athletic physique, she had taken Lord Armstrong for a man more suited to masculine pursuits like rugby or rowing. But he proved to be a dancer of finesse and grace, twirling her expertly about the floor. Uttering not a single word, he gazed down at her, his green eyes half-lidded. His slumbered look could not, however, hide the sharp glint in coal-black pupils bespeaking a mind in action—surmising, scheming . . . plotting her demise.

Well, he didn't frighten her.

Amelia gave an involuntary shiver and in flustered haste, shifted her gaze from the heat of his perusal. Was it her or had the temperature in the ballroom risen several degrees since the waltz had commenced?

Minutes and too many thundered heartbeats later, when the final notes of the waltz arrested the air, Amelia could hardly believe her punishment was over. That was it, only one dance for her insult? She'd receive no reprimand or belittlement on her conduct as a lady?

In a state of bemusement, she allowed him to escort her off the dance floor. And she dared not look up at him for fear her relief was too palpable to be disguised. Poking a sleeping lion while within moments of escape would be the height of stupidity.

"Come and join me. It would be a shame not to take this time to get to know one another better." Cupping her elbow in the palm of his hand, Lord Armstrong steered her in the opposite direction of where Miss Crawford stood alone next to a large potted fern.

Amelia started at his words, instinctively tugging her arm back. "No thank—"

"Uh-uh, perhaps you think I'm issuing you an invitation." He shook his head, his manner awash in the kind of parental admonishment that instantly caused everything in her to rebel against his authority. "No, that was an order." He retained a firm hold on her arm while keeping his tone conversational and smiling down at her with a hard, unyielding glint in his green eyes. "You didn't think it would be that easy, did you? I fear you'll have to suffer my presence a little longer."

As much as Amelia despised surrendering control, she gave up the fight almost as abruptly as it had begun. The man outweighed her by at least six stone, and she'd discovered during their dance that under the cut of the finely spun fabric of his evening jacket were hard, muscled arms.

"Whatever for? I'm quite certain you don't actually wish for my company," she said, endeavoring to keep her tone neutral.

Lord Armstrong laughed in amusement. "The first true thing I've heard come from your mouth this evening," he said, as they threaded through the crowd toward the refreshment room. "What I am attempting to do is save your father from embarrassment. I believe he's been through enough this past week, wouldn't you agree?" He cocked one eyebrow and leveled her with a censuring look, which effectively wilted her indignation.

The heat suffusing her face told Amelia she'd added a new hue to mortification. Of course, he knew. It shouldn't come as a surprise. Who else would her father have confided in when she'd run off with Lord Clayborough but the man who had usurped her in her father's affections and the man he no doubt wished was his flesh-and-blood son? She could well imagine what else her father had told him. Another wave of heat washed over her. Blast her father, and double blast this wretched man.

He kept her tight by his side as he retrieved two glasses of punch from a liveried footman. He thrust one into her hand. "Here, it appears you need this. You look quite flushed. Perhaps this will cool the fire in your cheeks . . . and other such places." He directed a pointed look at her décolleté, raising her ire *and* color, the latter to her consternation.

It required every bit of control she possessed to stop herself from throwing the contents in his face. She managed by a gossamer thread, taking a sip of the tepid punch to occupy her mouth, lest she say something else she would regret that evening.

Lord Armstrong didn't spend nearly the amount of time drinking his punch as he did eyeing her neckline. In two trips to his mouth, his glass came away empty while hers remained hardly touched. His arrogance, his proximity, his presence had obliterated her thirst.

"It's not every day that I have a woman cast aspersions on my abilities in the bedchambers, especially in such a public venue." So casual was his tone, he could have been speaking of the weather.

Some might have winced in embarrassment at having uttered something so raw and emasculating. Amelia felt no such emotion but instead clutched the glass as if her entire existence depended on her not upending it all over his head.

"So how do you intend to *prove* you've won the wager?"

Startled, she shot a look up at him, her desire to see him dripping in overly sweet punch forgotten for an instant. "What wager? What, pray tell, are you talking about?"

Guileless eyes regarded her as he batted decadent lashes. "Did you not wager your friends your dowry that I was not close to my rumored prowess in bed? By the bye, what exactly do the rumors say of me in that arena?" His hooded gaze dipped for a leisurely perusal of her form. "I suppose you'll want to sample my abilities for yourself." He spoke in a low purr as he directed his gaze back to hers. "I wouldn't want you to have to depend on hearsay."

A choked breath wheezed past her lips. The blasted man was thoroughly enjoying exacting his pound of flesh. Relished it, in fact.

"Not if you were—"

"Please don't say the last man on earth; it sounds so trite. I would think a woman with your penchant for wit and scorn would have come up with something more original. More biting."

Amelia sputtered, and her hand commenced shaking, nearly spilling her drink.

Gapping the distance between them so that he stood close enough for her skirt to brush his black trousered leg, he gently extricated the glass from her hand.

"You seem unnerved." He paused, and then said in lowered tones and a throaty rumble, "I should kiss you senseless right here . . . right now." He dropped his gaze to her lips, before lifting it back up to her eyes. "But perhaps that's what you want."

Before she could respond to his taunt, he bent his head, the warm, clean scent of his breath feathering her ear. For a brief moment, she feared he intended to make good on his threat.

"Contrary to what you may believe, I *am* a gentleman and I will not heap any more embarrassment upon you this evening by making you eat your words."

He then delivered the coup de grace in a very, *very* soft whisper. "That must be saved for another time, for what I have planned for you won't be fit for public consumption."

Amelia's mouth went dry. She shivered despite the unaccountable heat that scorched through her to settle low in her belly.

And then as if he'd not just threatened—promised—to commit untold debaucheries upon her person, he straightened to his full height and inclined his head in a bow. "Good evening, Lady Amelia." With that, he sauntered off.

Chapter 5

Thomas had left Lady Amelia just as indignation had begun to replace the shocked look on her face. But he didn't venture so far as to miss the graceful sway of her bottom as she crossed the room, her head set at an angle that expressed no signs of embarrassment or remorse. Haughty to the end.

"I see Harry's progeny is quite taken with you."

He turned at the witless remark his friend tried to pass off as humor, and acknowledged Lord Alex Cartwright with a baleful look. "I should have known better than to allow you to drag me here tonight. For all I know, you staged the whole thing with that little—"

"Uh, uh, uh, a gentleman should never speak ill of a lady," Cartwright chided.

Grown men had quaked at Thomas's glower. Cartwright didn't bat an eye; nor did it ruffle one strand of black hair on his head.

"As much as I'd like to take credit for this entire affair, sadly I cannot. The honor of delivering you the set-down of the decade shall be held wholly and solely by the fair Lady Amelia."

Well aware that his friend couldn't have enjoyed the spectacle more had he been caught bare-butt with a woman of questionable morals trying to coax his limp cock to life,

Thomas said nothing. He returned his gaze to Lady Amelia as she and her chaperone weaved their way toward the ballroom doors. Slinking away. As well she should.

"So are you going to tell me what you did to the lady to cause her to malign your manhood in the fashion of scorned lovers? Although, now that I think on it, Missy did say prior to your initial tête-à-tête with the lady, you'd been sizing her up like a gourmand at a banquet."

Thomas slowly turned his head to regard Cartwright. For a moment, he was tempted to use his fist to wipe the smug, self-satisfied smile off his face. "My sister was at the time, and is still, a besotted female. She imbues every glance between a man and a woman with her silly romantic notions. Apparently, now I can't even look at a woman without it being misconstrued as something more."

"Still, I do recollect weeks after the incident, your next mistress bore more than a passing resemblance to Lady Amelia. I believe I mentioned it a time or two." Cartwright's brows rose, his expression displaying the innocence of a card shark holding a winning hand.

Thomas made a peeved sound in the back of his throat. The man hadn't made the observation once or twice—he'd harped on it so often Thomas had been forced to end the arrangement just to shut him up. No more mistresses with coffee-brown hair and sapphire blue eyes. "One hadn't a thing to do with the other, and to suggest so is imbecilic even for a man of your limited intelligence."

"I may be dumb as a stone," Cartwright said, tongue firmly planted in cheek, "but I, for one, don't have women holding up my manhood for the ton's derision."

"From my vantage point, only the men were laughing. Spiteful bunch of sods. Women are astute enough to know a falsehood when they hear one and observant enough to spot a shrew at a dead run. Good God, everyone is aware of her reputation. I'm certain both Cromwell and Clayborough still suffer the frostbite from having taken her to their beds. And just who is *she* to judge any man's performance—in or out of bed?"

Cartwright winced. Thomas shifted the course of the conversation.

"Yesterday Harry asked me to keep her in Devon during his trip to America. I, of course, declined. But . . ." Thomas cast a contemplative look about the room.

"But?" Cartwright prompted after several seconds of silence.

"But I now see the error of my ways. I owe Harry this."

An amused glint appeared in Cartwright's silver-grey eyes. "And his daughter?"

"Oh her, I owe a great deal more."

"So, what's your game? Entertaining plans of seduction are you? God help you if Harry discovers it. He'll have your hide. And then he'll give you a violent handshaking and welcome you into the family."

Thomas shivered. The thought of marriage to Lady Amelia was the stuff of nightmares, plain and simple. But any male worthy of the title "man" would pleasure her until she lay whimpering and moaning incoherently—and make certain the pillars of society witnessed every lurid moment. Unfortunately, however fitting a punishment, a scheme of that sort was too ignoble for his tastes.

"Take that little wretch to my bed? Good God no. I intend to punish her, not reward her. I assure you, it won't be anything so pleasurable—or merciful."

Cartwright threw back his head and guffawed. "Then I pray you'll grant me a front-row seat to the festivities."

After a pause, his friend's expression sobered. "By the bye, I thought it might interest you to know there have been recent sightings in town of Lady Lou—beg my pardon— I mean *Her Grace*. She's back from France, and it appears for good this time. I've been informed that she's been making subtle inquiries in regard to your whereabouts."

Thomas stilled. What the devil could she possibly want

with him? After all that had transpired between them, she could have nothing to say to him—at least nothing he wished to entertain.

"Let her ask," Thomas bit out.

"I expect she'll be making an appearance here tonight. I've heard she likes to be fashionably late so she can make a grand entrance."

That was all Thomas needed to hear. "Then I shall leave unfashionably early this evening." He started for the door.

"Surely, you're not running from her?" Cartwright sounded amused and half-disbelieving.

Pausing, Thomas shot his friend a glance over his shoulder. "A wise man doesn't run, for that encourages a chase. What he does is avoid. I am avoiding."

Thomas could hear Cartwright's laugh ringing in his ears long after he took his leave of the ball.

The following day, while Amelia was still suffering the ill effects from a fitful night of sleep, Clemens interrupted her morning meal. Her father requested her presence in his study, the second footman conveyed. He then issued a deferential bow and departed with a click of his heels.

Goodness, midday hadn't even been reached and she had yet to see Miss Crawford poke her head from her bedchamber. Surely, word of last night's incident had not gotten back to him so swiftly.

With her heart racing and her appetite, which hadn't been substantial to begin with, now nonexistent, Amelia dabbed a serviette to her mouth, gathered her skirts, and rose from the table.

Given the tenuous nature of her circumstances considering the elopement attempt earlier that week, and now the unfortunate faux pas involving her mouth, Lord Armstrong, and a ballroom full of their peers, she thought it unwise to keep her father waiting.

As she made her way down the foyer, her steps a soft tap against polished wood floors, she thought back to her perfectly horrid evening, which had ended just as abruptly as Lord Armstrong had taken his leave of her.

She and Miss Crawford had managed a hasty but dignified exit, Amelia endeavoring to avoid eye contact with guests whose expressions ranged from mild rebuke to high amusement. She'd then endured a carriage ride home in oppressive silence, tumbling into bed after midnight only to have her sleep disturbed with dreams of the bloody man. Dreams of threatened kisses. Disturbing dreams.

Smoothing not-quite-steady hands over her loose chignon, Amelia drew in a calming breath before delivering two knuckled raps to the oak door. This time she awaited her father's muffled bid to enter before opening the door . . . slowly.

Harold Bertram sat ensconced in his wing-backed leather armchair, a pair of reading glasses perched low on his nose. Judging by his appearance, the world had righted itself back on its axis. His neckcloth looked as if painstaking efforts had been made to starch, press, and knot it to perfection, his bespoke garments immaculate, as always.

"Ah, Amelia, I feared I would have to send for you. Have a seat—we have things to discuss." He gestured to the chairs opposite him. Not exactly the manner of a father who'd heard scandalous news about his daughter. In fact, the curve of his mouth lit his face with the same pleased sort of smile usually brought on by the advent of a promising business venture.

A feeling of unease coursed the length of her spine as Amelia inched closer to his desk. He appeared too happy, too agreeable, not exhibiting his normal impatience when dealing with her. Their encounters normally consisted of few words, her father, at most, sparing her a preoccupied glance, before immersing himself back into his account ledgers.

Only when she was embroiled in a scrape that might affect her standing in society was she worthy of his full attention.

Amelia firmed her jaw, pushed back her shoulders, and took a seat in the chair closest to the door. She then occupied herself by arranging her skirt so the lace-trimmed flounces lay in perfect symmetry. If her father had called her here to inform her he'd accepted a marriage proposal on her behalf, he'd find himself up for the fight of his life.

Harold Bertram directed his gaze toward the back of the room. "Thomas, please join us."

With a start, Amelia twisted in her seat before she could stop herself, to find the man standing in front of a wall of teak bookshelves casually examining the spine of a leather-bound volume.

Her heart took off on a wild gallop as the dark corniced walls of the study seemed to close in on her, sucking all the air out in the process. The embodiment of her worst nightmare turned his regard to her, his air one of artless detachment. How was it possible she hadn't sensed him the moment she crossed the threshold when his presence permeated every crevice of the room?

"Good morning, Lady Amelia." His placid greeting rolled off his tongue as smooth as velvet.

"Lord Armstrong." She managed the address between tight lips, giving a vague nod in his direction before swiveling back around.

She hadn't actually thought he would do it. However, here he was, the dew on the grass barely dissipated by the early morning sun before he'd rushed to tell her father the tale of last night's incident. He was worse than the gossiping matrons of the ton, she thought, silently railing him with a string of epithets.

Unable to bring herself to look at her father, she cast her gaze about blindly. Unfortunately, no matter how hard she tried to focus on something—anything else—she sensed the moment Lord Armstrong came within feet of her. He approached with the stealth of a jungle cat, but his scent heralded his proximity just as loudly as a blast from a trumpet. Sinking his long length into the armchair beside her, he splayed legs encased in a forest green fabric before him.

"I told you I would apprise you when I found a situation appropriate for you during my stay in America," her father began, his words commanding her attention with mind-boggling swiftness.

Dread and disbelief coalesced on a wave in her belly.

"And Lord Armstrong has kindly consented to take you on."

An enraged gasp tore from her throat as she shoved white shaking hands into her lap, her fingers clutching swaths of sky blue pyramid silk.

Take me on! As though she were some—some *thing* to be managed. She tamped down a cauldron of emotions and stared back at her father while endeavoring to keep her expression void of emotion *and* make sense of the utterly senseless.

He intended she remain in London and work at the shipping company? The idea was preposterous. It actually went beyond that, trampling unhindered into the completely asinine realm. Wasn't she to remain in Westbury at Fountain Crest?

"But, Father, really, Wendel's Shipping? Surely—"

The marquess's hearty laugh filled the study, his shoulders shaking in mirth. "Good heavens, do you really believe I would send you anywhere near those docks?"

Finding nothing particularly amusing about any of it, Amelia narrowed her gaze. "But this makes no sense a'tall. Lord Armstrong isn't involved in any other business enterprises—is he?" She addressed the question to her father as if the viscount wasn't sitting a mere foot away and hadn't the capacity to answer for himself.

"As a matter of fact, I run a very lucrative horse-breeding farm."

Humph. Figures it would have to do with breeding. Her caustic observation was accompanied by a sidelong glance in Lord Armstrong's direction, where she encountered his bland, green-eyed stare.

"In Westbury?" The deadly calm in her voice did not belie the emotion surmounting her disdain, overtaking her, and rendering her insensate with horror.

Harold Bertram drummed blunt fingers against the surface of the desk. "I think perhaps you misunderstand the situation."

Amelia's narrowed regard swung back to him. "What am I misunderstanding, Father?" Her tone sharpened with each word.

The viscount cleared his throat, bouncing her attention from her father back to him like a spectator at a tennis match.

"What your father is trying to tell you, Lady Amelia, is that my farm is in Devon and you will be residing there on my country estate with me."

Chapter 6

Amelia shot to her feet amid the rustle of silk and one rather cumbersome crinoline, nearly toppling the chair.

"I-I cannot live with him at his residence," she said, struggling to catch her breath and bridle the panic threatening to career out of control. "Father, it wouldn't be proper. I will be ruined."

"I really don't believe it will come to that." A flash of dimples denting his chiseled cheeks betrayed the viscount's amusement.

Amelia hadn't thought it possible to despise a person more than she did him at that moment. His smile—no, it was more a taunting grin—laid that assumption to rest.

Harold Bertram's chest swelled beneath his black and grey checkered jacket. "Of course, I would not allow anything not sanctioned proper by society. You will be well chaperoned at Thomas's estate. Miss Crawford and Hélène will accompany you. In addition, during a portion of your stay, Lady Armstrong and her two teenaged daughters will be in residence."

His words neither registered nor penetrated her horrified brain. The only thing she knew without an ounce of doubt was that she could not—would not—live with *that man*.

"Father there must be someone—anyone else—whom you

could prevail upon so I may work this ridiculous punishment off." Never before had she pled for leniency, but the circumstances demanded she make an exception.

Her father's denial came with a hard shake of his head, as final and definitive as a judge bringing down his gavel. Inhaling a restorative breath, Amelia subsided right into the straight-backed chair. Arrowing a glare at the man seated next to her, she noted the barely contained look of satisfaction in his eyes. The urge to snatch up the marble weight from her father's desk and smash it repeatedly against his skull had her fisting her hands in her lap and clenching her jaw tightly enough to grind her back teeth into enamel dust.

"At Lady Stanton's ball, you knew that entire time," she said, her voice fierce and barely above a whisper. While she'd endured his touch and suffered his odious presence, he'd been relishing the prospect of soon having her at the crook of his finger.

Her father's gaze darted between them, his brow pleated, his expression perplexed. The viscount did not so much as blink at her accusation. "You give me far too much credit. I don't believe anyone has ever called me a soothsayer. No, I was more than happy to take up the ribbons your father offered."

"Ribbons? Ribbons! Are you comparing me to an animal—a horse?" Amelia clutched the arm of the chair with white knuckles.

"Never," he replied too quickly. "I meant no umbrage by that. Please forgive my ill use of that word, but this is what happens when one runs a horse breeding operation." He sent the marquess a small self-deprecating smile. In turn, her father beamed at the man as if he were the Savior sent down to restore earth to its natural order.

"I will have you know that Thomas initially turned down my request, so I am grateful he has reconsidered." Her father said it as if it meant something. As if she should also be oh so grateful for such a *magnanimous* gesture on the viscount's part.

Amelia yanked her gaze away, refusing to look at the blasted man, to watch the smirk lurking behind his feigned look of innocence. His reference had not been a metaphorical slip of the tongue. He did not intend to put her to work; he meant to break her just as one would do a fractious mount.

Never.

"How terribly considerate of him," she said in a tone drenched in sarcasm.

"We will return home in three days, and next month you will go to Devon."

Four whole months with the detestable man. While the knowledge caused her belly to clench in rebellion, Amelia sat erect, her mouth pursed in a tight-lipped, contentious line.

"If you have nothing else to say, Amelia, you may take your leave." With those words, her father dismissed her, much in the same manner as he always did. His attention withdrawn before she had barely risen from her seat.

She couldn't get out of there quickly enough, but tempered her strides so as not to appear like some cowed and beaten figure fresh from a sound trouncing. Just as she grasped the knob of the door in her hand, she heard *him,* his voice low and as benign as a declaration of war. "Lady Amelia, I look forward to your arrival in the coming month."

Her step faltered. She had to forcibly resist the urge to turn and confront him. To engage him in a war of words would be pointless. Instinct told her it would be best she save her energies for the battles that undoubtedly lay ahead. Amelia glided through the doorway without looking back.

"She is not happy." Harry asserted the obvious upon his daughter's exit.

"I believe that is why it's called punishment. It's not expected to be pleasant." Thomas's dry response came with a casual lift of his shoulders.

"Yes, but when Amelia is not happy, usually neither are those around her."

Thomas's mouth curved at one end. "That might indeed be the case in her dealings with others; however, I can assure you, any misery that befalls her will not affect me whatsoever." He'd barely reached his maturity the last time a woman had caused him emotional distress. And the day some spoilt, snake-tongued brat caused him to lose even a minute of sleep would be the day he'd give up his viscountcy.

"That is why I asked you. I knew if anyone could control her, you could. Unfortunately, since her mother's death, I have allowed her too free a hand when a firm one was required."

The warning bell didn't chime, it created a deafening cacophony in his ears. "Harry, I hope you're not taking my change of heart as an indication of interest in your daughter." Well, certainly not an honorable or genuine interest.

There was no mistaking the absurdly pleased expression on the marquess's face. If Harry was counting on a match between them, he'd be woefully disappointed. His goal was to deliver her comeuppance, nothing more, and assuredly nothing less.

Harry chuckled softly. "Certainly not. A more agreeable daughter is all I am hoping for."

However, the marquess's assurance did little to alleviate a sense of foreboding gnawing at his gut. Thomas immediately gave himself a mental kick. What could Harry do from thousands of miles away?

"I have a feeling that by your return, she will be much changed—hopefully for the better."

"I sincerely hope so. You would think with her beauty and dowry, I would have excellent prospects wearing a tread to my drawing room. Instead, she has completed her second Season with only five proposals from gentlemen too insipid to be borne. Not a handful of sense among the lot of them."

"I will do what I can with her." No other female in his association more deserved what he had planned for the little miss.

Ten minutes after bidding Harry farewell, Thomas headed south down St. James Street toward his bachelor's residence. He must send word to his mother to expect a visitor for the next several months. But should he tell her to ready a space for Lady Amelia in the servants' quarters or a chamber in the guest wing? Thomas smiled. Tricky business this thing called *just desserts*.

You will be residing there on my country estate with me.
With the ring of those words playing a most ominous tune in her mind, Amelia had escaped the study to her bedchamber to think . . . to plot. The urgency of her situation had had her mind working furiously. With her father's plans for her barreling forth like a coach-and-four with a broken axle—the outcome certain to be a catastrophe of grand proportions—this matter had to be dealt with without a moment's delay.

She had immediately shot off a letter to be delivered to Lord Clayborough posthaste. He might well have the pitiable distinction of being heir to an impoverished barony in Derbyshire, but what he lacked in funds, he made up for in gumption. Few men would dare cross her father. He'd done so—albeit without success—but the attempt certainly spoke of a strength of character. Certainly more character than the likes of Lord Armstrong, no matter how society appeared to esteem the man.

So at half past ten the following morning, Amelia, accompanied by Hélène and Charles, the first footman, awaited Lord Clayborough's arrival on the southwest side of Hyde Park.

His reply to her note requesting they meet, which she'd

received an hour later, suggested the location of the park by the large elm situated between Rotten Row and the river. Well, she had been waiting at the tree thirty minutes gone with nary a sighting of him or his landau.

Using her hand to shade her eyes from the glare of the August sun, Amelia scanned the vicinity again. She certainly could not have missed his tall, lanky frame. By this time of the year, the enormous crowds, which normally converged on the hundreds of acres of lush greenery and stately trees, had retreated to their homes in the country. At present, only a smattering of ladies and gentlemen were taking their constitutional on Hyde Park's well-kept foot paths. The baron unfortunately not being one of them.

Another glance down at the timepiece clutched in her hand told her it was only half a minute later than when last she'd checked. Snapping it closed, her mouth stretched into a grimmer line.

"Come along, Hélène," she said, motioning the woman back into the carriage with a gloved hand. She refused to wait a minute more in this heat. Just as they started toward the door of the brougham, the canter of horses alerted her to an approaching vehicle. Amelia turned to spot Lord Clayborough's blue and gray carriage cresting the hill up ahead.

The landau had barely come to a stop behind hers before the baron leapt out. Her very own knight, his armor pumice and brown wool instead of tempered iron plate and his equipage in dire need of paint and new springs. Well, better a poor knight than a wealthy, dissolute rake.

He reached her side within seconds, covering the distance separating them with loping strides. Amelia attributed his choppy breaths and flushed visage to anxiety rather than exertion. It wasn't as if he'd had to make the journey from his residence on foot.

"Good morning, Lady Amelia. Please excuse my tardiness, but a horse lost his shoe in the middle of Piccadilly. Caused quite a bit of confusion. I pray you haven't been waiting long?" His mouth curved up at the corners, softening the sharp contours of his face, making him appear younger than his twenty-nine years.

At his chagrined smile, Amelia put aside her pique. He could hardly control the vagaries of London traffic. "Good day, Lord Clayborough. That is quite all right," she said graciously. "Come, let us walk toward the bridge." Turning to address Charles, who was acting as her groom for the morning, she said, "We shall return shortly."

From the driver's seat, the ever-loyal Charles bobbed his head in acknowledgement. Having befriended the fair-haired, ruddy-faced young man when he was just a boy working in the stables, Amelia had received his eternal gratitude when she'd rallied her father on his behalf. Charles had promptly ascended to the rank of a footman. Her father's paltry effort to appease her after her birthday had come and gone without him offering even a token acknowledgement of the special day.

With Hélène trailing behind just out of earshot, Amelia and Lord Clayborough started down the walking path leading to the river.

They walked in silence for several seconds before she peered up at him from beneath the shallow brim of her bonnet. "My father is sending me to Devon." She made the announcement abrupt and dramatic in an effort to jolt him from his seemingly perpetual state of bonhomie.

His brows shot up as his brown eyes grew round with surprise. "To Devon? Pray tell, what business have you there?"

Well, it was certainly better than a placating smile accompanied by words of reassurance.

"No business at all. My father's idea of punishment involves putting me to work."

Lord Clayborough's eyes widened another fraction, his strides slowing, only to quicken to keep pace with her when her own continued brisk and unbroken.

"Work?" He uttered the word as if his tongue found it unpalatable. "You cannot be serious."

First Lady Jane and now him? Did she at all resemble a court jester? "I assure you, I do not sport about such things. For the duration of his trip commencing next month." This time when his strides slowed to a halt, Amelia followed his lead and turned to face him.

"My dearest Lady Amelia, I can only offer my sincerest apologies."

"It's hardly your fault," Amelia dismissed his apology with a wave of her hand. "My father is, as usual, being quite unreasonable. And this—this punishment is barbaric. In light of these events, it is imperative we wed immediately."

Pushing his brown hat up with the tip of his gloved finger, he furrowed his brows. "What about your father, your chaperone . . . ?"

Amelia could make out minute beads of sweat dotting the line on his forehead where his hat had recently sat. This would be a most inopportune time for him to start having second thoughts about going up against her father. It wasn't something that had troubled him before. And really, what could her father do? He hadn't the power to strip him of his title or entailed properties.

"Miss Crawford returned to Yorkshire early this morning. She received word last night that her mother has taken ill." Though, surely a distressing ordeal for her chaperone, it had made the task of meeting Lord Clayborough this morning a great deal easier.

"I do hope it's nothing serious," he said, with a look of concern.

Amelia resumed walking, Lord Clayborough instantly falling in step at her side. "I don't believe so. She is expected back next week. Now getting back to the matter of our wedding—"

"Well—"

"We have only 'til year's end to marry, given the new law

in Scotland." A gust of wind billowed the skirt of her walking dress. With both hands, Amelia clasped the striped muslin close to her legs until the wind subsided.

"If we have until then, why be hasty? I mean, is that really prudent given the disaster of this past week?" Lord Clayborough asked, trepidation lacing his tone.

"I'm returning home the day after tomorrow. We don't have the luxury of time." Amelia wondered if he had heard her. She was being put to work. If that did not necessitate haste, she did not know what did.

Removing his hat, he drew out a handkerchief from a pocket inside his jacket and dabbed his forehead. "Don't you think it would be to our advantage if we were to wait until *after* your father leaves for America? I should hate to risk a reoccurrence of Wednesday's incident."

Taking his hesitancy as an unacceptable show of weakness, Amelia angled her head and fixed him with a look of reproach. "Well, you must ensure that he does not discover us until *after* the ceremony."

A heavy sigh escaped his lips as he returned the handkerchief to his pocket and jammed the top hat back on his head. "If it were that easy."

Lord Clayborough was the antithesis of her father in the ways that mattered most to her. He'd make a splendid husband, attentive but at the same time undemanding. He had no ambitions of amassing Croesus's wealth, and he had a manner that told her he'd be a caring, concerned father.

Since they'd become acquainted, rare were the times that she could say that he had vexed her. That he should choose to do so now, the one time she needed him most was in alarmingly bad taste. "We shall just have to be more careful this time. Once I leave London, eloping will be a far more difficult endeavor."

"But to make another attempt so soon would not only be indiscreet, but foolish." He spoke in a fierce whisper, his gaze darting about the quiet of the dale.

If he thought they might be overheard, he could put that fear to rest. While the sounds of the Serpentine's flowing waters created a natural impediment to the breeze carrying their voices, the handful of ladies strolling farther up were well out of hearing range.

In a flash of pure brilliance, the idea came to her. "I will tell him that you have compromised me."

Madame Tussaud's Chamber of Horrors drew less horrified looks than the one that contorted Lord Clayborough's paled visage.

"Good God, we'd no sooner marry than you'd find yourself in widow weeds." His Adam's apple gave a frantic bob. "Or at the very least, your father would have one of his hired brutes make a eunuch of me."

The Marquess of Bradford would never resort to anything as base or illegal as murder or maiming. However, knowing the kind of contempt her father held for Lord Clayborough and all gentlemen he considered of his ilk—men of little financial means—he would in all likelihood send her off to a convent . . . for life. It wasn't as if she was his heir. Now, if she had been born a male—

Breaking that particular train of thoughts—for they were tracks bound to nowhere—Amelia focused her attention once again on the matter at hand: the cause of the lines of strain etched into the planes of her would-be husband's face and dark strands of hair plastered wetly to his forehead.

His mouth opened. Before he could continue with a litany of the excuses why what she'd suggested was not sound in its reason, she held up her hand to stay the words. "You are correct, of course. When it comes to the matter of his son-in-law, my father will not be threatened or coerced." How splendid it should be the one time she'd welcome his disinterest.

Relief appeared to slither down the length of Lord Clayborough's frame. It was there in the way his shoulders came unhitched, loosening his rigid stance, and the resumption of color in his face.

"I am glad we are in agreement." He smiled, but he still appeared a trifle uneasy.

"As we cannot marry immediately, you will have to come to Devon after my father has gone. By then I will be in residence at Lord Armstrong's estate."

The baron stumbled with his next step, but managed to remain upright. "Armstrong? You will be residing at Armstrong's estate?"

Amelia shot him a sharp look. Had his voice just cracked upon uttering the viscount's name? Surely he couldn't be suffering from anything as preposterous as jealousy, for she'd not tolerate that sort of emotion in respect to her. It conveyed a possession no man would ever have of her. Not even her own husband.

"Yes, who else would you expect? In my father's eyes, the man can do no wrong."

Frowning, he raised his hand to his chin and began stroking the line of his jaw. "But Armstrong—"

"Oh please, I beg you, let us not discuss that odious man. It's enough that I'm in this wretched situation. I'm well aware of the viscount's reputation, but my father doesn't appear to hold that against him. Men are allowed most liberties denied women."

As if he feared the bitterness tainting her words would somehow turn on him, Lord Clayborough's expression cleared, his hand dropping to his side. "Come, let us start back. I wouldn't wish for your father to send his men out to bodily retrieve you should you stay too long," he said wryly, his hand hovering beneath her right elbow as they turned and proceeded back in the direction of their waiting carriages.

"I will contact you after my father has left and I have settled in Devon. By then I should have a reasonable idea of how best to proceed with our plans." Amelia slanted him a glance. He affirmed her statement with a slow, deliberate nod.

"Have you contemplated what would happen if your father refused you your dowry when we marry?" He delivered the question insouciantly, given the importance of the response.

"My father's guilt will not allow his only child to live in genteel poverty, as he refers to your unfortunate circumstance," she said dryly.

A brittle sound emerged from Lord Clayborough—one she presumed he meant to pass off as a laugh. Amelia was well aware that he did not like to speak of those particular circumstances. And she certainly understood his embarrassment, for truly, what self-respecting man countenanced the public airing of what many in the ton considered his rank inadequacies.

If a gentleman could not afford to support a wife and children in the manner befitting a member of the privileged aristocracy, he was a man of little value. The gentlemen in this unenviable situation could only hope to marry well, and Amelia knew that a marriage to her would be marrying very well indeed. Lord Clayborough wanted to marry her for more than just the financial resources she would bring to the marriage. He understood her need to retain her independence. He understood theirs wasn't a marriage that would be ruled by passion but one built on the foundation of respect and companionship. Truly, the ideal marriage.

They exchanged few words once they reached the carriages, agreeing he would await her communication upon her arrival in Devon. Then with a light squeeze of her hand, he assisted her back into the plush, burgundy interior of the brougham. By the time Charles flicked the reins to set the matched chestnuts in motion, Lord Clayborough had disappeared into his older model landau. There were no lingering looks or longing glances, which was precisely the way Amelia preferred it.

Chapter 7

Thomas thought his mistress's parlor overly feminine—even for a female dwelling—cluttered with enough frippery to make an unsuspecting guest blanch and fall into an appalled silence at the ostentatious display of taste—or lack thereof. From the showy velvet curtains and a plethora of figurines and bronzes mounted on the chiffonier, to footstools, and a sewing box littering the floor, it was hard to move about in the small space. He couldn't even speak about the jarring his visuals endured upon taking in the gaudy flowered, red, green, and gold paper covering the walls.

Thankfully, his offended senses were not forced to suffer the sight long. Within moments of his arrival, Miss Grace Howell swept in through the doorway. She was a beautiful woman: petite, voluptuous, fair-haired, and hazel-eyed. Tonight she had donned a pale, green chiffon dress, worn off her shoulders to plunge at the neckline in a daring décolleté.

"Hmmm, Armstrong you look good enough to eat," she murmured, her voice low and sultry. Looping her hand about his neck, she dragged his head down for a kiss. It had been a fortnight since he'd seen her last and the way her tongue delved and tangled with his in a long, lusty mating of the mouths, it was apparent that she wouldn't satisfy easily that evening.

Thomas allowed himself the luxury of losing himself in the kiss, but when her hands began to roam to the front of his trousers and discovered the thick ridge of his arousal, he reluctantly broke the kiss, holding her straying hands gently but firmly at her side.

"I will not be discovered by one of your servants making love in the parlor," he murmured, his voice throaty.

Flashing him a coquettish smile, Grace fluttered her lashes up at him, her eyes heavy with desire. "Then, my darling, what are we still doing down here?" She took his hand in hers, offering him her back with a sensual spin on her heel, and led him down the narrow hallway and then up the stairs.

Thomas appreciated the sway of her lush hips. Upon reaching the bedchamber, they made straight for the canopied bed. Grace fell back onto the mattress. With a quick tug of her hand, she pulled him down atop her.

Lips met, open and hungry, tongues tangling in wet demand. In no time, clothes lay scattered across the carpeted floor. Just as Thomas had guessed, Grace was insatiable in her lust, clutching his buttocks and moaning loudly minutes later when he slid his length into her.

For Thomas, it too had been a long two weeks. He plucked at her peaked, dusty nipples, wringing a string of whimpers from her lips, her head twisting in abandon against the bed linens as he pounded relentlessly into her. She came with a wail of pleasure, the high-pitched sound reverberating off the walls as she convulsed helplessly, endlessly beneath him. And while she still trembled in the aftermath of her orgasm, he found his release with a harsh grunt and clenched teeth.

Spent and sated, Thomas flung himself from atop Grace's limp form and onto his back, his chest falling and rising as he luxuriated in the pleasure of his release. From the corner of his vision, he saw her turn slowly on her side toward him, and felt the languid slide of her hand over his chest. She was in the mood to cuddle, and now satiated, he yearned for his own bed—alone.

Then in his head, Lady Amelia's voice rang out crystal clear in that scathing tone as she announced to everyone within hearing range, that he was too self-involved to care for anyone else's pleasure. So, with her words rattling about in his brain, instead of bounding to his feet, throwing on his clothes, and going home as he was wont to do, he lay acquiescent under his mistress's caresses.

"Will you stay the night?" Her voice purred with satisfaction.

"I can't. Tomorrow I will be leaving for Devon," he said, turning his head on the pillow to face her. "That was my other reason for coming. To tell you in person."

The moment her hand stilled just above his navel, Thomas knew he had made a mistake. Grace bolted upright, her plump breasts bouncing against her ribs.

"You are going to Devon?"

Thomas suppressed a wince at the shrillness of her voice. Lord, why hadn't he simply sent her a note once he'd arrived?

Raising himself to a sitting position, he dragged his hand through his hair. "I told you when we started our arrangement that I routinely go home this time of the year to tend to my business interests."

However, his reminder was to no avail. For the next several minutes, Thomas listened with half an ear while Grace bemoaned the fact that his visits to her had dropped off over the past few months. She complained of feeling neglected. The bloody woman sounded more like a wife than a mistress. And truly, he had no idea what she need fret about. He'd set her up in a quaint townhouse in a fashionable part of London. Each month he parted with a good sum of coin to pay for her creature comforts, and he had opened accounts in her name at some of the best shops in town. She possessed a healthy supply of jewelry and he escorted her to some of the best entertainment to grace this side of the Atlantic. What more could she possibly want? Well, except for more of his time, which he had no inclination to give her, and she had no right to ask of him.

"Would you rather my visits not decrease but stop entirely?" He asked the question in a world-weary voice that conveyed his impatience all too clearly, while shooting her a look that said he was within minutes of ending their arrangement.

By the speed at which Grace ceased her fretful prattle, her expression immediately becoming contrite, she had taken heed of his warning. Soothing him with her hands, they fell back onto the bed, her fingers wrapping around his cock as she worked to coax it back to life.

Thomas stilled the movement of her hand and brought it up to his mouth for a kiss. At the moment, he had no desire for another bout of lovemaking. And once again, Amelia Bertram assailed his thoughts.

Clayborough might have won her affections, but Thomas sincerely doubted the baron had been able to elicit in her one iota of passion. A task surely more difficult than wringing blood from a stone. How was he, a man of questionable temperance and patience, and an inordinate amount of pride, supposed to accomplish such a feat? How was he going to make her want him—better yet, crave him, his touch, his kisses, yearn for the very thing she'd scorned? Were his acting skills truly up to the part of the smitten gentleman?

At present, the answer was an unequivocal no. But he'd need to hone those skills quickly enough if he was to see his plan to its completion.

"Apart from my title, my wealth, and my appearance, what is it that you find appealing about me?" All of the attributes the chit had discounted with a disdainful tilt of her chin. He surely had more to offer a woman than those things, didn't he?

He could feel Grace's hazel eyes boring into his profile. Angling his head to view her fully, he quirked a brow.

Silence met his question head on. Thomas laughed dryly. "As those are things largely out of my control, I'll try not to feel insulted at your speedy response."

"No, darling, I guess I just find it a strange question," she said, smiling, tiny wrinkles fanning the corners of her eyes. "Don't tell me you have been reconsidering your charms?"

"You still have not answered my question."

Removing her hand from his grasp, she began playfully tugging at the hairs on his chest. "You present a challenge, and women love a challenge. Secretly, women would love to bring a man like you to heel." She placed a kiss on his chest. Turning her face, she rubbed her cheek against the mat of hair, her gesture like that of a needy cat. "And women love being conquered. Especially by a man who knows just how to bring her to pleasure."

Another kiss landed on his abdomen. "You, my dear man, know exactly how to do that. To add to that, you're very generous. None of my previous protectors ever cared about such things as birthdays and holidays."

Thomas knew she referred to the ruby pendant he'd given her for her birthday several weeks back.

"How utterly thoughtful you can be when you want."

And thoughtless when he wanted, but he knew that complaint would go unsaid—at least for the evening.

But would such qualities be enough for a cold fish like Lady Amelia Bertram? He had never tried—in all actuality, he'd never had to try—to seduce any woman. In England, young, rich, and passably attractive (he could humbly claim to be at least that) gentlemen of the ton were pounced upon with the same speed and determination as one would an up-ended barrel of guineas in the midst of Covent Garden Market. He had certainly never faced the prospect of *having* to exert the full force of his charm on any female with a disposition like that of Lady Amelia.

"Why do you ask?" Grace inquired, her hand inching down his chest to where the hair arrowed, then thickened.

"Perhaps I'm wondering if more than my money keeps you here." This time he allowed her fingers to wrap around him and work his stiffening rod with long, firm strokes. Quickening pleasure pooled under the smooth glide of her talented hand.

Grace slid down the length of his body, taking his shaft into her mouth and twirling her tongue eagerly around the sensitive tip. Seconds later, she lifted her head and regarded him through passion-drugged eyes. Her mouth curved into a seductive smile, as her hand continued to work his turgid length. "This is what keeps me here."

Parting her lips, she took him deep into her mouth. With a low groan, Thomas threw his head back, all coherent thoughts having fled from his mind.

Chapter 8

Amelia might have bargained her soul to the devil himself to halt her departure from Westbury entirely, had she not feared the eternal fires of damnation. Though, in actuality, sharing a roof with the viscount would be its own form of damnation on earth.

However, no amount of praying or wishing could deter her father from his course. The month following her return to their country estate, he dispatched her from Fountain Crest with the rapidity and sanguine relief one would a guest who'd stayed months too long.

A broken axle interrupted their journey to Devon. Then they—she, Hélène, and George, her father's trusted manservant—missed their connecting train to Torbay, causing them a day's delay. A delay that vexed George mightily but a respite she welcomed. By luncheon time the next day, Amelia had arrived at her destination, her spirits having worsened with every mile that had brought her closer to imprisonment. Closer to her gaoler. Thankfully, it was his mother, and not he, who awaited her under the vaulted ceiling of the grand foyer of Stoneridge Hall.

After her father's initial introduction to the viscountess years back, he'd claimed her one of the most elegant women he'd ever met. Given such singular praise, Amelia expected to find a woman of unparalleled beauty. In that, the viscountess did not fall short.

Above average in height, Amelia was accustomed to peering down at most females and standing eye-to-eye with half the gentlemen of her acquaintance. The viscountess, however, topped her by an inch or so, her slim figure wrapped in a burgundy gown of fine merino wool. Her complexion, creamy and unblemished, had done well in weathering the wrinkling and dulling of age that had wreaked havoc with many of the fading beauties of the ton.

"Lady Amelia, welcome. I'm relieved to see you have arrived safely. Your father sent word expressly notifying us of your delay. I pray things went better this morning."

At the offering of a smile of such genuine kindness, Amelia's heart sank. How easier this whole ordeal would be if the viscountess was as arrogant and disagreeable as her son. But her manner, her tone, the warmth of her green eyes indicated quite the opposite.

Amelia dipped in a stiff curtsey. It still wouldn't be wise to grow fond of the woman, blood being all that it was. "Good afternoon, Lady Armstrong. Yes, I must admit we fared a great deal better today."

"Wonderful. You had us quite worried. Thomas was—"

A scant second before Lady Armstrong broke off and shot a glance over her shoulder, the air became charged. Even before Amelia saw him appear in the stretch of hall in front of her, she'd perceived him. Like some malevolent being, his presence filled the surroundings, causing her senses to shift into high alert.

"Ah, Thomas, there you are. Just in time. Lady Amelia has only recently arrived." It was clear by the softening of the viscountess's expression, she loved her son in the blind, unstinting way only a mother could love her offspring.

I was loved like that once. Just as quickly as Amelia felt the pang of pain, she ruthlessly quashed all thoughts of her mother. To remember was to open up a well of hurt.

"So I see," he drawled, closing the gap between them with unhurried strides and a lord-of-the-manor swagger. He appeared as if he'd just come from outside, attired in dark brown riding clothes with his thick mane windblown. Halting in front of her, he dropped at the waist in a bow. A most uncalled-for bit of gallantry, but one Amelia believed he'd performed purely for show.

"Welcome to Stoneridge Hall, Lady Amelia."

"Lord Armstrong." Amelia gave a stiff nod but managed to keep her tone neutral. It wouldn't do to have her dislike of the viscount obvious to members of his family and household.

Perhaps to his mother, and Hélène and George, who hovered discreetly behind her, the smile the viscount bestowed upon her might appear gracious, but she knew better. His green eyes held a mocking glint, his expression, a sly look of satisfaction.

"I pray your travels today progressed without further mishap."

Aware that Lady Armstrong watched their exchange with heightened interest as evidenced by her intent regard, Amelia inclined her head in a polite nod.

"Wonderful, then we best get you settled." Turning to the viscountess, he asked, "Mother, which room did you have prepared for Lady Amelia?"

"The blue room, my dear."

In brusque tones, he instructed the footmen, who had just hefted one of her larger trunks through the front door, to carry her things up to the designated bedchamber.

"And your chaperone . . . I believe it was Miss Crawford?" His gaze briefly strayed to Hélène and George.

"Unfortunately, Miss Crawford was forced to return to Yorkshire. Her mother is failing." And Amelia's father, the Marquess of Bradford, a man who had a sense of propriety rivaled only by the patronesses of the convent of Almack's, had had no qualms in sending her off to the residence of a known rake without a chaperone.

Lord Armstrong elevated a brow. "Indeed? Your father failed to mention that bit of news in his communication. Am I then to presume this is your new chaperone?" he asked, directing his attention to Hélène, his expression dubious.

Given her maid's youth, she hardly suited the role, but it was clear introductions were in order. Amelia motioned Hélène and George forward. "No, my lord, this is my maid, Hélène, and my father's manservant, Mr. Smith. Mr. Smith acted as our escort, but he will be returning home posthaste."

Son and mother greeted the servants amiably. Hélène and George responded with an exaggerated curtsey and a deep bow.

"Mother, why don't you have someone show Lady Amelia's maid to her chambers and have one of the footmen show Mr. Smith where he can refresh himself before he departs. I need to speak to Lady Amelia about some important matters pertaining to her father."

While Amelia's stomach recoiled at his words, the viscountess was already going about the business of acceding to her son's wishes.

"Come, we will go to the study." With that, he started down the hall as if expecting she trot obediently along beside him. Amelia followed but at a sedate walk not a trot, stubbornly hanging back a distance.

As they traversed down the wide corridor, with nowhere else to focus her attention but at the back of his form, Amelia inspected her surroundings. Large framed oil portraits dominated the silken walls. On the opposite wall hung several glass topiary pieces and elaborate brass sconces. She found the décor elegant and understated, a fine representation of the viscountess herself.

Several years after her mother had died, her father had had Fountain Crest done over from top to bottom. All vestiges of her mother had been carted off and discarded much like the dated furniture and the heavy window coverings.

Lord Armstrong came to a stop in front of the double doors of what could only be the study. With a sweep of his hand and an inclination of his head, he said, "After you."

Amelia swallowed and thrust thoughts of her mother from her mind. She preceded him into a room as wide as it was long.

"Please, do make yourself comfortable," he said, striding across the room, giving a pointed look at several of the armchairs in front of the oversized mahogany desk.

"After sitting nearly two days straight I would rather stand." Oftentimes sitting left one at a disadvantage, and with every passing minute, Amelia grew ever more certain that in dealing with Thomas Armstrong she'd require more than just her wits about her.

Thomas suppressed a smile. He'd expected nothing less than a refusal, but it was always good to test the boundaries.

"Then I hope you won't mind if I do. Unlike you, I'm on my feet much of the day." He took a seat behind his desk.

She watched him, her blue eyes the cold of the Russian tundra.

Far too many women tended to prattle on ad nauseum. But this one was an altogether different matter. Thomas continued. "I hope you'll find your accommodations adequate."

"Your concern for my comfort is—is *touching*, however, I assure you it is most unwarranted."

Well, she certainly hadn't lost her talent for biting sarcasm, Thomas mused. Perhaps she would prove to be as amusing as she was infuriating.

"I thought this would be a fine time to work out the details of your duties, which I might add have met with your father's stamp of approval."

"I don't doubt that whatsoever," she muttered under her breath. Thomas caught every word.

"Tell me, my lord, you say 'work out the details.' I assumed my punishment had already been set in stone. Am I to have a say in the matter?"

He let out a mild chuckle. Such a refreshing blend of churlish gentility. "Touché. I guess I should have said we need to discuss my expectations of you. But before we get into that, I would like for us to put our past differences aside. To that end, I hope you will address me as Thomas, or Armstrong if you prefer. Under the circumstances, I think it would be silly for us to stand on ceremony. By the same token, I'm sure you'll permit me to address you as Amelia."

"I can hardly prevent you from addressing me however you please, but under the *circumstances*, I prefer to keep my contact with you very much on ceremony," she said coolly.

Thomas hoped she strained her neck from having her chin tipped so high. "I may address you as I please? Then I should choose something fitting, wouldn't you agree?"

He relished the flash of anger that sparked in her eyes, darkened to a blue so deep he could barely make out the pupils.

"Several names do come to mind. However, I had best forgo those and settle with one equally suitable . . . Princess."

She went ominously still and branded him with a look so feral, he was surprised his jugular remained intact. Then she drew in a breath, drawing his attention to the rise and fall of her breasts.

A shock of arousal hit with sudden force, causing his member to test the seams on the front closure of his trousers. Her breasts weren't too big or inadequately small, but the size of a nice handful. He flexed his fingers. Yes, and they would be firm.

Good Lord, what was wrong with him? He didn't even like the girl. When had his sexual appetite become so indiscriminating? Certainly he'd been in the presence of more agreeable women with breasts equal to hers without being accosted by a full-on cockstand.

Annoyed at his reaction, his voice took on a crisper tone. "I shall expect you to be in this study promptly at eight o'clock every morning. You will be assigned various duties, and each I shall expect you to complete without a demur."

Her jaw clenched.

"As for your meals, I expect you to take them with my family."

Her eyes grew wide, he imagined with both surprise and displeasure. "I am to work for you *and* take my meals with you? Is that done?"

Propping his elbows on the desk, Thomas angled his head to the side, a small smile playing over his lips. "No, but then I don't have another member of the peerage in my, er, service."

"Well, I prefer to take my meals in my chamber," she said, as though she had a choice.

"Then perhaps you'd prefer to take your meals in the servants' hall or in the steward's room with your maid? And while we're to ensure proper protocol is followed, I can also ask that a different chamber be readied for your occupation." If she truly wanted to be treated like a servant, he had no qualms in obliging her.

Her eyes flared briefly, and for a moment Thomas thought she intended to respond. She said nothing and moved not an inch.

"I thought as much," he said, satisfied. "Let us get one thing very clear before we begin on this course. I am not your father. I will not condone your antics with even a quarter of his tolerance. You will conduct yourself in a manner above reproach while you are under my care. Do we understand each other?"

The silence that followed was of the variety of an insult being thrown just before a brawl ensued. Thomas didn't know whether to expect her accession or a dagger through his heart. Then as though a puppeteer controlled her actions, her head jerked in something resembling a nod.

Ah, sweet, divine acquiescence. A truly glorious, if somewhat painful, sight. He smiled and reclined back into his seat. "Then I see no reason that this experience should not be at the very least a tolerable one."

"Will that be all?"

Her voice was cold, but the heightened color in her cheeks said she was hot. Hot with anger and capable of a blaze to rival the Great Fire of London. More than ever now, he was convinced her frosty exterior was merely a layer of ice only in need of the proper handling to bring about a spring thaw. He grew hard again at the thought and seriously considered bedding her for real.

Thomas continued to watch her, his eyes skimming the length of her lithe figure. Soon she began to shift beneath his gaze, her hands flittering over the folds of her skirt. He liked her off-kilter. He liked that she was trying desperately not to be the one to break the stare. Finally defeated, she looked away, her face pomegranate red.

"Yes, that is all." Turning, he jerked the tasseled bell pull near his desk. "I will have one of the servants escort—"

He turned back in time to see the flutter of checkered brown skirts disappearing through the doorway, a light flowery scent left to linger in her wake.

Chapter 9

Amelia had run away from the hideous boarding school, but she'd never *run* from anyone. The pig on one of the tenants' farms didn't count because, of course, that was an animal, and a girl of twelve would certainly run from one the size of a—well very big pig.

She'd run from Thomas Armstrong. And just as quick as her legs could take her.

Finding a servant to show her to her bedchambers had been the easy part of her escape. Now, secured in a room done in many varying shades of blue, Amelia slumped against the door, her heart racing out of control.

One moment she'd been vexed beyond comprehension and the next she'd stood fidgeting under his perusal, his green eyes glittering with a brilliant intensity. His look hadn't held the scorn, annoyance, or gloating satisfaction she'd grown accustomed to from him. What it had held was something infinitely more dangerous, for it had had the power to unnerve her enough to forget herself. What remained back in that study was her poise, plain and simple.

Amelia gave her head a shake hard enough to cause a thick lock of hair to spill down her back. Pushing off the door, she crossed the room to the mahogany four-poster bed.

The viscount might be able to charm all the women of

London, but his attractions were lost on her. She knew that with unshakable certainty. But her reaction to him was troubling. For over a year, she'd managed minimum contact with him. And it had been a mutual avoidance. On the rare occasions they'd both attended the same ball, no less than a league was sufficient distance enough to separate them.

However, the circumstances were quite different now. There would be no avoiding. And with every minute she remained in his company, it grew ever apparent this wasn't just a man she should steer clear of but one that should have her running pell-mell in the opposite direction.

Passing the three trunks sitting at the foot of the bed, Amelia dispensed with her petticoats, kicking them onto the carpeted floor, and clambered onto the mattress.

It was clear the two days of travel had finally taken their toll. It hadn't been him she'd been reacting to but the circumstances. Obviously, what she needed was some rest. Perhaps when she woke her world wouldn't seem like it was whirling out of control and she'd be herself again.

Four hours of sleep taken at midafternoon should have left Amelia pleasantly rested. Instead, she awoke long after the sun had made its descent below the horizon, still weary, her head pulsing behind her eyes.

Squinting, she inventoried the room, noting her trunks now sat beside the large wardrobe against the wall and her toiletry lay spread on the adjacent vanity. Hélène had unpacked and put away her belongings without disturbing her, a sign of a truly efficient lady's maid.

No sooner had Amelia made the observation before a knock sounded at the door and Hélène bustled into the room.

"Ah, *oui*, you are awake," her maid said with a smile. Striding over to the wardrobe, she threw both doors open and immediately began to contemplate several of Amelia's supper dresses, her fingers skimming over one with a gauzy, pale yellow skirt.

"Shall I pick out a dress *pour vous*, mademoiselle?"

Coaxed by a headache that had gone from a dull throb to sharp and unrelenting, it took only seconds for Amelia to make up her mind. "No, I would like you to convey my most contrite apologies to Lord Armstrong that a malady will prevent me from joining the family for the evening meal." And as that was the truth, there wasn't much he'd be able to say or do about it.

Hélène's head jerked in her direction. "You are unwell, mademoiselle?"

"No need to look so alarmed. 'Tis just a headache, nothing more. A good night's sleep should set things right."

Nodding, Hélène dropped her hands from the tulle silk dress, and closed the wardrobe doors. "As you please, mademoiselle. Shall I ask a tray be brought up *pour vous?*"

It was at that moment her stomach voiced its protest, churning indelicately—and quite loudly. Lord, she hadn't eaten a thing since before luncheon time. "Yes, please do. Apparently, lack of food is contributing to my migraine."

Hélène's mouth edged up slightly at Amelia's grumbled response. With a nod, she turned and exited the room, her departure coinciding with the chiming of the supper bell.

Five minutes later, a knock sounded at the door.

"Come in," Amelia called out while sliding her legs from the bed onto the floor, her feet sinking into the plush pile of Brussels carpeting. The food had arrived much faster than she had anticipated. Her stomach growled its approval.

The door opened, but no servant greeted her bearing the much anticipated tray of food. The viscount himself stood framed in the doorway like Apollo on the cusp of the Trojan War—sans the bow and arrow. He had changed, now more formally attired in a sage jacket and waistcoat and tan trousers. The white cravat knotted about his neck contrasted sharply with the gold hue of his skin. An irrelevant observation, but one she'd made despite herself.

"You look well enough to me," he stated with no preamble.

Amelia halted abruptly at the foot of the bed. It took a moment for her to collect her wits enough to understand just what he intimated and respond in kind. "Your concern is overwhelming."

Without removing his gaze from hers, he entered, and the room seemed to shrink in size. Casually, he reached behind him to push the door closed, the click of the action loud and menacing to her ears.

With a start, Amelia swallowed hard and could only gape at him for several moments of incredulity. "What are you doing?" she said, recovering her speech and embracing her indignation.

"Is that what you do, get your servants to carry your lies for you?" He started toward her. "You are very much mistaken to think I believed a word of it."

"You are in my bedchamber, my lord." Her tone had shifted from heated to brittle as he drew closer. "Perhaps you are accustomed to treating females in this fashion. But I am a lady and I expect to be treated better than one of your trollops. I'm quite certain your mother would not look kindly upon your actions."

Lord Armstrong halted in front of her. He stood too close, and Amelia yearned for the distance two arm's lengths would have brought her. But after fleeing from him hours before, her pride wouldn't allow another retreat.

"You of all people will lecture me on impropriety?" A dark blond eyebrow rose with his question. "Did I fail to mention that your father gave me leave to acquire you other accommodations should this—um—situation prove too trying for me? I believe the sisters at a very remote convent in Westmorland would gladly welcome your arrival." He shook his head slowly and made a tsking sound. "It would be such a shame if it came to that."

The pain in her head was forgotten—or perhaps it fled in light of the anger that overwhelmed her. Directed both at her father and the loathsome man standing before her, it was the kind of anger that had men carrying a pistol to the fields at dawn in the company of their second. Amelia inhaled deeply.

His gaze dropped to her breasts. Then his regard snapped back to her eyes. "Now, I believe that in my office I was explicit in my instructions as to where you're to take your meals."

Amelia swallowed a breath, her anger broken by the pitching of her stomach. He made it sound inappropriate. Intimate.

That he did not believe she was ill was obvious by the look in his eyes as he took another step toward her. Forcing herself not to retreat, Amelia tipped her chin to stare him directly in the eye. It annoyed her that this close, his shoulders were wide enough to block her view of the door. Her only exit.

"Do you really want to begin a battle with me? On your very first night?" He bent his head, his face mere inches from her own, his voice low and taunting.

For the first time since she'd initially laid eyes on the man, Amelia experienced a pang of fear hitherto unknown to her. He represented a threat. She recognized that now. But what kind of threat was not as yet altogether clear. And that made her resent him all the more.

"Then I guess you would rather I come down to dine ailing?" Goodness, what was she doing? Trying to appeal to his sense of . . . decency? It was obvious granite had usurped anything he might at one time have had resembling a heart.

"If you are ailing, then I am the king of England."

"Then I will ask Your Highness to please remove yourself from my chamber."

"Princess, let us get one thing perfectly clear."

Amelia's jaw locked, and her hands curled tightly around a swath of her skirt. It was clear he took great delight in drawing out the name, knowing just how much she resented his use of it.

"This"—he gestured about the room with his hand—"and everything in this house is mine. You occupy this space at my hospitality. Moreover, I'm sure this isn't the first time you've been in a room alone with a man and a bed. Remember, I know about both Cromwell and Clayborough, though I'll wager Cromwell wasn't even the first."

If Amelia didn't fear he would retaliate in kind, she would have slapped him—no, she would have balled up her fist and pummeled him to the ground. No one had ever—not ever—cast aspersions on her character in such a manner. Did he think because he had the morals of an alley cat, so, too, did everyone else?

"While you are in *my* house, you will do as I say. Do we understand each other?"

His expression, his eyes, his entire demeanor told her he expected her to respond with a rousing display of feminine defiance. She refused to give him the satisfaction of responding to his slur.

"Oh, I very much understand," she replied softly.

Lord Armstrong stilled and stared as if he found her ready capitulation not to his liking—and not a capitulation at all.

"Now that you have my assurance, I am asking you to leave. I pray I will at least be permitted the privacy a bedchamber should afford anyone. Even someone in your service, I daresay." She wouldn't be at all surprised to discover he imprisoned the servants in their chambers. But then, how many of the female servants would actually call it being "imprisoned"?

Straightening with a languid grace, the viscount retreated several steps, a lazy smile in place. "You needn't worry in that regard."

Grateful that he no longer crowded her with his proximity,

Amelia chose to ignore the amused and knowing look in his eyes.

"Will I be permitted to eat this evening, or do you intend for me to starve?" The churning of her stomach had not allowed her to forget its current state of emptiness.

"I will instruct one of the servants to bring you something *this* time. Beginning tomorrow, I expect to see you in the dining hall."

To respond as she wanted would simply delay his departure, so Amelia remained mute.

Lord Armstrong was at the door in long, fluid strides. Before exiting, he turned to her and said in a clipped, unyielding tone, "Be in the study tomorrow morning at eight o'clock. If you keep me waiting for even one minute, whether you're dressed fit for company or not, I will come and fetch you myself." He paused and without so much as a glimmer of amusement said, "On second thought, don't sleep in a stitch tonight, that way that little exercise will rouse us both."

He left her standing stock-still by her bed, eyes wide and mouth agape, fairly reeling at his audacity. But his words conjured up an image in her mind that left her flushed and hot for an altogether entirely different reason.

Supper with his family had been a relatively quiet affair. Eaten up with curiosity, his sisters had set upon him, firing question after question about their newly arrived guest. To their questions, he'd replied, "You can ask her yourself when you meet her tomorrow." After receiving five such responses, Emily and Sarah had lapsed into silence.

Now retired to the library blissfully alone, Thomas crossed over to the sideboard and set about pouring himself a much desired—much needed—glass of port.

Soon he was settled in his favorite chair where he could freely assess his problem. One, Amelia Bertram. As evidenced by her behavior thus far, this might prove an even greater challenge than he'd imagined.

Thomas took a swallow of the drink. His plan had been simple enough. Make her eat her words. And he'd manage this by not actually bedding her. He imagined a kiss or two would be called for, perhaps even one heated embrace, but that was all. Just enough to leave her yearning for something she'd never get—at least not from him.

The logical part of his brain told him a smart man would send her to Westmorland as soon as the sun rose tomorrow and let the sisters deal with her. However, the part ruled by his pride demanded her requital must come at his hands. It was only fitting. And if that meant he'd have to put on a performance that rivaled the best the St. James Theatre had to offer, so be it. Though given his body's response to her, the physical intimacy aspect of it wouldn't require any acting on his part. She was desirable, he'd give her that.

"I thought you had already retired," came his mother's voice from behind him.

Angling his head, he watched as she made her way toward him, the skirts of her mauve gown fluttering around her.

"Not as yet."

"Good, because I would like to speak to you about Lady Amelia," she said, taking a spot on the adjacent sofa. "Are the two of you planning to marry?"

In the midst of taking a swallow of his drink, the port went down the wrong passage, sending Thomas into a paroxysm of coughing. He quickly placed the glass on the table next to him with a clatter.

The viscountess patted his hand solicitously until the coughing subsided. "My dear, I didn't mean to rattle you."

"What on earth would give you such a notion?" he said, wheezing a bit.

"Honestly dear, it's really the only thing that makes any sense. You are a bachelor, and she *is* beautiful and very much a lady. That Lord Bradford should ask you to watch his daughter is like asking a fox to guard over a chicken coop. It simply defies all logic. The only thing that does make sense is that you intend to marry her."

"Well, I'm sorry to disappoint you, Mother, but I have no intention of marrying anytime soon, and I can guarantee you when I do it won't be to the likes of Lady Amelia Bertram."

The viscountess's brow puckered. "And just what is wrong with her?"

The trap had been so neatly set, Thomas hadn't seen it until he hung upside down squirming at the end of the rope. A reluctant smile pulled at his mouth. He had to admire a mind that crafty.

"You could simply have asked that instead of going through the pretense of believing I intended to marry her."

His mother smiled, looking not the least bit abashed. "But if I'd asked outright, you would have tried to talk circles around me, much like you do when I inquire about the women in your life."

"Amelia Bertram is *not* a woman in my life. She is merely the daughter of a friend. And you will meet the woman in my life when I decide to take a wife." And he hoped she wasn't holding her breath for that.

"So, are you going to tell me what is going on between the two of you?" his mother asked with exaggerated patience.

"Nothing whatsoever," Thomas replied, shifting in his seat. "And I believe I've already explained Harry Bertram's predicament with his daughter."

The viscountess gave him the sort of arched look that had coaxed many confessions from him as a child. He was no longer a child.

"Yes, but why do I get the impression that you are conveniently omitting pertinent details?"

Thomas shrugged, picked up his drink from the table,

and took a cautious sip. "I'm not certain. There is nothing else to tell."

The viscountess continued to watch him closely, her expression dubious. "After meeting her, I'm hard pressed to believe her father couldn't find someone more suitable to care for her. Although I had heard she was quite beautiful, I was surprised to find her so—so collected. Hardly the type of woman who would require such a close watch."

His mother was too much the diplomat to use the more appropriate term of haughty.

"And what is this business of her coming without a chaperone? You know that I cannot, in all good conscience, leave the two of you here alone. My word, what would people say?"

Crossing his leg so his foot rested on the opposite knee, Thomas reposed back into the chair. "Yes, well, that was something that I could not have anticipated. But have no fear, I shall find her adequate supervision before you depart."

The problem wouldn't be in finding someone, but in keeping this saint after she met Amelia. He certainly didn't delude himself into believing this would be an easy task. How could Harry have put him in this position without a word of warning?

But his assurance didn't appear to appease his mother as much as he'd hoped. "And I will let it be known that Amelia is here as your guest."

"But I will be leaving in a month."

"And an unfortunate calamity will befall her, which will prohibit her from joining you and the girls in America. A surprise her father could not have anticipated but one that will sadly never come to pass."

The viscountess regarded him, her green eyes flickering with an emotion he couldn't quite place. Reaching over, she patted his forearm. "You have obviously thought of everything. I just hope this whole affair doesn't result in unwanted consequences."

Thomas gave a hollow laugh. "You're worrying overmuch. I will ensure nothing untoward should mar Amelia's reputation in your absence."

If his mother dared pick up one of the gossip rags, she'd soon learn a red mark already existed. Over a month had passed since Lady Stanton's ball, and the London set still savored the incident with the same relish as a wine connoisseur did a glass of Bordeaux.

With a satisfied nod, the viscountess gave her skirt a pat and rose. "Good, then I shall take myself off to bed."

Thomas held up his glass to her. "Good night, Mother."

She strode to the door. Upon reaching it, she stopped and turned back to him. "You said once that her mother died when she was young."

"Yes," Thomas affirmed even though it hadn't been a question.

His mother sighed. "I did sense a sadness there. You will take care how you deal with her, won't you? I very much want her to enjoy her stay."

Caught off guard by the statement, Thomas was at a loss of how to respond. His conscience didn't need the reminder of a dead parent. He too had lost his father at a difficult age. As for sadness, he saw none of that. What he saw was a spoiled and difficult female who cared nothing for anyone but herself.

"Rest assured, Mother, I will treat Lady Amelia with all the respect and care that is due her."

His reply appeared to satisfy her this time, for she offered him a warm smile before quitting the room.

Thomas sat and pondered her parting statement long after she'd gone.

Chapter 10

The following morning, and hours after day had wrested itself from the night grey and dreary, Thomas watched the long hand on the ormolu clock inch to the next position in its sixty-second journey. One minute after eight. Amelia was now officially late.

Indecision warred like a tempest within him. His first instinct urged—no commanded—that he follow through on his promise. He should march upstairs to her chamber and haul her bodily from her bed. But he didn't believe he possessed the discipline such a task would require without wringing her beautiful neck. Then there was the matter of his family and the servants. All the commotion was sure to cause a disturbance of tongue wagging proportions.

He went to his desk and gave the tasseled cord of the bell pull on the wall an impatient tug. Within seconds of the pealed summons, Johns, the second footman, appeared at the study entrance.

"Sir?" Johns inquired with the proper deference.

Thomas had intended to instruct him to send one of the maids to locate Amelia but quickly thought better of the idea and snapped his mouth closed. Such insolence could only be by design. No doubt she was currently tucked snug in her bed, fairly champing at the bit waiting to see just what he would do next.

"I can't seem to find the posts from yesterday." It was the first thing that came to his mind—and completely inane.

"I believe they're on your desk, sir." Johns replied solemnly.

Thomas made a show of moving around the books and papers on the desk, before saying, "Ah, yes. Here they are, buried under my work. Very well, that will be all."

With a quick bow, Johns pivoted on his heel and exited.

Damn girl. Now she had him looking like a dimwit in front of his servants. While contemplating how best to deal with Amelia, he began to rifle through the stack of correspondence, most of which, he surmised at a glance, did not require his immediate attention. However, one of the envelopes—dark olive in color—caught his eye just as he was about to toss it back onto the pile with the rest. It was obvious by the handwriting the sender was female, but not one he was familiar with.

Curious, he tore open the envelope and extracted a single piece of paper. The words on the first line jumped out at him: *My Dearest Thomas*. His gaze shot immediately to the salutation at the bottom, which read *With all my affections, Louisa*.

Thomas froze, his hand tightly clutching the letter. A quick scan of the contents told him *Her Grace* looked to renew their acquaintance. And it appeared she'd abandoned subtlety in favor of a more direct approach.

Snatching up the discarded envelope from his desk, Thomas strode over to the stone fireplace and tossed both it and the letter into the flames. The fire made quick work of turning the whole matter to ashes. Dead and buried and long forgotten, which was exactly where it would remain.

His thoughts went back to his current problem. Just how exactly was he to manage Amelia? There was no way he could allow for such a flagrant display of insubordination.

It was clear they were presently engaged in a battle in which only a level head could and would prevail. Therefore, he would wait. If nothing else, he had time on his side. Rome might not have been built in a day, but he wagered he could break Lady Amelia Bertram in four short months.

"Mademoiselle?"

The sound of her maid's voice jerked Amelia awake. For a moment she didn't know why she felt so panicked and what had her gulping mouthfuls of air. Then everything hit her at once.

Light—bright light—streamed in through the windows of the bedchamber. Her gaze frantically sought the clock on the bedside table. Her breath hitched in her throat.

Nine o'clock! With a squeal and a flurry of arms and legs, she kicked off her covers and sprang from the bed. "Heavens above, how can it possibly be so late?"

Amelia had a vague recollection of the upstairs maid arriving to open the curtains and tend the fireplace earlier that morning. She'd intended to rise then, but had talked herself into another fifteen minutes of sleep. How had she allowed that time to run nigh on two hours?

Blast and double blast!

In her haste, she snagged her toe on the hem of her nightdress but managed to right herself before she went tumbling to the floor.

"*Qu'est que c'est?* Mademoiselle, what is wrong?" Hélène darted forward to steady her as Amelia tottered on her feet.

"I am late," Amelia snapped her reply, her panic having quickly given way to irritation. This was not how she'd intended to begin the humiliation that was her punishment.

"But it is still quite early."

Her maid's point was a valid one. Rarely, if ever, had she reason to rise before ten, especially when residing in

London. The social whirl of the Season made it impossible for one to sleep before two in the morning.

"I know, I know, but I was to meet with Lord Armstrong at eight. Please Hélène, make haste. I must bathe and dress quickly."

With her brows furrowed in puzzlement, Hélène released her arm and started toward the bathing room adjoining the bedchamber.

"No, I shall tend to my bath. Just prepare my clothes."

Hélène shot her a curious glance and then reversed course to hurry toward the wardrobe.

Precisely fifteen minutes and one gooseflesh-inducing bath later, Amelia stood outfitted in a velvet robe dress. As she didn't have time for anything that required more effort than a brush and some pins, Hélène had merely coiled her hair at the nape in a simple bun.

"You must wake me at seven every morning," Amelia said, slipping her feet into a comfortable pair of kid leather shoes.

Hélène paused in her task of straightening the dressing area, raising her head to stare at Amelia, her brown eyes the size of a crown and just as round. "Every morning, mademoiselle?"

Amelia nodded briskly. "Unfortunately, we shan't enjoy the same luxury as we do at home. But you needn't bother with my toilette. That I can handle myself. But as there'll be no time for me to take breakfast downstairs, unless"—she gave a mild shudder—"I'm prepared to rise at an obscenely early hour, please bring a tray when you come. It needn't be anything grand. Just enough to stave off hunger until luncheon."

"And zis morning, shall I bring you something *toute de suite?*" Hélène asked, ever the solicitous lady's maid. She'd not have her mistress go hungry if she could prevent it.

"No, this morning, I have no appetite at all."

"As you please, mademoiselle."

Already out of the chamber, the address floated behind Amelia, a faint whisper in her ear as she hastened toward the staircase.

Downstairs, Amelia reduced her pace and made the long trek down the marbled hallway. In the midst of performing their duties, servants paused, their expressions polite with only the barest hint of curiosity. Then, as she passed, like a line of falling dominoes, they acknowledged it with dips and nods with the courtesy due her status as a lady.

However, her position in the household—neither a guest nor truly a servant—was the equivalent of a queen forced to labor for her keep with the full support and encouragement from the king. In truth, her position couldn't be considered much above the people whose duty it was to serve her.

Quickening her steps, she made the final turn down yet another long stretch of floor. She passed the billiard room, the library, and another half dozen servants before she finally reached the study. She viewed the sight of the ornately framed double doors with a mixture of disapprobation and trepidation.

Was he angry? she wondered. Or more aptly put, just how angry was he? Well, in this her conscience was clear. It was not as if she'd done it deliberately. Not that he'd believe her claim that she hadn't been late intentionally were she to offer it. But truly, not only was this punishment grossly unfair, so too was its expeditious beginning. As far as *he* was concerned, her duration there would afford ample time for torment and misery. Though *whose* torment and misery was a matter yet to be seen, for she vowed she'd not bear the brunt of that alone.

Despite all her internal assertions, her belly coiled up tighter than a sailor's hitch in the Arctic cold when she delivered two short raps to the door—a courtesy she exercised more to announce her arrival than request admittance.

Shoulders back and chin high, Amelia inhaled a deep breath before entering, a grudging apology ready on her tongue. The man who was to receive it sat behind the mahogany desk, his head bent over a blue leather-bound book she instantly recognized as an accounts ledger. Around him, papers ran rampant, consuming almost every square inch of the desk's surface.

She ventured several feet beyond the door and awaited his acknowledgement. Only the rustle of paper and the rhythmic tick of a clock perched on a glass stand broke the silence.

A true gentleman would have already risen to his feet. A good half dozen seconds passed. A man would have at least glanced up. Several more seconds passed. Only an unmannerly brute would do neither.

The viscount did neither.

She was tempted to clear her throat, but her pride balked at the notion. The action carried with it a sense of desperation. *Look at me*, it begged. Truth be told, she didn't so much mind that he ignored her. What had her more piqued was that she was here at *his* behest.

With every moment she stood there unmoving, her spine grew stiffer, her breathing, deeper. After a half minute had elapsed, she knew her intended apology would never materialize. After a full minute, said apology could not have been pried from her tongue with medieval tools of torture.

The clock chimed on the half hour.

Enough is really enough! Turning, she started toward the door.

"Sit down." His voice cut the air with bladelike precision.

Amelia halted mid-stride, her right foot inches from the doorway. For a pregnant moment, she did nothing, her mind engrossed in the possible consequences of outright defiance. It took a few moments to decide that doing so wouldn't be worth the stir it was sure to cause. Turning sharply back to him, she found his position unchanged, his head still bent over the ledger, strands of hair glinting a brilliant gold shine beneath the sun's rays.

"I just assumed you had no need of me."

"Sit down," he repeated in clipped tones, waving his hand negligently toward the chair directly opposite him. He had yet to look up.

Amelia bit her lip and clenched her hands, striving for calm. She'd quit the place soon enough, she reminded herself as reluctant steps propelled her forward to take a seat in the designated chair.

His head came up slowly, revealing a regard as intense as she'd ever experienced. In haste, she dropped her gaze and took in his attire. She wasn't altogether surprised to find him wearing shirtsleeves much less that it was open at the collar, allowing for an eyeful of chest hairs. But what else was to be expected? He was a Lothario lacking Casanova's heart. Amelia jerked her gaze back up to his.

"I hope you found the accommodations to your liking." The viscount reposed back in his chair to make a lazy appraisal of her person, his regard lingering overly long at her breasts.

"I find your regard offensive, my lord." She dismissed the slow curl of heat in her belly as hunger.

Her rebuke did not in any way halt his scrutiny. Indeed it appeared to amuse him, a smile breaking the golden planes of his visage.

Slowly, he raised his gaze up to hers. "Does it disturb you? I imagine you'd be well used to male admiration." His tone held a suggestive quality that belied the innocence in his eyes.

He flattered himself to think a look from him could do anything but revolt her. Gentlemen had been looking at her for years. She'd grown quite accustomed to being surveyed as if she were under consideration for purchase. But she knew quite well he did so with the sole purpose of unsettling her for he disliked her as much as she did him.

"My lord, I'd have you not play at these games. In the end, it will do little else but distress us both."

He arched an eyebrow, his smile still in place. "Distress? Why should either of us be so afflicted? I was merely commenting on your appearance, which I'm certain you are well aware could lead even a monk astray."

A flood of warmth suffused her face despite her best efforts to remain unaffected. From any other man the compliment would have sounded as stale as week-old bread. But from the viscount's lips, it flowed in a poetry of words that might have brought praise from Tennyson himself.

"But you needn't fear I have any designs on you. My tastes have always run toward females of the warm-blooded variety. Outward beauty, while pleasing to the eye, isn't enough to hold my attention. A good disposition is essential, and, Princess, that is one area in which you sorely lack."

His poetry hit a discordant note, rendering her motionless and mute. Then the indignity of his set-down brought a flash of molten anger. Later, she'd undoubtedly regret the impudence of her response, but the words streamed from her without thought, just a to-the-bone kind of fury.

"And this from a man who can't keep his trousers above his ankles a minute longer than it takes the pastor to deliver his sermon."

The corners of his mouth performed a slow grin, spurring her to uncharted levels of viciousness.

"So please, *my lord*, do save me from the dubious distinction of being singled out by a man who has undoubtedly made it through every whore in every whorehouse in all of London."

Once she'd finished the vitriolic diatribe, she wondered at the glaring absence of her poise. The vow she'd made to herself after he'd left her bedchamber the prior night—that she'd not allow him to see even the tiniest fissure in her control—had bolted in the wake of his scathing indictment of her.

But for all her rancor, his grin only broadened, revealing a set of straight teeth, white and blinding. She was almost certain he wouldn't be nearly as handsome with the front set of them—top and bottom—missing.

"Then I can safely presume I needn't fear you'll attempt to entice me with your, er, charms, and you in turn are safe from my lascivious and most unwanted attentions?"

Want to entice him? Her? The idea was beyond absurd. "*You*, my lord, were never in any danger of that," she said, her tone scornful.

Leaning forward, the viscount rested his elbows on the desk. "Then I know I won't offend you by saying it wouldn't matter if that was your intention because *you* could never tempt me."

Having regained some of her calm, Amelia silently assessed the situation with more forethought and a clearer head.

He was lying.

Which was not to say that he liked her—or even desired her, for that matter. He could think her as cold as the Thames frozen over in the dead of winter, but he'd no more turn her down than a rummy would a bottle of liquor. His mission, as the reprehensible rake that he was, was to fornicate himself through vast pools of women, the willing ones making the task of attaining the goal that much easier. All his talk was bluster and bravado. Now had she been a spiteful sort of woman, she might have made a liar of him.

"Shall we now move onto a more pleasurable topic, like your duties for today?" His brow raised as if awaiting her permission to proceed.

For all his seeming nonchalance, no doubt he expected her to view him as a man of great restraint. Amelia wasn't fooled. Nevertheless, she was determined to match him in demeanor if nothing else. Ranting on like a fishwife would do little good.

"Your father tells me you have a good head for numbers. He believes you'd be the most use to me if I put you in charge of the accounts."

Ah yes, the one area her father thought she showed great

promise. It simply boggled his mind that a female could manage such a manly task without straining her inferior, insufficient brain. That "her gift" related to a matter in the financial realm came as no big surprise to her.

"Although I have a great deal of confidence in your father's opinion, I believe it completely ill-conceived to think of placing something of that importance in your hands."

Ill-conceived? The only ill-conceived thing—

"However, I see no harm in allowing you to put my files in order."

Harm? Amelia gritted her teeth, refusing to rise to his insults. It was what he wanted. She should collect his bloody files, dump them on a woodpile, and light the biggest blaze anyone in Devon had ever seen. Oh yes, the idea did have merit, she thought with a certain amount of glee.

"That should not tax me unduly," she said just to be contrary.

"Excellent." Like a well-rested lion, he unfolded his long length from the chair to circle the desk and stride over to the *secretaire*, which sat some twenty feet away, close to two towering arched windows.

Turning in her seat, Amelia watched his progress. If he'd had the decency to wear a jacket, she wouldn't have to endure an unfettered view of his backside—a part of the male anatomy to which she typically paid little mind. Black trousers molded trim hips, firm buttocks, and long muscled legs to proclaim him a very fine figure of a man.

Amelia quickly averted her gaze and gave her head a quick shake as if that would now dislodge the image from her mind's eye. Or perhaps she expected the action to jolt some sense back into her.

"You can start with these." He prodded a large open box by the desk with a black-booted foot.

Careful to avoid looking at his backside again, she rose to her feet and made her way to the desk to peer inside the box. What she discovered was utter chaos in the form of sheaves of black-inked papers, most of which appeared worn with age.

"And what am I to do with this?" she asked coolly. The man was the devil incarnate.

He paused before replying, "Why, organize them of course."

"These papers, documents, whatever they are, don't appear to be well kept at all."

"I see your father was right. You are intelligent. How quickly you've grasped the need for an organized work space."

Amelia bristled under his condescension and clamped her bottom lip between her teeth to stifle a response.

His shift to a businesslike manner occurred with the suddenness of a passing summer storm. He proceeded to explain what he wanted done and exactly how she should go about doing it.

The box—the first of many, he informed her—contained years of contracts for services pertaining to his breeding farm. He indicated where and how they would be filed: in a tall, six-drawer cabinet, equipped with metal dividers. He would be available for any questions that may arise. At that statement, a sense of relief overwhelmed her, for it indicated he had no intention in remaining there with her. No matter how grand a study this was, it would have felt like a broom closet if she was confined in it with him for the duration of the day.

"I will be down at the stables if your need is urgent."

Amelia's regard immediately snapped to him. Though his tone was not in the least bit suggestive, his choice of words begged a sharp look. But he was already halfway across the room, seconds later his tread a fading echo beyond the study doors.

Alone in the room for the first time, Amelia heaved a sigh of relief and cast an abstracted look around. The French Rococo influence was prominent in the serpentine-backed sofa and a plum brocade armchair at the far end of the room, which created an intimate sitting area around a black walnut fireplace. Four arched windows, topped by gold tasseled curtains, were evenly spaced along the length of the north and east walls, making little need for artificial lighting during daylight hours. Built-in bookcases consumed at least half of the wall space, its dark wood and clean lines giving the room its masculine appearance.

Amelia circled what could now be considered *her* desk and seated herself in the high-backed chair. Plucking a handful of papers from the box, she surveyed the first sheet. Faded with age and smudged from frequent handling, her eyes strained to make out the name at the top of the contract, all to no avail. Why wait for a ceremonious bonfire? She had a mind to toss it in the fire right then and there.

Amelia could see this would indeed be a long and frustrating day—*days*, perhaps even weeks. Tonight she'd pen a letter to Lord Clayborough; then tomorrow she'd acquaint herself with every conceivable avenue of escape the sprawling Stoneridge Hall possessed.

If a purgatory of smudged black ink on sheaves of paper existed, Amelia could rightly say she was trapped in it. Her day, which normally clipped on at a steady pace, lumbered relentlessly onward and was broken only by the luncheon meal and an afternoon snack she'd eaten at her desk. By the time six o'clock arrived, she'd suffered every second of every minute of every hour—the tedium of her task nearly lulling her to unconsciousness.

The only bright spot in her otherwise dreary day was that Lord Armstrong had not come back to check on her progress.

As she straightened her desk, the opening of the door had her turning with a start to view the man himself. He had changed since the morning, a neckcloth, waistcoat, and jacket adding much-needed formality to his attire. Suddenly a clothed version of Myron's Discobolus came to mind. The viscount would be the same under all that wool, silk, and lawn, all lean, sinewy muscle over golden flesh. Amelia immediately wanted to knock herself senseless for allowing another such image to enter her thoughts. What had come over her? Good looks had never impressed her—did not impress her still.

"How have you managed thus far?" He shot her a glance as he headed toward his desk.

"As well as expected, I imagine," she said pertly before turning to straighten the last stack of documents. "I shall finish what remains in the morning." She retrieved a handkerchief from the desk drawer and began wiping herself clean of what ink had gotten on her hands.

He had opened the account ledger and had begun to flip the pages. At her words, the rustling of paper ceased and the room went quiet.

Curious, Amelia darted a look in his direction to find him staring at her, the book suspended in his hand. "Tomorrow? Why tomorrow when you can do it now?"

Amelia blinked rapidly, her eyes widening. "Now?"

"Yes, do you have a problem with that?" He closed the account ledger and placed it on his desk.

Did she have a problem with that? The hour was late, her hands and back ached, and the majority of the day she'd spent sitting. Her bum had grown numb from overuse. Ridiculous man, of course she had a problem with it!

"Surely this can wait until the morning?" Her brittle tone cracked under the weight of her irritation.

Shifting, he propped himself on the edge of the desk and folded his hand across the expanse of his chest. "My dear Princess, there is still the matter of this morning to contend with. An hour and a half to be precise. You didn't think I'd forgotten your tardiness did you?"

Amelia's fingers tightened around the handkerchief much the same way she yearned to do to his neck.

"While I may have exercised restraint this morning," he

continued softly with a thread of steel in his tone, "I won't should there be another occurrence. I will not countenance disobedience."

Yes, how dare she thwart his expressed orders? A fact that had undoubtedly gnawed at him the entire day and would haunt his dreams tonight. Amelia dropped the handkerchief on the desk.

"So oversleeping is now a capital offense?" she asked, endeavoring to sound as if he hadn't just managed to set every one of her nerves on edge.

He shook his head, his expression vaguely amused. "We'd be hanging them in droves in the town square. However, for you, while not a *capital* offense, consider it an offense that carries with it certain consequences."

Was she now supposed to tremble in fear? She'd simply have to fight to contain herself. "And supper this evening? Am I to join your family or am I to work? You simply cannot have it both ways."

He pinned her with the kind of look that robbed grown women of breath, reason, and propriety. In that order. "Princess," he drawled, "you can scarce imagine all the ways I manage to have *it*."

Never had the word *it* sounded so very wicked. A sinful utterance. And for that very reason he robbed her of speech; she had no caustic response primed and ready to cut him to ribbons. She even forgot to bristle at the hated manner in which he addressed her.

But if his intention was to render her mute, he did not linger nor appear to gloat over his victory. "Supper does not commence until eight, and as it's only six now, you should have ample time to finish."

He pushed off the desk and came to his full, impressive height. "If you find yourself in need of me"—he paused ever so slightly, but long enough to infuse the words with a breadth of meaning—"ring for Reeves. He will know of my whereabouts."

While she busily gathered her wits and composure and summoned back some of her suspended indignation, he strode from the room, with the unstudied air of a man who hadn't just performed a sort of verbal intercourse with her.

Amelia dropped back into the chair, landing on the cushioned seat with a soft thump. She was angry, and agitated that her anger was threefold.

Firstly, Thomas Armstrong was a loathsome man. Secondly, he aggravated her more than any person should have a right or power to. And lastly, but the one which distressed her most, she was angry with herself. That he should have the power to fluster her with not just his words or his regard, but at times with his very presence, was an excruciating blow to a woman who'd always thought herself immune to his overstated charms. Humiliating if she considered just how unaffected he appeared by their exchanges.

The knock on the door jarred her from her damning admission. A young girl whose age Amelia estimated at no more than fifteen, entered and eagerly approached her. If the color of the girl's hair—which was a shade lighter than the viscount's—hadn't proclaimed her an Armstrong, then her green eyes certainly would. Moreover, she possessed a striking resemblance to the viscountess.

"Hello. Lady Amelia." The address seemed more an afterthought, as though the girl had suddenly remembered her manners. And perhaps if the young Miss Armstrong knew Amelia would rather be troweling under the hot desert sun, she'd have saved her greeting for someone who could more appreciate her exuberance.

She halted beside Amelia's desk, an impish smile wreathing her face. "We had so hoped to meet you yesterday—my sister and I. I'm Sarah. Thomas never mentioned how pretty you are."

Amelia was at a loss as to which of her hodgepodge of statements to respond to first. "Um—hello, Sarah. Perhaps that's because your brother doesn't believe I am."

Sarah laughed as though she'd just heard the most amusing tale, her braid swaying at the jostling of her shoulders. "One thing my brother does know better than most is a beautiful woman, and I'm sure he finds you so."

Amelia stifled a laugh. No diffident female was Miss Sarah Armstrong. "Well then, thank you. I shall take that as a compliment coming from a beauty such as yourself."

Most girls—women—would have simpered at the compliment or made sounds of feigned denial. Sarah merely smiled, her eyes bright with delight. Her attention then moved to the contracts stacked neatly in front of Amelia.

"What are you doing?"

"Getting these documents in order," Amelia replied, resuming her task. "And if I intend to make supper this evening, I can't afford to dawdle."

"I think it's admirable that you've offered to help Thomas with his charity work."

Amelia covered an eruption of laughter with a cough. So that's what he'd told his family. He'd painted her as the saintly do-gooder instead of the daughter whose father had passed her off to the viscount like unwanted baggage.

"Indeed it is," Amelia replied dryly.

"Perhaps I could assist you," Sarah offered, her expression so eager and earnest, Amelia regretted that she had to refuse her.

Or did she? Amelia took in what represented almost two hours of work on her desk and in the box. Work that would take her right up to the supper hour. She would not even have time to dress at leisure.

"Won't you be missed?" Amelia inquired, angling her head to gaze up at her.

"No, for the next hour Mama will be practicing the piano, and Emily is still with Miss Jasper completing today's lesson."

"Then should you not be taking lessons also?"

"I've already completed the lesson. Emily despises

French because her enunciation isn't terribly good. She'd be there all night if Miss Jasper didn't have to eat and sleep."

Amelia suppressed a smile while she considered the offer. Why not have the girl help? She was obviously willing. The viscount hadn't told her how she was to complete the task, just that she should. And two pairs of hands would certainly speed up the process. Surely that should please him. It would certainly please her.

"Well, if you insist." Amelia rose from her chair. "Come, you may have my seat while I instruct you."

Chapter 11

"Ah, Lady Amelia, so good of you to join us," Lady Armstrong said upon Amelia's entry into the dining room at precisely two minutes to eight that evening.

The viscountess, resplendent in a double-skirted gown edged with velvet vandykes, stood beside two women—well, the younger female might not be considered a woman just yet.

"Good evening, Lady Armstrong," Amelia replied.

"Please, allow me to introduce you to my dear friend, Mrs. Eleanor Roland, and her daughter Dorothy. Eleanor, Dorothy, may I present Lady Amelia Bertram. She will be our guest while her father is out of the country."

Mrs. Roland was a tall, stocky woman with dark, graying hair suffering from too much pomade, her face, too much powder. The latter, undoubtedly, to hide the pockmarks riddling her cheeks, forehead, and chin. Despite her size, she gave the illusion of a woman three stone lighter. Donned in a dark blue dinner dress, she'd opted for fabric that draped her figure instead of trying to squeeze her body into something that idealized the feminine shape as many ladies of grander proportions were wont to do.

The daughter was the antithesis of the mother, possessing a shock of curly red hair the texture of which made humidity its natural enemy. Small and slight, she spoke in monosyllables, her voice hardly more than a whisper.

"Lady Amelia, it's a pleasure to make your acquaintance," Mrs. Roland said politely, but her voice lacked sufficient warmth to declare it a friendly greeting. But then, women rarely welcomed her with open arms.

"The pleasure is mine, Mrs. Roland, Miss Roland." Amelia gave each a nod.

Mrs. Roland appeared preoccupied, her attention focused elsewhere. Amelia followed the woman's gaze straight to the hooded stare of the viscount.

Since her arrival, she'd done her best to ignore him, conscious that he stood only feet away in front of the mahogany cabinet, watching her, making her feel as if he could see through her tulle silk gown and cotton undergarments straight to the bare flesh below. Amelia quickly averted her gaze.

"And I believe you have met my daughters." Lady Armstrong gestured to where they stood by their brother, both dressed in pretty lace-trimmed frocks.

"Yes, ma'am, earlier this evening."

Amelia certainly would not divulge under what circumstances she became acquainted with the youngest. Emily, three years older than Sarah's fifteen years, Amelia had met as she'd returned to her chambers after leaving the study. Though not inclined to her sister's chattiness, Emily had been welcoming and kind. And like her brother and sister, she had inherited the viscountess's green eyes, golden hair, and good looks.

With the introductions completed, they took their places at a table covered with a white linen tablecloth. In proportion to all the other furniture in the room, it was solid and large.

To Amelia's chagrin, she was seated to the left of the viscount, who sat at the head with the viscountess on his right. She would have preferred the opposite end of the table.

The entry of the footmen bearing silver trays, laden with food tasty enough to tempt even the most particular palette, diverted her attention.

Within minutes, bowls and dishes were filled, red wine in every glass.

"And how did you enjoy the Season?" Lord Armstrong asked, addressing Miss Roland after the footmen had taken up their post at the back of the room and everyone was intent upon the first course.

Miss Roland stilled, her spoon poised near her lips. She quickly lowered it into her bowl of turtle soup.

"Do tell his lordship how you enjoyed your Season," Mrs. Roland prodded, impatience edging her tone when her daughter didn't offer up an immediate reply.

"If I were prettier then I'm certain I would have attracted more suitors . . . well, at least one suitor." Miss Roland let out a heavy sigh. "I fear I shall end up disappointing Mama."

Amelia nearly choked on her wine. Honesty among the aristocracy was usually harder to find than a lady with an eighteen-inch waist—without stays—and looked upon with just as much skepticism, envy, or lecherous delight. But no one could doubt Miss Roland's sincerity. Not with the droop of her narrow shoulders and the forlorn look in her hazel eyes.

A swift glance around the table gave testament to the fact. Though Mrs. Roland looked mortified, every member of the Armstrong family observed her as if they'd just witnessed a puppy being kicked.

However, it was Lord Armstrong who galloped in on his white horse in full knight armor, polished and glistening.

"You're much more than pretty. And if the gentlemen of the ton can't see your other wonderful qualities, they don't deserve you."

Miss Roland lifted her gaze from her plate to regard him. If he'd told her she was Aphrodite immortalized, she couldn't have looked more dubious. "I can't imagine anything better than being pretty enough to attract a gentleman."

In response, he placed his utensils down, dabbed the corners of his mouth with a serviette and gave Miss Roland a measured look. Obviously a man so filled with his own self-importance, he expected Miss Roland to accept his every word as fact.

"I really must disagree. I've met my share of beauties who would have made a tour of duty seem like a picnic. Without divulging the name of a certain lady of the ton, I will tell you a story about my introduction to her the year past."

The ting of utensils against the white porcelain plates halted. All eyes were riveted on the viscount, who needed only his crown to claim his position as the noble prince. The hairs on Amelia's nape reared up as her unease began its ascent.

"She was quite beautiful. I would say almost as handsome as—" He paused as if in search of the right comparison. His gaze found hers. "Lady Amelia, I would wager. Certainly a stunning beauty by all accounts."

All eyes in the room fell on her. She quickly gave her bowl of vermicelli soup her undivided attention. Her cheeks warmed with every extended moment of silence.

Amelia wasn't naïve enough to think he'd intended to pay her a compliment. With this grand show in front of his rapt audience, she was certain he planned to make her the moral example of his little tale.

"Well, this young *lady*,"—he stressed the last word as if the term in regard to said "lady"—her—was suspect—"and I had no prior acquaintance. I won't offend your sensibilities with the particulars of what she said to me during our introduction. Needless to say, it was the sort of thing you'd find in the gossip rags. Groundless, unfounded rumors maligning my character."

"You mean there is a woman alive who can resist your

charms?" the viscountess asked, the grave sincerity in her tone contrary to the amusement in her eyes.

At their mother's remark, Sarah and Emily, who had been trying to stifle their laughter by covering their mouths with serviettes, abandoned all efforts to remain poker-faced and let out a torrent of girlish giggles.

"Abominable behavior," Mrs. Roland exclaimed with a disapproving sniff, her back visibly stiffening, pushing back her plump shoulders. "Some of the young ladies these days are lacking in good breeding." Turning her regard from the viscount, she beamed a smile at her daughter. "Now Dorothy here has what anyone would consider exemplary manners. Don't you, dear?"

"But what good does all that do me? Manners alone won't find me a husband. Gentlemen prefer pretty wives," Miss Roland muttered, her gaze downcast.

The viscountess and Mrs. Roland looked primed to voice their replies. However, it was again Lord Armstrong who prevailed. "An intelligent man prefers much more desirable qualities in a wife. Qualities such as kindness, humility, warmth, and a good character. A beautiful wife who is disagreeable is hardly the sort of woman a man wants to remain chained to for the rest of his life."

In a move that held all the innocence of a highwayman telling the magistrate he'd merely stopped the carriage for a ride while touting a gun and a mask, he shifted his gaze to her. "Don't you agree, Lady Amelia?"

Just what was his game, to embarrass her? Didn't he know one had to actually *care* for that to work? Besides, she hadn't said anything that hadn't been the unvarnished truth.

"Certainly, if in fact the lady in question was truly disagreeable. I, for one, did not witness the incident so I have no knowledge as to the circumstances under which the lady, um, insulted you, as you say. And as you haven't enlightened us on exactly what she said, it would be unseemly of me to offer my opinion."

"You have my assurances that this lady was indeed insulting." The intensity of his regard could have seared a hole through her.

"Well, before I condemn the woman, I would have to hear her account of the events. As you know, there are always two sides to a story." With that pert statement, Amelia spooned some soup into her mouth.

Silence befell the table. Amelia pretended to be oblivious to the gazes darting between her and the viscount.

"It's good to know that you, Thomas, a gentleman of good taste and judgment, appreciates the finer, less obvious qualities in a woman." Mrs. Roland endowed him with the smile of a woman who was closing in on her prey.

Then it all made perfect sense—touting her daughter's exceptional manners, singing her praises to Lord Armstrong. Mrs. Roland wanted the viscount for her daughter, which would be the equivalent of teaming Little Red Riding Hood with the wolf.

But that being said, Amelia felt duty bound to aid in such a worthwhile endeavor. *Let's see how he likes having the tables turned on him.*

"Yes, Lord Armstrong is truly remarkable in that respect. I'm quite certain he too is in search of a woman exactly like Miss Roland. But wait, if Miss Roland is willing, I daresay he won't have to look very far." Amelia sent the aforementioned parties a look of pure guilelessness.

The crystal chandelier soaring above them was lit by at least four dozen candles. There were gas-lit wall sconces and two candelabras on the dining table. Mrs. Roland's smile shone brighter than the light of all combined. Everyone else remained mute.

"I must say—"

"How good of you to offer your matchmaking services, Lady Amelia," Lord Armstrong cut in before Mrs. Roland could finish. "However, I've known Dorothy since she was a child—a babe really. I look upon her as I do my own sisters, and I'm sure she feels the same."

The viscountess gave a faint smile, appearing relieved her son had handled the delicate matter so tactfully. His sisters exchanged a look Amelia couldn't decipher. Miss Roland slowly nodded her agreement to his assessment of their relationship. But poor Mrs. Roland sat motionless in her chair, rendered mute by his gentle yet unequivocal refusal to entertain a match with her daughter.

Suddenly, Amelia was contrite. In her zeal to embarrass Lord Armstrong, she'd included others in her wide-reaching net. Blast it all. It was he who had started all of this with his "The beauty who is an utter shrew" tale. And because of that, Mrs. Roland now bore the pained expression of dashed hopes and misspent dreams.

"Well, if not the viscount, a far luckier gentleman will have the privilege of taking Miss Roland as his wife," Amelia said, in an attempt to temper the—albeit gentle— rejection.

The girl, seventeen if she was a day, still had a couple years more to add some flesh to her figure. The men would come calling then, for her complexion was clear and her features quite regular. Though she might never be considered a rose, she certainly wasn't the least bit objectionable. With the appropriate dowry, she'd fair well in the marriage mart.

"Do you really think so?" Miss Roland asked, a faint note of hope in her voice.

"I wouldn't say it if I didn't mean it. You are only, what seventeen, eighteen?" *Sixteen?*

"Seventeen."

"I was quite a fright at that age." An out-and-out lie, but Miss Roland would never know that. The viscount knew; his eyes told her so. But he said not a word, merely watched her in contemplative silence.

"I don't believe that for a second. I thought . . ." Sarah trailed off at the quelling glare from her sister.

"You can ask anyone." There was no one to ask, save some of the servants. Cloistered at their country estate with only one friend to speak of, Amelia hadn't been seen by anyone in society until the past year.

Miss Roland regarded her with an expression close to awe. As if she could barely believe the transformation that had turned a fright into the female who now sat opposite her.

"And look at me now, finished my second Season with no marriage prospects as yet." Which was technically true if one asked her father. "You're still very young and have many years to find a man worthy of your affections."

"Yes, dear, plenty of time," her mother echoed, having come out of her stupor of silence. "I'm certain next Season Thomas would be happy to introduce you to some of his friends. I believe Lord Alex is still unattached. And so very handsome."

In the midst of taking a sip of his wine, a coughing fit seized the viscount. Amelia smiled and resumed eating.

Three courses and an hour and a half later, the women rose to retire to the drawing room for tea. Amelia politely demurred an invitation to join them. Indeed, it had been a long day, and she yearned for the privacy of her bedchamber.

"Lady Amelia, might I have a word with you before you retire?" Lord Armstrong called out from behind her as she proceeded to exit the dining room.

Amelia stopped, her belly knotting as the women disappeared beyond the doors and into the hall. Reluctantly, she turned to find him advancing toward her, only stopping when he stood close—too close. His scent, wholly masculine and provoking, assailed her nostrils in a rush. She stood quietly while he made a sweep of her body with those green eyes of his, her heart lurching in traitorous and maddening response.

Unsettled by his nearness but loath to betray her feelings,

Amelia raised an eyebrow, fixing her expression into a cool mask of sufferance. "Can this not wait until the morning?"

"No. Come let us go to the study." Without further explanation, he started toward the door. When he realized she hadn't moved, he paused and shot a glance at her over his shoulder. "Do you require a written invitation?"

The sarcasm in his tone was just the thing she needed to tamp down her heightened senses, the hammering of her heart. The man was insufferable far above all his vaunted appeal.

"Fine," she snapped, "but do be quick about it. I would like to get a proper night's rest tonight. I do have to rise frightfully early in the morning, and the lord of the manor is a stickler for punctuality." She lifted the weight of her three-tiered silk skirt and swept past him.

Amelia reached the study in long, angry strides. He followed her in a moment later, his mouth curved at the corners into a semblance of a smile. Leisurely, he made his way to the opposite end of the room near the fireplace, stopping at the sideboard to pour himself a drink.

Determined to maintain her composure, Amelia waited quietly as he took a deep swallow, then turned and sauntered back to where she stood, still and rigid on the edge of the Oriental area rug.

"I returned to the study at quarter to seven to find you gone." He spoke softly without a hint of emotion.

That was what all this was about? That she hadn't been here when he returned? The man was impossible. "And your point?"

His jaw tightened. "Am I to understand that you completed your task in that brief time?"

"Look for yourself if you don't believe me," she said, jerking her head toward the cabinet. "You will find every document filed and in order. And you can check the box. You will find it empty."

This time, Lord Armstrong tossed his drink back with a

gulp. He was either thirsty or angry. She imagined it was the latter. A sweet sense of triumph flooded her.

When he lowered the glass from his lips, it was empty. Perhaps he had been thirsty after all. Amelia quelled the smile threatening her hard-fought stoicism.

"You were to work for an hour and a half," he stated, rotating the glass in his hand.

"Your mandate to me was to complete my task. I achieved that. What did you expect me to do after I'd finished, sit at my desk and twiddle my thumbs?"

A mirthless laugh rumbled in his throat. "It appears then, I've greatly misjudged how effective and efficient you would be. I can see that if I'm to have you duly occupied, I'll need to give you more work."

The fleeting, sweet taste of victory turned acrid in her throat.

Without removing his gaze from her, he placed the empty glass on a nearby table. For what seemed like an interminable length of time, he stared at her, his eyes darkening to the color of cut emeralds of the flawless variety. "You really must learn to temper your words. Your mouth always seems to get you into trouble. Have you not learned that yet, Princess?"

Amelia swallowed at the huskiness of his tone, the sensual intent of his gaze. When his attention shifted to focus on her mouth, she took an instinctive step back. He instantly countered, coming even closer than before.

Lowering his head a fraction, he whispered, "It provokes a man in dangerous ways."

His voice was seduction encased in velvet heat. Her gaze drifted to his mouth—his fuller lower lip. Amelia swallowed again and nervously ran her tongue over her bottom lip.

It happened so swiftly, she didn't have a chance to blink. A light tug of his hand, and she was in his arms. There was nothing to stop peach silk from meeting sage wool; her breasts from crushing against the unyielding wall of his chest. Amelia stiffened, her heart a jackhammer in her chest as his head began an unhurried descent.

Move. Scream. Do anything except stand there like a ninny. But the languor stealing over her body turned her limbs as useless as a swimmer's against a powerful undertow. Then his lips found hers, and the tide of feelings dragged her under.

Unlike the fumbling efforts of Lord Finley, the viscount did not try to pry her lips apart with brute force or the fervor of his passion. No, he managed that with seductive finesse, nipping then soothing her bottom lip until her lips parted with a tiny gasp. At her submission, he drove his fingers into the heavy weight of her hair, anchoring her head in his hands. Then he fit his mouth to hers.

Her knees buckled, and her hands clutched the silk lapels of his jacket. For a fleeting moment, she surfaced from the fog of passion, and thought about stopping or at the very least offering some resistance. The slow thrust of his tongue persuaded her otherwise, acting like a drug on her senses and turning her mind to mush. Amelia opened her mouth wider. She wanted more.

He let out a low groan and obliged her, his hand now at her hip pulling her closer until their lower bodies were flush. The strength of his arousal lay stiff and throbbing against her belly, the intimate contact sending a flood of warmth and embarrassing moisture to her center.

There had been times when she had overheard girls titter and engage in whispered discussions out of earshot of their chaperones. The subject of those discussions invariably involved men and such things as kissing, sometimes even fondling of an improper nature. *Had they? Would they? How did it feel?* Amelia would listen, silently pitying their naivety. In her experience, though limited it might have been, kissing did not have the power to move her physically or otherwise. Or so she had thought.

Never could she have been more wrong.

Then her hands were sifting through the golden locks of his hair, silky and thick between her fingers. Uncertain what she should do with her tongue, so bewildered by the torrents of pleasure coursing through her body, she'd been content to receive his passionate ministrations. Now she wanted to participate just as fully. She began with tentative probes, then wide sweeping forays of his mouth. Before long, their tongues tangled in wet demand, the kiss feeding a hunger of which she hadn't known herself capable.

Heat consumed her everywhere. She clenched her thighs, but the action failed to alleviate the ache in the place she burned the hottest. His hand trailed from her hip to the underside of her breast until he palmed the pebbled mound over her bodice.

That was what it took to bring her back to reality with a jarring thud. Appalled, she wrenched herself from his embrace, staggering back until she achieved enough distance from him to begin to gain control of her senses.

"Don't," she said weakly, her breaths ragged puffs of air. Dislodged from the security of the pins, her hair streamed past her shoulders and down her back. She imagined she looked the very picture of "the lady who doth protest too much." She knew she felt it.

Contrarily, except for a faint blush staining his cheeks, the viscount appeared unaffected by their embrace, undoubtedly accustomed not only to kissing women senseless but to doing a great deal more. What they had shared was probably as commonplace to him as a peck on the cheek.

"Who'd have thought such heat existed under all that ice?" He adjusted his jacket as he spoke.

"Never, *ever* touch me again." She ground out every word.

Lord Armstrong chuckled softly. "Are you sure? From my position, you seemed to be enjoying yourself thoroughly."

Bastard!

"And what of you? Just this morning you claimed to be

immune to my charms?" She wanted—needed—to wipe the mocking smile clean from his face.

"Oh, I am," he replied softly. "But I believe I've just discovered the most efficient manner in which to deal with you."

"It didn't feel that way to me," she snapped, remembering the hard ridge of his erection against her belly. How dare he try to make it appear as if she had been the only one affected, the only one who had lost her head for those heated moments.

The viscount gave a hearty laugh and gestured down to the front of his trousers. "You mean this?"

Shocked, Amelia blindly averted her gaze but could do little to halt another flood of heat from blistering her cheeks.

"I would hardly call this the barometer of good taste. Didn't you know, these things have minds of their own? Sometimes it requires merely a comely face and a shapely figure. Discriminating these are not."

Amelia wished she'd been born a big hulk of a man so she could pummel him senseless. But then if she were a man, she wouldn't be in this position.

"If you refuse to keep your hands to yourself, I'll be forced to take the matter in hand. And I guarantee you this, my lord, you will not like the outcome." Her warning carried all the weight of a hummingbird, but at the moment, she did not care.

"And just what do you plan to do? Appeal to your father? If I compromised you, he would have us wed before the onset of winter. A prospect I'm certain neither of us desires."

Of course, the blasted man was right. And nothing short of increasing his wealth threefold would please her father more. "Now I see why my father admires you so much. You and he are just the same."

Thomas stiffened. It was clear in her tone that her statement wasn't meant as a compliment. The creep of anger began to steal over him. His affront was for Harry not himself. Hadn't the poor man endured enough because of her?

"I suggest you watch your tongue. Your father is one of the best men I've ever known."

Amelia's head jerked back, her eyes widening as if surprised by the vehemence of his response.

"Which isn't saying much, I daresay. But as far as I'm concerned, the two of you suit each other well. You both care nothing for anyone else unless it's to your financial or personal benefit. It's a shame you weren't my father's son—how much simpler life would be for everyone involved."

Thomas schooled his features. This spoilt brat dared to condescend to him. What did she know of money other than listing expenses in the credit and debit column? She'd never had to look his mother and three sisters in the eye and tell them not only hadn't they money enough to keep up their properties but hardly enough for the barest necessities.

If she had people she considered friends—and that was very much in doubt—who ceased to have anything to do with her, it was because of her surly disposition, not because a lack of funds had suddenly deemed her unworthy of their company. Her father had saved his family from certain financial ruin.

"My heart goes out to your father. God help me should I have a daughter like you." Contempt laced his every word.

Amelia's body stiffened on a softly indrawn breath. A look of some indiscernible emotion flashed across her face as she stood motionless, her eyes unblinking.

"When he returns, I'll be certain to give him your condolences. On the other hand, since you do see him more frequently than I, perhaps you can offer them yourself." With that, she turned, lifted her skirts, and calmly exited the study.

Thomas made no attempt to stop her. Further conversation might just end in a full-scale war. Raking an unsteady hand through his hair, he slumped back to rest on the edge of the desk, a dull ache radiating in his chest.

Chapter 12

The longcase clock in the hall announced the top of the hour with eight strident chimes just as Amelia entered the study the day following. She expelled a small sigh of relief when a quick scan of the room revealed that she was indeed alone.

"I see you managed to arrive on time," the viscount drawled from behind her, his voice containing no residue of displeasure from yesterday's unpropitious ending.

Or had been alone.

Amelia turned her head to find him framed in the doorway. He looked remarkably rested—and wretchedly handsome. Never had brown tweed and camel wool had a more strikingly masculine form to cover. Her heart gave a tiny flutter.

"What did you expect? I've heard you flog your servants. I like my back unmarred thank you very much," she replied crisply before taking a seat at her desk. If he could act as if they were at their acrimonious normalcy, as if the kiss had not occurred, so certainly could she.

"Oh, I wouldn't flog you. I'd paddle your bare behind."

A gasp escaped her lips as her gaze flew to his. Amusement danced in his eyes, but he looked perfectly capable of carrying out such a punishment.

"You my lord, are the most—"

"Yes I know, arrogant, horrible, et cetera. You needn't continue. I get the idea."

Three days ago, she would have bristled at the interruption and seethed over a remark infused with a boredom bordering on insolence. Then she would have delivered him a set-down that would make her remarks at the ball tame in comparison. Today, embarrassment heated her cheeks to blistering degrees. Amelia snapped her mouth closed.

He crossed the room, not coming to a stop until he stood wide-legged in front of her desk. Amelia's heart had started to beat faster when he'd bypassed his desk; now it galloped along at unheard-of speeds. Yet she still maintained the fortitude to acknowledge him with a supercilious raise of her eyebrow.

"Is my mother hosting a party in your honor?"

Amelia wished she didn't know of what he spoke. But she did. She treated him to a blank stare anyway.

"Your hair. Your dress. Isn't it a bit fancy for all this?" A jerk of his head indicated *all this* was the narrow scope of her current existence: the study.

So what if she'd had Hélène take the irons to give her hair some bouncy curls?

Outward beauty, while pleasing to the eye, isn't enough to hold my attention.

And so what if the pale violet, silk dress with trimmings of puffed ribbon might be more suited for an elegant supper party? It wasn't a crime that she chose to wear it today.

You could never tempt me.

But as much as she tried to convince herself of that fact, she knew he saw right through to her damaged pride and silently mocked her.

God help me should I have a daughter like you.

He let her stew in her foolishness a second longer before turning on his heel and heading to his desk. "Before you get settled there, I'll need some coffee." He tossed the remark over his shoulder with a casualness meant to give the impression that such a request was a common occurrence.

Amelia gave her head a violent mental shake. *Fetch him his coffee? Has he gone completely daft?*

"Then I suggest you ring for one of the servants."

"And why should I do that when I have you?" He now sat ensconced behind his desk.

"Why should I get you coffee when you employ a team of servants whose express purpose is to cater to your every whim?" He'd now taken his petty vindictiveness to a level of which even he should be ashamed.

The viscount didn't immediately respond, his attention focused on ostensibly searching for something on his desk. When he spoke, he sounded distracted. "But I want you to do it. Every morning Mr. Wendel's secretary brings him his morning beverage. It is not an uncommon practice."

"I do not particularly care what occurs in Mr. Wendel's office," she said, bearing down on her back teeth.

Lord Armstrong lifted his head to regard her. "You are correct. The only thing that need concern you right now is bringing me my coffee. Two cubes of sugar with just a dash of cream. And Amelia, make no mistake about it—this is not a request." He returned his attention to the clutter on his desk, effectively dismissing her.

Amelia silently cursed him in English, French, and the smattering of Italian she'd learned from an Italian governess. But damn it, she had little choice but to do as he said. He had her at a disadvantage. This was his estate, his family, his bloody everything. Here she was nothing but another servant in the guise of a guest. Imprisoned for having a mind of her own and wanting a life of her own.

Although she took pains not to glance in his direction, she felt the intensity of his gaze as she rose and crossed the room to the door, her pride smarting with her every step. Like everything else, she'd attempt to get through this with as much aplomb as she could muster.

In the hall, Amelia immediately located the butler, a dour, portly man with graying hair, who treated her request for the beverage with a monotone "Yes ma'am." He summoned a footman from the drawing room and dispatched him to the kitchen. The confusion came when she insisted on taking the coffee to the study herself. Puzzled looks were exchanged between the two men until with a nod, the butler permitted the footman to hand her the tray.

The same silence of her leave-taking met her return to the study. Lord Armstrong stopped what he was doing to watch her approach, his expression shuttered.

If she was truly the hoyden he and her father believed her to be, he wouldn't be drinking the hot liquid; he'd be wearing it.

The sequence of events that followed would make that very thought appear as rehearsed as anything performed in Her Majesty's Theatre, the execution the stuff of accolades. In trying to find a place for the tray amongst the clutter of papers, books, and various writing accoutrements, one corner of the tray tilted and sent the cup careening like a drunken sailor in a storm. All of her frantic efforts could not prevent what happened next: hot coffee—fixed to the viscount's specifications—all over his lap.

A roar and a series of blistering curses added to the carnage as he bolted to his feet and toppled his chair to the wood floor. The empty cup landed on the rug but miraculously came through the fall unscathed, leaving only one human casualty.

"I-I-I'm dreadfully sorry." Amelia gulped, flustered and out of sorts. She stared at him—his wet, coffee-stained trousers an untrammeled horror.

"You little brat, you did that deliberately," he ground out, and pulled open one of the many drawers of his desk, yanking out a white handkerchief.

"I swear to you, I didn't mean to—" Amelia abruptly

broke off when her mind fully comprehended what he had called her. Stiffening, she drew her shoulders back.

Brat?

And here she was practically tripping all over herself to apologize. "Well if you're going to be a boar about it, I shall withdraw my apologies."

"Milord." The breathless address came from behind her.

Amelia turned to see a footman hovering anxiously at the doorway.

"I heard—" The footman broke off when he saw the nature of the calamity that had sent a string of colorful expletives echoing down the corridors.

"I will send someone from the kitchen directly," the young man said, before disappearing back through the door.

"If the desk wasn't such a mess, this would not have occurred. Where was I to put this?" Amelia gave the tray she still held in her hand a pointed look.

Lord Armstrong growled low in his throat. "You should have taken the damn cup off the tray is what you should have done." With one last dab of the once-white handkerchief at a wet spot on his upper thigh, the viscount tossed the soiled linen on the floor with a hiss of disgust.

"My lord, you are in the presence of a lady, whether you will admit the fact to yourself or not. Please do keep a check on your tongue," she reproached him in her frostiest tone.

His head jerked up, and suddenly his green eyes glowed with predatory intent. "Me? *I* am the one who needs to check my tongue?" he asked softly.

Rounding the desk, he advanced toward her, and with each stride forward, Amelia instinctively took one step back. She held the tray in front of her as if tempered silver was enough to ward him off.

Their dance of advance and retreat continued in silence until Amelia saw they were nearing the bookshelves along the south walls—where she would be trapped.

"Milord." The footman announced his return, and in front

of him stood a petite girl whom Amelia swiftly assessed as the kitchen help by her white food-stained apron. She carried a pail in one hand and a cloth rag in the other.

The footman directed the girl with a motion of his hand. "Anna will clean up."

Lord Armstrong had stopped, and Amelia took that opportunity to place the tray on her desk and distance herself from him, far enough away that his presence—utterly male and overwhelming—didn't continue to unnerve her.

"No." The word emerged clipped and harsh. He strode over to the maid and relieved her of the bucket.

All eyes in the room snapped to him, containing varying degrees of bewilderment. With a solicitousness he'd never once shown her, the viscount removed the cloth from the maid's hand and set the bucket on the floor. "You may leave. I shall have this dealt with." At his nod of dismissal, the girl curtsied and scampered from the room.

"As you wish, sir." The footman bowed before following the maid's hasty departure.

The soft click of the door closing indicated they were once again very much alone. The viscount directed his attention to her. Only when he extended the hand holding the cloth rag, did she realize what he intended.

Stupefied, Amelia could only shake her head in mute denial. He simply could not be serious.

In response to her vigorous head shaking, he gave a slow, deliberate nod to the contrary. "Oh, yes, you will. And after every single drop of coffee is wiped clean, you may mop the entire floor."

It would have been thigh-slapping, chortling, snorting funny had it not been quite so apparent he was serious—and obviously as mad as a hatter.

Amelia held up her hand, splayed her fingers for him to take in their unblemished, perfection and manicured nails, and then gestured to her dress, which was a color that could only be described as pale salmon. "If you expect me to get down on my knees to perform menial servant work, you, my lord, are sadly mistaken." What would he do, physically force her to her knees? As heinous a man as he was, that seemed several levels beneath his character.

"Oh, I don't just expect it—I shall relish it." He tossed the rag in the water and started toward her, his movements lithe and controlled.

Amelia stood her ground, commanding her legs not to move. When he drew within several feet, she balked and stammered, "If you dare lay one finger on me, I shall create so much noise, everyone will think someone is being murdered."

The viscount came to a smooth stop in front of her, his expression implacable. As if to test the sincerity of her threat, he stroked the curve of her cheek with his finger in a feathery caress. Amelia's stomach plummeted the same way it had done when she had once lost her seat on her mount. She vividly recalled the terrifying feeling of hurtling forward to meet the hard earth. At least when she had hit the ground unharmed but shaken, the sensation had stopped. In this case, there appeared to be no end to her fall.

Wide-eyed, she regarded him, unable to move, incapable of protest.

He lowered his head until she could feel his breath, lemon-scented and warm, on her forehead. "This is my finger," he whispered. "Maybe I've gone deaf, but I can't seem to hear your screams."

It took a moment for his words to register, her thinking having been momentarily suspended by the lull of his dark, silken tones. Amelia took a hasty, if somewhat jerky step backward, breaking the heated contact as she endeavored to collect herself.

Really, this whole situation was laughable—or perhaps one day she'd look back upon it and feel so.

"That's because you are not listening closely enough."

Certainly one absurd statement deserved an equally absurd response.

Lord Armstrong answered her with one undaunted forward movement. When Amelia attempted another step backward, she encountered the hard edge of her desk.

He was going to kiss her, his intent clear in his eyes. A silent yearning had taken root within her, setting her blood pulsing wildly and starting a dull throb at the apex of her thighs. She watched, transfixed, as his mouth drew closer. Not only was he about to kiss her, she was going to permit him the liberty . . . again.

Then, in a flash, he was gone, his movements a blur. By the time she regained a portion of her bewildered senses, he was beside his desk looking the picture of equanimity.

Then she heard it again. The knock. The sound she'd thought was the frantic beating of her heart had been someone knocking on the door. Her face went up in flames. She sat down with an abruptness that knocked the next breath from her, laid her hands flat on the desk and willed them to stop their god-awful trembling.

Lord Armstrong issued the terse command to enter and made a show of sopping the coffee from his trousers with a clean handkerchief.

The door flew open. Sarah entered with her smile and sunny disposition. If Amelia had been inclined to grand shows of physical affection, she might have hugged her.

"Good morning, Thomas, I wondered if—" Sarah halted. Espying her brother, her eyes grew round and her mouth formed a perfect *o*. Then she giggled, a girlish sound that reminded Amelia of innocent mischief making. "What happened to your trousers?"

The viscount shot her a dark look and ceased his ineffectual wiping. "I'm glad I'm able to amuse you this morning. What do you want, brat?"

How different the word sounded when used in reference

to his sister, exasperated but warmly affectionate. Certainly not the tone he'd used with her.

"I—well, I came to find out if I could assist Amelia again today."

Amelia nearly groaned aloud. The innocence of youth also had its drawbacks. How she wished the girl knew when to keep her mouth shut. She half expected a bolt of lightning to zigzag down from the sky and impale her right where she sat. That was just the sort of day she was bound to have.

"What do you mean 'again'?" the viscount asked in a deceptively soft voice. Though he addressed his sister, he affixed his regard on her.

Amelia swallowed hard.

Sarah's gaze bounced between them several times before responding. "Um—I helped Amelia with some . . ." Her voice trailed off as a storm gathered in the viscount's eyes.

"Did I do something wrong?" Sarah asked, after a moment of charged silence.

"No, you did nothing wrong. If anyone—" Amelia began.

"Amelia will not require your assistance any longer," the viscount cut in smoothly.

Sarah shot a glance at Amelia as if she expected her to contradict her brother.

"Yes, Sarah, I shan't be requiring your help again."

Sarah sighed in the dramatic fashion of a girl who could turn even the most minor events into something fit for a fiction novel. "Fine, then I shall have to find something else to do today since Miss Jasper is sick in bed with a cold." She turned back to her brother. "Oh, and mother says she hopes you don't intend to keep Lady Amelia holed up in the study all day."

Amelia choked back a bitter laugh. If only the viscountess knew the full of it. Lord Armstrong's response was low and unintelligible.

Sarah issued them a cheery farewell and went on her way.

The viscount wasted no time after the door closed before

stalking toward her desk. Standing, he had her at a disadvantage, and he knew it. But she'd be damned if she'd acknowledge it by bolting to her feet looking the least bit intimidated and defensive.

"If you ever use my sister again, I'll paddle you so hard you won't be able to sit for days. Now, you have two choices, you can either clean up the mess you made or you'll be rubbing elbows with the scullery maids. Which is it to be?"

If he'd delivered the first smack of the threatened paddling, Amelia couldn't have been more horrified.

"What, not the two choices you expected? What did you think, that I would kiss you again?" He searched her expression, and whatever he found there made him exclaim softly, "Lord, is that what this was all about? You wanted another kiss? Well, you're going to have to work on your approach. There are much easier ways to get what you want, and dousing a man with coffee is definitely not one of them. However, since you've gone through all this trouble, it would behoove me to oblige you."

Of all the things he'd ever accused her of, this was by far the worst. Not to mention it made her appear pitiable and utterly pathetic. With little but her pride to act in her defense, Amelia sprang to her feet in a rustle of skirts and marched over to his desk. She snatched up the rag from the bucket of soapy water and with as much dignity as one could manage in the given situation, began to lower herself to her knees.

But her knees barely brushed the floor when she was hauled to her feet and into Lord Armstrong's hard embrace. The wet rag fell from her startled hand to the floor.

"What——" She let out a gasp and clutched his shoulders for balance.

"Damn, but you are the most obstinate, willful, exasperating female——" He covered her mouth in a searing kiss. Amelia resisted for the time it took his tongue to penetrate the wall of teeth guarding the inside of her mouth, a task requiring only seconds. With that citadel breeched, her lips parted in helpless wonder, in hunger. She felt completely out of herself, drifting on a plane of pleasure that grew with every slow thrust of his tongue. Then his hands were on her bottom, squeezing and dragging her closer until she could feel his erection nudging her center through the inconvenient bulk of silk and cotton petticoats. Amelia whimpered and strained to get closer.

He abandoned her lips, which elicited a moan of protest. His mouth scored her cheek and then her chin, anointing every spot with a feathery kiss. Her head fell back with a soft groan, and he took advantage of the full access he now had to the long line of her neck. Her nails scraped his scalp, the feel of his hair soft and silky between her fingers as she pulled him closer.

She'd never known the spot behind her ears was so sensitive until his mouth settled there, the surge of his breaths its own caress. Amelia drank in the sounds of his pleasure and the scent of male heat, starched linen, and—coffee.

Reality descended down on her with pride crushing force. Her body immediately became rigid as she jerked her hands from his tousled strands to give his shoulders a hard shove. With a grunt and a bewildered look, he took a step back, his hands falling to his sides.

Good Lord, what was she doing? What was wrong with her? Earlier, she'd thought him mad when in truth *she* had to be the mad one.

For several moments, neither spoke, her labored breathing the only sound to fill the lengthening silence. If the viscount had been at all affected by the kiss, his expression revealed none of it.

"I need to change." His gaze flickered down to her skirts. "And so do you." With that, he strode from the room.

Amelia glanced down, and on her silk skirt, plain for all to see, was a large coffee stain.

Chapter 13

That evening under the light of the tallow candle in her bedchamber, Amelia penned a letter to Lord Clayborough. The pen pierced the paper in several places as if her words weren't enough to convey her growing sense of urgency. And she despised that feeling of desperation.

Amelia was also tempted to write to Elizabeth, but could not bring herself to burden her with the horror of her circumstances when her friend, the Countess of Creswell, happily awaited the birth of her first child in four months.

After sealing the letter and placing it on the bedside table to give to the footman to post, Amelia crawled into bed doing something she rarely did: she fretted. She'd always thought it was nothing but a wasted bit of emotion signified by heavy sighs and persistent worry, which accomplished little and solved nothing. However, she had to concede that the matter of her physical reaction to Thomas Armstrong did call for something, if not fretting itself, then something close in association.

The truth of it was she couldn't trust herself around him—alone with him. Nothing seemed to be able to change that. The kiss that morning had punctuated that point quite emphatically and her dress—the coffee stain raising not an eyebrow from Hélène—acted as a glaring reminder. She was no better than the women he'd taken to his bed. In actuality, she was worse, for hers hadn't been a courting with the expected flowers, pretty words, or gestures of adoration. No, he had her succumbing when only two minutes before she would have gladly seen him hung, drawn, and quartered. Embarrassment didn't come close to describing her feelings.

If only she could send the letter to Lord Clayborough by messenger as she had done in London. A story of a farmer who'd found two bags of letters near his barn—letters two years old—had circulated through London two months ago. Since then, Amelia hadn't fully trusted the post. However, this wasn't her house and these weren't her servants to utilize at will. Moreover, she'd never be able to manage something like that with the viscount in residence.

The morning following, Amelia had been at her desk a full fifteen minutes before the viscount arrived. With yesterday's kiss still vivid in her mind, Amelia kept her gaze focused on the papers in front of her, feigning a concentration that had all but abandoned her the moment he'd stepped foot in the study.

"Good morning, Amelia."

The way her senses responded to his polite greeting—the words tripping over every nerve end—one would have thought there'd been an intimacy in his tone. Amelia sent him a quick glance and issued a brisk nod. Two things about his appearance registered immediately, the first of which she'd have done well not to notice: His dimples made him look ridiculously appealing. Secondly, he was wearing riding clothes, which suggested he would be spending most of the day down at the stables instead of in the study with her. Certainly a comforting prospect.

"Put away the contracts," he said, striding over to his desk. "We are going riding this morning."

Amelia's head snapped up to stare at him wide-eyed. He gazed across at her, a mild smile shaping his mouth.

"I would rather not," she said in lemon-tart tones, having recovered from her bewilderment.

He chuckled. "Think of this as part of your duties, although I thought you'd enjoy the fresh air. Your father spoke many times of your skill on a horse. I rather thought you'd be eager to take up the reins again."

That her father had anything kind to say about her was preposterous. The viscount was fabricating things as usual.

"I do not recall going riding with you listed on the duties you presented me with when I arrived."

He laughed again, the dimples in his cheeks deepening. "I believe I mentioned there would be additional tasks. Think of this as one of those."

Amelia viewed the work on her desk and then the accursed filing drawers. This was like being asked to choose between strawberries and cream drizzled with chocolate and boiled mutton and potatoes; there was no question as to preference. "I'm hardly dressed to go riding." She gestured at her flowered dress in a halfhearted protest.

The lucid, sane part of Thomas wished he hadn't seen the reluctant yearning in her eyes. It added a dimension of vulnerability to her otherwise prickly disposition.

Quietly, he asked, "Will it help if I tell you this isn't a request but an order given by the viscountess herself?"

Thomas, my dear, why don't you take Lady Amelia riding? I can't imagine the poor girl intended to be cooped up in the study for most of the day.

She stood, the movement as graceful as a ballerina. Apparently, a combination of his mother's backing and the lure of the outdoors was an inducement she could not refuse.

"Well, as it's under the viscountess's directive, I shall go and change into something more suitable."

The other part of him, the one that had him semi-hard watching the innocent provocation of hips and legs moving in feminine unity as she crossed the floor and exited the room, could have made a meal of her right then and greedily come back for more.

Lord, he was in trouble.

Nothing was turning out as he planned. Although her response to him was more than he'd hoped for, the ferocity of his response to her could have split the Rock of Gibraltar clean in two.

The answer to his dilemma was quite simple. Just stop kissing the damn woman as each kiss turned him inside out, upside down, the memories living on to torment him endlessly.

Stop kissing the woman. This time the command echoed in his head with more force. He'd just have to accomplish his ultimate goal without further physical intimacy. A rather novel idea and one he'd do his best to employ.

However, fifteen minutes later, Thomas began to seriously doubt whether he had the required restraint to follow through on his recent vow. The erection straining the brown wool of his riding breeches forced him to remain seated behind his desk.

She strode into the room, a mass of dark silken hair, long limbs, and pert breasts. Her attire was nothing short of scandalous. But for two slits in front and back running from hip to hem, what she was wearing resembled a skirt. And beneath the heavy, dark blue material, fitted leather breeches encased a pair of legs finer than any that had ever graced the Argyll rooms. A man had never envied a pair of breeches more than he did at that moment.

Now he understood why trousers on women were not permissible in society. Swallowing hard, he tried to keep his expression blank while lust, raw and primitive, accosted him from all sides.

"I am ready." She had stopped just inside the room.

"Yes, most assuredly you are." His words were an indiscernible utterance under his breath while he entertained lurid thoughts of spreading her out on his desk and taking her, driving into her body until she reached her peak, convulsing around him in a mass of quivering flesh and silken limbs. Then he'd find his own release in the tight, wet clasp of her body.

Thomas surfaced from his reverie to find her staring expectantly at him. He came swiftly to his feet. A surreptitious glance down revealed no betraying bit of bulges marring the clean line of his jacket, though his erection still lingered about as if hoping for some form of appeasement.

"Will you require a sidesaddle for your mount?" Long strides carried him to her side.

"No, I ride astride."

Her statement conjured up images of her atop him, her long legs straddling his hips in wanton abandon. He didn't dare allow his gaze to venture below her neck. "Why is that?"

She paused and cleared her throat before she spoke again. "My mother believed sidesaddle to be unsafe."

"A suffragette, was she?" he teased. It was either make light of it or take her where she stood.

"No!" Then as if she realized the sharpness of her tone, she continued mildly "Merely a sensible woman."

Thomas detected in her an unspoken distress and knew there was something far deeper in her simply spoken words than Amelia would ever reveal.

"Come, let us walk down to the stables. It is not far from the house." And a walk on a crisp, cool autumn day would do wonders for his unflagging libido—or so he hoped.

They completed the walk down to the stables in relative silence. They spoke nothing of the kiss—and again, would not. The viscount had said not a word about her attire. Again, it appeared that was not to be mentioned or discussed.

Minutes after the groom had left them with two of the finest horses she'd ever seen, Amelia stared up at a beautiful chestnut mare and a black thoroughbred. Now she and the viscount would ride the grounds together as if the kiss had already faded into the annals of time, and the practice of women parading about in leather breeches and riding a horse astride were a common enough occurrence.

While Lord Armstrong affectionately stroked the thoroughbred's mane, the mare poked its mouth around the pockets of his riding jacket, as if hoping to find some kind of treat. "This is Lightning. You will be riding her today." He nodded at the mare.

Amelia reached up and gently rubbed the silky, brown hair just above her muzzle. "She's beautiful," she said, in a quiet soothing voice. The horse nickered softly, pawing at the dirt with her front hoof.

Securing the thoroughbred's reins on a wooden post, Lord Armstrong retrieved the mare's reins. "Lightning is eighteen hands. You'll require some help to mount."

"I can manage on my own." Then she looked at the height of the foot strap for the saddle, which was a far cry higher than what she was accustomed to.

"Don't be stubborn. I've had grown men unable to mount her on their own."

"Well, I can," she said her teeth gritted in determination. Jerking the reins from his hand, she raised her leg, and neatly inserted her booted foot into the stirrup, but found she lacked sufficient leg strength to pull herself up. Undaunted, she tried again, hoisting herself a little higher, but not enough to propel her onto the saddle.

Lightning remained perfectly still while she attempted to mount a third time, also to no avail. Amelia sent a fleeting glance in Lord Armstrong's direction. His expression was blank save a knowing glimmer in his eyes.

He cleared his throat the last time she came back down on one leg, the other still propped in the stirrup, her breath heavy from her exertions. "Will you allow me to assist you or do you mean to waste away the morning struggling to prove you are more accomplished at this than most men?"

Amelia threw him a disgruntled glare over her shoulder and then jerked her head in an angry nod. "My horse is not quite this tall," she muttered.

"Then should I locate a mount of a more appropriate height?" He appeared to be holding back a smile.

Why the blazes hadn't he done that from the onset? Amelia emitted an indelicate snort. "Hardly."

"Then let us get on with it."

His assistance, however, consisted of his hands coming in contact in some form or another, with the entire length of her leg. When she finally sat atop the horse, her flesh was prickly hot and her composure somewhat shaken.

"How is that?" He watched her as he took his time removing his hand from her leather-clad leg. But she was too busy fighting the discomfiting sensations coursing through her body to slap his offensive hand away. Agitated, she hastily tried to adjust her skirt so it covered her leg. However, the movement sent her foot into the mare's side and sent her off in a canter while she desperately fought to gain full control of the reins.

By the time she managed to halt her horse, Lord Armstrong atop his mount, had thundered up alongside her.

"What the blazes are you doing?" His eyes flashed with fury. "Trying to get yourself killed and maim my horse in the process?"

Amelia turned the mare until she faced the irate, red-faced lord. "There is no need to shout. My leg slipped, that is all."

"You should have better sense than to jerk your leg like that while sitting atop a horse."

"Well, if you'd removed your hand from my leg, there would have been no need for me to jerk it." As soon as the statement was out, Amelia would have given anything to snatch it back. She'd just given him enough ammunition to arm an entire cavalry. And the lazy smile that replaced the anger on his face told her it was a fact he was well aware of.

"I will remember that for next time."

"There won't be a next time," she growled.

His smile broadened. "Come, let's commence our ride," he said, edging his horse forward.

What followed was sure to be the highlight of her stay thus far at Stoneridge Hall. Lord Armstrong took her on a tour of the most picturesque acreage she had yet to see.

Unlike their usual encounters, today they managed to surpass civility to venture cautiously into the unknown realm of mutual cordiality. Ever the efficient guide, the viscount pointed out the various crops growing on the leased properties. They passed through a meadow, rode by a valley, and skirted a pond well stocked with fish.

By the conclusion of the tour, the two hours had felt like a mere twenty minutes had passed. The groom met them upon their return to the stables.

With her inauspicious start with the horse still fresh in her memory, Amelia hurriedly dismounted before Lord Armstrong could offer a hand. She might have required aid in mounting, but she could get down fine on her own. His rueful smile told her he well understood her haste.

"I'll take 'em, milord," the young man said, retrieving the reins from Lord Armstrong, one in each of his sunburned hands. Then he led the horses to the side of the building, where they drank from a large tub of water.

"Come, I imagine you'll want to clean up some and eat before you resume your duties this afternoon."

Amelia could only imagine the sight she made. Despite the cool temperatures, she was flushed hot and strands of hair lay wet against her forehead. She could think of nothing better than a long soak in a warm bath.

He, of course, looked no worse for the wear, his golden locks ruffled in a manner that only made his strikingly handsome visage all the more compelling. The light sheen coating his face didn't make it shine in an unbecoming manner, but made it glow that golden hue that was so much a part of his Greek god image. It was really quite unfair that he managed to look good after several hours on horseback while she felt as attractive as a dairy maid milking a cow.

On their return to the main house, the viscount led her on a small detour to show her a shedding elm tree he claimed to have planted as a young child.

"Let me show you where I carved my initials." He grasped her hand and led her toward the tree, their boots crunching the dried leaves around the thick, knotted trunk. Amelia tried to ignore the spread of heat where his hand lightly clasped her arm.

He didn't release her when he stabbed his finger at the area on the trunk that clearly had the initials TPA etched in it.

Without thinking, Amelia asked, "What does the P stand for?" Then she could have kicked herself three times for expressing any interest in him whatsoever.

"Phillip. It is a family name," he said.

Amelia knew, from her father, that his father had died when he had just reached his maturity, and he had carried his title and the responsibilities that went with it since he was only a young man. It was one of the things her father most admired about him. One of the many, she reminded herself, tamping down an acridness rising silently within her.

"We both lost a parent young," he continued, holding her gaze.

Swallowing, Amelia could only nod while unobtrusively trying to ease her arm from his hold. She preferred it much better when they were either ignoring one another or shooting daggers at each other. When he was nice to her, she didn't like how tongue-tied she became, or the way she tensed up at his proximity. And right now he was much too close for her equilibrium.

It was at that moment that Amelia realized that there were

far more frightening things than being on his bad side. And that was being on his good side.

With her hand firmly back at her side, Amelia took a step back from beneath the branches of the towering tree, only to be brought up short when the viscount smoothly slid a small knife from inside his knee-high leather boot.

"Go ahead, carve your initials." He extended the knife, the metal handle facing her.

"Why ever would I want to do that?" She gave the blade a pointed stare.

Teeth flashed white in his sun-darkened face, and her stomach plummeted in much the same manner as it did when he'd kissed her.

"Don't you ever do anything just for the sheer enjoyment of it? Wouldn't you like to know that there is something that will bear your mark for the rest of its life?" His eyes darkened to a forest green as his gaze focused on her mouth, sending an army of heat waves coursing through her.

"Not particularly," she said, sounding and feeling slightly breathless.

"Then I shall do it for you." He pulled back the proffered knife and then with great care, etched the initials ARB below his. After he finished, he slid the blade back in his boot.

"How did you—"

"Your father. He's spoken about you at length."

Suddenly an unaccountable pain washed over her, as bitter as it was debilitating. In that same moment, Amelia recalled, with a clarity that had too often escaped her since her arrival at Stoneridge Hall, not only the reasons, but the intensity of her dislike for Thomas Armstrong, smashing the truce they had reached that morning into pieces no bigger than particles of dust.

Rose was her middle name—her mother's name. Her father hadn't a right to share such personal information with the viscount. Especially him of all people.

She found strength in her rage. "Yes, while he cannot

recall my birthday, knows nothing of anything that is of
the vaguest importance to me, and has now carted me off
to be served up on a bride platter to a man I'd sooner
bludgeon than marry, I'm exceedingly grateful he's somehow managed to remember my full name."

The viscount's eyes widened as though he'd been am-
bushed. Slowly, all vestiges of amiability disappeared, and
his expression shuttered to a mask of stone. "Marry you?"

Any other woman might have been insulted at the amount
of distaste infused in those two words.

"I don't know which half-witted jackass has imparted
you with the notion that I would ever have you on a plate
much less a platter, but I shall gladly disabuse you of
it now."

"Anyone with half a brain can see through my father's
machinations. You're the son he never had, and if he can't
claim you by blood, then come hell or high water he'll attempt to do so by marriage. And if you can't see that, I can
tell you right now who that half-witted jackass is."

A vein throbbed in stark relief against his temple. He
held his hands clenched tight at his side.

"Only you could make me regret my gesture of kindness
today."

"Ha! You weren't being kind, you were conceding to your
mother's wishes."

His eyes sparked like green bolts of lightning. "Yes,
taking my parent's wishes into consideration, something of
which you have no concept. Well, *you* should consider yourself lucky you ungrateful little chit. At least your father
would see you married to a gentleman who won't fritter
away every shilling of your dowry at the hazard tables. If I
were him—which I thank God every day that I'm not—I'd
gladly give you the rope to hang yourself by allowing you to
marry that no-account Clayborough. But I'll tell you this,
the Bank of England doesn't possess enough coin to entice
me to marry you, so you can rest easy on that score."

Amelia swallowed hard, remembering the last time she'd cried. It had been the summer of her thirteenth year. She'd been in bed with the fever awaiting her father's return. He hadn't come. Five days she'd cried for him. She'd cried for the loss of her mother the year before. She'd never shed another tear since.

What she wouldn't give now to be that thirteen-year-old child who'd been able to cry without fear of revealing the depth of her pain and hurt. But she knew she couldn't. Not here, not with him, perhaps never again.

Amelia mustered up some of her dwindling composure. "You're correct. Tonight I'm certain to sleep much easier." She then turned and made the walk back to the house alone.

Chapter 14

At the library door, Thomas bid the woman adieu, sent the footman escorting her out a curt nod, then made his way right to his desk and dropped into the high-backed leather chair. He ran a weary hand through his hair and pondered his options with the same concentration a surgeon would wield his scalpel.

Two weeks, ten perfectly amiable women later, and the right chaperone for Amelia continued to elude him. Deliberately, he was almost certain.

"I gather she won't do either?"

His mother's voice drew Thomas's attention to the door. She proceeded in, in a rustle of silk and satin.

"Would you have the woman give notice before she has enough time to put away her belongings?" he asked wryly.

"Oh, you're too hard on her. Lady Amelia is a lovely young woman. Why in the past month, I've seen a marked change in her. And she has been wonderful to the girls, so I won't hear another word against her."

Yes, a whole month had passed since her arrival and she'd warmed to everyone—including the servants—save him, of course. Since their last exchange during their outing, a chasm now existed between them, unbridgeable and empty. And frankly, he was glad of it. He wanted as little to do with

her as conceivably possible. But as it was apparent his
mother had become her staunchest defender, Thomas wisely
kept such opinions to himself.

"Have you considered Miss Foxworth?" his mother continued. "She's of an appropriate age and is as respectable as
they come. I'm certain you need only ask her and she would
agree. Remember, with only three days until our departure,
you haven't a lot of time. I absolutely refuse to leave the two
of you here without a proper chaperone."

Ah, Camille! Though somewhat self-effacing, she was
loyal to a fault, which would do him well in dealing with
Amelia.

"Yes, you might be right. She could suit the position adequately. I'll send off a letter to her today," he said, and settled into the deep pocket of his chair.

"Then perhaps you will come with me and your sisters to
London and escort Camille back. You can make a trip of it."

"And what, pray tell, would I do with Amelia?" He'd be
damned if he'd leave her here alone. Lord only knows what
chaos would await him upon his return.

"Well, why else do you think I'm suggesting the trip?
Of course, Lady Amelia would come along. Honestly,
Thomas, you have the poor girl like a prisoner in your study
all day long. And don't give me any nonsense about her
wanting it so. A young girl needs her amusements. I'm certain she would welcome the change."

Yes, and therein lay the problem. She'd enjoy it too much.
But perhaps his mother was right. A trip to London would
give him an opportunity to visit Grace. Over a month without sex had begun to wear on his nerves and temper.

"As you wish," he acceded.

The viscountess's gaze skittered around the room. Several times she turned to him, her mouth open as if to speak
only to snap it closed. Her hands began to fidget with the
gauze net of her skirt.

Once again, she shifted her gaze back to him, a smile fixed on her face. "Thomas, I've been thinking. . . ."

In the context of many women, these were ominous words in and of themselves, but added to the gravity of his mother's tone, they sent a jolt of trepidation through him. Thomas swallowed and indicated she continue with a brief nod of his head.

"When I was speaking to Amelia yesterday—"

And just like that, Thomas could add another phrase to the list of the most dangerous terms in the English language.

"—she asked me what I intend to do with myself when the girls are gone. I must confess, I am embarrassed to admit I hadn't a response."

Thomas emitted a heavy sigh. "Mother—"

"No, dear, I have given this much thought. It has been eleven years since your father's death, and I am not growing any younger."

"With your beauty and grace, a woman half your age would be considered fortunate." And that was no empty praise.

A blush heightened the color of her face. Pivoting on her heel, she strolled over to a side table and picked up the intricately carved ivory horse she'd given him last Christmas. She examined the figurine as she spoke. "In just three years Sarah will make her debut, and soon after I shall be alone."

His mother gazed at him, and in that instant he saw something in her eyes he had never seen before: loneliness. When his father had died, he'd witnessed her sadness, her hurt, and her fear. But never this. She'd had responsibilities then: an estate to run, three young daughters to raise to maturity, and a son going off to Cambridge.

Thomas was out of his chair and at her side within seconds, his arm wrapping tightly about her shoulder. "You will never be alone, not with the brood of grandchildren Missy will give you to spoil," he teased and lightly brushed his lips against the smooth skin of her temple. He slowly released her and took a step back.

The viscountess offered him a faint smile. "Yes, but the care of a grandchild is hardly the same. No, dear, it's past time I started to carve out a life of my own."

Thomas furrowed his brows. Just what did a life of her own entail? Increasing the frequency of her calls and engaging in endless hours of cribbage and whist? It took several seconds more for his slow-witted mind to comprehend his mother's meaning.

"Oh, Thomas, do not look so appalled. One would think I just told you I've decided to join the theater."

"No, no, that's not it at all," he hastened to assure her. It was just that—well, she was his mother. There wasn't a man alive good enough for her.

"The only reason I'm even broaching this subject with you is because—well, I will be in America for the next two months and I expect I'll run into Mr. Wendel and Lord Bradford."

At the mention of Derrick Wendel, the president and majority stockholder of Wendel's Shipping, Thomas began to understand his mother's discomfiture. The men had recently travelled to America to negotiate the deal to purchase a steel company; a deal that, if successful, would cut their operating costs by 20 percent.

The viscountess placed the ivory horse back on the table. "Mr. Wendel has asked if I would allow him to escort me about town a time or two."

Knowing his friend, Thomas thought his mother's estimate low. Wendel would likely charm his mother into as many outings as his schedule and hers would permit. Since Thomas had introduced them the year past, Wendel had taken an inordinate interest in the viscountess. And who could blame the man? Besides her obvious attributes, his mother could disarm a gentleman with just a smile.

Lord, he'd seen it happen often enough, even when his father was alive.

"Well, I've known of his interest for some time, but I must admit, I hadn't thought it was reciprocated."

His mother's blush deepened. She looked away briefly. After a pause, she said, "I am not admitting to an interest. However, *if* there were, would that be of concern to you?"

"Why, because Wendel is not a peer?"

The viscountess shook her head. "No, because he is your friend and business partner. And of course, there is the matter of your father."

"Mother, as much as I love and miss Father, I would hardly expect you to live your life like a nun." Although, a part of him had expected just that. "And Derrick Wendel is a good man. There are few I admire more."

A relieved smile wreathed her face, taking ten years off her already youthful forty-eight years. Reaching up, she pressed a soft kiss on his cheek, the faint scent of gardenias tickling his nose. "And he's very handsome too."

Thomas emitted a dry laugh and gave her slender hands a gentle squeeze.

The viscountess withdrew her hands from his and then smoothed the folds of her voluminous skirt. She was every inch the lady of the manor again. "Now that the matter is arranged, I must go and settle the house accounts. And pray, do not dawdle over the letter to Miss Foxworth. Lady Amelia must have a chaperone before I depart."

After his mother had gone, Thomas returned to his desk, and his thoughts returned—as they did with increasing frequency—to Amelia.

He didn't want to admit that he was at all bothered by the new distance between them. While they might not have shared dark secrets or their innermost thoughts that day, he'd felt they'd reached a truce of sorts. Then she'd spoiled it with her firestorm of insults. It was obvious she saw him as the usurper of her father's affections. What had brought her to such a ridiculous conclusion was beyond him. The marquess seemed to spend a great deal of time worrying over his daughter's welfare. Over the years of their acquaintance, Harry had bent his ear on numerous occasions about what to do with her unruliness, as she appeared hell-bent on ruination. Amelia's resentment of him was as well founded as the belief that the Earth was the center of the universe.

Good Lord, what did she expect from her father? For him to cut all others from his life so she could have his undivided attention? From what he'd seen, Harry denied his daughter nothing. Not the horse that had cost what the average person could comfortably live on for three years. Not the conveyance, which was equipped with frills enough to impress royalty. And certainly not her wardrobe, which Harry had once admitted was in excess of fifteen hundred pounds per annum.

While he berated himself for not being able to get the blasted woman from his thoughts, he snatched up the morning's correspondence from his desk. His eye caught a flash of green. Thomas stilled and his agitation mounted. He swiftly removed the dark olive envelope from the stack of letters. The gold ducal seal glittered under the light of the gas lamp. Suddenly, he wasn't agitated, he was in a blazing temper.

Damn Louisa. Why couldn't the blasted woman leave things as they were? One beautiful, selfish, manipulative female was all he could manage at one time. Even the task of responding to her to tell her to go to blazes was more contact than he wished to have with her.

Thomas didn't bother to read the letter—not this time— for it would only worsen his mood. Like her previous letter, this one saw its speedy demise at the hands of the flames roaring in the fireplace.

Amelia heard the familiar fall of his footsteps approaching the study. Inhaling a deep breath, she mentally composed herself for the coming encounter.

Her stomach took a little dip when she saw him. Fine, so he looked exceedingly well this morning dressed all in blue. He wasn't the first handsome face she'd ever beheld. So why in heavens was her reaction to him so excessive, so embarrassingly visceral?

He didn't speak immediately when he entered but caught and held her gaze as he proceeded to her desk. Then he was standing at her side with only a couple of feet separating them. An inexplicable sense of panic washed over her that she did her best to tamp down.

"Was there something else you required of me? I still have yet to complete the tasks from yesterday." She spoke with a hauteur polished to perfection over time.

"Friday morning we will be travelling to London with my mother and sisters." The crease in his forehead and the tightness around his mouth indicated he was none too happy about the situation.

"We? Am I to accompany you?"

"Well, I certainly can't leave you here by yourself," he muttered, in a tone as dark as his mood.

"As it's clear the prospect is not pleasing to either of us, why must I go? Just what exactly do you think I'll do while you're gone? Abscond with your silver?" It was the most she'd said to him in a month.

"No, however, I wouldn't put it past you to run off with one of the servants," he snapped.

Amelia's face burned at his snide inference to Joseph Cromwell, whose father owned two large textile factories. She endeavored to keep her pique from coming through in her voice. "I'd have thought by this time you would know my interest lies in the ranks of tradesmen and destitute aristocratic gentlemen. And certainly you of all people, my lord, should have nothing to say in regards to members of the working class. Not when I've heard you avail yourself to the services of women of a—dare I say—certain trade."

The tightness around his mouth eased as he chuckled

softly. "Why so coy, Princess? You've already accused me of having been with every whore in London. But I think it's time I disabused you of your erroneous assumption. Despite what you believe, I have never utilized the services of a whore."

Amelia barely contained her laugh.

"Why would I pay for something I can get for free?"

"Do you not keep a mistress? Do you not in fact have to pay for her patronage?"

The viscount's eyes narrowed. "I hope you're not trying to compare a mistress to a common whore."

"No, not a common one, to be sure. Mistresses, I gather, have wealthier prospects and need only service one man during their contract. But I wager the price of all of those manners, sophistication, and beauty is steep indeed."

Lord Armstrong didn't speak for several seconds, he just stared at her, his expression shuttered. "My, you seem to know quite a bit about mistresses. Considering the option for yourself?"

He clearly meant to offend. Amelia refused to take the bait. "I might be young, but I'm not naïve. Though these things may be whispered about in society, they are hardly a secret."

With the casualness of a personal acquaintance, the viscount pushed the documents aside and sat down on the desk—her desk—one leg dangling a hairbreadth from her arm, the other firmly planted on the floor.

"And the only thing more expensive than a mistress is a wife. But I could have had you without a mistress contract or a betrothal agreement and you're not a woman of the streets, so what does that make you?" He spoke in a low, intimate voice, which made his question all the more outrageous.

Amelia's breath hitched, indignation bubbling to the surface. The movement caused her hand to brush the navy fabric of his trousers. She nearly bolted from the chair. But her pride kept her rooted to her seat. She'd responded to two of his kisses, and now he thought she'd lay the world at his feet?

"Don't flatter yourself."

He laughed, a husky sound that sent an unwanted shock of awareness through her. "Why, Princess, I do believe you're trying to goad me." He stared at her as if he'd discovered her every weakness and planned to exploit each one to his advantage. Suddenly, Amelia was afraid—terrified.

"Prove it," he whispered, a challenge lighting his eyes.

"Pardon?" Flustered, Amelia blinked repeatedly.

"Prove I can't make you want me."

"I-I don't have to prove any such thing."

He gave a short laugh. "Oh, I'm not so certain of that." Then his hand was cupping the base of her neck and easing her closer as he lowered his head.

She could have easily broken free of his hold and ended the madness right then. There'd be no need for endless recriminations afterward. But she did no such thing. She just watched him as he drew ever closer, his eyes seductively intent on her. Never in her life had she been the focus of such heat. Never had she been so entranced by a man.

Then she was free, his hand abruptly withdrawn. He levered himself to his feet, a satisfied smile curving the lips she'd so desperately wanted on hers. She stared up at him and saw her own stark look of horror reflected back in his eyes.

"You see, I'm sure I could have already had you in a hundred different ways." Thomas shoved his hands deep into his trouser pockets because they shook. They shook with the urge to pull her into his arms, lower her onto the floor, and take her in at least one of those ways—the front, the side, from behind, he didn't care how as long as he could assuage this hunger for her that had been practically eating him alive the past month.

He turned away to hide his reaction, his bloody erection.

"Why did you do that?" She sounded hoarse.

Thomas half turned back to her, surprised at the question, the bluntness of it.

"To prove a point," he replied after a long moment of silence.

She rose from her chair and started toward him.

Thomas wanted to close his eyes against her allure but knew he couldn't afford to betray any weakness. She'd use it against him and eat him alive.

"Which was what?" she asked, her voice cooler, more composed.

What the hell was he to say? To prove he was in control? Given his current feelings, fiction of such magnitude deserved its own stage.

Before he could collect his thoughts enough to offer an articulate response, she was pressed against him, her slender hands on the nape of his neck tugging his head down.

His senses were bombarded, overrun with the scent of something delicately feminine and the feel of soft female flesh. Painfully aroused, Thomas had neither the strength nor the desire to fight her—much less himself. He cupped her face in his hands and assumed control of the kiss before their lips met.

Desire and hunger obliterated every bit of his restraint. A month of denying himself and a month of wanting went into the kiss. With her head tucked into the crook of his shoulder, his hands scored the slim length of her torso. His palm grazed the tip of her breast before closing around the firm thrust of female flesh.

The nipple peaked to a hard nub beneath the silk bodice as he began to pluck at it. Her breath hitched, and then she let out a strangled moan.

He yearned to bare her breasts to his gaze. In his dreams,

he'd imagined sucking the rosy, pink tip. Thomas bit back a groan. God, when had he ever wanted a woman more? It seemed like forever ago.

She returned his kisses with the fervor of an innocent, her mouth parted, her untutored tongue capable of bringing a man to his knees.

"God, I want you." He used his free hand to pull her hips flush with his. Too many layers of clothes stood in the way of the kind of fit he most desired.

Just as quickly as he'd found himself locked in the passionate embrace, she was out of his arms.

Reflectively, he reached for her, but she hastily stepped out of his reach, backing up to her desk. Thomas emitted a low, tortured groan.

Her lips were still pouty from his kisses, her coiffure mussed so clumps of hair hung past her shoulders in a stream of dark chocolate silk. She pressed trembling fingers to her lips and stared at him with eyes still heated with passion.

"What was the meaning of that?" He barely recognized his own voice.

She didn't reply for several seconds. Perhaps she couldn't, given the dramatic rise and fall of her chest as she drew gulping breaths. "I kissed you because you are an arrogant, presumptuous man who believes he can make a fool of me because he's dedicated his entire adulthood to the art of learning to pleasure a woman. Well, I think you'd have to be a complete simpleton if you didn't have your skills honed to perfection by now. Congratulations, my lord, you are not a *complete* simpleton."

Thomas knew he'd just been insulted but didn't care. His body had yet to recover from the feel of her. His hands ached to snatch her back into his arms and continue where they'd left off. Heavy with arousal, all he could think about was locking the door and taking her up against the wall, the floor, the desk, the rug in front of the fireplace. Sliding into her slick heat. Driving into her repeatedly until she didn't know her own name and he could claim only a passing acquaintance with civility.

"I understand that what I said at the ball injured your pride," she continued evenly. "But as you can see, my response to you has proven me wrong. There, I've conceded to your superior sexual prowess. Now, will you leave me alone?"

Thomas could barely comprehend what he was hearing. He'd not anticipated her admission would come quite like this. The shattering climax had her saying it with more humility as she begged him to end her torment and take her. Of course, that's when he would deny her. Nowhere in the script was she supposed to admit she was wrong and then calmly ask him to leave her alone.

"Given what you've just confessed, are you certain that's what you want?"

Amelia looked away and smoothed a hand over her hair. "Yes."

Later he'd tell himself it was all for the best. He'd made a discovery of his own: that he no longer wanted to be party to his game of seduction. She'd made him feel petty and small, and he'd be exactly that if he had continued on his course. So it was done, the game officially over. Now he must act the role intended for him. Her guardian cum employer. Which meant he must leave . . . now.

"Then it shall be as you wish," he said solemnly.

Her gaze shot back to him as if she feared duplicity.

"I will leave you to your tasks. Tomorrow, you can take the day to pack for our departure on Friday." With a swift bow, he was gone.

The instant the vis—Thomas disappeared through the doorway, Amelia sank back into her chair, inhaling a lungful of air. The man had had his tongue in her mouth, his hands on her breast, and parts of him knew parts of her almost as intimately as she knew herself. She could scarcely think of him so formally anymore.

Dear Lord, what had possessed her to kiss him like that? All she knew was that when he had pulled away and left her still wanting, she couldn't see anything beyond the hypocrisy of his actions. How she'd wanted to prove to him that the powerful pull of their physical attraction wasn't confined to her alone. But knowing didn't make things better; in fact, it could make things a far cry worse.

How vastly different he was from Lord Clayborough. The baron didn't elicit even a fraction of the physical reaction in her that the viscount did. But that was all it was, merely a physical response to an attractive—stunningly beautiful— man. What she shared with Lord Clayborough was more important than that. Which was why his lack of response to the three letters she'd posted since her arrival was so troubling. He'd always been overly solicitous of her, so his behavior now was very much out of character. Something was wrong. And to add to her problems, she was now expected to travel to London with Thomas and his family.

Just as she was beginning to despair that things could not possibly get worse, she remembered that Lord Clayborough was in London. She made the connection with the staggering relief one would feel in finding solid ground in a bed of quicksand, as opposed to the giddy excitement a woman might have at the prospect of seeing her betrothed. But her feelings were immaterial here. The only thing that mattered was that after over a month, she and Lord Clayborough would finally have a good chance to meet. The viscount couldn't possibly know the gift he'd just given her. One she intended to utilize to the utmost.

Chapter 15

The trip to London was uneventful. Their arrival at the viscountess's residence in Mayfair occurred at precisely two o'clock in the afternoon. And as Amelia should have expected, her argument with Thomas occurred an hour later, five minutes after the viscountess and her daughters exited the townhouse.

Amelia faced him across the expanse of his mother's drawing room. As if by tacit agreement, they both now gave one another a wide berth when circumstances demanded they be in each other's company.

"Your mother invited me to go with her and your sisters. I should like to have gone."

"Your father didn't send you to me so you could traipse about enjoying the pleasures of the city."

"So I shall be denied a shopping excursion on Bond Street? I'm in need of some personal items. What do you expect me to do?"

"Make a list, and I'll have someone procure them for you."

Amelia silently counted to five, resisting the urge to bash him with one of the candelabras on the fireplace mantel. "So I'm to be kept a prisoner in this house?"

"Well, let's see. You're confined to this house until we

depart on Sunday. Yes, I'd say that's an accurate assessment of the situation."

He didn't smile, and the firm set of Thomas's jaw, the cool directness of his gaze, told her that on this, he would not grant her even the slightest bit of latitude. Just how she was to get word to Lord Clayborough of her arrival in town was growing to be a task of monumental proportions.

"If you will ready that list . . ."

Amelia glared at him, tight-lipped and angry. And not solely angry over his obstinacy in the current matter but at his treatment of her. When he spoke to her—as infrequent as that had been in the last several days—he did so in clipped tones to the exclusivity of instructing her on her duties. No doubt she could have paraded about the place naked for all the notice he'd taken of her. And despite repeated reminders to herself that this is what she wanted, at times her words seemed a hollow resonance of a fervent, ill-fated prayer. She wished it didn't bother her, but the sad fact was, it did.

"Don't bother. I shall take care of it myself," she snapped before turning on her heels and exiting the drawing room.

The sharp click of her heels echoed loudly on the planked floors of the hallway. As she spun to take the stairs to the first floor, reflexively she darted a glance back at the drawing room entrance to find Thomas watching her. He acknowledged her regard with a slight bow, his gaze steady, his features inscrutable.

Amelia raced up the stairs, her heart beating in tandem with her footsteps.

Unlike many of the more accomplished ladies of the ton, Amelia hadn't an ear for music, couldn't carry a note any further than she could a piano, and would surely bleed to death if she attempted another needlepoint sampler. But she did enjoy reading, fiction novels being her greatest indulgence. So it would stand to reason she'd be drawn to the library. The works of the most esteemed and prolific authors graced the viscountess's bookshelves. The room was a librarian's dream, and where she found herself an hour later.

She ran her finger down the spine of *The Taming of the Shrew* and debated whether she'd rather a Shakespearean farce or something tragic and romantic like *Jane Eyre*.

The sound of someone clearing their throat startled Amelia from her reverie, causing her head to swivel sharply in the direction of the door. Framed at the threshold was the tall—very tall—footman, Jones, if she remembered his name correctly.

"I beg your pardon, ma'am, but his lordship begs your presence in the morning room."

Her heart skipped a beat, and she couldn't quell the frisson of anticipation that shot through her. She gave a brief nod. "Please tell his lordship I will be there in a moment."

"Yes ma'am." With a stiff bow, he departed.

Thomas hadn't gone? She'd thought he'd left an hour ago. The viscountess had told her he would be staying at his bachelor's residence. But he was still here. And he wished to see her.

Amelia would have gone there directly if the immediacy of her response didn't make her appear too eager and willing to bend to his will. Let him cool his heels. He couldn't have everything to his liking. Ten minutes seemed an appropriate amount of time to make him wait.

Nine minutes later, she breeched the morning room threshold, halting abruptly at the sight of Camille Foxworth conversing with Thomas.

Leave him alone, he's mine. Perhaps it was the unexpectedness of the woman's presence there that stirred such a primitive reaction in her. Inhaling deeply, she ignored the voice and proceeded toward the pair.

"Ah, here she is, Camille," Thomas said, turning his attention to Amelia.

Despite his easy manner, Amelia felt she'd interrupted a private conversation, which made her as belligerent as a child who'd had her toy taken away long before she had finished playing with it.

He wore the first smile she'd seen in days, she noted with some rancor. Apparently, Miss Foxworth brought out the bonhomie in him.

"Lady Amelia Bertram, I would like to introduce you to Miss Camille Foxworth."

Amelia forced her limbs and the muscles in her face to relax. When she was able to wade her way through her pique, a sobering question reared in her head. *What is she doing here?* Then a horrifying thought struck her with the same force of Lord Stanley coming down on her toes during an energetic polka dance—he was eighteen stone if he was an ounce—surely Thomas didn't intend for her . . . ? No, the idea was preposterous.

Miss Foxworth smiled and executed an elegant curtsey. "Good day, Lady Amelia. I believe we were introduced on another occasion. The Randall ball earlier in the Season."

Lest she wished to appear lacking in the basic societal niceties, Amelia acknowledged the woman with a dip of her head, endeavoring to keep her emotions from her expression. She received a sharp look of censure from Thomas for her efforts.

"Yes, I do recall," she replied, her voice having acquired a thin layer of ice.

Amelia ignored another one of his hard stares.

"Miss Foxworth has agreed to be your chaperone while my mother is away." Thomas's features instantly softened when he turned his regard to Miss Foxworth—who stared up at him as if he were a deity, and she his worshipping subject.

In turn, Amelia stared at the woman, her horrifying suspicion confirmed. She took in her thin figure in a dress more appropriate for an elderly matron, and her eyes, blue beacons amid a ghostly complexion, and became inexplicably angry.

"Is that so, indeed? I would assume that Miss Foxworth would have infinitely better things to do than to take on such a task." Amelia paused in an effort to stem the words and the rise of bitterness within her. But it was to no avail. The desire—the need—to cut the woman down to an insignificant, paltry existence was such that she'd never experienced before. "But then again, I imagine being a single woman with no marriage prospects might leave you with quite a bit of time on your hands."

Once the final word ended the most egregious statement to ever pass her lips, Amelia would have given anything to take back the insult. She cursed whatever it was that had taken over her, turning her tongue into a vehicle of insolence of the worst sort. But her wave of contriteness came too late.

Thomas's breath escaped in a hiss, but Miss Foxworth's only reaction was a brief gaze downward as if to hide the effect of her words.

Amelia willed the floor to open up and envelop her whole. Miss Foxworth had never personally done anything to her. Her only crime appeared to be her association with the viscount and her apparent adoration of him. And since Amelia managed to rub along quite well with the viscountess and her daughters, surely she didn't consider even that a crime.

"As you can see, Lady Amelia has not yet learned the manners of polite society," Thomas said through clenched teeth. He gave the woman an apologetic half smile. "If you will please excuse us, Camille, I would like a word with Lady Amelia in private. I'll call for you once I'm finished here."

Miss Foxworth nodded slowly, and with her gaze chasing the area rugs and the parquet floors, she quietly exited. The soft click of the door closing echoed her departure.

Thomas's handsome face could have been carved from stone. Amelia didn't have the courage to meet his eyes when she spoke, but she was defensive nonetheless.

"I know in its entirety what you're going to say, so please spare me the lecture. I'm quite aware that what I said—"

His hand shot out and grasped her forearm, his grip unyielding. With a jerk of his hand, he brought her inches away from his rigid form. He had only a six-inch advantage in height but seemed to tower more than that above her. "Don't you ever insult my guest in my presence," he said, his voice a grated whisper. He was furious. He was red-faced. He looked as if he would happily throttle her within an inch of her life.

Had she not come from sterner stock, she might have recoiled in the face of the kind of ire that undoubtedly had many men shrinking in their own shadows. She winced as fear crept inexorably to settle in her bones.

He immediately loosened his grip but did not release her. Amelia made no move to further extricate herself from his hold.

"Why did you choose her of all women, for heaven's sake? Is your ego so grand you must have someone fawning over you night and day?" There, she'd laid bare the crux of her objection.

Thomas didn't reply at first; he drew back and stared at her, his anger now replaced by something cryptic and unnerving to behold. "What exactly do you believe I intend to do with her?"

"I don't particularly care what you *do* with her. I just have no desire to be party to whatever it is."

Releasing her arm, he took a step back. Amelia relished the breathing room. She didn't like the fact that when she stood so close to him her mind muddled and every nerve ending stood at attention.

He continued to observe her closely, his dark gold lashes fanning the tops of his cheekbones. "Good God, I do believe you're jealous." Awe threaded the softly spoken words. If he had been Petruchio reveling in Kate's obedience, Thomas could not have looked more satisfied.

Amelia sputtered a laugh before finding her voice. "You

couldn't be farther from the truth. But I'm certain the notion does wonders for your bloated ego."

"Oh no? Well, you give a very good impression of it." His eyebrow inched up. "What have you against Miss Foxworth? Why should it bother you if she is—as you quaintly put it— fawning all over me?"

"That is not what bothers me about the situation. I simply have no desire to be used."

"And pray tell, how exactly are you being used?"

"Well, to-to-to—" Dear Lord, she was sputtering again.

He looked at her as if he could read her mind and delighted in what he found there. "If you are worried that there is something going on between Miss Foxworth and I, let me put your fears to rest in that regard."

"I don't care—"

It required only two steps, and he stood inches from her, his masculine scent enveloping her in a sensual prison. He pressed his forefinger gently to her lips, stilling her words. "You might be the most vexing woman I've ever met, but the one thing I'd begun to admire about you was your candor. Don't spoil it now," he murmured.

Staring up at him, Amelia wasn't certain what kept her mute, his audacity or his finger on her lips.

"Now," he continued, as casual as you please, "If you're going to pitch a jealous fit, at least have just cause. Case in point, the appointment I have this evening."

"No doubt a bed romp with your wretched mistress." Abruptly, she stepped back and swatted at his hand.

His hand fell to his side. "Why should you care who I sleep with, mistress or otherwise?"

It was only at his softly spoken question that Amelia realized she must have given a voice to her thoughts. Heat flooded her from head to toe as she wished she could snatch back those renegade words.

"I don't care who you bed," she said coldly.

Thomas threw back his head and emitted a dry laugh.

She suppressed the overwhelming urge to slap him clear into oblivion.

"So you say. However, I'm getting the distinct impression you care more than you like or will ever admit."

"Believe what you choose." Avoiding his gaze—the knowing glint in his green eyes—Amelia turned sharply and stalked from the room with the sound of his laughter, a taunting trail behind her.

Thomas glanced around Grace's parlor and wondered again what he was doing there.

The idea of an uncomplicated evening of sexual release had been foremost in his thoughts when he'd set out from his townhouse. More than a month had passed with nothing but his hand to relieve his sexual urges. He should be fairly frothing at the mouth in anticipation of an encounter with Grace. He wasn't. And he dare not examine the reason why.

"Darling."

Thomas started, and then turned at the soft lilting exclamation. Grace swept into the room, her hands outstretched. She wore a silky robe over an equally silky, pale pink confection of lingerie, which skimmed her lush figure. Before he could respond, she enfolded him into her arms, her neck angled back for her kiss.

Thomas pressed an obligatory kiss on painted red lips and then hastily extricated himself from the embrace and the overly sweet scent of her perfume. The pleasure on her face dimmed. She quickly offered him a smile too bright, too wide-eyed to be genuine. "You didn't tell me you were coming to town," she scolded lightly, trailing her hand up his arm.

Her touch failed to elicit the normal rush of desire. At that moment Thomas knew what he had to do and couldn't help an inward cringe.

Thomas caught her hand with his, and drew her down to the chintz, floral sofa. "Come, we must talk."

Grace subsided without a demur, her nightwear pulling taut over womanly hips and thighs, but her hazel eyes held a glimmer of unease. "You want to talk before we retire to the bedchamber?" Again her smile appeared forced.

"I'm not here for that. I've come to tell you I'm ending our arrangement," he said in a matter-of-fact tone, while retaining his hold on her hand.

The force of the slap caught him unawares, causing a stinging pain in his left cheek. That was when he wished he'd captured both hands.

"You wretched bastard." Fury contorted her features, turning what he'd always thought was a comely visage into something not quite as comely. Not with her pupils dark pinpoints of rage and her red mouth drawn into a feline's angry hiss.

She sprang to her feet and commenced raining blows all over his shoulders and arms.

The instinct of self-preservation surged to life and sent Thomas to his feet to capture the small hands before she managed to do any real damage. "Good God, Grace, get a hold of yourself." He held her hands firmly while she tugged in vain to free them.

"A year I have saved myself for you. An entire year when I could have had any gentleman in London. They all wanted me, you know. Do you know how many men offered their protection? Men I turned down waiting for you, and you could barely see your way to call on me in the last three months."

In an abrupt and unexpected move, she stopped struggling, her body going limp. She dropped back down onto the sofa. Thomas released her and quickly positioned himself on the other side of the center table opposite her, well out of her arm's reach.

A violent shudder wracked her body as she covered her face with her hands and began a noisy sobbing.

Thomas could bear almost anything but a weeping,

distraught female. And it had been at least three years since he'd had to endure such a scene. One of the reasons he had chosen Grace was because she'd not appeared the sort of female prone to crying fits. She'd handled herself with the kind of aplomb he admired and wanted in a mistress. With her, there'd be no histrionics. She'd keep to fulfilling his sexual needs and being the model escort when he desired one. Or so that's what he'd thought. Four months into their arrangement she'd dispelled that assumption when she began to complain as the frequency of their meetings began to wane. From that point on, Thomas knew the clock on their arrangement was winding down. But obviously the end hadn't come soon enough, he thought, rubbing his smarting cheek as he flexed his jaw.

"You've known from the start these sorts of arrangements are temporary," he said, shifting on his feet. He watched her body heave as she inhaled and exhaled long, shuddering breaths.

At his words, her head jerked up, her hands dropped from her face, and he saw red swollen eyes and tear-stained, mottled cheeks. "It's that woman, isn't it? She's demanded that you give me up, hasn't she?"

Thomas's thoughts flew immediately to Amelia. How could Grace possibly know about her? "What woman?" he asked sharply.

"The bloody Duchess of Bedford. The one who was here three weeks ago. Oh, she went on as if she'd mistakenly called on the wrong house. Said she thought a Mrs. Franklin lived here. But even after I told her there was no woman by that name around here, she didn't leave. She started asking me questions about you. Were we acquainted? She told me how you and she had been close." Grace stopped to swipe the tears from her cheeks. "I'm not stupid. I knew why she was here."

Shocked but careful not to betray his alarm, Thomas stated calmly, "I'm not involved with the duchess nor do I desire to become so." *Never, ever again.*

"You're lying." Her statement was bitterly accusing.

"Why on earth would I lie to you? You are not my lady wife. I have nothing to hide." The letters were naught but a small nuisance. Her temerity, however, in calling on his mistress was a different matter altogether. One he intended to put a stop to immediately.

"You have had no discussions with her in regards to me?" Still disbelieving.

"I've had no contact with the woman in well over seven years. I was barely a man when we became acquainted."

Faint hope flared in eyes still glassy from tears. "Then why—"

"But that changes nothing between us." He sighed a long weary sigh. "I made no promises, Grace. You are acting as if I offered more than what we had. I did not."

"Yes, just someone to scratch an itch when the need strikes you." Tears choked her voice.

"That's what a mistress is for." Thomas didn't want to sound callous, but in that she left him little choice.

"I've fallen in love with you." She slowly rose to her feet, continuing to swipe at the tears rolling down her face.

Briefly, Thomas closed his eyes. As he'd feared, she imagined herself in love with him. He quickly consoled himself with the knowledge that in a few months time she'd imagine herself similarly in love with her next protector.

Miss Grace Howell, with all her worldly airs and invulnerability—or so that's how he'd seen it when they'd first met—didn't have what it took to be a good mistress. She too easily became emotionally entangled. What she needed was a husband, not a protector, which was something he should have seen from the onset. But this knowledge came one bruised heart too late.

"I'm sorry to hear that." He could think of little else to say.

Instead of dissolving back into tears, she visibly collected herself and treated him to a hard glare.

"You are even more heartless than I was told. Does

nothing affect you? Save your precious mother and sisters, is there not a woman you care enough about to feel anything for?"

A vision of Amelia pushed to the forefront of his thoughts, a place she tended to linger all too frequently in. He forcibly shoved it back. "I will ensure there is enough money in your account to keep you until you find a new situation. Three months should be adequate." Three months should be more than plenty. In two weeks or less, the Earl of Chesterfield would snatch her up. He'd been waiting impatiently for Thomas to tire of her. Or so Grace had told him on more than one occasion.

"Keep your damn money."

If he had handed her a bank draft, he could see her ripping it to pieces and crushing it under her rosette embellished slippers. As soon as he'd gone, she'd be on her knees frantically collecting every jagged scrap. Pride and anger would elicit the former reaction, practicality and logic the latter.

"I will put it in your account. Do with it as you will." By then, her temper should have cooled.

Thomas exited her residence for the final time with the grim thought, *Women are more trouble than they are worth.*

Instead of an evening on silky linen sheets, Thomas sat in the small library at Cartwright's residence on John's Street. Each man cradled a glass of port in their hand and lounged in brocade armchairs in the respective colors of deep green and burgundy in front of a blazing marble fireplace.

"She pounced on me like a cat." Thomas slanted a glance at his friend, feeling fatigued by the whole affair. "By tomorrow I'm sure to bear some of the scars of our encounter."

A small mirror in the carriage had already revealed a faint bruise appearing near his jaw.

"Who the hell told you to do it in person?" Cartwright chastised, lifting his legs to rest his stockinged feet on the ottoman in front of him. "Some flowers and a note should have sufficed, or perhaps a little trinket."

"Yes, well, it was not my intention to break it off when I set out."

His remark drew a quirked brow from his friend, who tipped his glass back for a sip of the port. "Then why did you?" Cartwright asked, placing his drink on the redwood side table next to his chair.

Yes, why did he? Thomas had pondered that question often since he'd left Grace's residence. He lifted his shoulders in a helpless sort of shrug. "I don't know. I guess because I'd been getting bored with her and she was becoming too possessive. Too demanding of my time."

"Yes, that does happen. But in your case, much sooner than usual. How long had it been with her? Six months? A year?"

"What does that matter? She's over and done with. At present, my most pressing matter is that damn Louisa."

"And just what has our fair duchess done now?" Cartwright asked dryly, his grey eyes alight with interest.

Thomas quickly recited what Grace had told him.

"To seek out your mistress, at her residence no less, was bold beyond words. And with her husband gone not even three months." Cartwright tsked. "The passing years have changed her. I don't believe she'd have attempted anything so blatant when we made her acquaintance. Although, there was the incident with Rutherford. . . ."

Yes, the incident.

Thomas had been foolish enough to believe Louisa when she'd said she loved him and claimed she'd marry him without a shilling to his name. At that time, his bank account contained little more than that.

He'd been completely taken with her blond beauty and coquettish innocence. But her veil of innocence came down with a mighty tug when he'd caught her pressing herself up against Rutherford at a ball Thomas hadn't been expected to attend. At first, he'd stood there in shock, hidden behind the hedgerow in the garden. Then he'd waited in growing rage and watched to see just how far she intended to go.

Despite the fact that Rutherford had gently but firmly pried her hands from about his neck and left the scene shortly after, the incident had caused a small rift in their friendship. He'd confronted Rutherford the day after, but by the time he'd swallowed his pride enough to confront her, she was already betrothed to the Duke of Bedford.

Thomas had had to face the truth then. He, a young, penniless viscount with nothing but his name to recommend him, and his mother and younger sisters to care for, had been nothing more than a flattering diversion until she could worm a proposal from one of her two intended victims. Never mind that Thomas had meant to marry her.

"So how do you mean to handle the situation?" Cartwright continued.

"Well, I bloody well have to talk to the damn woman now, don't I? She's given me little choice, which I'm certain is exactly what she intended." Thomas bowed his head and ran a weary hand over his face.

"Then you should come with me to Lady Forsham's ball. I have it on good authority Her Grace has deigned to make an appearance."

Thomas raised his head and eyed Cartwright skeptically. "You expect me to confront her at a ball? I don't want to be more fodder for those damn gossip sheets."

"Would you rather go to her home or worse yet, have her meet you at your residence? I would advise against being alone with her for any reason."

Cartwright did raise a good point. No good could come of that. And the more thought he gave the idea of the ball, the better it was beginning to sound. Louisa was too aware of her position in society to create a scene in such a public venue.

"Very well, I will go, but don't expect me to remain for the duration. As scintillating as I find these events, I have other duties to attend to. Since I had to retain a chaperone for Amelia *and* bring her into town with me, I'm forced to keep a close eye on her. I'm almost positive she'll try to contact Clayborough, and while I'm confident Camille will be circumspect in her duties, I don't want to leave anything to chance."

A burst of laughter came from Cartwright. "A positively seamless foray into the discussion of difficult females as I've ever heard. But truly, Armstrong, Miss Foxworth chaperoning Lady Amelia? Have you gone soft in the head? If things are that bad, perhaps I could be of assistance. I wouldn't mind keeping an eye on her for you." His grey eyes glinted appreciatively as he waggled black eyebrows.

Thomas didn't find him the least bit amusing but nonetheless forced a smile under the vehement protest of his facial muscles. "Thank you, but I believe I can manage."

Angling his head, Cartwright narrowed his gaze. "And by managing you mean . . . ?"

Thomas abandoned his relaxed posture and came up straight in the chair. "What the hell do you think I mean?"

Cartwright held up his hand in mock surrender. "Whoa, no need to get yourself into a state over a simple question," he said, laughing. "The last I heard, you intended the fair Lady Amelia receive her, er, comeuppance at your hands. She did, after all, question your sexual prowess. I'm merely inquiring how things are coming along on that front."

Given his overwrought reaction to Cartwright's teasing, Thomas could only imagine what his friend must be thinking. He forced a low chuckle from his throat, relaxed back into the chair, and offered Cartwright a dry smile before taking a deep swallow of his port.

After resting the etched glass on the table to his left, Thomas said, "I've come to see she isn't even worth the bother."

Cartwright barked a laugh, his eyes dancing. "That bad, eh? Well, I'm certain there are a number of ladies prime for whatever you had in mind for Lady Amelia. Though if you want a mistress who won't become too attached, someone like Lady Amelia would suit you admirably."

A dull suffusion of heat warmed Thomas's face. He quickly shuttered his expression, hoping Cartwright would mistake the reddening for distaste and not guilt. "The one thing I do require from the women I take to my bed is that they don't despise me. It would also be nice if I had some liking for them."

After draining the last of his port, Cartwright lazily pushed to his feet and padded to his desk to pour himself another. Turning, he silently held up the crystal decanter to his friend. Thomas declined with a shake of his head.

"When are you returning to Devon?" Cartwright asked, as he made his way back to his chair.

"Sunday."

"Perfect. I'll need somewhere to go while the duke is in town. If I remain, he'll expect to meet with me. I'd rather spend time in Newgate than see my father."

Normally, Thomas would not have had an issue with his friend staying at Stoneridge Hall—he had been a frequent guest there since their youth—but this time . . . it just didn't feel right. Couldn't he avoid the duke without leaving town? Good Lord, his friend acted as if London wasn't a big enough city for the two Cartwright men.

At his silence, Cartwright asked, "It won't be a problem, will it?"

Thomas quickly shook his head. "No, no problem at all." However, something inside him refuted the claim—loudly.

"Wonderful. It will also give me an opportunity to become better acquainted with Lady Amelia. Of the handful of times we've met, we've exchanged scarcely more than a polite greeting." Cartwright appeared to be watching him closely for a reaction.

A thousand words of protest sprang to his lips. Thomas voiced not one word and flickered not one eyelash. "I'm certain she'll be delighted for the company."

On second thought, perhaps he could use that second drink.

Chapter 16

There were no two ways around it; Amelia knew what she had to do. And if she did it now, she might be able to avoid awkwardness at supper.

With nothing to bolster her flagging courage but the deepest sense of remorse, she knocked on the bedchamber door and waited in dread.

The door was opened quickly. Camille Foxworth stood on the other side regarding her with eyes widened in shock—or perhaps it was horror. Amelia really couldn't take issue with that. No doubt the poor woman believed she had come to divest her of her last shred of dignity. Finish the job, so to speak. Amelia could well understand why; her remark had been the veriest of insults.

"Lady Amelia, I-I—"

"Might I have a moment of your time, Miss Foxworth?"

"Yes—yes, of course." She appeared flustered and not only a little nervous as she hastily moved aside to bid her entrance.

The bedchamber was on par with hers in décor as well as size: roomy, adequately heated, with solid, elegant furnishings and an exquisite canopied bed. Apparently, like hers, Miss Foxworth's accommodations were more those of a guest than servant.

Quietly, Miss Foxworth closed the door before turning to face her. Amelia swallowed hard.

"Please allow me to apologize for my behavior this afternoon. I don't know what prompted me to say something so unkind, so unwarranted. My rudeness was inexcusable and utterly reprehensible." Amelia could barely stand to meet the woman's gaze after she ended the contrite and rushed apology. Humble pie did not go down as easily as chocolate-dipped strawberries, nor did it come even remotely close to pleasing the palate.

For a moment Miss Foxworth stood motionless, her expression that of someone who'd received a hard knock on the head. Then she was fluttering her hands about and speaking quickly. "Lady Amelia, you needn't apologize. Believe me, at my age and circumstance, I've heard much worse. All you did was speak the truth."

Such self-deprecation. No one should be so inured to insults as to be resigned to them. Make light of them. A stab of shame hit her square in her conscience, one Amelia felt down to her bones.

"No." Amelia said quite emphatically. "I have every need to apologize. What I said, how I acted, was beyond reproach. I remain more than a little ashamed of myself."

Miss Foxworth smiled tentatively lighting up her blue eyes and accentuating cheekbones Amelia only now noticed were attractively high. It struck her then, that the woman wasn't as nondescript as she'd first thought. Yes, her appearance certainly could be improved, and the first thing Amelia would suggest was a change in her wardrobe, which seemed to consist primarily of pale colors that did nothing for her pallid complexion.

"You have such lovely eyes and cheekbones."

Miss Foxworth averted her head in a quick dismissal of the compliment, but her face turned the color of a ripe apricot. "Please, Lady Amelia, you do not have to—"

"I'm not saying so to make up for my behavior. Believe

me, I'm not that kind." Well, perhaps she was being a little kind, for she had much too appease for.

"I believe you're kinder than you think."

"And I believe there are others who would not agree with you," Amelia answered with a little laugh. After a shared moment of amiable silence, her regard went to the bed, where a newspaper lay open atop the flowered counterpane. "I see I've interrupted you. I shall allow you to get back to your reading."

Miss Foxworth glanced somewhat guiltily at the newspaper. "Oh, that is nothing but a gossip sheet. They say if one is to indulge in scandal, the preference is to have it on paper in black ink involving others."

It appeared Camille Foxworth had a sense of humor. A surprise, given what Amelia had seen of her and the little she knew of her, but a welcome one nonetheless. "Yes, I suppose that's the only way one would find it palatable. I hope the scandals are keeping you properly entertained."

"Nothing terribly scandalous at the moment. However, the town is abuzz over the ball tomorrow evening."

"And whose ball is that, pray tell?" Amelia asked more out of curiosity than anything else. After her last appearance at a ball, she wasn't overly eager to attend another.

"Lady Forsham's ball."

Amelia stilled. Could it be the stars were aligning in her favor? Not only had she and her father received an invitation to the gala months before, but Lady Forsham was Lord Clayborough's aunt. From his account, he and his aunt could have only been closer had she actually birthed him herself. Amelia had no doubt he'd be attending the ball.

"We should attend." Amelia silently vowed she'd find a way, come hell or high water, though neither option was preferable.

After a perceptible pause, Miss Foxworth smiled as if caution should be preserved at all costs. "But, of course, you must have been invited. I will confer with Lord Armstrong when he returns. He might well be inclined to act as our escort."

"Lord Armstrong informed me himself that he has other plans for the evening." *With his mistress.* Not that it mattered to Amelia. It did not. But if the poor woman was foolish enough to be taken with him, a warning of this nature could save her in the long run.

"Then perhaps we shouldn't—"

"And if we attend, I shall have my maid fix your hair. She is quite proficient with the tongs. I think curls will suit your face admirably. Of course, there is the matter of your gown." Amelia gave her dress a critical stare. "I think a brighter color will go best with your complexion."

A flicker of excitement sparked in Miss Foxworth's eyes. There was nothing like flattery to bolster a woman's self-image. *And a handsome viscount to lead an innocent to scandalous behavior.*

"I have a blue gown that will look divine on you. I can have Hélène take the hem up a few inches and take in the bodice, and it should fit you perfectly. We'll also experiment with some cosmetics. A little color on your cheeks would be quite flattering. What do you think?" Amelia would simply overwhelm her with the tremendous possibilities to such an endeavor.

Thankfully, it worked, for Miss Foxworth appeared to have gone on the journey of her transformation with Amelia, her eyes shining with girlish excitement. And just like that, the matter of going to the ball without the viscount's permission or escort ceased to be a concern.

The scent of perfume and candle wax hung heavy in the air. Certainly, Thomas had had to contend with worse smells in his lifetime, but tonight he felt practically suffocated by the cloying mixture. Or perhaps his sensitivity had more to do with just how much he had no desire to be there.

After only a few minutes at the ball, Lady Stanton, with her daughter in tow, had pounced upon him and Cartwright like an oversized cat sprigged in an elaborate headdress, claws drawn. She'd taken one look at his expression and wisely turned to Cartwright. *Lord Alex, would you be so good as to take my dear Georgiana on a swirl about the room?* Cartwright had acquiesced without a fuss. And he so often complained that he—being a second son and all— found himself being dragged off to the dance floor with such regularity. Stupid man. Escaping the clutches of ruthless, socially ambitious mothers was not for the faint of heart and certainly not for a man who strived to comport himself like a gentleman at all times—at least publicly. Cartwright was hardly the saintly pillar many thought him to be.

The only squared edges to be found in the circular ballroom were on the thick, grooved support columns running the periphery of the room. Thomas stood near the one closest to the door, scanning the guests with a dispassionate eye. The joviality around him didn't entice him. He'd come for one singular purpose.

Thomas spotted said purpose a minute later amid a buzz of activity at the entrance. He checked his timepiece. Ten o'clock and fashionably late. He didn't have to see Louisa to know it was she who had created the stir. Who else would have gentlemen effusively bowing like wooden toy soldiers, and women practically genuflecting, their crinolines colliding with every object and person within a fifteen-foot radius?

The object of their reverence—perched obscenely high on her self-appointed pedestal—glided into the room, much too imperial to walk like lesser mortals.

She was still beautiful, sheathed in a ball gown of ice blue silk and white lace, her hair a profusion of pearls weaved in between ringlets of blond curls. But he'd expected as much. Louisa possessed too much vanity to permit time to taint her God-given looks.

During their last encounter, his emotions had been in a state of upheaval, his pride in tatters. He was gratified to discover he could now observe her with a detachment only time and distance could bring.

Surrounded by some of her boot-scraping admirers, Louisa accepted their attentions with the due of a queen. In the midst of the gaggle of fawning peers, she shot an idle glance about, her smile masking bored sufferance—he now knew that pasty smile for what it was. Thomas angled himself in her direct line of vision. She would spot him soon enough.

As evidenced by the brief rounding of her eyes, she did so moments later. But her smile didn't falter and their eye contact was brief. She calmly continued to nod imperious greetings to the guests surrounding her.

Motionless amid the swirling masses, Thomas was certain it would only be a matter of time. Before long, she lightly touched the gloved arm of Lady Forsham and with the tip of her chin, gestured in his direction. Within seconds, she and their hostess were making their way toward him.

The speed at which she'd separated herself from a group that included the ranks of the Earl of Radcliffe and the Marquess of Stratford brought Thomas no satisfaction. Once upon a time, he would have experienced a sense of triumph, of vindication. Currently, he felt nothing save the irritation that she'd succeeded in forcing him to seek her out.

They reached his side after several unsuccessful attempts by other guests to waylay them.

Lady Forsham reached out and lightly touched the sleeve of his jacket as she beamed a wide smile up at him. "Lord Armstrong, Her Grace has requested an introduction."

"I daresay, I don't believe we are in need of an official introduction. Her Grace and I met many years ago, did we not?"

Louisa merely inclined her chin, a small smile on her lips

as Lady Forsham's gaze darted between them before a dawning look of comprehension altered her expression. "Then this is altogether truly delightful. I am certain you will want to reacquaint yourselves."

At this point, Thomas thought she would have gone merrily on her way, but she did not. Instead, she remained rooted in place wearing an expectant look on her face. An awkward silence followed. Then, as if the countess finally realized they would hardly be inclined to renew their acquaintance with her standing in avid earshot, she executed a small curtsey before turning and disappearing into the throng of partygoers.

What followed her departure was a silence the width and breadth of the Andes. Louisa effectively bridged the silence, stepping closer, her mouth set in a moue. "Would it have wounded that accursed pride of yours to respond to even one of my letters? You, sir, are a fiend to put me in a position that I should be forced to take up pursuit. That is supposed to be the gentleman's privilege."

Thomas cocked his brow and retreated a step. So refreshingly forward. Good, it gave him leave to be just as forthright.

"And here I thought my lack of response would clearly indicate my disinterest. If I'd known you required I put it in writing, I would have done so immediately."

She winced. A bit of a farce if he'd ever seen one—as if she'd taken an egregious hit. After their acquaintance had met its dramatic demise, he'd thought of her as the queen—or duchess as it were—of deception. That's when he could think about her without the rage and the feeling of betrayal and humiliation.

"Perhaps you'd care to find somewhere more"—Louisa shot a glance around at the ebullient crowds—"private to talk. It's much too noisy in here for us to carry on a proper conversation. I've much to tell you. Much I think you might wish to hear."

Thomas deliberately took in their position by the colonnade and the potted plants, which offered as much privacy from the crush as they would get anywhere in the room. "This looks to be private enough for me to say what I must." He paused a beat. "I want you to stop."

Two faint lines appeared on her forehead as though the final word bitten out through his clenched jaw surprised her.

"Calling on my mistress was low even for you."

Her brown eyes darkened at the insult.

"I want you to cease the letters."

Her mouth tightened into a red, pouty line.

"I want you to cease the inquiries of my whereabouts. I believe I've made it plain that I have no desire to renew our acquaintance."

She wrinkled her nose delicately, as if her nostrils had just been accosted by an objectionable scent.

"Have I made myself clear?"

A myriad of emotions expressed themselves in her eyes, her mouth, the angle of her chin and her form. Finally, she offered up a smile teetering on the fringes of irritation and exasperation. "It makes me wonder, Thomas, why you're so angry with me after so many years. Such strong emotions may suggest that you still have feelings for me. Feelings possibly as strong as mine for you. I hear you're still unwed."

The only thing more staggering than her arrogance was her cheek. As if his marital state had *anything* to do with her. Thomas's own sense of propriety—and the group of debutantes casting interested looks in his direction—prevented him from delivering her the dressing-down she deserved, but something in his expression must have conveyed his derision.

With the suddenness of a shift in the wind, her eyes went from a contrived woefulness to shards of ice. But that too was gone just as quickly, though her displeasure couldn't be completely disguised. He knew the signs: the jawbone protruding slightly, the indrawn breath, and a quick flaring of her nostrils. Rejection could never be considered an aphrodisiac.

"I can't help if your overwrought imaginings have you misconstruing my indifference for some sort of pent-up longing. I will, however, ask that you cease your pursuit. Now!" The last word was a growled command, brooking no opposition.

With that, Thomas gave a sharp bow, pivoted on his heel, and started toward the exit. He could see her in his mind's eye, her eyes wide in disbelief and then quickly narrowing to slits. How dare he walk away from her, a duchess, the daughter of an earl? He had, the penniless viscount who wasn't penniless anymore. But her pride wouldn't permit her to pursue him so publicly. After all, she was all she'd ever aspired to be. A duchess, queen of the noble realm.

As he'd accomplished what he'd set out to do, he could now take his leave of the place. There was just the matter of informing Cartwright of his departure. They'd come together so he could at least offer his friend transport home if he was inclined to leave now.

Thomas skirted the dance floor, evading a group of ladies who appeared ready to pounce on the next passing eligible male. As his gaze swept the room, a figure near the set of French doors leading to the terrace caught his attention. Although she stood a fair distance away and had her back to him, she possessed the kind of figure a man would have to be blind or a eunuch not to appreciate. And there was something familiar about the dark silken coif of curls pinned atop her head, and the set of her slender shoulders.

She angled her head. The view of her profile caused him to stop in mid-stride.

Damn her!

Someone bumped him from behind.

"I beg your pardon," he said instantly, only giving the gentleman—Mr. Wright—an impatient glance. By the time he turned his attention back to the woman, the shifting masses now obscured his view.

Behind him, he could hear Mr. Wright launch into a profuse apology, for it was certainly his fault. Should he not have anticipated that his lordship would halt so abruptly in front of him? And if he hadn't been in such a rush and following his lordship so closely, the unfortunate contact would not have occurred.

Thomas started toward the terrace, a maelstrom of fury propelling him forward as Mr. Wright's ingratiating apology droned on behind him.

Thirty minutes after their arrival at the ball, Amelia watched as Mr. Glenville escorted her chaperone to the dance floor. In viewing the results of her and Hélène's efforts, she conceded with more humility than conceit, that they had done a wonderful job in her transformation.

Miss Foxworth's hair had been curled and strategically coiled about her face to accentuate her cheekbones and minimize her forehead, which Amelia had belatedly discovered upon closer inspection, was a fraction too long. She wore a rich blue taffeta gown with lace flounces, and the corset Amelia had chosen for her helped to create a cleavage out of modest-sized breasts, although the term modest in this instance might be an overly generous one. Miss Foxworth was almost unrecognizable, and looking very much improved. One could say she happily bordered on pretty.

And with Miss Foxworth now occupied, Amelia was free to search out Lord Clayborough. She knew he had to be in the crowd somewhere.

It took all of five minutes, in which time she refused three offers of refreshments, and four requests to dance. He was entering the ballroom through the doors leading to the terrace with a drink in his hand. Clad in a black jacket and trousers, and a white waistcoat and cravat, he moved with a sense of purpose in his strides.

She was practically on top of him when he finally noticed her. He could scarcely hide his shock, his mouth moving without the effect of sound. He quickly recovered his speech. "Why, Lady Amelia, what are you doing here? I thought you were in Devon."

Amelia didn't give an immediate response, instead she first steered them to a more private spot by the terrace doors. "Why have you not responded to my letters?" she demanded once they were safely out of earshot. There were too many women present who would like nothing better than to see her total ostracism from society. The cuts she'd received since her arrival told her some had not forgotten her last attendance at a ball.

The baron's eyes widened in what appeared to be genuine surprise. "What letters? I've received no letters from you."

"I've sent you three letters since I arrived in Devon. For over a month I've been awaiting your response."

"Lady Amelia, I swear to you, I've received none of them." The baron had a tendency to look away when he lied—as he had when he'd said he would marry her with or without her substantial dowry. His gaze was alarmingly direct.

Amelia was too piqued to find any solace in his assertion. "Would it behoove *you* to try to contact *me?* I did tell you I would write upon my father's departure. As you well know, my father left the country over a month ago."

Lord Clayborough could offer no response because he hadn't thought of it. When he could have taken the initiative, he hadn't done so. Amelia dearly hoped this did not speak of things to come. *Now Thomas would have* . . . She broke off the thought, for it didn't bear completion.

"Well, in the future, you needn't wait for me to contact you. You know precisely where I am. You own your own

conveyance, and public transit is well within your means."
*In other words, you can rescue me without an expressed
written invitation.*

A stricken look flashed across his face. "Yes, of course. I
was just under the assumption that we—"

"Well, in the future, do not assume." She didn't mean to
snap her reply, but she was beginning to draw comparisons
between Lord Clayborough and the viscount and the baron
was coming up wanting—which just wouldn't do. Again,
she did her best to quell further such thoughts. "But as I am
in town, all of that may be a moot point."

"Begging your pardon, Lady Amelia, but I have left Lord
Barnaby waiting for me in the game room. If you'll give me
a moment, I must excuse myself from the game."

The baron regarded her as if awaiting her permission to
depart, which only succeeded in vexing her all the more.
Nonetheless, she assented with an irritated nod. Lord Clayborough executed a polite bow and strode off, soon swallowed
by the press of the crowd.

Conscious of some disapproving stares from certain matrons of the ton, Amelia stoically started toward the refreshment room. Narrowly focused on her destination, which was
conveniently situated next to the game room, Amelia didn't
see the person bearing down on her until it was too late.
They collided with unforgiving force. Masculine hands
grasped her upper arms to steady her and remained long
after she'd established her balance was sound.

"Beg my par—" A glance up caused the words to still in
her throat and her heart to give a horrifying thud. Amelia
had never seen an emerald burn, but as she viewed the green
eyes staring down at her, she imagined it would look exactly
like that.

Chapter 17

Thomas didn't breathe a word; he simply retained a firm hold of Amelia's arm, and began steering her toward the exit. And sadly, there wasn't a thing she could do to prevent him from hustling her from the ball like a disobedient charge.

At some point during her unceremonious leave taking, Lord Alex materialized at his friend's side. He gauged the situation with a single look and then assumed the role of an emissary.

"Now, Armstrong, don't go getting all—"

With neither a break in his stride nor a glance at Lord Alex, Thomas severed his friend's efforts to negotiate peace. "This is none of your concern. I will handle the matter as I see fit." He lowered his mouth to her ear. "Where is Miss Foxworth?"

Ignoring the quaking of her legs and the violent turning of her belly, Amelia swallowed hard and replied in a small voice, "Dancing."

"Do you have any idea how much this little escapade will cost you? Do you even have the sense to be terrified?"

Nothing noisy or dramatic from the viscount, he issued his threat in the kind of dangerous soft tone that undoubtedly had men—or case in point, a lady—hoping the punishment would be carried out swiftly and with minimum fuss.

Amelia had sense enough to wait until they'd exited the ballroom before trying to free herself, but she was ever conscious of the servants and the guests milling about in the hall.

"Oh, for heaven's sake, do unhand me. You're hurting my arm, and if you're not mindful, you'll cause a scene," she said in a fierce whisper.

The only indication he gave that he had heard her was to ease his hold so his fingers weren't digging into her flesh.

"Cartwright, please inform Miss Foxworth that Lady Amelia has taken ill and I have escorted her home. When she is ready to leave, please see her safely back to my mother's residence." Thomas spoke with a barely controlled kind of rumble in his voice as he peered down at her, his eyes slits and two slashes of red coloring his cheekbones.

Lord Alex gestured beseechingly with his hand. "Armstrong—"

"Damn it, man, just do as I ask and don't interfere."

Lord Alex appeared genuinely concerned. She glanced at Thomas. Perhaps, she really did have something to fear.

Lord Alex halted abruptly. "For God's sake, do remember she's Harry's daughter." After sending her what she took to be a resigned look, he turned and proceeded back to the ballroom.

Thomas continued toward the front entrance, forcing Amelia to quicken her pace to what felt like a trot. Trotting was for horses not ladies.

Within minutes, they had donned their respective outdoor garments, Amelia's a thick wool cloak, and the viscount's, a black great coat.

Outside under the moonlit night sky, cold air nipped at her face, creating visible vapors of air with each exhalation. Thomas curtly dismissed the footman, his hand clasping her elbow as she mounted the step to his brougham. She glared back at him over her shoulder, her mouth drawn, her form taut.

Near the gothic front entrance with its high gables and iron finials, a movement caught her attention. Lord Clayborough watched them, half hidden behind one of the thick plaster columns. Her heart didn't know whether to sing with joy or leap to her throat in fear. This was a confrontation she'd never anticipated, the victory leaning heavily in the viscount's favor.

Thomas turned and followed the direction of her gaze. By then, the baron had stepped back behind the column. Humiliated, Amelia turned and allowed Thomas to herald her into the coach.

Lord Clayborough had done absolutely naught to interfere. He had merely watched her with dull, impotent eyes. Even if it would have been a losing cause, should he not have tried? Was she not worth the effort? So much for her knight in silver-plated armor.

But Amelia refused to give into her disillusionment. Her fury roared forth like a cyclone, to destroy everything in her path. One Thomas Armstrong.

She sat down and jerked her arm from his hold. "You miserable, sanctimonious bastard." Those four words encapsulated all the emotions she'd kept in check while he had all but dragged her from the ball. "Don't you ever lay your hands on me again."

The viscount gave a mild start and regarded her with raised brows. Then with great deliberation of purpose, he took the seat next to her, trapping a portion of her skirts beneath him.

Amelia instantly started to rise, intent on sitting in the opposite seat—the one the gentleman should have taken—but was forestalled with his snakelike swiftness as he yanked her back down beside him.

"I am *this* close to tossing you across my knee," he said softly, holding up his hand, his thumb and forefinger almost touching. "Make another move away from me and you will feel the palm of my hand."

Despicable brute. Rage bloomed hot in her face as she freed her trapped skirt with several hard tugs, then moved to hug the cold metal door.

Thomas narrowed his gaze. "I don't know how you managed it, but in the span of one blasted day, you've corrupted Camille. And for that, you will pay."

"Pay! Pay for what? I wanted just one evening in the company of a man I actually like. I hardly think that's a crime."

Lord Armstrong barked a harsh laugh. "Who, Clayborough? I thought he was auditioning to be a ghost the way he tried to melt into that plasterwork."

Her head jerked up, and her face flamed in embarrassment. He had seen him too? Another bit of shame to heap on her.

"What? Did you think I didn't see that cowardly good-for-nothing? If that's your idea of character in a real man, then I can see you require very little in a husband."

Amelia despised his high-handedness. She hated his derision. She loathed even more that he'd found a fault in her choice of husbands he could use to render any defense of Lord Clayborough as ineffective as legs on a fish. But she refused to concede him a thing. "And what would you have him do? Make a scene and get into a brawling match with you?"

He met her bristling glare directly and replied calmly, "For the woman I intend to take as my wife? Yes. I would have done so."

His response knocked the wind from her, leaving her in disconcerted silence. For the woman who managed to secure his love—if one existed—she could well imagine he'd move heaven and earth. The thought of what that would be like, to be loved by a man like him, evoked an unwanted longing in her. Like a cook with a rolling pin spying a mouse in the kitchen, she bludgeoned the feeling just as swiftly.

"Your father will never allow you to marry that blackguard." His low-pitched voice broke the quiet of the carriage. "*I* will not allow it. Not while you are under my care."

"I am not under your care—I am your prisoner."

"Then as your warden it appears I have to expand your duties to keep you occupied. Tomorrow you'll report to the cook. I believe we can use some additional help in the scullery."

"You must be mad."

"I assure you all my faculties are intact and functioning efficiently."

"I won't do it." The words were ripped from her throat. "When I tell my father—"

"Your father will do nothing once I explain the circumstances. He too wouldn't approve of you appearing in public so soon after the spectacle you made of yourself at Lady Stanton's ball."

Before she took the time to consider the recklessness and futility of her actions, Amelia launched herself at him.

Thomas instinctively threw up his hands to cover his face. Two women attacking him in the span of a day? Good God, had the whole world gone insane?

After several ineffectual blows to his shoulders and upper chest, she caught his lower jaw in a glancing blow. He quickly captured her flailing hands before she succeeded in doing any real damage.

"For God's sake, get a hold of yourself, you bloody hell-cat," he muttered. Exerting little force, he used one hand to secure hers behind her back, finally ending the attack.

Thomas held her in a position that left one inhalation's distance between their upper torsos. And to show him how little his body cared about her insolence, her woeful disobedience to his orders, his loins surged to life, growing hard behind the fall of his trousers. Reflectively, he bore her down onto the seat.

"Let me go." Ragged breaths feathered his cheek, while she twisted beneath him, further encouraging his arousal.

"Stop moving," he said harshly, his control slipping with the feel of her soft, womanly flesh.

Amelia stilled. She stared up at him, her blue eyes wide and wary as if she feared even a breath would draw attention to the way their bodies meshed from shoulder to hip.

"Right now I'm beyond tempted to lift your skirts and take you. Give me one good reason I should not." His gaze dropped to the pink lushness of her lips and the avaricious hunger that had started weeks ago, threatened to consume him whole. He had to taste her again.

"Don't." The plea squeaked from her throat.

"Not good enough," he murmured before lowering his head and smothering her breathy sounds of resistance with his mouth.

Blood, hot and thick, coursed through him, pulsing strongly between his thighs, his erection near to bursting. Impatient and hungry, he thrust deeply into her mouth. A shudder ran down the length of his frame when his tongue touched hers. He tried to temper his need, but it required only one delicious swipe of the cavern of her mouth before she eagerly, almost helplessly, joined in the sensual tongue play.

Thomas released her hands, dealt with the buttons of her cloak, and smoothed it from her shoulders without so much as a demur from her. The garment spread beneath her like an altar, with her as the offering.

Tracing the curve of her hip up past the indent of her narrow waist, he found the underside of her breast. Amelia let out a low moan and wrapped her arms tightly about his neck.

Lust had him in its grip, making his mind merely a vehicle of his physical needs. Mewling sounds escaped her lips when he angled his head for a more thorough and carnal access to her mouth.

One hand inched up and palmed the firm thrust of her breast, his thumb swiping repeatedly across the nipple, causing it to pebble against the pale green bodice of her gown. Thomas didn't only want to feel them in his hand, he wanted to feast on them with his eyes and taste them with his lips.

A guttural sound emerged from his throat as he lifted his mouth from hers to gaze into her shadowed, flushed face. Taking in her swollen lips and closed eyes, he started on the row of pearl buttons marching down the front of her gown, deftly releasing them to reveal a white silk corset barely containing her breasts . . . and firm, smooth, creamy skin. He grew harder than he thought possible.

Slowly, her eyes, dark with desire, drifted open and she gazed up at him. It only took a few moments for her to lose the look of a woman lost in the deepest regions of passion. His fingers were releasing the buttons at her waist when her eyes widened in alarm.

What the blazes am I doing? Amelia began frantically batting at his hands. "Stop! Do not—don't touch me."

Thomas halted and stared down at her with a dazed expression of unappeased hunger. For a moment she thought he intended to override her weakened defenses, mute every protest she would make. Slowly, however, he removed his hands from her dress and levered his muscular frame from hers.

Amelia immediately bolted into a sitting position, caught both edges of her cloak, and jerked them together in a desperate attempt to shield herself. There was no time to struggle with her buttons, not with his gaze blistering her with its heat.

Moving to the opposite seat, Thomas watched her silently, a derisive smile now twisting his mouth.

In the past when she'd seen him in public, he was usually dressed as he was now, in dark colors that only succeeded in accentuating his goldenness. How well he wore the façade of the honorable gentleman. If his adoring admirers could see him now, lounging back against the leather seat, his legs splayed, his gaze hooded and hair tousled, no one would mistake him for anything less than the rake she knew him to be.

"Doesn't it ever get tiring?" he drawled.

"Pardon?"

"You want me physically. You've already admitted to that. So why the performance of the affronted virgin every time I kiss you? I imagine it gets tiring after a while. I know it does to me."

"Per-performance! You believe that I enjoy you taking unwanted liberties?" Her voice rose with every indignant word.

A dry laugh emerged from his lips. "Taking unwanted liberties, Princess?" he said in that manner she most despised—not that he'd ever said anything in a manner she liked. "Then it's a very fortunate gentleman who can show you true enjoyment. Do you make the same panting sounds when he kisses you?" His gaze dropped to her breasts. "When he touches your nipples?"

"I did not," she croaked, but the memory of the truth shamed her.

"Would you like me to show you again just how easy it is to make you wet?" His voice was a sultry challenge.

Amelia jerked the cloak tighter about her in a fruitless effort to halt the tremors wracking her form. "Do not touch me again." The command, however, sounded as if it came from a woman fighting a losing battle of retaining a semblance of her control.

It seemed an eternity until Thomas spoke again. He casually gestured toward the window at his side, its curtain closed. "We've been stopped well over five minutes now. Something you failed to notice, because you were, er, otherwise occupied. Oh, don't worry, Johns will only open the door if the curtain is drawn."

Swinging her gaze immediately to the window beside her, she pushed back the curtain. Surrounded by high railings of fortifying iron, its tops spearlike in shape, was the viscountess's red-bricked townhouse.

Without uttering a word, Amelia threw open the door and scrambled out. In her hasty exit, she caught the hem of her skirt on the carriage step. The fragile material rent under her impatient tug, but she didn't care. She would have gladly shredded half her wardrobe to get away from Thomas Armstrong and every wretched emotion he elicited in her.

Chapter 18

In the morning, Amelia was surprised to see their traveling party had acquired an additional member: one Lord Alex Cartwright. It appeared he too would be a guest at Stoneridge Hall. Thomas had been vague as to the duration, but the time—a day, a week—was immaterial. Anyone who could create a buffer between her and the viscount would be more than welcome.

Miss Foxworth appeared genuinely disappointed that Amelia had been too unwell to remain at the ball, but did indicate, in that subdued manner of hers, that she had enjoyed herself thoroughly. Lord Alex greeted her kindly while Thomas treated her with a studied indifference, which was just fine with her.

En masse, they departed Mayfair to Paddington Station. The women rode in the comfort of Thomas's carriage while the men followed in a hired hack. Traveling separately from the viscount was another added benefit to having Lord Alex accompanying them.

On the train, the men discussed the latest methods of shipbuilding and the merits in acquiring stocks for a steel company lately trading on the London Stock Exchange. On that stretch of the trip, Amelia read a novel she'd brought with her, taking a short break for lunch when

Thomas produced sandwiches, biscuits, fruit, and lemonade prepared for them by the viscountess's cook.

They changed trains at Newton to go on to Totnes, where upon their arrival at the station, Thomas hired two hacks. At seven that evening, they concluded the ten-hour journey back to Stoneridge Hall.

"Will you be joining us for supper?"

Amelia paused on her way up the stairs, shooting a look at Thomas over her shoulder. Given he had spoken precisely five words to her the entire day—*Good morning* and *Are you hungry?*—the question surprised her.

"I think I'm going to retire for the evening." Feeling travel weary and with her stomach unsettled from the long journey, she had absolutely no appetite.

Thomas's gaze flickered over her briefly, his expression inscrutable. He nodded curtly. "You may resume your duties on Tuesday. Take tomorrow to rest."

Coldly polite was an apt phrase to describe his manner toward her, yet his abeyance of her duties suggested something else. Something she'd be a fool to examine too closely.

Amelia turned quickly and made her way up to her bedchamber, where it would require another three hours to find escape in sleep.

A morning walk had been a mistake. Amelia realized it the moment her belly contracted in the second wave of pain. She should have heeded the signs when she awoke still feeling queasy from the night before. A mug of hot chocolate at breakfast had done nothing to settle it. And when she started to feel warm, instead of getting herself back to bed, she had decided fresh air—cold though it might be—and a quick walk would be the thing. She'd clearly been in denial.

The truth was, she had been all too eager to leave the house before anyone else arrived for breakfast. She also hated being sick. She hated the helplessness of it. Memories of fevers wracking her body and the smell of mint water could still elicit the odd niggling sense of fear. Stubbornly ignoring the signs would change nothing. She was ill, plain and simple.

As Amelia turned to go back to the house, she caught sight of Lord Alex cresting the hill before her. He looked exceedingly handsome, his lean muscular frame donned in tan and brown riding clothes.

Halting in front of her, he greeted her with a dip of his head and a tip of his hat. "Lady Amelia."

"Lord Alex," she replied, suddenly aware that this was the first time they'd ever been alone together.

"I wasn't aware that you would be out walking this morning." He took in her attire. "I assume you have come out for a walk?" he queried politely.

"Yes, one does get tired of being indoors for an extended length of time." Even if one wasn't feeling quite up to par.

A faint smile tipped the corners of his mouth—a full mouth, especially for a man. "Given my friendship with your father, I can't believe we aren't better acquainted. I hope to rectify that during this visit."

Disarmed, Amelia could only stare at him, at a loss for words. She quickly collected herself. "Yes, well, that is-is surprising."

"But I see no reason we cannot further our acquaintance now. I pray you won't hold Armstrong's behemoth-like behavior against me?"

In her weakened condition—and indeed she did feel weak—Amelia couldn't gauge whether he was toying with her or not. His handsome face was everything to be found in gentlemanly solicitousness.

"Certainly not."

"Good, glad to hear. I hadn't pegged you as one to judge me solely by the company I keep." He smiled a slow, thoroughly engaging smile. "Given a chance, I can be charming and agreeable—or so I'm told."

Amelia chuckled softly despite the cold penetrating the thick wool of her cloak and beginning to seep into her flesh. She imagined he was everything he claimed and more with his silver-grey eyes and his dimpled chin. Thankfully, Lord Alex didn't affect her senses as his friend did.

She emitted a pained gasp as another shooting pain nearly doubled her over.

"What's wrong?" he asked sharply.

Amelia briefly closed her eyes to fight the dizziness threatening to engulf her. "No-no, I'm fine. I must not have gotten enough sleep." The last thing she needed was his sympathy.

Lord Alex was immediately at her side, concern etching his features. "Is it your stomach? You look ready to keel over."

"I-I'm fine." Then to make a complete liar of her, she clutched the sleeve of his jacket, his forearm steady and hard beneath her gloved hand. "I can't imagine what could be the matter," she murmured as another dizzy spell sent her head into a spin.

Amelia closed her eyes against the weakness in her limbs. Lord Alex swiftly removed the glove from his hand and pressed his palm to her forehead.

"Good Lord, you're burning up," he said, his voice raised in alarm.

"I think I may be ill," she said faintly.

"Oh really?" he asked, a touch wryly. "Come, let's get you back to the house."

The house was about fifty yards away, but she began panting at the prospect of the walk.

She started forward, resting more of her weight on his arm than she intended. With a swiftness that left her gasping, he hoisted her up in his arms, high against his chest.

"No," she said—a feeble protest a man with any sense of gallantry and the strength to carry eight stone would ignore. "Please put me down, I can walk just fine on my own."

Another roll of her belly had her promptly dropping her head back on his shoulder as her entire body contracted sharply against the breath-stealing pain.

"You don't even have the strength to hold up your head and you think I will permit you to walk. What you need is your bed and a physician."

Amelia closed her eyes and inhaled the frosty air. She had never been particularly fond of physicians. Hélène was apt to take better care of her. But her protests would be futile. Much like his friend, Lord Alex looked like a man rarely refused anything. Both men carried themselves with an inherent arrogance, but could command goodwill without a word.

It took him only a few minutes to cover the required distance, carrying her as if she weighed nothing at all. They entered the house through the rear and were immediately enveloped in its warmth.

"You can put me down now," she murmured, her eyes fluttering open.

"I will put you down when——"

"What is going on?"

In unison, their heads jerked in the direction of the viscount's steely quiet tones. He loomed just outside the billiard room, his expression containing all the outrage of a husband catching his wife with her lover.

"Send for a physician. Lady Amelia is ill."

At his friend's barked command, Thomas strode swiftly toward them, placing himself in the direct path to the staircase.

Lord Alex's black brows drew over narrowed grey eyes. "Move aside, man. I'm taking her to her chamber."

Thomas's gaze flew to take in Amelia's wan visage. Her eyes fluttered, the spread of dark lashes fanned above the crest of her cheekbones.

"Give her to me," he demanded, his hands already reaching for her.

Cartwright's mouth formed a tight, displeased line as he pulled her tighter against his chest. "Damn it, man, I have her. Just direct me to her bedchamber."

What bloody gall! And damn if he needed Cartwright's permission. Amelia was his. *His guest*, he quickly corrected. He and he alone was responsible for her. "I will take her." His words came out a growl. And since Cartwright remained unwilling to give Amelia to him, Thomas took her, extricating her smoothly from his friend's arms.

Cartwright relinquished her without another word of protest. He did one better. He watched him, all sober-faced and assessing.

With Amelia securely in his arms, Thomas studiously ignored him and headed for the stairs. He ascended to the first floor with swift, sure steps.

He glanced down at her again to find her peeping up at him. "You needn't act like such a boar. He was being a gentleman. In any case, you can put me down. I'm quite capable of walking unassisted. It's nothing more than a bellyache and perhaps a touch of a fever."

"We'll let a physician determine that," he said grimly.

In her chamber, he placed her gently on the bed. Seconds later, Amelia's maid came rushing to her bedside, anxiously peering at Amelia from behind him.

"*Oh, mon Dieu, qu'est qui s'est passé?* Monsieur says zu are ailing. What 'as 'appened to mademoiselle?"

"Your mistress is unwell. Find Alfred and have him send for the physician."

"Monsieur has already sent for a physician."

By monsieur, Thomas assumed she meant Cartwright, whom he was relieved to see was nowhere in sight.

"Mademoiselle, iz it your belly? Your appetite has not been right."

Amelia nodded slowly. "And some dizziness, but I'm sure it's nothing a day in bed won't cure."

The maid sighed softly, then turned and made her way to the adjoining bathing room.

Thomas's gaze flew to Amelia. He began to mentally catalogue her symptoms. Dizziness and stomach pains? Brought on by what, nausea? Suddenly the possible cause of her illness had *his* stomach dropping and his head spinning.

"Are you with child?" Behind his harshly bitten-out question lay a fear so distasteful he found it hard to swallow.

Her eyes rounded. "Good Lord, you shall always think the worst of me, shall you not?"

He'd been holding his breath in anticipation of her response. He expelled that breath and swallowed the lump in his throat. She wasn't breeding. Not even Amelia could feign that kind of affront.

Thomas shifted on his feet, momentarily averting his gaze. "Not an impossibility given your history."

Her eyes darkened, and then she abruptly fell back against the pillow, her pallor stark against the navy bed sheets. "Please go. I don't want you here."

Amelia's maid returned to her bedside with a rag in her hand. "If zu would pardon me, my lord." She sent him a tentative glance, as if not wanting to offend. Thomas hastily moved aside to allow the woman access to her mistress.

Pregnant indeed! The cool rag on her forehead was a balm against her fevered skin, but the wretched man was impossible.

Hélène began to remove the pins from her hair. Shortly, Amelia's hair lay fanned about her head. Thomas, who had taken to pacing at the side of the bed, halted and stared at her.

"My lord, I will attend mademoiselle, and tomorrow she should be, as you English say, good as new, *non?*"

Thomas didn't reply to Hélène, just continued to stare at Amelia. She blinked against the intensity of his gaze.

"Worried I won't be well enough to resume work tomorrow?" she whispered in an effort to blunt the sudden tension in the air.

Her voice seemed to snap him to attention as if coming out of a daze. "Don't be absurd. What do you think I am, a tyrant?" he asked briskly.

"Oh, don't scowl so. Just leave so I can rest. I can hardly do so with you hovering over me. And Hélène can—"

The knock at the door was followed immediately by the entrance of Lord Alex and a man who could only be the physician, given the black physician's bag in his hand. Moreover, the older gentleman, tall and elegant with a thick thatch of snowy white hair, entered the chamber with an air of authority.

"Dr. Lawson was belowstairs treating one of the servants who appears to be suffering from something similar," Lord Alex announced to no one in particular, advancing into the room as if anointed by some authority that he too was at liberty to be in attendance.

Leprosy might have received a warmer welcome than Thomas offered the arrival of his friend. Amelia noted the stiffening of his jaw and the coldness now glazing his eyes. Thomas gave Lord Alex a curt, dismissive nod.

"Good morning, Thomas. I gather this is the patient?" The doctor spoke with an informality that told Amelia he'd known Thomas many years, probably long before Thomas had gained his title.

The doctor advanced to her side and gazed down at her in a medically assessing manner.

"Yes, Dr. Lawson, this is Lady Amelia Bertram. She's running a fever and is complaining of stomach pains."

"Hmm. Well, let me take a look. Don't worry, my dear, this will not hurt." He gave her a reassuring smile, which did nothing to allay Amelia's worries. Doctors had a way of mucking things up before eventually curing you. Of course, that's if they didn't kill you first.

Thomas turned to Cartwright, who stood several feet behind him. "I believe Dr. Lawson has this in hand." In other words, *You've done your good deed for the day, so run along your way.*

In the midst of removing an instrument from his bag, the physician angled a look over his shoulder, and followed Thomas's gaze with a discreet clearing of the throat. "Um, if you gentlemen would give me some time alone to examine Lady Amelia."

Like the crack of a whip, his statement made Thomas more aware. He was standing by her bedside like that of a concerned spouse. "Yes, of course. We will confer once you're done with the examination."

Thomas reluctantly trailed Cartwright from the room. Once in the hall, Cartwright immediately confronted him. "What the hell was that all about?"

"Now is neither the time nor the place," Thomas responded in clipped tones. "Why don't you go and wash off that stench of horse from you?"

The quick flaring of his nostrils was the only indication that Cartwright was perturbed. They stood eye to eye for several seconds before his friend abruptly pivoted and walked away, his tread muffled by the velvet-pile carpeting.

Thomas intended to return to the main floor to await Dr. Lawson after Cartwright left to go to his chamber at the opposite wing of the house. But instead, he found himself pacing the hall outside Amelia's chamber.

The door opened twenty minutes later, and Dr. Lawson emerged. He started when he saw Thomas standing there.

"What's wrong with her?"

"Oh, Thomas, I was just on my way down."

"What is wrong with Amelia?"

The familiarity of his address did not escape the physician's notice as evidenced by the slight raise of his brow.

"I can see it's nothing several days of bed rest won't cure. I could hear no obstruction in her lungs, and her heart is strong. There is some swelling in the glands at her neck, but that I expected because of the fever." Dr. Lawson switched his black physician's bag to his other hand. "Now, if the fever hasn't abated in the next two days, send for me again. I haven't seen a reoccurrence of scarlet fever, but stranger things have happened."

Thomas's brows jumped. *Scarlet fever?* "What do you mean a reoccurrence?"

"Since her bout with it at the age of thirteen. Did she not tell you? She's a lucky one as it appears she suffered no lasting effects. In the past year alone, I've lost four patients to the fever."

Thomas's panic must have shown on his face because Dr. Lawson added hastily, "Rest assured, that is not what's ailing the young lady now. What she has is influenza of the stomach. She's the tenth patient in the past two weeks. As I said, in two, three days at the very most, she should be back to normal."

Thomas tried to convince himself his concern was normal. She was his friend's daughter and an acquaintance—of sorts. Of course, her well-being would be of some concern to him.

Some concern? a voice inside of him mocked. In the past twenty minutes, his anxiety had taken on that of a husband awaiting the safe birth of his heir.

"Lady Amelia shall have the best of care."

Dr. Lawson inclined his head in a nod and touched his hand to his neckcloth in what seemed an unconscious gesture. "In that, I have no doubt." He pulled a watch piece from his jacket and gave it a quick glance. "I must be on my way. Call immediately if the young lady's condition worsens. Good day, Thomas." Tucking the watch back in his pocket, he started toward the stairs.

Good manners compelled Thomas to escort him to the door.

Without breaking stride or turning, Dr. Lawson said, "I've frequented this house for well over thirty years now. I can see myself out. I'm certain you'll want to see for yourself that your guest is resting comfortably."

Dr. Lawson needn't have told him twice. Before the doctor could reach the stairs, Thomas was standing in front of Amelia's chamber pressing the door open with the tips of his fingers. The hinges gave a betraying creak.

The maid was sitting at Amelia's side and angled her head when he entered. Thomas strode to the bed, keenly aware of the silence and the maid's gaze following his progress. This was his residence, Amelia was in his care, so yes, he had every right to be here, to see to her welfare.

"Monsieur, mademoiselle iz sleeping," the maid whispered.

Thomas halted at the side of the bed, his chest compressing at the sight of Amelia. Her head rested amid a froth of feather pillows. He took in the fan of dark, curling lashes against her fevered cheeks. With her features softened by sleep, she looked unbearably vulnerable. Beautiful.

Without removing his gaze from her face, he said, "So I see."

"Did the doctor give her anything for the fever?" he asked after a long pause.

"'e left laudanum *pour* the belly pains." The maid continued to stare up at him, her expression quizzical and expectant.

He nodded slowly. He'd come to ensure she was resting comfortably, and from his observation she was. He should leave, yet his feet refused to obey his silent command.

"Then I shall leave you to tend to her." Still he didn't budge as he followed the rise and fall of her chest comprising her shallow breathing. "Notify me immediately if she worsens—am I understood?"

The maid responded to the hard note in his tone and his sharp look with two rigorous nods.

Thomas gave Amelia's sleeping form one final glance before taking his leave.

Chapter 19

Thomas found Cartwright in the library, sitting in one of the armchairs, forearms braced on his thighs. He'd since changed from his riding clothes and the dampness of his hair indicated he'd taken the advised bath.

Cartwright shot to his feet upon Thomas's entrance. "How is she? What did the physician say?"

Instead of offering an immediate response, Thomas strode over to the sideboard and poured himself a dram of rum, heedless that the appropriate drinking time still loomed hours away. As irrational as his feelings were, he hadn't liked it one bit to see Amelia in Cartwright's arms or his friend in the intimacy of her bedchamber. He sensed a familiarity there that the brevity of their association could not justify.

Throwing his head back, Thomas drained the contents of the glass in one burning swallow.

Cartwright sidestepped the center table and made his way to the edge of the rug spread beneath the sitting area. After waiting in silence, no doubt expectant of a reply, he flicked a glance at the door. "Am I permitted to see her? Miss Foxworth has also expressed great concern regarding her condition. I assured her I would keep her apprised."

He would keep her apprised? The bloody gall! Thomas

dropped the glass back onto the sideboard with such force it was surprising the glass hadn't shattered as his composure was perilously close to doing.

Cartwright's eyebrow slowly rose as he folded his arms across his chest.

"She's asleep," Thomas replied curtly. "Dr. Lawson says it's nothing more than a stomach ailment which should clear up in a few days."

"I see." Cartwright dragged out the latter word as if he saw too damn much. "And I suppose you're going to tell me what the devil is wrong with you? You're carrying on as if I intend to ravish the girl. Give me some credit for possessing some kind of tact. If that's what I had in mind, I'd at least wait until she wasn't burning up with a fever."

"I'm glad you can joke at a time like this." Of late, Thomas found very little amusing about his friend's sense of humor.

"Do I appear to be amused? I assure you, I'm perfectly serious." Cartwright said, his countenance lacking his trademark dry half smile.

Some emotion in him—one Thomas dare not identify—bubbled to the surface in molten fury. "You will leave her the hell alone, is that understood? She's not to be trifled with. She is my concern, and I will deal with her."

"I thought you could barely tolerate her. I'd think you'd be relieved to have me take her off your hands for *any* amount of time."

A slew of curse words sprang instantly to his lips, but Thomas bit them back with a violent oath. "Go to bloody hell."

"Why, in need of company?" came Cartwright's rapid-fire response, his mouth quirking at the corners in a manner that had Thomas glancing around for something to bludgeon him with.

He eyed the thick crystal decanter of brandy. How unfortunate it was one of his mother's favorite pieces. He had to content himself with silently counting to ten as he fought to retain the last vestiges of his control. "I'm glad you continue to find humor in this situation."

"Lady Amelia ailing I don't find the slightest bit amusing. You, however . . ." Cartwright's voice trailed off as if he needn't say more, his omission an indictment of Thomas. "And truly, Armstrong, this cavemanlike behavior toward a girl you claim no fondness for."

Neatly boxed and gift-wrapped, his friend placed the argument before him tied with a bow. Juxtaposed, even Thomas could see his words and recent actions lay in sharp and damning contrast.

"Regardless of how I feel about her, she is a guest in my home and under my care."

"Good God, man, you practically ripped her from my arms. I think that's taking your role a tad bit too far, wouldn't you say?"

When Cartwright became fixated on a notion, he refused to let go, which meant Thomas would have to accomplish the task for him. "I am going to the study. I will see you at supper."

As it was only nine in the morning and supper wouldn't be served until eight that evening, Thomas's message rang as clear as it was loud in the echoing silence that followed him as he exited the room.

At first, Amelia didn't know what had awakened her. Her chamber was dark and silent. She felt hot and cold all at the same time. After several seconds, her eyes adjusted to the darkness. She perceived the presence just before she heard the movement at her side.

Her head snapped in the direction of the sound. A startled cry escaped her dry lips when she spotted a form reposed in the chair at her bedside. For an instant, she hovered between confusion and terror before recognition set in.

Thomas.

His head rested against the cushion of burgundy brocade, and the deep, rhythmic whisper of his breath indicated he was asleep.

Her fevered mind tried to rationalize his presence there but couldn't quite make the enormous leap as to what it signified. She could only lower her head back onto her pillow and watch him silently, her gaze drifting along the shadowed planes of his face. There was a certain vulnerability in his restful state that made him appear younger. Tender even.

No more than a minute passed before he moved and slowly raised his head. Had he sensed her watching him? Suddenly, he bolted up straight in his seat, his form alert and his green eyes glittering bright in the sooty night as he focused on her. "Is something wrong? Should I call for the physician?" he asked in a tone that didn't convey he'd been asleep only moments before.

Weakly, Amelia shook her head, now aware of a parched feeling in her mouth. "I would appreciate some water." Her words were whisper soft and her voice hoarse.

He was out of the chair and at the dresser before she could fully comprehend he'd gone. Soon, light suffused the chamber in a dim glow, and the slosh of water filled the air. Thomas returned to her side with a glass in one hand and a candle in the other. He set the candle on the night table by the bed. Awash in candlelight, Amelia could now see the fatigue on his face. His fatigue did not, however, detract from his masculine allure. Even in her illness, she clearly saw that and felt the inexorable pull of his appeal.

Instead of handing her the glass, Thomas sat on the edge of the bed. She started when he gently slid his hand beneath her head and lifted it up. "Here, drink," he said, tipping the glass to her mouth.

Amelia automatically parted her lips at his softly spoken command. The water was neither cold nor warm, but it felt like heaven sliding down her throat. She drank the glass's entire contents before slumping back onto the pillows.

Thomas didn't remove his hand immediately. She felt the pressure of his palm, the weight of every finger with a keenness that had her skin tingling—a sensation not caused by her fever or body aches.

"Would you like me to get you anything else?" He stared at her with a quiet, disturbing intensity.

"No, I'm feeling much better now."

"Your stomach is no longer paining you?" He removed his hand from beneath her head. Amelia felt the loss like a flower would miss the warmth of the sun on a frigidly cold winter day. But she wasn't to be bereft of his touch for long. He placed the back of his hand against her forehead. "Hmm, while you're not as hot as before, you're still a little warm. But I am glad to see you've improved."

Perhaps tomorrow, she would tell herself her weakened state had left her vulnerable to a bedside manner every physician should endeavor to emulate. But it wasn't tomorrow, it was tonight, and her pulse pounded erratically. His nearness, the masculine scent emanating from his very pores, had her dragging in air as if it were a scarce element of nature.

"Yes, my—my stomach is much improved," she said, her voice above a bare whisper. Her throat was no longer dry and she wasn't feeling as poorly as she had been earlier, but it appeared she now suffered a different sort of sickness— one that could be every bit as dangerous to her as another bout with scarlet fever. Thomas Armstrong.

He removed his hand from her forehead, and he asked, "Are you certain? You look somewhat distressed. Are you not comfortable?" His hooded gaze skimmed the length of her body outlined beneath the counterpane and bed sheets. Amelia didn't think she could have been more conscious of her body had she laid there naked.

"I am fine. I'm sure I just need some more rest." *And I need you to leave so that I may regain my senses . . . my sanity.*

"Then I will leave you now." At the softly spoken words, Thomas stood, the wood of the bed frame creaking faintly at the removal of his weight. His face was immediately cast in shadow, the candle's light illuminating the dark blond bristle of his jaw.

"I will see you in the morning." His gaze seemed to linger on her before he turned and quit the chamber, closing the door softly behind him.

Don't go, hovered on her lips long after he'd gone.

Chapter 20

Thomas was relieved Amelia's fever lasted only twenty-four hours. But, despite its brevity, he instructed her to remain in bed until he determined she was fully recovered. She could fret and moan about it all she wanted—which she did. His position didn't waver.

In addition to her maid, who cosseted her like a newborn, Thomas instructed two of his servants to cater to Amelia's every need and ensure her every comfort. He himself, made it his duty to check on her twice during the day—visits he limited to the times he knew she was asleep.

By the third day of her confinement, and much to Thomas's satisfaction, she did appear restored to full health. Only then did he finally grant her leave to venture beyond her bedchamber walls. And he, like a drunkard resisting the silent call of a bottle of alcohol, spent the better part of the day down at the stables with his latest purchase, a majestic grey thoroughbred.

That evening, she presented herself at the dining hall looking vibrant and fetching in a lavender dress and a neckline whose appeal lay in what remained hidden rather than what it revealed. Thomas had to physically steel himself from going to her and touching her, as he mentally stripped her down to bare skin and pink nipples.

Cartwright, who should have departed Devon the day
before but had insisted on staying until he was certain of
Amelia's full recovery, brightened noticeably at her appearance. Thomas scowled, and his annoyance with his friend
sparked anew.

"Good evening, Miss Foxworth. My lords. I hope you'll
forgive my tardiness." She sent them a warm, all-
encompassing smile.

Cartwright hastily came to his feet. Thomas belatedly followed. The effervescent glow about her that cast so many
women in her shadow had unsettled him several moments
too long.

She laughed lightly. "Oh please, my lords, do not stand
on ceremony on my behalf." The second footman followed
her dutifully to the table to seat her in the empty chair beside
Cartwright.

"I didn't think you would be up to joining us for supper
this evening," Thomas said as he wondered what their reaction would be if he insisted she and Cartwright exchange
places to have her sit at his elbow.

After she settled in, he and Cartwright resumed their
seats. "And as I told you this morning, I'm perfectly well. If
you hadn't been so stubborn, I would have been up and
about yesterday." She treated him to a teasing look, something she'd never done before.

"I'm simply relieved to see you looking so well," Camille
said with a smile.

Amelia smiled in return, and not the kind of smile generally reserved for Thomas. This one held no trace of ire or
mockery, just pearl-white teeth shown in contrast against
succulent pink lips. Thomas's loins began a painful and
pleasurable throb.

"I'd say looking well is a vast understatement. In my
opinion, Lady Amelia looks radiantly stunning. The picture
of beauty, health, and prosperity."

Thomas shot a look at his friend. *Radiantly stunning?*

Beauty, health, and prosperity? Good Lord, with only a little more wax, his friend could single-handedly seal all the envelopes in London. Just how bloody cozy had they become during their time together? It appeared it had been time enough to turn Cartwright into not only her protector but a doting suitor. Thomas was revolted by the thought.

Amelia made a sound like the faded remnants of a full-bodied laugh. "Truly, Lord Alex, you gift me with far more admirable attributes than I deserve."

Thomas's gaze darted to her. By God, was she actually falling prey to that balderdash? "Yes, don't you think you're plying it on rather thick?" Thomas said, unable to keep the sardonic note from his voice.

Cartwright merely laughed. "I'm a second son. I haven't the luxury of subtlety."

Amelia dipped her chin to hide a smile. Lord Alex was witty and charming beyond words. Thomas, on the other hand, looked anything but pleased. He wasn't scowling—at least not anymore—but his face was set in such a mask that anything as beguiling as a smile would fall victim to a cold, hard death.

If she claimed any intimate knowledge of him, she'd say his behavior held the green tinge of jealousy. But perhaps that was her exalted opinion of her own charms. He could very well have entirely different reasons for his surly disposition. Perhaps he didn't think her good enough for his friend.

Although, that notion certainly wouldn't explain what he'd been doing slumbering in a chair at her bedside when she was ill. In the grip of her fever, she'd thought she'd dreamed him there. However, along with the cold light of day the next morning, she'd awoken to the lingering scent of bergamot in her bedchamber, proof she hadn't conjured him up on the sliver of a wishful thought. Something inside her had melted with the knowledge, her opinion of him irrevocably changed. He wasn't in *every* way like her father, as he'd actually come to her in her time of illness.

Yes, perhaps he was jealous. And for him to succumb to that emotion, he had to care for her at least a little beyond their undeniable, potent physical attraction.

While she and Thomas fell silent, Cartwright inquired politely to Miss Foxworth of her plans for Christmas, which was only a month away. Amelia had no special fondness for the holiday, at least not since her mother had died.

"Today, I received a letter from my brother. He hopes to be home for Christmas this year." Miss Foxworth did not so much as respond to Lord Alex as announce the news to the occupants of the table.

"Foxworth finally coming home? Truly a reason to celebrate this year, eh Armstrong?" Lord Alex said, flicking a glance at Thomas before returning his attention to Miss Foxworth. "I can only imagine how eager you must be."

Miss Foxworth's pale cheeks flushed to apricot as she bobbed her head in agreement, a stark longing flaring in her eyes. "It has been almost two years since I've seen him. I wonder how much he has changed. But certainly my biggest hope and prayer is that he come home safe and unharmed." Her gaze then flew to the viscount's expressionless face. "Lord Armstrong, I hoped perhaps you could spare me some time during Christmastide?"

Thomas seemed to snap to attention as if her question had jerked him from deep thoughts. "Forgive me. I'm afraid my mind was occupied with a business matter. Did you say your brother is due home?"

"He expects to arrive back on English soil three days prior to Christmas. If you could spare me for three or four days that would—"

"Three or four days? Absolutely not. You will remain with him as long as you wish. How long is he to remain in London?"

"He wrote for two months—or that is the hope." Camille turned to Amelia. "Marcus is the only family I have."

"Oh, no need to explain yourself to me. I think it's wonderful that he should have such a devoted sister." Oftentimes, when she was a child she'd craved a sibling.

"Missy has invited us to spend Christmas with her and her family. However, I can see that would in no way compare to seeing your brother."

Amelia shot a wide-eyed look at Thomas. They would be spending Christmas with his sister? Why was it only now she was hearing of this?

"Why, that's wonderful. I want you to know that in my absence, I fully intended to find a replacement. But if you will be in Berkshire with your sister and Lord Windmere . . ." Miss Foxworth's voice trailed off.

"And as my mother and sisters will be back by the New Year, there will be no need for you to return. That should give you as much time as you please to spend with your brother."

"Yes, then it all works out perfectly." Miss Foxworth's gaze dropped to her plate but not before Amelia noted the faint yearning in her eyes. She wanted to return, that much Amelia could see. It was absurd, really ridiculous, as she'd never seen Thomas treat Miss Foxworth in anything but a brotherly manner, but in a moment of her own twinge of jealousy, she could hardly wait for the woman to leave.

In an effort to veer from the unwanted feelings, Amelia shifted her attention to Lord Alex. "And you, my lord, how will you be celebrating Christmas?"

Cartwright's shoulders rose and fell negligently. "Not entirely certain. Perhaps I'll take Lady Windmere up on her invitation."

"My sister's invited you too?" Thomas heard the sharpness in his own voice and regretted it.

"Actually, Rutherford mentioned it when he was in town on Parliament business."

Normally, Thomas would have welcomed the company of his friend during his stay at Rutherford Manor. He couldn't count the number of times Cartwright had celebrated various holidays and celebrations with his family. He was, for all intents and purposes, a surrogate member of the Armstrong clan, the two having met when they were young boys at Eton.

But this Christmas was different. This Christmas Amelia would be there, and the thought of Cartwright and her spending that much time together, and in such close proximity, rankled more than it should. Thomas could summon only a stiff nod.

Cartwright chuckled dryly. "You don't look pleased. Am I no longer a welcome guest?" He placed his spoon in his soup bowl and edged it forward as an indication he was finished with that course.

"Of course not," Thomas snapped, angry with himself for making his displeasure so evident. Amelia was driving him crazy—completely mad. And that he should allow her to come between he and Cartwright was paramount to a betrayal of their twenty-year friendship. "I was just surprised since you said your father wanted you home for the holidays this year." When the Duke of Hastings summoned his son, Cartwright usually abided, although always reluctantly due to their strained relationship.

His friend's silver eyes grew cool at the mention of his father. "Yes, well, as you know I have no desire to see the duke. Now or during the holidays," he said in a tight voice.

Thomas quickly changed the subject. The duke was the one person who could put the even-tempered Cartwright in a foul mood. This had been the case for at least ten years now. And Thomas had learned not to ask the reasons as to what had caused the rift.

"Do you play cards, Lord Alex?" Amelia asked, ending the taut silence.

Cartwright's expression instantly eased. "Not for money, but I've a knack for vingt-et-un or blackjack, and I have been known to dabble in whist."

Thomas didn't like the course of the conversation, nor did he like the sudden brightening of his friend's mood as he lazily surveyed Amelia.

"Don't you think it best if you rested? You've only recently recovered," Thomas objected.

"My lord, I hardly think a game of cards will put my health in jeopardy," Amelia replied with a laugh.

"Nevertheless, it's better to be safe. And I'm sure Cartwright wouldn't want in any way to be party to the cause of your decline."

Cartwright's gaze turned to him. For a moment, Thomas thought he intended to challenge him—scoff that his argument was beyond ludicrous. After studying him for several seconds, his friend shifted his attention back to Amelia. "Yes, I have heard parlor games are known to cause an illness of sorts, and I certainly wouldn't want you to fall victim to it."

In this instance, Cartwright's barely veiled mockery was acceptable. It was infinitely better than a row, Thomas thought with the full knowledge that what he spouted was nothing shy of grasping at straws. He also knew everyone at the table was aware of it too. Luckily for him, they were too civilized to call him on it.

"Well, since it appears I'm too fragile for a game of cards, I shall take myself off to bed. Suddenly I'm feeling rather fatigued." Cartwright made a move to rise. Amelia stayed him with a wave of her hand as she stood. "Oh, do remain seated."

A footman materialized at her elbow to assist her from her chair. Thomas hadn't intended to send her so early to her bed; hadn't intended to deprive himself of her company. He sat mute as she smoothed the folds of her velvet skirts, trying to quell the image of those slender hands sliding lovingly over his hard, bare flesh, wrapping around him.

"I shall see you all in the morning." Her regard flickered to him. "That is, if I have not gone into decline." A teasing light glinted in the sapphire blue of her eyes, and a smile tipped the corners of her mouth—a smile whose effects Thomas felt from his chest right down to his loins.

After Amelia quit the dining hall, she didn't walk but floated up the stairs. She hadn't really wanted to play cards with Lord Alex. She'd only been seeking proof that Thomas didn't want her to. Who would have guessed—certainly not she—that she was the type of woman who would stoop to engaging in games of jealousy? And who would have guessed upon eliciting the desired response, she'd be left feeling giddy and dizzier than she had when she'd been swooning about the place with a fever.

Leaving the dining table had been a matter of survival, for if she'd stayed, she would have sat there looking as besotted as she felt. He cared enough about her to be jealous of his friend. He cared enough about her to sit at her bedside when she was ill. Thomas, Viscount Armstrong, cared about her, period, and right now that was all that mattered. Tomorrow, she decided with steadfast determination, they would begin their relationship anew.

Amelia was still in a euphoric glow when she heard the unmistakable sound of a cat as she made her way to her chamber. Turning in the direction of the plaintive meow, she saw a blur of fur dash in the direction of the opposite wing.

No animals resided in Stoneridge Hall, of that she was certain. Undoubtedly a stray sneaking in from the cold. The poor dear was probably hungry. Amelia proceeded in search of the cat.

After much coaxing and whispered pleas of, "Here kitty,

kitty," she found the cat huddled beneath a hall table with a heavy base that came half a foot off the floor. And she discovered it wasn't a cat but a tiny, frightened kitten with camel-colored fur. Soon, Amelia was on her knees, her right hand stretched out to capture the skittish animal, her voice soothing and low. As her fingers made contact with the downy fur, the kitten darted from beneath the table and through the closest open door.

Sighing, Amelia scrambled to her feet. She hesitated at the threshold. Then she heard the kitten's cry. She would be quick about it. Miss Foxworth and the men were occupied downstairs and none of the servants were about.

Quashing every single one of her misgivings—and she harbored quite a few—Amelia inhaled a deep breath and entered the room. Save for the blaze in the fireplace, the chamber was shrouded in shadows of varying shades of grey. It took several seconds for her eyes to adjust to the darkness. The chamber was large. With a fresh wave of trepidation, she realized fate, with its sometimes macabre sense of humor, had deposited her in the master's suite. Thomas's bedchamber. If she had any sense at all, she would leave. A quiver of anticipation coursed through her as she ventured farther into the room.

Amelia took in big, dark furniture, including an enormous four-poster bed. She shivered again. There was nothing fussy about it. No softening contours or feminine embellishments, just polished mahogany and a dark green counterpane covering the mattress.

A flash of fur darting from under the bed to somewhere in the darkest corner of the room caught her eye, yanking her back to her purpose for being there. Before Amelia could move, she heard a faint creak, then saw a splinter of light originate from the area in which the kitten had disappeared. The light lengthened and broadened across the carpeted floor in front of her.

With no time to think and only a second to act, Amelia

made a dash to an area in the chamber where she saw no shadowy grey just the blessed oblivion of black. She braced up against the wall beside a towering wardrobe. Her nostrils were immediately assailed by the scent of starch and something else . . . bergamot.

The kitten emitted a pitiful meow. Amelia barely dared to breathe.

"How on earth did you get in here?"

Thomas. Amelia's breath left her.

"Lord, aren't you a tiny little thing. I bet you're hungry?"

It took her a moment to realize he was speaking to the cat. As much as a human was capable, she plastered herself against the wall.

"Come, let's get you something to eat. Perhaps Cook has some leftover fish. What do you think?" The kitten purred as if in agreement.

He was leaving. With her fingers splayed against the wall at her back, Amelia waited. She heard muffled footfalls, then the sound of the door opening, and then silence. Blessed silence. She quickly darted a glance around the wardrobe to ensure all was clear. It was.

Amelia had never moved so fast in her entire life, the soles of her suede shoes scarcely touching the floor. Unfortunately, fast wasn't quite quick enough.

Chapter 21

"Why do you continue to turn up in all the places you shouldn't?" Thomas stood framed in the doorway, bathed in the iridescent light of the gas wall sconces in the hall, and spoke in a tone of dark amusement.

Shuddering to a stop, Amelia sought safety on the laddered rail of the footboard behind her—she'd only managed to get that far. The wood was solid and smooth under her fingers unlike the erratic beat of her heart. This was not at all the way she'd imagined their new start.

"I-I didn't see you—I thought you had gon—I mean, the cat—" Amelia ceased speaking. What was the point? She'd heard animals could smell fear. In that case, she was amazed that every animal in the environs of Devon wasn't growling at her feet.

He chuckled softly, slowly closing the door before turning to advance toward her with measured strides. "Oh, please do continue. I do love it when you stutter."

Amelia quelled a dismayed groan, edging away from the safety of the footboard, intent on reaching the door, but a glance deemed her exit too far away to risk a mad dash.

Thomas shot a glance at the door and then back to her. He circled to come and stand behind her. "Is that really what you want to do—run?" His voice had a rumbling, sensuous quality. "You know what I believe, Amelia?" he whispered, lowering his head until his mouth feathered the rim of her right ear and his masculine scent infused into every pore of her body in sensual suffocation.

He was taunting her, damn him. "No, I don't care to know." But the hitch in her voice belied her words. She gave her head two determined shakes, as if that would sufficiently rid her of the languor that stole through her, softening her, weakening her.

"I believe you're here awaiting me." He kept his voice low and soft, his every word misting her ear in a sweet caress.

Amelia's nipples tightened and pushed against the soft muslin cloth of her dress. "I came because of the cat," she whispered, ducking her head to escape his warming breath on her face.

"Then why are you making no real effort to escape?" He turned her around to face him and placed one finger lightly on her parted lips when she attempted to speak. It would be a mistake for them to start like this. "No, don't utter another word. We both know you're here for this."

Without giving her a chance to object, he pinned her arms to her sides while his tongue breeched the boundary of lips and teeth. When his tongue touched hers, Amelia's knees wobbled. He tasted that rich and decadent; it felt that right. She encouraged him with an impassioned slide of her tongue over his. A shudder rifled through his body sending an answering heat pulsing between her thighs. This kiss had no limit. It blotted every thought from her mind, except the hard male form gathering her ever closer and bending her neck back.

Never had she experienced this kind of passion except in his arms, with his lips on hers. His hand moved to cup her breasts, and the layers of fabric covering her could not mute the kind of pleasure that caused her to whimper and tear her mouth from his, only to desperately seek it out again after she caught her breath and needed him again.

Nothing had prepared Thomas for the sheer wildness of their embrace. She was on fire for him, and he couldn't get enough of her mouth, of her tongue, of her breasts, of everything she had to offer. Plastering her against the length of him, his erection stabbed at her belly with hard insistence as his hips imitated a sexual dance older than time.

Amelia responded with a slow, helpless roll of her hips, threatening to send him over the precipice of sanity. With a harsh groan and his breathing already laboring as if he had just run a mile, he tore his mouth from hers and swung her effortlessly up into his arms. He strode to the bedside, deposited her onto the mattress, and wasted no time in joining her. Under his deft fingers, he removed the dress from her body with the ease of a man who had more than a passing knowledge of women's garments. Each scrap of silk and muslin he removed revealed breathtaking creamy flesh. Legs, long, slender, and exquisitely formed, snagged his breath, but it was the sight of the dark triangular patch of hair at the apex of her thighs that threatened to rob him of all reason and control.

His cock reared up and fought to split the seams of the front placket of his trousers. So intense was the sensation snaking through him, Thomas had to grit his teeth to contain a groan. He could think of nothing beyond driving himself into her, burying himself as deep as he could.

He managed to remove his hands from her quivering form long enough to divest himself of his clothes. Several shirt buttons popped in his haste, as Amelia lay sprawled on her back watching him with a decidedly bemused look on her face. He paused, momentarily transfixed at the sight she made, her lips parted and her eyes darkened to navy orbs.

The glide of her tongue along the edge of her kiss-plumped lips jolted him from his daze and back into action.

He tossed his shirt to the floor, and came briefly to his feet to kick off the black wool trousers. His drawers came next, shoved over his hips with impatient hands. Amelia gave a sharp inhalation at the sight of his arousal springing out, so swollen and hard as to be painful. Debilitating him in a pleasurable kind of pain.

Amelia couldn't take her eyes off his erection, long, thick, and heavily veined. Panic welled up inside of her. He could not possibly think he could put *that* in her. Dear Lord, there was no way it would fit. Her gaze flew to his taut visage. She instinctively tried to shield her nakedness from his devouring stare, one hand flying to try to span both breasts, while the other covered her privates.

"No, don't hide from me," he soothed, gently prying her hands from her body to secure them above her head while wedging a place for himself between her thighs. The heat of his erection settled heavily on the tender skin above the fleece of hair covering her sex, the contact inflaming her senses, sending her back into the intoxicating arms of passion.

He lowered his head and began tracing soft kisses from her shoulder to the swell of her breast. His mouth tracked up to a ruched nipple. Amelia clamped down hard on her lower lip. He swiped the taut bud with his tongue until her back bowed, forcing both the nipple and surrounding aureole into his mouth. With a muffled groan, he ended the torment and began to suckle. Amelia let out a whimper, her breath rhythmic pants. Jerking her hands from his grip, she plowed her fingers through strands of golden hair to imprison him against her breast.

For endless minutes, he urged her squirming body to a heightened state of arousal. Amelia had never known such pleasure existed. Thomas now took her on a journey of hitherto untapped sensations, which had her keening and gasping beneath him. Widening her legs, she arched her back and writhed as she tried to trap his hard flesh where she needed it most—inside her.

"Easy, Princess, easy." Despite his soothing words, his voice came out strained, as if he was holding onto his control by the slimmest of margins. "I will give you what you want."

If she had been in her right mind, she would have been appalled at his words. Appalled at her wanton exhibition. But she was mindless. Nothing mattered but the fire he had started that now raged hot between her thighs.

With one final flick at her pink bud, he sent shards of sensual pleasure from her nipple straight to the heart of her. Thomas continued his trek downward, dotting her quivering belly with languid kisses. A puff of air rushed uncontrolled from her mouth. Her eyelids fluttered closed, her hands still clutching the back of his head.

He reached the downy tuff of hair between her thighs, and scooted down, widening them in the process, giving him the most intimate view anyone had ever had of her. His tongue came out and touched his upper lip.

Amelia realized his intent and immediately tried to push his head away. Her face flamed with embarrassment. "No, no, you can't. You shouldn't—"

The first probe of his tongue on the swollen folds of her sex nearly sent her senses spinning. Shock and embarrass-ment quickly gave way to the most delicious, unbearable pleasure that shot through her like a lightning bolt. Her hands fell to her sides as he took full reign, using his mouth to master her body.

Long and languid strokes of his tongue continued un-abated on her slick, wet flesh. Amelia couldn't think, she could only feel. Being loved in this fashion was lurid and shameful . . . and exquisite. While he feasted on her, her hips tilted forward to offer him more. The sensation of a band being pulled tighter and tighter gripped her, refusing to release her. Her body spiraled upward, searching for something else. Then he parted her pink flesh and flicked the little nub at the hood of her sex and Amelia let out a high, keening cry as she heaved beneath him, nearly dislodging his mouth. But he held on, his tongue wringing a cry from her that ended in a long lusty moan. A paroxysm of pleasure overtook her, and she could do nothing but succumb blissfully, helplessly.

Spent in the aftermath of her first orgasm, Amelia was insensate to her surroundings, everything, until she felt the thrust of his manhood at her entrance. Then he was plunging into her. She winced and gasped at the burn of his possession. It had come so unexpectedly. She hadn't had time to prepare herself for the stinging pain, nor the tightness of the fit.

If Thomas hadn't been so caught up in the sweet, unbearably tight clasp of her body, he would have halted—or at least paused—when he met the resistance of her maidenhood, before tearing through it like a marauding bull. But with Amelia, he had no such restraint. And even when his mind fully grasped that he had just taken her virginity, he could not stop the advance and retreat of his hips as he plowed into her. All he could do was try to make it as good for her as he could.

He sought her lips and caught her anguished sob in his mouth as his tongue mimicked the mating of their bodies. She had initially gone stiff with the pain of his penetration, but under his avid ministrations, her body began to relax. Soon Thomas was tearing his lips from hers, ducking his head, and encompassing her nipple in his mouth to suckle strongly. Amelia let out a hoarse moan, allowing her legs to encircle his hips, drawing him deeper into her.

Thomas quickened his pace, now slamming into her with such ferocity he had no doubt he'd leave her sore. The knowledge, however, did not stop him. And to his disbelief, he felt her stiffen and claw at his shoulders as she reached her peak once again. With that, his body convulsed and shattered in a release so staggering in its intensity, he let out a guttural cry that exclaimed his unadulterated satisfaction.

It took a while for him to recover from what had just been the most mind-blowing climax of his life—thus far. Only then did he realize he was resting heavily on Amelia's delicate frame, his mouth nuzzling her breast.

Not a man who liked to cuddle as so many women craved after sexual intercourse, Thomas was disconcerted to discover he didn't immediately want to bolt from the bed. Yes, it was his bed, but he had no desire to hustle Amelia back to her chamber. This, of course, was downright terrifying.

Good Lord, what have I done?

Amelia lay stiff beneath Thomas as he remained buried inside her. Lord, there hadn't even been talk of the future, no promise of marriage, just the most exquisite pleasure her body had ever known. This was not how it was supposed to be.

Slowly, he slid from atop her, his chest hairs abrading her nipples, his sweat-dampened abdomen sliding over hers in a sensuous dance. Once again, Amelia could feel herself drowning into the misty haze of passion—lurid, decadent passion.

"A virgin."

His tone said it all, hushed and incredulous. But it jerked her back to the harsh edges of reality. *Not anymore she wasn't.*

Soon mortification replaced the vestiges of ardor. Amelia couldn't bear to look at him, much less respond. She heard, rather than saw, him get out of the bed, taking all of his heat with him. She caught the edge of the counterpane and draped it over herself.

Thomas came into view as he padded toward the dresser. Amelia knew she should avert her gaze, but the sight of his buttocks, flesh and muscle sculpted to magnificence, captivated her. He opened the top drawer and yanked out a small piece of toweling and with it, several envelopes fluttered to the carpet.

Clasping the counterpane tightly to her breasts, she came up on the bed, her attention now riveted to the floor.

Thomas shot a quick glance at her, let out a mild curse, and started grabbing for the envelopes.

"No!" Heedless of her state of undress, she scrambled from the bed to his side, having discarded the cover in her haste. She grabbed his wrist, stopping his hand in midair, and stared at the now crumpled papers in his hand and the third, which lay on the carpet pointing at him like an accusing finger.

"These are my letters," she said softly. While her mind reeled, her heart echoed a hollow beat in her ear. In black ink, Lord Clayborough's name and address stood in stark relief against the pale yellow envelopes. Her handwriting. He hadn't been lying when he'd said he hadn't received them. Thomas had had them all along.

"Amelia—"

Amelia dropped his wrist as if she held a vile object in her hand. Blindly, she turned, now acutely aware of her nakedness. Her eyes searched the floor frantically until she spotted her discarded clothes. She quickly donned her dress in several jerky motions. She had no time to waste on petticoats and flimsy undergarments when her sanity depended on removing herself from his chamber as expeditiously as possible.

Before she could move out of arm's reach, Thomas's hand shot out and caught her by the upper arm. Amelia halted but kept her head angled from him. She'd learned it was useless to fight against his strength.

"Amelia, listen to me. I was—"

"Save your excuses, my lord." Her civil tone masked her growing hysteria. All she wanted to do was throw something, rage and scream at him.

His hold on her arm tightened. Amelia turned to regard him directly for the first time since she'd discovered the depth of his deceit. He didn't look guilty. He looked like a frustrated, angry man whose coming defense of his actions would ring as absurd as he appeared indignant. He wore the expression her father had worn when she'd discovered, weeks after her attempted elopement with Joseph Cromwell, that he had been confiscating his letters.

"I gather you did this under my father's directive?"

Thomas didn't immediately respond, and that in itself was response enough for her. She tugged her arm free. He relinquished his hold and then snatched up the piece of toweling that had fallen on the floor and secured it about his waist.

Amelia turned away not only because she couldn't bear the sight of him, but because he stood there arrogantly unselfconscious. "He'll be proud to know you intend to follow in his footsteps in every way."

"Can you honestly say you would be happy with Clayborough?" He snorted in disbelief. "Would you have given your virginity to me if you truly loved the man? Right now you should be thanking me for preventing you from making the biggest mistake of your life."

Amelia whipped around to glare at him. "You pompous bastard! I've just made the biggest mistake of my life, and far from preventing me, you spurred me on and had a grand time while you were doing it."

"I wasn't the only one," he said darkly.

Too angry to be embarrassed, her response was fierce. "As long as this remains between just the two of us, we are safe. More than anything, I want to forget this ever happened. We'll not speak a word of this again, agreed?"

For many moments, Thomas stared at her without answering, his expression unreadable. He ended the silence with a slow nod. "Yes, I suppose that would be for the best. No one wants to be reminded of their mistakes."

His words clobbered her, effectively releasing her from the invisible hold he had on her. Amelia hastened from the room, allowing herself the luxury of a ragged breath only once she was secured within the thick walls of her bedchamber.

Chapter 22

When Hélène awakened her at the dreadful hour of seven, Amelia contemplated remaining in bed. Thomas could hardly fault her given her recent illness, but he would know her absence had everything to do with last night . . . the debauching of an innocent. For that reason alone, she forced herself to rise.

Except for a cup of tea, she hadn't touched the contents of her breakfast tray. And now as she sat alone at her *secretaire*, the rumble of her belly proclaimed the morning was destined to be a long one. But, it would have been regardless of the state of her appetite, for neither time nor sleep had blotted the memory of the time she'd spent in Thomas's bed . . . in his arms. When sleep had finally claimed her, his kisses, his touch, the feel of him inside her had chased through her dreams to her waking moments and dogged her still.

In an effort to block the torrid images of his aroused, naked body from her thoughts, she tried to focus instead on his duplicity. Although she'd mentally severed ties with Lord Clayborough weeks ago when she'd realized he was not the man for her, that did not excuse Thomas's deceitful machinations. She needed to remain angry. Anger didn't make her feel weak inside or cause her to yearn in ways she'd never dreamed of.

Amelia was firmly resolved to forget the incident. She'd allowed a handsome face, a few passionate embraces, and a token gesture of concern to cause a ruinous lapse in her judgment. Despite the good she'd seen in him these past months, taking—no stealing—her letters was proof of his true character. With a new resolve, Amelia did her utmost to busy herself with the work on her desk.

Ten minutes later Thomas arrived, and with that her heart sank. Had she really believed his allure could be muted or its effect controlled? He was the kind of man females clamored to like Christians to church. But how many women knew that beneath his good looks and surface charm lay such a lying, conniving soul—an attribute undoubtedly honed and perfected at the feet of her own dear father.

"Good morning, Amelia." He spoke briskly, barely sparing her a glance as he strode to his desk.

Amelia hid her surprise, managing a crisp nod. He didn't appear uneasy, his expression displaying not one iota of guilt. He had taken the innocence of a lady. He had plenty to be guilty for. An honorable gentleman would already have the ring fitted and polished, and her father's blessing. Not even she could have anticipated he'd treat her with such disregard. She tipped her chin and lengthened her spine.

"As you can see, the work has accumulated in your absence." He sounded distracted as his gaze roamed over the piles of paper littering his desk. "I will be working in the library if you require my assistance." He regarded her. "File these." He gestured broadly about his desk. "And once that task is complete, I have a contract requiring translation. Oh, and try not to tire yourself." Without a backward glance, he picked up the ledger and exited the room.

Amelia didn't know how long she sat there frozen, her composure crumbling. While she railed at herself for being a hundred different kinds of fool, she swallowed the lump in her throat. She wouldn't cry—desperately willing herself not to spill bitter tears of disbelief and regret. She hadn't cried last night, so she certainly wouldn't cry now. He had duped her once, but she'd take the veil before she ever allowed it to happen again. He wasn't worth her precious tears or another dram of wasted emotion. Moreover, this was what she herself had insisted on. The sooner they both forgot about the incident, the better. She expected nothing from him. Nothing.

A shuffled sound drew her attention to the study door. *Blast, he's returned.* She quickly picked up a stack of contracts and lowered her head in the pretense of deep concentration.

"I hope I'm not interrupting."

At the sound of Lord Alex's voice, Amelia raised her head, a wave of relief flooding her. He looked as handsome as ever, freshly shaved and clad in olive trousers and waistcoat, and a matching cravat was knotted about his neck. A pair of black leather gloves hung from his left hand.

"Good morning, Lady Amelia." He greeted her with an easy smile, advancing toward her before halting in front of the desk.

"Good morning, Lord Alex." She tried her best to adopt an amicable tone that wouldn't reveal her inner turmoil. "And no, you're not—at least nothing that can't wait." He was a friendly face, one she could desperately use right now.

"I've come to say good-bye. I believe I've overstayed my welcome."

Don't leave, she wanted to plead, but of course, her pride would never permit her to utter such words. At the understanding smile that tipped the corners of his mouth, she wondered if her expression looked as stricken as she felt.

"If I'd known you would be such pleasant company, I would have arranged to stay a month. As it is, business matters compel me back to London. As no sensible woman will have me, I must continue to work for my keep."

Amelia let out a throaty chuckle. "I hardly believe things are quite that dire." Her father had once told her the profits from Wendel's Shipping alone would have the future generation of Cartwrights exceedingly well cared for. In addition, with his stunning good looks, second son or not, she imagined there weren't many women who would refuse him.

"I've managed to keep myself off the streets, so I guess things could be worse," he replied with a wink.

"Perhaps, I shall see you again before I leave."

"That, Lady Amelia, would be my dearest wish." Then with an exaggerated bow, he took her proffered hand to his mouth, his lips treating the back of it with an airy kiss.

"I also need to have the—" Thomas's voice broke off as he came to a jarring halt in the doorway.

Amelia instinctively snatched her hand back and then cursed herself for acting like a thief caught in the act. Peering over Alex's bowed head, she met Thomas's gaze. His green eyes narrowed and his mouth firmed.

"I thought you were on your way out?" Although he addressed Lord Alex, his gaze held hers.

Straightening, Lord Alex turned to him, his expression unperturbed. "How could I depart without saying good-bye to Lady Amelia?" he asked, a note of mocking, chastisement in his voice.

Thomas observed them, his features set in a severe cast. "Don't let me stop you." The chill in his voice and his stance—wide-legged and bold—emitted a challenge. A pregnant silence followed, the atmosphere thick with the kind of tension capable of destroying friendships.

Alex returned his friend's regard before moving back to her, a wry smile on his face. "I'm getting the distinct feeling I'm being ushered out. Once again, my dear Lady Amelia, I hope we can further our acquaintance in the near future."

"I would be so honored, Lord Alex," Amelia replied, ever conscious Thomas loomed behind them like a menacing prison guard. Perhaps, that's what goaded her on. "I do hope you'll join us for Christmas in Berkshire. It would be lovely to see a friendly face—never mind one so handsome."

As if he understood the reason for her flirtatious compliment, his smile stretched the full width of his jaw. "You make it impossible to refuse." Grasping her hand again, he brought it to his lips for another kiss.

"Don't you have a train to catch?" Thomas bit out each syllable.

Lord Alex peered up at her, and with another audacious wink, he released her hand, executed a shallow bow, and turned to Thomas. "I see I have greatly overstayed my welcome. Don't get so worked up—I'm leaving."

"Amelia has important work to do. Bid your adieu and go."

Lord Alex strode to the door, passing his friend's stiff form without a word. At the threshold, he shot a glance back at Thomas. "I gather then I'll see you at Rutherford's." With that parting shot, he was gone.

"I'm surprised you have any friends at all," Amelia said, peeved and perversely pleased at his highhanded manner.

"You will stay away from Cartwright, you understand me?" Gone was the stoic man of minutes before as was his veneer of civility.

"I believe I can manage that now that he's gone."

His hands, fisted at his sides, moved spasmodically. His green eyes blazed as if he wanted to wring her neck and only the thought of hanging from a rope in the middle of Trafalgar Square prevented him.

"That you find me objectionable for your friend but availed yourself of me is truly the height of hypocrisy." Amelia hadn't intended to say a word about the prior night, but too frequently the man caused her to speak without thought.

"When I discover an uninvited woman in my chambers, I'm obligated to have my way with her." His reply came back with biting promptness. "And as I'm sure you recall, my intentions were welcomed with great enthusiasm. But I'm sure that's the part you most want to forget."

Smug, arrogant cad. He'd find every opportunity to throw the incident back in her face. "I unfortunately lack your vast pool of experience as to what is de rigueur in that particular situation."

His mouth quirked in a fashion she found infuriating: smug yet grim. "It certainly didn't stop you from scratching my back and howling like a cat in heat."

Reflectively, Amelia lowered her head to hide the blush scorching her cheeks. Her father had always said she was impetuous. This was one conversation she wished she hadn't broached.

"Ah, I see you have no response to that."

She could hear the amusement in his voice. He sounded like he was rubbing his hands together in glee.

Amelia jerked her head up and pinned him with a withering stare. "You are deplorable."

His smile broadened. "I don't believe that's what you said last night. If I recall, you could barely speak. There was all that gasping, whimpering, and moaning. Whoever thought you would be such a lustful bedmate. Thankfully, I discovered before it was too late, the best way to—"

The chair toppled wildly as Amelia sprang to her feet. Her heart pounded madly. "Stop! Stop! I will not sit here and listen to this. You are the most—the most—" She broke off, the right word failing her. At that moment, there wasn't a word strong enough, heinous enough to describe Thomas Armstrong.

"Skilled lover you ever had?" he asked innocently.

"Ha!" she shrieked. "The only one I've had thus far. And I'm certain you will shrivel in comparison to the next man."

The speed at which he reached her desk and hauled her into his arms was staggering. And the speed at which her mouth parted to accept his tongue even more so. Her only excuse was he had caught her unawares. She hadn't had the time to fortify her resistance. And her stupid body didn't know it wasn't supposed to succumb to this man again. And again, and again.

She tasted like peppermint. She felt soft and firm in all the right places—her delectable bottom, her beautiful breasts. And God, she could kiss. She knew how to use her tongue for such an innocent. She had a way of capturing his between her lips, and languidly sucking, coaxing, sipping on it as if she were enjoying one of those flavored Italian ices that were so popular.

Thomas adjusted their positions so he could fit his erection against her sweet mound, silently cursing the endless swaths of grey fabric of her skirt. His cock jerked at the contact. He ached for nothing more than to take her right there on the study floor.

Again, he was experiencing a loss of control. Amelia had somehow managed to turn him into a simpleton when it came to matters of the flesh. He dragged his mouth from hers and feathered down the smooth line of her neck back up to the sensitive spot behind her ear. At his kisses, she began to pant and moan. His mouth then sought the indent of her shoulder. She moaned again.

Drowning, that sound was his lifeline back to sanity. Summoning up a will he required in Amelia's presence, Thomas released her. His release was so abrupt she stumbled backward. Her hands caught the edge of the desk to steady her. She stared up at him, her blue eyes unguarded for a moment. Surprise, lust, and yearning were all there on her face. She quickly turned her back to him, her breath ragged, her slender shoulders heaving with the exertion of unspent passion.

Thomas thought to say something—anything. He could think of nothing. He cleared his throat, his heart pounding as if he'd been holding his breath under water until his lungs threatened to burst. And each drawn breath didn't bring him the relief he sought. Slowly, carefully, he turned from her bent figure, and made his way from the room as if she were opium and he, addicted.

Amelia straightened only when the door whistled closed. Her breath escaped her lips in an audible, jagged hiss. She tentatively put her hand to her throat and then touched her face to ensure she was still there. Then the knowledge rushed through her with the force of a wave crashing against the shores. It had been he who had called a halt to the kiss, not her. He who had pulled away.

Her face burned; her hands trembled. What was this man doing to her? She had offered little to no resistance when he'd taken her virginity. She had liked it. Who was she fooling, she'd been like a gourmand at the most lavish spread in all of London, gorging herself to satiation, and then wishing she could go back for more.

Chapter 23

Amelia's gaze toured the bronzes and Staffordshire figures on the rosewood étagère in the drawing room. The ornaments displayed were not so plentiful as to give it a cluttered appearance. She herself preferred sparse simplicity rather than a hodgepodge of knickknacks laying claim to taste and money. Yes, Lady Armstrong had made Stoneridge Hall a place anyone would be proud to call home. Which was one of the other reasons Amelia so desperately needed to leave—the sooner, infinitely the better.

She hadn't intended to become comfortable here. More important, she and Thomas had crossed a line in their relationship and couldn't go back. With the heat of his touch and kiss . . . his possession, he could send her high as a kite in flight, ascending the dizziest heights. But all too soon, she was cast down low to the darkest depths of despair. Never in her life had a person affected her so. She feared the risk of remaining would somehow include her heart—a risk she wasn't willing to take.

Since Lord Alex's departure three days ago, they now circled each other like strangers. Their conversation—such as it was—extended to staggering five-word sentences. *Good morning. I'll be at the stables.* And the moment he finished, he'd vanish and not return for the remainder of the day. She worked the hours in solitude. Rarely did he speak to her during the evening meals, choosing to converse almost exclusively with Miss Foxworth, who proved to be a most captive audience. He'd committed the grievance, yet she was being ignored. More glaring evidence of his arrogance.

"Lady Amelia?"

Amelia started at the sound of her name, quickly turning to view the pale, wisp of a woman hovering at the entrance of the drawing room. Speak—or in this instance think—of the devil and she was sure to appear.

Since Miss Foxworth's arrival at Stoneridge Hall, she'd continued to follow Amelia's advice, managing to unearth from her wardrobe brighter colored dresses more suitable to her complexion. Today, she wore a chartreuse dress with raglan sleeves and a full, billowing skirt.

"Is anything wrong? You've been so very quiet lately." Miss Foxworth edged into the room and daintily sidestepped a rogue footstool.

Amelia summoned a small smile. "Nothing really. You've just caught me deep in thought."

"Are you missing home?"

"Yes, perhaps a little." At this point, lying was easier than a game of twenty questions . . . or the truth.

"May we sit? I would like to speak with you." Miss Foxworth motioned to the dark blue sofa flanked by a balloon chair on her left.

Dear Lord, this all sounded quite ominous. Amelia took a seat in the balloon chair and tamped down any show of apprehension by busily arranging her skirts around her.

Miss Foxworth sat on the edge of the sofa with her hands clasped neatly on her lap, her expression earnest. "I would like to assure you that Lord Armstrong has no designs on me whatsoever."

Amelia's jaw went slack. Of all the things she had expected the woman to say, this hadn't even made her mental list. "Pardon?"

Miss Foxworth studied her with sage eyes. "From the beginning, I've gotten the impression you don't particularly care for my association with Lord Armstrong. Oh, don't get me wrong," she added hastily, "I certainly don't fault you for your reaction. I might be moved to act in a similar fashion for his affection. That is why I felt the need to assure you, he cares nothing for me—at least not in a romantic sense."

Amelia choked out a laugh, endeavoring for a smooth recovery from the shock of the woman's words—and the accuracy of her observation. "You are very much mistaken. Nothing could be further from the truth." She then held her breath to see if a bolt of lightning should appear in the crystalline, blue, winter sky. After a minute pause without the scent of burning flesh, she continued. "And truly, it is none of my concern what the true nature of your relationship is with the viscount."

Miss Foxworth now appeared puzzled. "So your grievance is with Lord Armstrong, not me?"

"No—I mean—yes—what I mean is my grievance is with no one. Lord Armstrong is free to associate with as many women as he pleases. It is not my concern." Of all the characteristics Amelia would have attributed to Miss Foxworth, tenacity hadn't been one of them.

"You see, we've been getting on nicely since our time in London. I just didn't want—"

"Truly, Miss Foxworth, I don't think it's any of my—"

"Does your disapproval of him stem from what you said at the ball?"

Dear Lord, did the woman know when to stop?

"If that is the case, I must disabuse you of the notion that Lord Armstrong indiscriminately goes about town bedding any and every woman who happens to cross his path. That is your assumption, is it not?" Miss Foxworth appeared so utterly confident of what she spoke. As if Amelia were the sadly ignorant girl and it was she who was schooled and learned in the inner workings of human behavior. Amelia didn't very much like the feeling.

"The man is hardly a saint, so if that's what you hope to convince me of, please save your breath."

Miss Foxworth nodded. "That is true. He isn't a saint, but then show me a man who is. Lord Armstrong is kind, loyal, and generous beyond fault. Were you aware he gave my brother the money to buy his commission? He is also paying for the lease on our flat in town. He has been doing so since Marcus entered the military." Her voice softened with emotion. "Thomas Armstrong has been a saint to Marcus and me, and we owe him a great deal."

She gave a short self-deprecating laugh. "Don't mistake me, it would be far too easy to fall in love with Lord Armstrong." Miss Foxworth lowered her gaze to her lap where she stared at her intertwined fingers. "But for me that would be a foolish act. Although he likes me just fine, he is not interested in me like that. He would deny it, of course, for that's the kind of gentleman he is, but to him I am merely Marcus's rather unfortunate spinster sister who is in need of support while her brother is away fighting wars. And that is fine with me, you know." She peered up at Amelia. "I would never do anything to damage our friendship."

Why had Miss Foxworth told her all of this? Such outpourings were better reserved for broken dams and rain downfalls. She'd already said she had no interest in the nature of their relationship. But her heart did lighten and flutter in the most abominable fashion at what she'd just heard.

Despite the fact he would be spending the Christmas holiday at his sister's home in Berkshire, Thomas allowed the servants to decorate the hall much in the same manner as his mother would have done. A Christmas tree was magnificently displayed in the morning room, its sturdy branches holding a ponderous amount of ornaments of bronze and silver. Against the backdrop of the night sky, candles lit the tree like a festive beacon in the bow-shaped window.

But for all the outward signs of Christmas cheer, he was feeling anything but in the holiday spirit. The last three weeks had been the most tension-wrought he'd ever spent, Amelia being the source of his disquiet. Like a festering sore, she seemed to affect everything he did. His sleep—or lack thereof—could only be considered fitful at best. The guilt of taking her virginity couldn't escape him. The unquenchable need to have her again had him keeping as far away from her as physically possible.

So many times he'd wanted to go to her and explain his reasons for taking her letters. But two things had always stopped him, the first being he could offer no acceptable excuse. He hadn't had to take Harry's suggestion that he monitor her correspondence. The second was that he could clearly see in her manner toward him that any kind of peace offering on his part would not be well received. She treated him like a pariah, and it was obvious she regretted giving him her innocence.

Raking a hand through his hair, he weaved his way between the side table and the settee, and dropped into the damask armchair facing the tree. He silently watched the flickering candles dance under the light of the crescent moon outside. He was too wide awake to take to his bed, and a book couldn't distract him from the things he wanted to do more. Even a drink had done nothing to soothe his nerves or ease the tension in his muscles. No, nothing had worked the past week.

Thomas dropped his head back against the cushioned chair and closed his eyes. But Amelia's beautiful face remained firmly implanted in his mind and thoughts.

In the tortured silence, he heard the rustle of cloth. Snapping his eyes open and jerking his head up, his gaze flew to the entrance. The unmistakable figure of the woman who now haunted his dreams by night and thoughts by day appeared, gliding into the room to stand in front of the Christmas tree. Flicking a glance at the longcase clock adjacent to the stone fireplace, Thomas was surprised to note it was much later than he first thought—fifteen minutes to eleven.

What was she still doing up? And good God, why hadn't she the sense to don more than the blue, silky cover-up that draped her from her slender shoulders to the tip of her stockinged feet and had him aching like a man too long deprived of a woman's touch.

Thomas shifted to rest his forearms on his splayed legs. She started at the movement before swiveling sharply. Her eyes widened when she spotted him tucked in the shadowed corner. Her hand flew to her throat.

"Oh Lord, I didn't realize anyone else was up," she said in a breathy voice. She immediately began to edge toward the entrance. "I was—was getting a book from the—the library, when I noticed the tree. . . ." She trailed off with a gulp, her face flushing a becoming pink.

"Don't allow me to stop you from looking your fill." In that moment, he decided it was time to end the standoff.

Amelia's instincts urged her to leave immediately. But foolhardy she must be, for she halted at his words. Thomas looked too . . . masculine, his hands hanging between his muscled thighs, and his jaw shadowed from a day's worth of growth. And his eyes, dark and vibrantly green, watched her from between lids lowered to half-mast. If any man should keep the aura surrounding him bottled to keep all the females of the world safe, it was Thomas Armstrong.

"I just wanted a closer look at the tr-tree," she said, stuttering like a child who had just learned its way around its tongue.

Two craterlike dimples creased his bristled cheeks as a

smile tipped the corners of his mouth. Lord, he was more beautiful than any fully grown male had a right to be. Amelia's gaze skittered away in a show of keen interest in the garland decorating the fireplace mantel. She hated this new nervousness that struck her when around him.

"You are beginning to remind me of your father." He made no attempt to keep the amusement from his voice, coming to his feet in one lithe, fluid motion.

Amelia's gaze narrowed. What on earth did he mean? She was not at all like him—in any manner.

"You both have a tendency to stutter when you're anxious."

Her father was never anxious; therefore he never stuttered. And neither did she! At least she hadn't done so until she'd met the viscount.

"I am not stuttering," she managed to say without the embarrassment of stumbling over her words. "The air down here is quite chilly. I should have realized the servants would have already put out the fires." She could think of nothing else to say so as to not appear completely ridiculous.

"Why are you so nervous?" With every word from his sensuous lips, he advanced a step. Self-preservation urged her to close her eyes and keep them shut.

"I—" Amelia was forced to stop when she realized she was about to do the very thing he'd just accused her of. She cleared her throat, and began to edge toward the entrance. "What you're mistaking as nervousness is fatigue, as it's late and I'm tired." She tried for a bit of hauteur, but failed miserably as he drew closer, causing her throat to lock up and the last several words to trickle out low and breathless.

"You can't be that tired if you were just looking for a book to read."

Amelia's face burned. *Blasted man.*

"You're running from me," he said softly.

Just a few steps and he would be within arm's reach. Amelia turned but didn't make it one step before his hand locked around her upper arm. His hold was firm and unyielding . . . and warm. Hot sparks shot through her.

"What are you doing?" A breathless gasp emerged from her lips.

"I want to know why you are so nervous." He pulled her inexorably closer. Amelia turned away from the sight of his chest, shoulders, and the ridged line of his neck.

Amelia swallowed. "Thomas, do not do this." She winced at the weak note in her voice. Weak of mind and of body.

"Don't do what?" he murmured, his voice seductively low.

Now he was standing within a hairbreadth of her, the male scent of him scrambling her thoughts, his nearness sending a cacophony of sensations coursing through her body.

The last time they had been this close, his hands had been on her breast, his tongue tangling with hers. And it had been he who had pulled back, not her, the weak, weak woman that she was. But only with him. She couldn't allow him this sort of control over her.

He lowered his head, his hooded gaze focused intently on her lips. She immediately clamped them shut tight, and angled her head to the side. Her feet, though, felt glued to where she stood. *Move. Move. Move.*

Then the faint shuffle of movement came from the hall. A thread of light soon seeped across the floor outside the room. Thomas quickly stepped back, straightening to his full height. In the next moment, his face was set into one of self-possession.

Amelia sighed in relief and turned away, clutching her cover-up around her as if it could shield her from his potency. She knew it could not.

"Good night." She didn't look at him—dared not—and quickly started toward the exit.

"We will be leaving on Saturday for Berkshire."

She halted abruptly, her head swiveling back around. "Must I go?"

"Do you believe I would leave you to spend Christmas here by yourself?" He actually sounded as if the thought was quite absurd. Her own father had never had a problem with it. After her mother had died, Christmas stopped having much meaning to her father. If he happened to be there on the day, he would invariably hole himself up in his study going over business documents and account ledgers.

"I'd really rather spend it alone."

Thomas eyed her as if he didn't want her to come any more than she did. "You haven't a choice in this, Amelia. You're coming to my sister's with me."

Amelia gave a jerky nod before making a hasty departure, wondering how she was going to survive a holiday with Thomas Armstrong without losing herself completely.

What the hell was wrong with him? He'd have kissed her and God knows what else if one of the servants hadn't unknowingly saved him from himself. The damned woman was making him crazy.

He recalled, with a clenching of his heart, the expression on her face as she stood there looking fragile and alone, gazing up at the tree. He'd glimpsed a poignant sadness in her eyes when she'd turned to him. He wondered at the cause of the sadness. Then she had started to retreat from him. Something in him, perhaps the predatory instinct that kept mankind from becoming extinct, had risen in him, and he'd pursued with the age-old lure to mate and possess surging wildly through his veins.

He gave his head a hard shake. He had to get a hold of himself. They would have two weeks in the confines of Rutherford Manor with Missy, her family, and Cartwright. His mouth instantly tightened. If for no other reason than for appearances, he needed to curb his baser needs when it came to Amelia. Whatever spell she had cast over him had to be temporary. Not to be overlooked was the fact he no longer had a mistress, which obviously left him vulnerable to her charms. How often had he ever had a young, beautiful, and desirable woman living under his roof for months on end? Never. No wonder he'd gone a little crazy. But in Berkshire, he could only hope his feelings would dissipate as quickly as bats scattered at the hint of daylight.

Chapter 24

The smoke swirling from the black-rimmed chimneys of Rutherford Manor seemed to morph into the clouds hovering above—grey ominous clouds foretelling a heavy snowfall. Amelia turned from the carriage window, taking great care to keep her regard from straying in the direction of Thomas, whose gaze burned her with a quiet intensity.

"Mademoiselle, are you unwell?" Hélène inquired from beside her. "You look piqued."

Piqued would be a blessing if one considered she'd been anticipating their arrival there much the same way Marie Antoinette must have embraced her fate: with stalwart resignation.

"You have no need to be nervous."

Her gaze snapped to Thomas, surprised at his oddly soothing tone and the sincerity in his eyes. "I am hardly nervous," she replied, her voice unusually high. Lord, what was wrong with her? She'd never ever made a sound so missish in her life. She immediately lowered her voice. "I'm merely anxious to arrive so I can change. I feel molted, traveling a full day in this gown."

There, she sounded like herself. A minor victory when it came to her quickly vanishing self-control in all things pertaining to Thomas Armstrong.

The door at her side opened, permitting an icy blast of air into the already cold interior of the brougham. A footman in a livery of navy blue and green waited to assist them from the carriage. Amelia quickly offered him her gloved hand, eager to quit the viscount's disquieting presence.

A short time later, she was standing in the center of the three-storey foyer of the red-bricked structure. Amelia gladly relinquished her bonnet, coat, and muffs to the attending second footman. As Thomas was handing the young man his great coat, a high-pitched squeal pierced the silence.

"Thomas!"

A woman—slim, tall, and blessed with an abundance of chestnut hair—flew past Amelia to launch herself into his arms. He caught her fast and held her secure.

Amelia instantly recognized her from several portraits at Stoneridge Hall—Lady Windmere, or as her family so affectionately called her, Missy. The portraits, however, hadn't done her justice. She possessed a vibrancy the artist hadn't quite captured, giving the real flesh-and-blood woman a rare, indefinable beauty.

"God, Missy, you're smaller than you were before you got with child," Thomas said, releasing her after a prolonged embrace and setting her before him, his hands clasping her lightly by the waist. Amelia had never seen him smile quite like that before, a smile that rivaled the sun on the brightest day and the glitter of the stars against the darkest and clearest of nights. Her belly dipped sharply.

"Try taking care of two infants and you'll see how little time you have for anything else. Of the choice between eating and sleeping, sleeping has been winning handily," his sister replied with a laugh and then pulled him to her once again. "I'm so glad you've arrived."

Thomas's expression sobered some when he turned to her. "Missy, Lady Amelia, I believe the two of you met the year before. Although at the time my sister was not yet the Countess of Windmere."

The chestnut-haired beauty turned to her. The woman's eyes, an arresting mixture of slate grey and blue, glowed in genuine welcome, and she looked positively radiant from her flushed face, right down to her festive hunter-green wool and satin gown. And if the countess had indeed given birth only months past, one would be hard pressed to tell, as her waist couldn't be more than twenty inches.

"Lady Windmere." Amelia dipped into a shallow curtsey. How could she ever forget the circumstances under which they'd met? And Amelia was certain the countess remembered the woman who had insulted her brother at their introduction. A brother of whom, she might add, the countess appeared intensely fond. Her actions then, coupled with the warmth of her reception now, shamed her. Unfortunately, it was one year too late for regrets.

The countess, however, would have nothing so formal. She took Amelia's hands in hers and patted them with the familiarity of old friends.

Nonplussed, Amelia could think of little else to do but allow it. Not since Elizabeth had a woman her age touched her in kindness. If an indication existed that Lady Windmere wouldn't hold her past behavior against her, this was it. This relieved Amelia to no end.

"Of course, I remember Lady Amelia." The countess sidled an impish grin at her brother. "I'm so pleased you could join us for the holidays. This is so much better than tea, don't you agree, Thomas?"

Thomas's mouth tightened at her question. Amelia's gaze darted between the siblings. *Better than tea?* "Pardon me?"

"After our introduction last year, I urged Thomas to invite you over for tea. But I think an entire fortnight is much better, wouldn't you agree?" She gave Amelia a guileless sort of look and gave her hand a final pat before releasing it. "And please, none of this Lady Windmere nonsense. I am Missy to any friend of my brother's." She shot her brother a look of pure mischief.

Any friend of Thomas's? She certainly was not his friend, she was his—Amelia halted, refusing to complete the thought. Their situation was too confusing and discomfiting to be mused about at the present time.

Amelia forced a smile. "I would be more than happy to dispense with the formality of titles."

In response to her invitation, Missy appeared more than a little pleased. Thomas, on the other hand, raised his brow, clearly surprised by her willingness to do so. She had held a rather hard line with him. But why shouldn't she? Just because the countess—Missy—was his sister. She'd far outgrown the stage when she'd hold a person's association with him against them. She wasn't nearly that petty . . . anymore.

"Thank God you're finally here, Armstrong. I thought my wife would expire awaiting your arrival."

Amelia started as the deep male voice sounded from behind her. Twisting on her heel, she took in a *very* handsome, tall dark-haired man casually attired in shirttails and black trousers. The Earl of Windmere. The only member of the dimpled trio she had yet to meet. Goodness, Thomas and his friends must have kept the females of London in a constant state of wanting. And undoubtedly still did.

The men greeted each other in the manner of longtime intimates. After they concluded the Englishman's form of an embrace—a brisk handshake and some masculine shoulder slapping—Lord Windmere turned to her. He then exchanged a brief inscrutable look with Thomas. "And this must be the fair Lady Amelia." He watched her with a teasing glimmer in his pale blue eyes. Beautiful eyes.

No one spoke in the ensuing silence. Amelia's cheeks warmed. If tales of her verbal exploits hadn't reached the earl's ears through the gossip mill, then of course, Thomas would have eagerly informed him. She could well imagine how badly they'd bandied her name about.

"James, do behave. You'll have Amelia believing you're

as impertinent as I am," Missy admonished lightly. "Since my brother seems to have forgotten his manners, Amelia, may I introduce you to my husband, James, the sixth Earl of Windmere."

"Lord Windmere," she said, dipping in another curtsey.

The earl dropped at the waist in a formal bow and grasped her hand in his, raising it to his lips for a kiss. "The pleasure is mine," he said, slowly relinquishing her hand.

"Come, Amelia. You must be perfectly exhausted from your travels." Addressing the footman who stood by the double staircase behind them, several large portmanteaus at his feet, Missy said, "Stevens, please take Lady Amelia's baggage to the pink guest chamber and my brother's to the green."

"Yes, milady." Stevens hefted one of the portmanteaus in his hands and proceeded up the stairs.

"I'm sure you would like to get out of those clothes and take a nice warm bath," Missy said, her gaze skimming over Amelia's wrinkled claret-colored traveling suit with its simple lines and full sleeves.

Suddenly self-conscious of her appearance, Amelia tucked several stray hairs into her once pin-neat coiffure. Too much napping had dislodged one too many pins from her chignon. "Yes, as you can well imagine, it has been a tiring day."

She certainly wouldn't tell the countess how excruciating the journey had been due to her brother's brooding presence. As much as she'd tried to ignore him, she had found her gaze frequently drifting back to him, only to hastily look away as soon as he turned his regard to her.

"Come then. Let me show you and your maid to the guest quarters. I'm sure the men have much to discuss." Missy smiled at her brother and then cast her husband a look so blatantly adoring Amelia averted her gaze. The feeling of intruding on something rare and intimate washed her in a cloud of melancholy.

With a familiarity no woman, save Elizabeth, had ever shown her, Missy hooked an arm through hers and proceeded up the stairs to what would be her bedchamber for the next two weeks.

"So that's the infamous Lady Amelia," Rutherford commented dryly, his eyes sparked in appreciation. "While no woman can hold a candle to my wife, she *is* a beauty."

Rutherford was as enamored of his wife as any man Thomas had ever seen, which was just as well for she suffered just as badly as he.

"I couldn't very well leave her at Stoneridge Hall," Thomas muttered.

Rutherford chuckled. "Is that what you convinced yourself?"

Before Thomas could offer a response in his defense, the door sounded. Another footman quickly appeared to answer the chimed summons. Everything within him stiffened at the sight of Cartwright breezing through the doorway, hat in hand.

His friend's presence normally would have promised a good time filled with great conversation—raucous and intelligent alike—and the ease of a long-held friendship. Or so it had been until Cartwright's last visit. What the hell was wrong with him? Years ago, they'd all promised each other nothing, especially a woman, would ever come between them. Especially since the incident with Louisa. Pushing aside his feelings, Thomas forced a smile. If it lacked in authenticity, so be it. He was at least making the effort to be cordial.

Cartwright stopped to hand the footman his hat and coat before advancing toward them. Upon his approach, Rutherford thrust out his hand in greeting. "Missy told me you weren't going to arrive until tomorrow."

The two men smiled and shook hands warmly. "I left

early to avoid the crush, as every fool I know intends to take to the roads tomorrow. And damned if I'm not glad I did. I practically had the entire first-class section to myself."

"Seems more deliberate on the part of the train riders than a matter of happenstance." Uncertain of his reception, Thomas kept his greeting in keeping with the sarcastic manner in which they often joked.

Cartwright's expression instantly sobered as he turned to eye him silently. The seconds on the longcase clock outside the drawing room ticked inordinately loud throughout the hall. Just as Thomas's smile began to falter, Cartwright raised his eyebrow. "After the way you tossed me from your home, I wasn't sure you were still speaking to me."

Rutherford's gaze darted between them, his expression bewildered. "Would one of you be kind enough to fill me in? It's obvious I'm missing something."

With his eyes trained on Thomas, Cartwright peeled off his gloves, one finger at a time, his movements unhurried. Extending his right hand to him, he said, "Nothing that bears repeating. Isn't that right, Armstrong?"

Thomas grasped his friend's cold hand in his, accepting the peace offering in the spirit in which it was given. "It's already forgotten. "

"But—"

"Leave it alone, Rutherford. It was nothing." Thomas used a tone that clearly conveyed he'd entertain no further discussion on the matter. The earl eyed them for a few seconds longer before snapping his mouth closed.

As far as Thomas was concerned, the incident *was* forgotten. "Will supper be served at eight?"

Rutherford gave a short nod.

"Good, then I think a bath and a change of clothes are in order. I will see you both then." With a nod toward his friends, Thomas departed.

* * *

"What the hell was that about?" Rutherford asked the moment Armstrong disappeared up the stairs.

Cartwright gave his friend a feigned look of innocence. "Where is the lovely Lady Amelia?"

"She's upstairs with Missy," Rutherford replied automatically. Then a look of comprehension dawned in his eyes. "Is that what—or to be more precise—whom that exchange was about?"

Cartwright idly tapped his gloves against his trousered leg. "Let's just say the most effective way to get to Armstrong is by showing an interest in Lady Amelia. You wouldn't imagine the time I had of it. Just be prepared to defend yourself though. You know the man's temper."

Rutherford grimaced, no doubt remembering the pummeling Armstrong had given him last year when he'd discovered the earl had compromised Missy. A beating Alex would no sooner forget and one he had no desire to ever be on the receiving end of. He could very well have broken something trying to break the two up.

"Ah," Rutherford whispered after a moment of silence. "I should have suspected as much. He has always been just a little *too* violently opposed to her. Too much a Shakespearean element to his protests."

Cartwright barked out a laugh. "My thoughts precisely."

"And something tells me you're up to something."

"Well, I have been known to be a risk taker, as you are aware. And what would Christmas season be without me to liven things up?"

"If you do anything to spoil mine and Missy's first Christmas with our children, I'll beat you to a pulp myself," Rutherford said, but the ghost of a smile softened the sternness of his warning. There was probably no one more eager to see Armstrong squirm because of a female.

"Uncle Alex ruin Christmas for my favorite twins? Absolutely not," he said, theatrically aggrieved. "I'm just going to have some fun with their dear Uncle Thomas. And I know you'll enjoy watching the show."

Rutherford conceded the point with a wry chuckle. "You mean the damn spectacle. You're a daring man, Cartwright."

Alex smiled. He'd been told that a time or two, though under considerably different circumstances. "I know."

The countess had summoned one of the maids to escort Hélène to her sleeping quarters after she'd shown Amelia hers. When the three departed, Amelia properly surveyed the room. Included in the mahogany and enameled furnishings were a large canopied four-poster bed, a winged wardrobe with inset glass on the center door, and a chintz flowered armchair. The walls were covered in silk paper of embossed pink and gold flowers, and the ceiling was an elaborate bead and floral molding. Everything appeared comfortable and infinitely pleasing to the eye.

Amelia's plans for the evening were simple enough: a hot bath, a short nap, and supper, in that order. But the moment her head touched the pillow, her plans collapsed under the weight of her fatigue. Her allotted hour-long nap ran unabated until a knock on the door pulled her from a dreamless sleep.

Two things registered immediately: the curtains were drawn, permitting in a profusion of wintery light. And this, of course, led to Amelia's other very astute observation: it was morning. *Morning!*

She bolted up in bed just as Hélène entered the chamber.

"*Bonjour*, mademoiselle." Her maid's tone brimmed with joie de vivre.

"Hélène, it's morning."

"*Oui*, mademoiselle." Hélène replied as if Amelia hadn't just stated the obvious.

"Why didn't you wake me for supper?"

"Lord Armstrong told me to permit you to sleep."

Did he indeed?

A half hour later Amelia was making her way down the stairs continuing to ponder Thomas's motivation. Had his gesture been one of kindness, or had her exhaustion simply presented him with a way to avoid her company? She disliked not knowing. But more than ever she disliked that his reasons so concerned her.

As Amelia started toward the breakfast room, Lord Alex rounded the hallway and headed toward her.

He stopped in front of her, and dropped into a deep bow. "Good morning, Lady Amelia. You look lovely as always." A roguish smile tugged at the corners of his mouth. "I was completely heartbroken to discover you wouldn't be joining us for supper last evening."

Amelia laughed. Such effusiveness was hard to take seriously. "And certainly if I'd known you were here, neither illness nor a natural disaster would have prevented my attendance."

"Well, thank heavens for that. Last night I thought I'd lost my touch." His grey eyes sparkled with amusement.

"Will my company for breakfast suffice, or would that constitute a poor substitute?" she teased, something she found easy to do with him.

"If you'll give me fifteen minutes to make myself presentable, I would be more than honored." He motioned to his riding clothes and punctuated his tongue-in-cheek formality with a wink.

"I guess I can stave off hunger for that long, but not a moment longer," Amelia replied, only half joking. After all, she hadn't eaten since the afternoon snack the day before.

"Am I interrupting something?" A thread of steel ran through Thomas's tone, giving its mildness a deceptive ring.

Amelia started and turned at the question. The blasted man needed a cowbell to alert her of his presence. He had stopped outside of the drawing room, his arms folded, his form taut, looking the very picture of the Archangel Gabriel, all golden, handsome . . . and entirely too forbidding. No man should look *that* good in precisely cut and stitched wool and cotton. And certainly not when it appeared he'd used his fingers instead of a comb to tame those silken locks. Why did he have to look so . . . so damnably appealing?

Lord Alex regarded his friend, looking, by all appearances, unperturbed. "Actually, I do believe you are. Is that not right, Lady Amelia?" He shot her a glance, his eyebrow raised in question.

Amelia did her circumspect best to quell a burst of laughter that bubbled to the surface. She gave a choked cough and offered no response.

Thomas's glower grew as he eyed Lord Alex. After a pause, he regarded her. "You must be hungry. Allow me to escort you to breakfast."

"Lady Amelia has just agreed to join me for breakfast as soon as I clean up."

The only thing worse than two boys fighting over a toy, was two fully grown men treating a woman in the same manner. And currently, Thomas was the guilty party in this childish tug of war, although Lord Alex could easily be accused of his own bit of mischief making.

Amelia started to speak, as she should have some say in the matter. "I really—"

"Then we'll make certain to chew slowly," Thomas said, dismissing Cartwright with a turn of the head and motioning for Amelia to come to him.

No one moved and no one spoke during the deafening silence that followed. Amelia was simply too struck dumb to do anything, the situation simply too unbelievable to be real. Both men watched her, their expressions expectant.

Finally, Lord Alex turned to her. "The decision is yours. I would certainly understand if you chose to accompany Armstrong."

Thomas's intake of breath was audible, his anger visible

for all to see. Two red slashes stained his cheekbones as his eyes turned into emerald chips. His chest rose and fell the way one did when striving to maintain control. Apparently, he didn't appreciate his friend's magnanimity; didn't like that Lord Alex's manner was a great deal more civilized than his.

"Amelia, please leave us. I need to speak with Cartwright . . . privately." Thomas had his friend fixed in his gaze.

"Whatever you wish to say, I'm sure it can be said in front of Lady Amelia." Lord Alex ruined what would have been a smooth retort when a smirk caught the corners of his mouth.

Once again, Amelia stood rooted in place, unable to make herself leave and miss the coming confrontation. *Lord, you must be touched in the head.* But not even that self-reproach made her go.

"I assure you, it cannot," Thomas managed to utter despite his locked jaw and clenched teeth.

Thomas's cavemanlike behavior caused a heady bit of excitement within her, which she valiantly tried to ignore. Her gaze darted uneasily between the two men. Lord Alex had an indolent look about him, currently braced against the balustrade, his feet crossed at his ankles, his arms across his chest.

"You look angry. Are you angry with me?" A perfectly legitimate observation and question if Lord Alex possessed the diseased brain of a half-wit.

Thomas's eyes snapped and a growl rumbled in his throat. "You will leave Amelia alone." Each word, distinct and precisely enunciated, exploded from his lips.

Amelia gasped. He had actually said it aloud. She experienced another heady rush. Thomas immediately stiffened and clamped his mouth shut. He'd said too much, but the effects of the blast reverberated throughout the hall, turning the air so dense it seemed to take on a solid form.

Cartwright's laughter broke the silence. "If you're staking

a claim, I will gladly bow out. But if this is a case of 'dog in the manger,' I'll have to object strenuously."

Dog in the manger? She'd heard the phrase before and had always wondered at its meaning. She wished now she'd weathered the embarrassment and imposed upon someone to elucidate her.

Thomas's expression hardened to granite. His eyes seemed to say, *Staking a claim indeed! The bowels of hell would be knee-deep in snow first.* However, what emerged from her mouth took him completely by surprise. "Bow out from what exactly? Is one mistress not enough for you?"

To this, Cartwright threw his head back, his Adam's apple bobbing under the bark of laughter loud and raucous.

Thomas scowled at her as if she'd somehow instigated the entire incident. But the glare he saved for his friend invoked an image of a coven of witches leaning over a boiling cauldron casting spells, its victim possessing silver-grey eyes and a dashing dimple in his chin.

"I'm the last person you want to toy with right now." Thomas uttered the warning with such deathly sincerity, a rash of gooseflesh chased up the length of her arms.

Lord Alex, however, was not a man who cowed easily. His laugh subsided into a cant of rhythmic chuckles. "Whose intentions worry you more, mine or yours?"

In a blur of movement, Thomas had his friend by the jacket, his hands clutching a fistful of dark green wool and satin. Thomas breathed fire and brimstone while Lord Alex maintained the composure of a surgeon wielding a cutting knife.

"Mine don't worry me one bit, as I have every intention of beating you to—"

"What on earth is going on down here?" A flurry of footsteps—those of the lord and lady of the house—descending the stairs accompanied the feminine voice raised in alarm.

"Thomas, what is the meaning of all this shouting?" the countess asked, halting at the foot of the staircase, her

husband at her side. Her eyes rounded as she took in the
scene before her: her brother clutching the shiny lapels of
Lord Alex's riding jacket.

"Cartwright." His friend's name growled from the earl
like an expletive.

In response, Lord Alex spread his arms wide and held
his palms up in supplication as he gave an innocent shrug.
"You will take careful note of who is holding *whom* against
their will."

With that, Thomas abruptly released him and took an
angry step back. Lord Alex made a grand show of straightening and smoothing his jacket.

"Will someone please tell me what's going on?" the
countess demanded. She stood with her hands akimbo, the
azure blue of her gown causing her eyes to flash more blue
than grey.

"Go ahead, Armstrong, tell Missy why you came within
inches of beating me to a pulp," Lord Alex instructed in a
smooth, unruffled tone.

"Cartwright." Another warning from Lord Windmere.

Thomas stared back at his sister. Like an overworked
motor, his breathing appeared subject to erratic fits and
starts, until he seemed to get it under control.

Then there was just the silence. Everyone watched
Thomas. With a scowl marring his handsome countenance,
he watched them right back. "Oh, bloody hell," he finally
muttered. With one last withering look at Lord Alex, he
started toward the front door. Before anyone could protest,
he had disappeared through the doorway.

In a bemused state of wonder, Amelia turned to Lord
Alex, who met her gaze with a sly wink. Though sinfully
handsome, on their initial introduction he'd appeared as mild-
mannered as a man of the cloth. But upon closer association,
it was clear this man could chew her up and spit her out with
such finesse she wouldn't even feel the bites—a talent of

only the truly dangerous. She was doubly glad he considered her a friend.

The earl approached Lord Alex on silent treads as the countess stared grim-faced after her brother. "I told you I won't tolerate you spoiling Christmas. Fix this with Armstrong and fix it now. You can save your chicanery for when he's visiting with *your* family."

Amelia shared a bewildered look with the countess.

"Now I have to go out in the cold and fetch the man before he catches his death." The earl turned from his friend, bellowed for someone named Randolph to fetch him two overcoats. Seconds later a bald man, short and muscled, appeared with two black wool greatcoats. The earl hurriedly shrugged one on and draped the other over his arm before departing the house, pulling the door closed with a resounding slam.

Chapter 25

Thomas didn't feel the cold. The heat of his blood warmed him against the biting wind sending his hair flying about his head in a whirlwind. He walked with no destination in mind; he just knew he needed to walk off the corrosive anger inside him, the primitive urge to do his boyhood friend bodily harm.

He shouldn't have allowed Cartwright to rile him. But in matters concerning Amelia, he *was* like a dog in a manger. And he bloody well hated that Cartwright had challenged him with the truth.

Rounding the hedgerows along the side of the manor house, a gust of bone-chilling wind finally penetrated his anger. To be out in this weather without a coat proved just how foolhardy he was acting. If he possessed one iota of sense, he'd go back. But as it stood, freezing seemed a better alternative than going back to face Missy, Rutherford, Cartwright . . . and, dear Lord, Amelia. He might as well have branded her with a KEEP OFF MY PROPERTY sign, sodding imbecile that he was.

Approaching footsteps sounded behind him. Thomas shot a glance over his shoulder. *Rutherford. Blast.* The last thing he wanted was company—even that of the well-meaning variety. He wanted to be alone. Then an involuntary shiver shook him as the cold crept under his shirt collar. Although he wouldn't refuse the coat his friend was carrying.

Without saying a word, Rutherford reached his side and offered him the coat. Thomas paused to pull it on, gratified to have the thick garment to defend against the winter elements. He then continued on his way to nowhere in particular.

Rutherford fell in step beside him. "Are you going to tell me what that was all about?" he asked quietly.

They walked a good half a minute in silence, their breath creating icy smoke trails in the air.

"It's nothing," Thomas finally replied. Even if he had the desire to do so, how did he explain himself?

"Has it to do with Lady Amelia?" Rutherford regarded his profile.

Thomas refused to look at him, his pace steady as their footprints disturbed the white tranquility of the newly fallen snow. "This is between me and Cartwright. Leave the matter alone," he said crisply.

Shoving his hands deep in his coat pockets, Rutherford stared at the ground. "I can certainly understand why you wanted to refuse Harry—Lady Amelia looks to be quite a handful. I bet she's even more petulant and spoiled than you'd thought."

Thomas shot his friend a sharp look of censure as something inside him instinctively protested his friend's unwarranted criticism of her. "I would hardly call her petulant or spoiled."

"But you did. The last time you were here. I believe you also referred to her as rude and insolent." The earl innocently returned his gaze.

And so he had. But that didn't give Rutherford the right to malign her character. Bloody hell, the man didn't even know her.

"She's not all that bad," he grumbled, somewhat annoyed at himself for his own defense of her.

A wry smile tipped the corners of Rutherford's mouth. "Well, she *is* very beautiful," he conceded.

"My mother and sisters are extremely fond of her. And she is as intelligent as she is beautiful."

A choked sound came from the earl, before he quickly cleared his throat. "Really? She sounds like a veritable goddess." Another choked sound emerged as Rutherford's shoulders began to shake in swells of amusement.

Good God, the bloody man was laughing at him. "Christ, if I'm going to have to deal with you too, I'll bloody well go back to Devon." Thomas pivoted abruptly to start toward the front.

"You're in love with the woman. Why can't you just admit it?"

It was Rutherford's words that caused him to halt, not the restraining hand he placed on his coat sleeve. Thomas slowly turned to face him, feeling as if he'd been struck in the head by a heavy instrument, numb from the bluntness of the question and the starkness of that word. Love.

"I ran from Missy for four years, and where did it get me? Bound to her for life—and happier than I ever thought possible. There's something to be said for beautiful, stubborn, willful, infuriating females. They can prove to be downright irresistible." As it always did at the mention of his wife, love lit Rutherford's eyes and softened his features.

It didn't take a genius to figure out what his friend was angling at. "Please don't compare your relationship with my sister to mine and Amelia's. I wouldn't even term what the lady and I have as a relationship, unless incessant fighting classifies it as such." *And passion with enough fire to reduce a thousand forests to ashes.*

Their unplanned trek had left them at the back of the house, next to a final line of hedgerows before the land gave way to gently rolling hills blanketed in shimmering white. Thomas fixed his gaze on a patch of clouds hanging incongruously in an otherwise crystal blue sky.

"Whatever is going on between you two must be strong if it has you like this." And they both knew that *this* was him acting the fool over that slip of a woman.

"This is Cartwright's doing." Thomas growled and jammed his hands into his coat pockets.

Rutherford chuckled dryly. "Well, he does like to have his fun."

"Has it come to your attention that this fun he's intent on having is at my expense? Who the hell told you to invite him for Christmas anyhow?" Thomas slanted him an accusatory look.

"You know damn well I haven't any say in these matters. Moreover, your sister adores the man."

Yes, Cartwright held a special place in Missy's soft heart. Lord, she had known him before she could crawl.

"So will you now admit you're in love with Lady Amelia?"

Thomas gaze snapped to his friend, his mouth poised to issue a forceful denial. But the commiserate expression on Rutherford's face stopped him cold. Although the words died in his throat, the very essence of who he was as a man begged him to bluster and prevaricate something—anything that would give him the appearance of being immune to the debilitating emotion.

As if sensing his turmoil, Rutherford gave his shoulder a firm squeeze. "If it's at all comforting, admitting it to yourself is the hardest part. After that it's just the matter of setting a wedding date and showing up at the church."

Marriage to Amelia? A dull ache started in Thomas's chest. He swallowed hard. "I would be a complete fool to even consider her for my wife."

Rutherford's lips quirked. "Perhaps not a *complete* fool."

Thomas's toes were growing numb from the cold and so too was his mind, for he wasn't just contemplating marrying Amelia, he was all but resigned to it. What else is a fairly honorable man supposed to do when he takes a lady's virginity? So what if the incident had taken place weeks before? He thought himself fairly honorable. She was already his, but marriage would legalize the union. Suddenly, what felt like a heavy weight fell from his shoulders. He wouldn't concede it was love, but he felt the emotion was strong enough to sustain a marriage.

"Well, let's see if the lady will have me." Thomas turned and started back toward the house.

From behind him, he heard Rutherford mutter, "I have the distinct feeling she already has."

After the door closed behind the earl, Amelia regarded Lord Alex, who appeared the very picture of guilelessness. But she knew quite well that if wickedness were a virtue, he'd by far be considered the most virtuous person there.

Missy peered up at him, a frown fixed on her beautiful face. "And just what, pray tell, is that smile all about? What did you do to my brother?" The countess punctuated her question by jabbing him in the shoulder—hard. He responded with an exaggerated wince. Missy possessed the litheness of a dancer and she was a half-foot shorter than Alex, but Amelia had no doubt she was more than up to the task of browbeating him silly.

"I didn't do anything," he protested, all mock innocence. "Your brother really needs to try to control that temper of his."

"He could freeze to death out there." Another jab of Missy's finger to his chest was followed by another unconvincing wince.

"You saw for yourself—Rutherford is bringing him an overcoat," he reasoned, still smiling.

The countess rolled her eyes. "You are impossible," she said, sounding thoroughly exasperated. "Just don't come complaining to me when Thomas beats you black and blue." With a sharp turn on her heel, she dismissed him as one would an exasperating younger sibling. "Come, Amelia, let us go and eat so that Alex can determine the best way to bring down swelling without a poultice."

If his fate involved a sound trouncing, as the countess inferred, the man in question didn't look the least bit concerned. He acknowledged their departure with an overly deferential bow and a playful glimmer in his grey eyes.

The countess led Amelia down the hall, hooking their arms at the elbows like longtime friends while grousing about what an unapologetic rapscallion Lord Alex had become. Amelia, who was little more than a novice at sharing this kind of intimacy with a female contemporary, permitted it, somewhat taken aback and too polite to react differently.

A short time later, they entered the breakfast room. Candles lit the room as only weak rays of sunlight streamed through three large windows.

"Please help yourself. We're generally only formal for supper," Missy invited her, angling her chin toward the sideboard, which was currently home to silver-covered platters of varying sizes. Amelia's stomach gave a celebratory lurch, growling at the bombardment of pleasant smells assailing her nostrils.

The countess laughed. "I told my brother someone should have awoken you last night, but he insisted you needed your rest more."

Amelia didn't know quite how best to respond. Though the countess made the statement without any apparent innuendo, his actions came across almost . . . protective. "I was quite tired," she said, busily piling her plate with crumpets, poached eggs, bacon, and oven-warmed bread. Hunger should not suffer the pretense of female delicacy.

After their plates were duly filled, the women took them to the linen-covered table, where the attending footman— a tall, sturdy young man with a shock of red hair—seated them. When he reached for the teapot, Lady Windmere lightly batted his hand away. "We are fine, Stevens. Please go and ensure Lord Alex has no hot water for his shower bath." She proceeded to pour two cups of tea before glancing at Amelia. "A cold one will do him good."

As though that kind of order were commonplace, Stevens gave a brisk nod and bowed out of the room.

The countess let out a soft chuckle at Amelia's raised brow and wide-eyed stare. "As fitting a punishment as that would be, Stevens has known me long enough to know that I am not serious."

Beauty and a sense of humor. In the past, Amelia wouldn't have thought the two traits together admirable in a female. Usually, it was the lack of the former that necessitated the latter.

They commenced eating, Amelia digging into her food with zeal. After a minute of companionable chewing, Lady Windmere said, "Would *you* like to tell me what caused that display out in the foyer? Is something going on between you and Alex?"

"N-No!"

"Between you and my brother then?" she asked pleasantly, picking up her teacup to take a sip.

Given the previous question, the second one shouldn't have surprised Amelia at all—but it did. It so discomfited her, her mouth couldn't form a denial. "Um—"

"You find me terribly forward, don't you? Ask my husband, it's a terrible personal flaw of mine." But there was no embarrassment or apology in the countess's admission.

Amelia slowed the chewing of her buttered scone to give her time to collect her thoughts. How did one articulate to the man's sister the complexities of their relationship? *He's taken me to bed, where we had scorching, passionate sex, but still we don't exactly get along.* Somehow that just didn't seem a wise thing to say. At least not at the breakfast table.

"Lord Alex has been kind to me. He is my friend—or at least I believe he holds me in that light." There, it was much easier to start with the initial question. The relationship she understood. She knew that whatever Lord Alex was playing at, he had no interest in her as a prospective wife, or even a conquest. But it seemed it would take the return of Christ to convince Thomas of that.

"And my brother? Why were we about to witness a brawl in my foyer?"

"I believe Lord Alex just enjoys provoking Thomas." Which was as apparent as a trunk on an elephant.

The countess's mouth curved in a secretive smile as she took another drink of tea. "Alex can be provoking, period. Although, only those close to him are aware of that fact. But rarely can he get a rise out of Thomas. They have known each other too long. But I wonder how long you will try to avoid my question about you and my brother." She flashed Amelia a guileless smile before popping a forkful of ham in her mouth.

The woman was absolutely relentless—an Armstrong trait, it would appear. "There is nothing between me and Thom–Lord Armstrong."

The countess's eyebrows rose innocently at her slip.

Amelia continued. "He and my father are very close. On the other hand, he and I don't particularly get along, but we will make an effort during our visit."

If Amelia expected the countess to lay the whole thing to rest, she would have been well advised not to hold her breath. A full-bodied laugh burst from Lady Windmere's throat. She laughed and laughed. And the longer she laughed, the more disgruntled Amelia grew. Lord, she hadn't said anything *that* amusing.

"Oh dear," the countess said, her slender shoulders still shaking as she wiped a tear from her eye. "For a moment, I thought you actually expected me to believe the two of you have no feelings for each other." She gave one final hiccupping laugh, her expression slowly sobering. Then her mouth formed a circle. "Oh," the countess breathed, "you *do* expect me to believe that drivel."

Amelia blanched. Some thought she had cheek, but it

appeared the countess was looking to best her in that arena.
Suddenly, she felt quite put upon and defensive. But she was
not about to go off, all half-cocked, as she would have done
in the past. Instead, she plucked the serviette from her lap,
and touched it to the corners of her mouth, the small action
giving her a measure of composure.

"I'm not certain I know entirely what you mean by that,"
Amelia said. Normally situations such as this would have
called for a swift and cutting response. Unfortunately, she
could think of nothing else to say.

The countess's slate-blue eyes softened, her expression becoming contrite. "Amelia, I didn't mean to disconcert you."

Amelia shook her head numbly, trying to ignore the
look the countess wore. It was that you-poor-girl-you-are-
fooling-yourself expression she knew so well because she'd
worn it herself and directed it at many deluded females.

Turning her attention back to her food, the countess
popped the last piece of marmalade-laden bread in her
mouth. Once finished, she washed it down with the remainder of her tea. Amelia followed suit, her near-empty stomach demanding she try to consume as much as she could.

"My brother has been known for his temper, but that was
in the past." The countess fixed her utensils on her plate to
signal her completion of her meal. "The last time I've seen
him so close to violence was with James." Her eyes lit at the
mention of her husband's name. A soft wispy sigh fluttered
past her lips. "But that was to be expected as Thomas had
just learned he'd compromised me."

Amelia blinked back another wave of surprise at the
latest revelation. For a brief moment, she wondered if the
countess had said it for shock value, but the frankness of her
regard told her differently as she appeared amused by the
memory.

"Unfortunately—or perhaps fortunately—my determination to have James as my husband was a thing to be seen.
I was in love, and terribly naïve. But as you can see, it all

worked out for the best, for I couldn't be happier with my life." Her smile displayed pearly white teeth, and a woman more than content with her lot in life.

"But getting back to the point I am trying to make. I think I've known since your introduction last year, you would play a significant role in his life." Amelia opened her mouth to speak, but the countess held up her hand to halt the words before she could issue them. "And when I heard word of what happened at Lady Stanton's ball back in August, I was certain of it. Your reaction to him is too volatile. And instead of dismissing you out of hand as Thomas does with most women he doesn't care for, he allows you to get under his skin. I have *never* seen my brother allow a woman to get under his skin. Quite the opposite in fact."

Amelia sat mute in her chair, trying to quell a rising tide of fear. Lord, how exposed she felt. What response did she give to this woman who—much like her brother—seemed to be able to see right through her and would no doubt scoff at her every denial and any defense she chose to mount?

"Are you in love with my brother?"

Months ago the question would have catapulted her into peals of laughter at its absurdity. Or perhaps had her elegant little nose turned up in affront at the sheer audacity of it. But months had passed. Time enough to lose her heart. Amelia didn't laugh. Instead she sat wide-eyed and stricken. Swallowing became a special process only performed by those possessing the coordination to do so. Or those who hadn't that same lost organ blocking the passage of her throat.

No. No. No. I don't love him. More important, I don't want to love him. But as loudly as the words reverberated within her, she could not get her mouth to cooperate and speak them. Why?

I can't love him, her mind continued to wail. *I will never be in control with him.* Amelia blinked and swallowed hard, the revelation hitting her harder than gale-force winds.

"I see I've discomfited you," the countess said. "I won't

continue to press you. Perhaps you yourself haven't realized it as yet. So now you'll have to think about what I've said." Patting her hand solicitously, she said, "Since we are finished with our meal, would you like to go up to the nursery and meet my twins?"

"I would love to meet your children," Amelia said, desperate to latch on to another topic of discussion, willing and ready to throw herself into any activity that didn't require her to see, think, feel, or speak about Thomas.

The countess gathered her skirts and came gracefully to her feet. "Then come with me."

Amelia spent the remainder of the day with Missy—as she had been instructed to call her when she'd slipped and addressed her as Lady Windmere. The countess claimed the title made her feel ancient coming from a woman her age.

They spent many hours with Jason and Jessica, the four-month-old twins. Sadly, Amelia's life hadn't given her many opportunities to be around children, much less babies. But, as she'd always believed, she took to them with the ease of a mother destined to care for her own. She adored everything about them: their rosy cheeks, their chubby little bodies, their gummy smiles, and their innocent neediness. She could have cuddled the babies for hours more had Jason not fallen asleep in her arms. It was at that point she and Missy placed both babies back in their cribs for their naps.

Missy then introduced her to the earl's sixteen-year-old twin sisters (twins appeared to be aplenty in the Rutherford household), Catherine and Charlotte. The girls were strikingly lovely. Exotic was the word that came instantly to mind as the only way to describe them with their honey-gold tresses and sun-kissed complexions. Their eyes were the same iridescent blue of their brother's with the same large, dark pupils. Amelia could see their coming out would set the gentlemen of the ton anxiously on their toes.

The sisters greeted her with an initial reserve, all finishing-school politeness and deference. But during afternoon tea, they lost much of that reserve, their liveliness bubbling to the surface.

While sipping her hot cocoa, Catherine revealed another aspect of her character when she cheerfully informed Amelia, she and her sister were in fact the earl's half sisters, the by-blows of the dearly departed fifth Earl of Windmere. The girl enjoyed a salacious tale. Once learning of their existence the year before, their brother, a saint to rival all biblical saints, had promptly taken them in. Their lives hadn't been the same since, Catherine concluded with a smile. Amelia expressed the desired surprise, although she'd heard varieties of the same tale through the grapevine some time ago.

Charlotte, on the other hand, seemed more concerned with Amelia's association with Lord Alex. But she was subtle in her approach. A question and comment here and there. Had they met? Was she aware he'd arrived a day early from London? No, Amelia had not. How nice. Alex and Thomas had been ever so kind to them. Did she know Alex was quite brilliant at fixing things? She'd not met many men with eyes like his. Lovely in the empirical sense. The girl had the vocabulary of a literary scholar. Although she said nothing terribly forward, her feelings were obvious. But the poor girl hadn't a chance. Her beauty, and even the promise of the diamond she would become in another year or so, couldn't make up for her youth and innocence.

After tea was concluded, Amelia retired to her bedchamber to rest until supper. What else had she to do? Thomas had made himself scarce throughout the day since he'd stormed out of the house. Nearly the entire day she had waited and hoped to catch a glimpse of him, her breath hanging on every footfall she'd heard out in the hall and her heart fluttering like a hummingbird's wings. But it had never been him, only the servants going about their daily chores.

Missy had been kind enough not to call her on her frequent inattentiveness, merely watching her, a sympathetic smile playing on the corners of her lips as if she too had experienced the same uncertain, anxious, crippling course of love.

As Amelia lay on her bed, stripped down to her chemise and pantaloons, her gaze idly, almost sightlessly, traced the blue gauzy material of the canopy. She was in love with Thomas Armstrong. There, she had admitted it. And if this was not love, it was a petrifying facsimile of some other heartrending emotion.

Surely it was only love that could take one from the summit of the highest mountain to the depths of the deepest valley. It could only be love that had her uncertain as to whether she was right side up or upside down, and had her every sense screaming for a cessation to the excess of feelings: the yearning, the anger . . . the passion roiling constantly inside her.

Lord, she had never felt so much and with such intensity since . . . yes, since her mother's death. Sometime after that—perhaps when she'd realized she'd lost not one but both parents—the numbness had claimed her. She had welcomed the numbness. She'd welcomed freedom from the pain that rent her heart at the thought of the mother she would never see again. She'd ceased to feel the pain, like tiny jagged knives into her skull, when her father's eyes would look right through her, if he chose to look at her at all.

Shifting on her side, she tucked her hands to pillow her cheek and let out a ragged breath. Feeling again was exhilarating, like coming back to life. But it had its dangers, especially now that she'd given her heart to a man whose feelings she was unsure of. He could make passionate love to her one moment and the next treat her as if he'd gladly see the last of her. Her choice wouldn't have made a whit of sense if she'd in fact had one. She'd be better off with the likes of Lord Clayborough: affable, courteous, and well-mannered. He would perch her high on some invisible pedestal and treat her like the vestal Virgin Mary. There would be no lustful passion, riotous kisses, or glorious lovemaking. With him she'd be safe from ever truly hurting again. But after a taste of the pulse beat of life, could she go back to having her emotions cocooned off for life? From life?

The question followed her into an uneasy sleep.

For the majority of the day Thomas had not been fit for company, his mood dark and brooding. After returning to the house with Rutherford, they had gone their separate ways, his friend more than likely gone to seek out his wife or children, or both. He had taken to his guest chambers, the need to be alone overwhelming.

Despite his intention, Thomas didn't go there directly, his attention caught and held by the sounds of feminine laughter and baby noises. He followed the sounds to the nursery. He stood outside the gaily decorated room, watching the scene silently from the hall.

Amelia was cuddling his nephew, cooing and scattering tender kisses all over his face. She looked happy and . . . maternal, which was mildly surprising. He'd never thought of her in that light. As a mother. Earlier, when he'd resolved to marry her, he'd been thinking about the physical side of things, having full and unfettered access to her body. The prospect of children would merely have been an inevitable result of that unquenchable passion.

But seeing her like this made him realize his feelings ran much deeper than he'd thought. Deeper than the Pacific Ocean. He could see only her as the mother of his children. Not only because he wanted her in his bed, but because he wanted her forever in his life. And he'd been unfair to her. She deserved better than a tumble, no matter how pleasurably explosive an experience. She deserved to be courted properly, as any lady of her rank should be. Even more so because she was his.

Chapter 26

Supper could be summed up in one word: Strained. At least on the part of her and Thomas, Amelia mused. Or perhaps strained was too ambivalent a word to describe the combustible electricity that simmered between them.

Thomas treated Lord Alex with surly politeness, which meant he only spoke to him when specifically addressed, and responded in curt monosyllables. It came as no surprise to her that Lord Alex didn't appear the least bit offended by his treatment.

Thomas spoke to her twice throughout the meal. The first time to inquire about her day, and the second to ask if she was finding everything to her liking. She replied to each question "excellent" and "yes," respectively, in as normal a voice as she could muster, considering that when he'd walked into the room, he'd literally taken her breath away, dressed to the nines, his scent a mixture of delicious clean male flesh and rosemary and bergamot. Thomas's own scent. If bottled, she'd purchase it by the caseload.

The silence between them after the last exchange was deafening and fraught with an indefinable anticipation, for thereon he took to watching her. And there was nothing informal, pleasant, or even polite about his regard. He watched her as if he'd like to devour her instead of the roasted fowl on his plate. And she was helpless not to do the same, snatching a glance here and there when she thought no one was paying her any mind.

Thankfully, the others at the table—the twins, the countess, the earl, and of course, Lord Alex—kept conversation from being in short supply.

At the conclusion of the meal, the men came swiftly to their feet as the countess rose. Amelia quickly followed, desperate to leave before she did something stupid to give herself away. No one but her need know how completely besotted she'd become over Thomas, especially the man himself. It was obvious he wanted her physically, but she loved him. And as always, love made all the difference. It made her the more vulnerable of the two.

"I hope you'll allow me to escort you to the drawing room, Lady Amelia," said Lord Alex, already making a move toward her.

Charlotte's gaze snapped to her and then back to him, a crestfallen expression now on her pretty face. Amelia's heart constricted in sympathy. Had Lord Alex a clue that he'd just diced the poor girl's heart in two?

"Amelia, I would like a word with you in private, if you please." Thomas blithely ignored his friend and clearly expecting her to do likewise.

Amelia stilled as her pulse tried to leap beyond the confines of her skin.

"Perhaps the study?" he queried, passing Lord Alex to stand next to her. She conceded with a small nod and departed the room at his side while the rest looked on in silence.

"Armstrong," Lord Alex called out just as they breached the threshold.

Thomas paused—as did she—and angled his head over his shoulder. He looked none to pleased at the interruption, but it appeared manners wouldn't allow him to ignore his friend.

"I will accept your undying gratitude at a later date." Lord Alex was all smiles and self-satisfaction.

The earl coughed in an effort not to laugh, and the countess tucked her chin to her chest to hide her smile. The twins looked on, wearing mystified expressions. Thomas made a grumbled sound in his throat that didn't sound at all appreciative. With the jerk of his head, he clasped her satin-clad elbow and steered her from the room.

In tension-wrought silence, they entered the study, where Thomas relinquished his hold of her. Amelia sought out the closest seating, sinking weakly onto a finely napped sofa of indeterminate color—something between green and beige—avoiding his gaze by fidgeting with her skirts.

A glass-encased clock ticked in time with the lengthening silence. *Don't look or you'll be lost.* Amelia kept her gaze fixed on her lap, her fingers now idly tracing the embroidered edge of her flounce.

"How can I talk to you if you refuse to even look at me?"

Somehow the gentleness of his tone put her at ease when she was certain nothing could. She drew a shaky breath and lifted her head to meet his stare. He wore a half smile, his dimples lending him a boyish appeal in the masculine planes of his too-handsome face. Lord, he was more potent than any wine she'd ever consumed.

"I gather this is in regard to Lord Alex." She really hadn't a clue as to why he wanted to speak to her, but his friend would probably be as good a place to start as any.

Thomas abandoned his post by the door and took a seat on the edge of the armchair by her. Leaning forward, he braced his forearms on his splayed legs. "I hope you're not taking his interest seriously. Cartwright has an unfortunate sense of humor at times."

Amelia wanted to laugh at the seriousness of his tone. His face was now all angles and hard lines, his mouth straight. He actually thought she believed his friend had an interest in her. Perhaps he even thought she returned that interest. Lord if he only knew that at that moment she could barely breathe properly, much less conceive a coherent thought with him sitting so close and his warm scent enveloping her. If he only knew that, if she allowed her emotions to run amuck, she could pounce on him like a woman in the throes of a Spanish fly overdose.

"I can assure you I have no designs on your friend, nor do I believe he has any on my person." She paused a moment to look at her hands clasped tightly in her lap. Peering at him from beneath her lashes, she asked softly, "Would it bother you much if such an interest existed between us?"

Thomas heard his own indrawn breath without being aware he'd taken it. Bother him? If she had taken a poker from the fireplace and prodded him with it—hard—the thought couldn't have pained him more.

Clearing the thickness in his throat, he took in her heart-stopping features, her flawless skin and her lush pink lips. Just the thought of her kissing another man sent his emotions rioting in rebellion. She was his, and the sooner she came to realize it, the better for them both.

"Yes, it would bother me." His admission came in a low voice, while pinning her with a look designed to indicate to her just how much.

Sapphire eyes widened before her hands became lost in the folds of her crimson skirt.

"And I think you know why," he continued softly, refusing to let her look away, to hide her feelings from him behind the mask she'd worn so long. He knew the passion simmering beneath the beautiful woman she was on the outside. He'd felt the hot, wet clasp of her sex on his as her body convulsed in orgasm. Just the memory of it caused his member to stiffen, urging him to satisfy its call.

"I'm not completely certain what you want from me. At

first I thought you intended to seduce me for revenge, but now things are so different between us."

The vulnerability in her voice was endearing, stinging his conscience with remorse. For the expediency of their courtship, he would not admit that initially that had been his intent. He'd wait until their relationship was on firmer ground. They might even be able to laugh about it in the future.

"Do you honestly believe I would bed a woman out of revenge?" Which was not a lie. He hadn't planned to actually take her. He'd made love to her because he couldn't help himself.

Her gaze probed his for a moment before a smile appeared. "But the thought must have crossed your mind. I'd given you ample reason to dislike me."

He chuckled at her gross understatement. "I think we've established I like you fine enough."

With his right hand, he stilled her fidgeting fingers and stared deeply into her eyes. "I made love to you because I desperately wanted you and for no other reason. Does that answer your question?"

The soothing stroke of his thumb on her palm and the warmth of his flesh had Amelia's senses clamoring in response.

She nodded as a fire ignited between her thighs.

"Good," he said, in a low, hypnotic voice. "I want there to be no misunderstanding between us. May I escort you to your chamber?"

His request sounded decadent and forbidden. Yes, and wonderfully sinful. Amelia said nothing, knowing her silence signaled her willingness. He rose still clutching her hand in a firm but gentle grip. She allowed him to assist her to her somewhat shaky feet, and they made the trek up the stairs, his hand hovering near the small of her back.

"What about your sister—the others? They are awaiting me in the drawing room." Her protest was as much an afterthought as one could be.

Thomas gave a husky laugh, lowering his mouth to her ear. "My brother-in-law is too newly married to spend time in the evening drinking port with Cartwright. He's already spent the entire day with him. Believe me when I say, everyone has already retired for the night."

Amelia didn't say another word but continued on to her room, anticipation unfurling inside her. At her chamber, she turned to face him, and he stepped forward, crowding her, forcing her back against the solid wood door. When he lowered his head, his intent was clear and so greatly anticipated she found herself reaching out to draw him to her. She hadn't his patience.

The light of the gas-lit wall sconce flickered. She blinked, suddenly struck by their location as they stood in the hallway where anyone could happen upon them.

Her arms stiffened and she pulled her head back. "Wait," she croaked, "what if someone—?"

He dropped a hard kiss on her mouth. Amelia went silent. Raising his hands, he slid his fingers into her chignon, dislodging several pins. His breath was warm against her face, his lips now feathering hers. "This wing of the house is just for non-family members, and Missy considers Cartwright a relation. No one sleeps here but you. But you're right—we need someplace much more private for what I have in mind."

The feel of his fingers tunneling through her hair and stroking her scalp would have had her sliding to the floor if not for the support of his arms.

When his lips finally made contact with hers, there was no pretense. She wanted it, craved it in the most absurd, mindless manner. She didn't wait, couldn't wait for his tongue to find hers, thrusting hers in a relentless search. But he pulled his head back a fraction, making her endure tiny nips to the corners of her mouth, the curve of her chin and the vulnerable line of her neck.

Then she was up in his arms and in her chamber. The heel of his boot kicked the door shut. Amelia tightened her arms around his neck, pulling his mouth down to hers, sealing his in a kiss. The firm, sensuous feel of his lips on hers drew a whimper from her throat. The clash came as tongue and teeth met. A stab of desire so sharp she wanted to wail, beaded her nipples into tight buds, blistering a path down to her center.

The mattress gave way under their combined weight as Thomas laid her in a luxurious spread in the center of the bed. His tongue continued to plunder her mouth, seeking out every nook and crevice in avaricious demand. Amelia angled her head to obtain deeper, more thorough penetration—if such a thing was possible. Sliding her hand from around his neck, she wedged her hands between their torsos to tear at the buttons of his shirt. The need to feel his flesh, warm and hard, beneath her fingertips, drove her.

The loss of his touch was momentary as he sat up and joined in helping her divest him of his clothes with ruthless efficiency.

He wanted her. If his impassioned kisses hadn't made it obvious enough, his erection certainly did. It was stiff and thick, thrusting out from a thatch of dark blond hair. Amelia clamped her thighs together, as if that would prevent the flow of moisture pooling her sex. Then he was straddling her, his erection rubbing against her lower stomach as he made quick work of the buttons of her gown. Staggering pleasure washed over her in inundating waves, making her every breath a pant followed by a gasp.

Her stays, petticoats, chemise, and drawers surrendered to his deft fingers. The feel of him, hard and scorching hot, dragging against her lower belly started a riot within her. She throbbed and pulsed where she wanted him to touch her the most.

"Heaven help me, you're beautiful," he groaned on a

labored breath. His eyes feasted on the soft thrust of her breasts. Cupping both in his hands, he flicked at the tips until she didn't think she could take any more. But she could if she had to. She arched her back to push her breasts firmly into his hand, her body urging him to take ever more liberties. She wanted his mouth there. She craved the feel of his mouth at her breast, licking and sucking on her nipple.

He watched her, his lids heavy with passion and lust. Her hand clasped the nape of his neck and pulled his head down. Thomas needed no further urging, his lips finding the berry tip with unerring accuracy.

"Thomas," she gasped, the band of pleasure tightening within her as she parted her legs to make a space for him there.

He raised his head and the loss of his mouth had her twisting beneath him, searching, wanting, yearning, and then demanding. "Tell me what you want." His voice was a deep rumble, his features contorted by constrained lust.

Amelia responded by thrusting her hips up, sending the tip of his erection to nestle into the patch of hair covering her privates. His groan rent the air. With his mouth still toying, nibbling, then suckling her nipple, his hand scored the smooth indent of her belly down to the notch of her thighs, his fingers urgent and tender as they parted the vulnerable lips of her sex.

She was wet, embarrassingly so. A ragged breath fluttered from her parted lips. Her breaths then just came in short pants. There was no way to fight the pleasure spurring her hips to lift and undulate in this helpless, needy fashion.

Thomas gave her nipple one last lingering lick, twirling his tongue around the berry tip before he made the journey across the flushed quivering skin of her belly, to follow his fingers to the place beckoning him to further delights.

He worked his finger into her small opening and was rewarded with the moisture of her passion. He jerked and rubbed his erection against her thigh as if her wetness further excited him. "God, you're tight. So tight. I hope I can make it," he groaned before his mouth was on her.

He had pleasured her like this the last time, the rasp of his tongue firm and tender and so wildly arousing against her slickened flesh, Amelia wanted to weep with the undiluted pleasure of it. Widening her thighs, she tipped her hips to give him better access to the moist folds. She knew she must look a complete wanton, but the need clawing inside her was enough to overcome years of sexual repression—most of it self-inflicted. With his other hand, he spread her open for her delectation. His tongue found the nub hooded by soft pink flesh, and she was lost. She soared, quivered, and convulsed in the kind of pleasure she had never known existed until Thomas.

Amelia floated back to earth dazed, her body spent. Then Thomas was on his knees, a limp thigh in each hand held wide to receive him. He entered in a single jolting thrust. The fit was snug. He filled her seemingly beyond capacity and had her sex humming back to life. Every push and pull had her body clamoring for more of the same, deeper, harder. He went from slow and excruciatingly long thrusts, her walls contracting and quivering in helpless pleasure, until he was pounding into her.

Pleasure, the likes he had only known in her arms with his cock buried deep inside her, coursed and built in him like a boulder gathering speed down a steep incline. Her head twisted on the pillow, her sapphire eyes glazed. The pace of his thrusts increased and grew more forceful in their demand. The sound of flesh colliding took on a rhythmic, powerful beat in the cool evening air of the bedchamber.

Amelia emitted a high cry and stiffened beneath him, her hips thrust up to take him deeper while she clawed at his back. Thomas welcomed the pleasurable pain that came when her nails finally sank into his shoulders as she found her release in a series of convulsions. Her feminine sheath tightened around his cock, the pressure, the suctionlike pull sending him spiraling over the edge when he could no longer hold off his orgasm. His peak was blissfully prolonged and all consuming, the tumble down nearly frightening in its intensity.

Dropping his head into the crook of her shoulder, he labored to catch his breath while holding her tight in his arms. He sought her lips in a slow open-mouthed kiss, and she returned it with equal amounts of need and want. His cock stirred inside her, and the tilt of her hips and arch of her back indicated she was more than willing and more than ready for him again.

The morning could have arrived amid a sun veiled in darkness, accompanied by frogs, locusts, *and* hail, and still Amelia would have welcomed it with a smile rivaling the light of the sun at its zenith in a cloudless sky.

Thomas. Amelia sighed the sigh of the truly besotted. He'd reluctantly dragged himself from her bed, donned his clothes, and departed her chamber. Of course, before he'd finally left, they'd shared a deep, lengthy good-bye kiss meant to hold them until the next one. The kiss had naturally progressed to the fondling of buttocks, and the nuzzling and suckling of breasts. When it appeared he'd end up right back where he started—the fourth time for the night—sinfully naked and buried between her thighs, he summoned the strength and halted the heated embrace with a muffled curse and a groan.

"If I don't leave now, I never will. And we can't allow your maid or one of the servants to find me here." With a short, hard kiss to her mouth, he'd quickly exited the room.

That had been four hours ago. Yet the anticipation of seeing him again had her wiping damp palms against her skirt just before she entered the breakfast room.

Thomas was there standing in front of the sideboard, in his hand a plate piled high with food. He stopped as soon as he spotted her and treated her to the kind of look that had everyone else in the room turning to watch her.

A wave of heat flooded her face and other places she dared not think of. Ever conscious of her audience, she was brief in her acknowledgement of him: a silent dip of her head. But even as she turned to greet the earl and the countess, she could easily recall the exact shade of green of his waistcoat and trousers, and was envious of the fit of his shirt and jacket over his muscled shoulders, chest, and abdomen. Never had a man stirred her blood so.

"And how did you enjoy your evening?" The earl's question ended abruptly with a grunt of pain. "Why—"

Missy condemned her husband with a sharp look, interjecting smoothly, "Good morning, Amelia." She spoke as if she just hadn't poked him in the side with her elbow—this contact the apparent source of his pain. The countess's reaction suggested she knew exactly how and *with whom* Amelia had enjoyed her evening.

"Good morning, Lord Windmere, Lady—I mean Missy," Amelia corrected upon receiving a look of mock reproach from the countess.

The earl seemed to quickly collect himself, clearly seeing the error of his ways. "And you must address me as James or Rutherford if you prefer, as it is obvious we will become well acquainted." He brought his cup of coffee to his lips, peering over the rim at Thomas, who in turn continued to watch her intently.

"I told you we are an informal lot," Missy chimed in.

Amelia rounded the table to the sideboard, feeling all three pair of eyes boring into her. More than anything, she could feel the heat of Thomas's stare.

When she'd finished serving herself and came to the table, Thomas bounded to his feet, took her plate, placed it at the setting beside his, and seated her himself. Her heart leapt at the combination of his solicitousness and proximity. She inhaled his scent and wondered how she could ever have been adverse to it—adverse to him. It would be a miracle if she survived the day without pouncing upon him like some sexually deprived widow.

To hide her embarrassment, Amelia concentrated intently on her food, never daring to meet Thomas's sidelong glances. If breathing was difficult, eating required Herculean efforts. Thomas had done this to her. Love had done this to her.

"Have you any plans for today, Amelia?" Again, Missy spoke to her as one would an intimate, very familiar and warm. To Amelia, even after such a short acquaintance, something in Missy's manner felt right.

"I—"

"Yes, I plan to take Amelia into town. I thought she would enjoy Windsor's shops, especially during the height of the season," Thomas cut in.

Now she did look at him. He intended they spend the entire day together. Joy gripped her and refused to let go. She grew dizzy with it.

Thomas offered her a half smile. His gaze became hooded when it drifted to her mouth. Her breasts peaked and her skin tingled, her body responding as if it had been a physical touch.

"Yes, I would enjoy that tremendously." She tried to sound not quite so much like an adoring simpleton.

James cleared his throat while Missy unsuccessfully attempted to hide a smile behind her serviette.

"I believe Catherine and Charlotte would enjoy a trip into town. Catherine in particular, for she adores the stores." Missy directed her statement to her brother, a dark eyebrow arched. Amelia understood the look immediately. The countess didn't trust him—them. While at her home they may enjoy their privacy; in public they would be circumspect, adhering to some form of propriety even if it was the chaperone of two sixteen-year-old girls.

A momentary tightening of Thomas's features indicated his chagrin, but he conceded with a curt nod. Obviously they would have to curtail any physical intimacies. Amelia couldn't help a stab of disappointment, her body already impatient for his next caress, his next touch, his next scorching kiss. Today would indeed be a very long day, her mind already on the homecoming. Her only solace was that she'd be spending it in Thomas's company.

An hour and a half later, Amelia, Thomas, and Catherine boarded the black-lacquered brougham. The weather was ideal for their trip. Snow, fluffy and light, lazily circled the air before settling on graveled roads and dormant foliage in a white blanket. Catherine fairly bounced onto the seat, her blue eyes sparkling with excitement. Peering out the window, she exclaimed, "The snow is so pretty."

Thomas took the seat across from them, his gaze flitting to Catherine's pink-cheeked face before returning a steady regard to her. Amelia had to look away. It was all too much. The wanting, the yearning, and not being able to have him at that very moment.

She needed a distraction. "Did your sister not want to come as well?" She thought all girls their age lived for things like shopping, baubles, and whatnot.

Catherine shoved her hands deeper into the muffs, yanking her gaze from a terrain of naked trees with snow-laden branches. Her mouth formed a pout. "She said she'd rather finish her book. But I know it's because Alex is here. Everyone knows it. She does it every time."

Thomas smiled dryly. "And you find this vexing?"

"I think it's terribly silly is all. Alex will never pay her any mind. Anyway, he's much too old for her." With her brows furrowed and her mouth set in a pink line, she resembled a displeased golden-haired Dresden doll.

Amelia could easily see how a young girl like Charlotte could fall for the raven-haired lord. He was dangerous enough to the women of London as the second son, Lord help them all if he had been born heir to the dukedom.

"Not that I am encouraging her, but I once thought the same about Missy and Rutherford. Now look at them. She set her sights on him when she was but ten years of age." Thomas reposed back in the velvet-cushioned seat, his legs splayed negligently, amusement lighting his eyes.

Was that what explained their easy familiarity, the connection between the two a stranger could pick up within seconds of observing them together? A pang of envy shot through her. She couldn't tear her gaze from Thomas, or he from her.

"I just think it's silly," Catherine mumbled, turning back to the window. "Oh!" she cried after a minute pause. "Notice how pretty the street looks."

Amelia reluctantly directed her attention to the scene beyond the window. The carriage was rumbling down a paved road leading to the main street. Not far in the distance, storefronts lined the street, the lampposts gaily decorated with miniature wreaths and shiny red bows, making for the quintessential Christmas tableau.

They spent the next several hours traipsing through almost every shop on Peascod Street. Thomas was solicitous in his attendance, escorting her about like a suitor on his best behavior. That is, save a smoldering glance and the lingering touch here and there that had her already-heightened senses in constant flux. Catherine appeared quite oblivious to it all, chattering on and exclaiming over every pretty trinket and ribbon she saw.

Amelia rarely purchased—or had need to purchase—presents for Christmas. Her father was generous with the servants, ensuring they were amply rewarded in their Christmas boxes. One year, when she was fourteen, she'd taken her allowance and bought a present for Mrs. Smith, their housekeeper, and Reese, their butler, because they had always been so kind to her. They'd both since retired. In respect to her, the marquess treated the day like any other. There were, of course, the token gifts for her bought by whichever governess was currently employed.

This would be the first Christmas since her mother's death that she'd spend with a family. A real family. The thought warmed her insides, flooding her with a sense of joy. Today she would purchase gifts for everyone.

A quiet word to Thomas and he was quickly whisking Catherine off to the nearest pastry shop. She'd told him she needed privacy to select Catherine's gift, which she did. But she also took that time to find something for him.

Amelia soon discovered finding something fitting for her lover was much more difficult than shopping for the others, as she desperately wanted him to like it. Then she spotted a miniature of a ship. Carved from a rich mahogany wood, it was intricately detailed and polished to a low shine. Given his involvement in manufacturing the real ones, this seemed exactly the sort of thing Thomas would like.

After she paid for her purchases, the accompanying footman took them to the carriage while she joined Thomas and Catherine next door.

They wandered the shops for another hour, sending the footman back several times to store their packages in the boot of the carriage. By this time, Amelia's feet began to ache and she was tired and hungry.

As if sensing her growing discomfort and fatigue, Thomas cupped her elbow and asked, "Shall we return home?"

At his touch, the layers of wool and varying weights of cotton could not prevent the spark of desire that shot through her. It was as if she'd spent her entire life unaware, then suddenly to be catapulted head first into stark, teeth clenching awareness.

Amelia turned to Catherine, but mostly to collect herself. "Shall we?"

The young girl nodded. "I can't wait to show Charlotte the hair ribbons I purchased."

"Then we can be off." She dared a glance up at Thomas. His eyes told her what he wanted; he wanted her. It was at that moment something inside her emerged. The reckless, abandoned side that understood the power of her charms. But not only understood it—reveled in it and wanted to flaunt it.

The trip home was silent, save for Catherine recounting their visit to every shop and detailing all the delightful things she saw but didn't have the money to buy, which proved to be quite a list.

Amelia listened to her with one ear, speaking when a response was called for. The rest of her attention focused helplessly on Thomas, meeting his gaze with equal intent, equal desire. If his emerald-green eyes consumed, hers devoured. With Catherine duly occupied and apparently oblivious to what sizzled between her and Thomas, what was the point of hiding it or shying away from it? She'd experienced the power of his passion and returned it in spades. Whatever was happening between them, she never wanted it to stop. This journey was hers for the taking, and she fully intended to take it to wherever it would lead.

Chapter 27

Thomas entered Amelia's bedchamber that evening as if he did so every night. As if it were his right. The entire day he'd spent leashed, exhibiting the control of a saint. He was no damn saint, so that control was all but taxed out.

The fire blazing in the fireplace helped to ward off the cold. Amelia, who sat upright on the canopied bed wearing a pale pink nightdress, her nipples prominent against the silky fabric, made him hot. His cock, which had been in a state of semi-arousal the whole day, roared to life like a steam engine picking up speed.

No longer reticent, she fairly oozed this potent sexuality, her blue eyes half-mast, her desire laid bare for him to see. He couldn't get to her quick enough.

"I never thought tonight would come." If he sounded tortured, it was because he was and had been the entire day. He quickly dispensed with her nightdress to urgently cup her breasts in his hands, squeezing, kneading, and luxuriating in their softness and firmness. He slowly rimmed the nipples with his thumbs.

Amelia's laugh came out sultry and low. "I want you naked." She let out a moan before launching herself into the task of helping him remove his garments. While he hurriedly worked on his shirt buttons, she tackled his trousers, her hands constantly brushing against his rampant erection.

Between urgent caresses and kisses so scorchingly hot he was amazed the mattress hadn't caught afire, they managed to divest him of every single piece of clothing. Only then could he have her underneath him, whimpering and gasping in rapturous delight. Her delectable breasts, her splendid thighs, and the notch there that promised endless gut-wrenching ecstasy, drove him ever onward, reaching for the satisfaction only the summit could bring.

Amelia was lost to everything but the man between her thighs, her body ready, wet, and awaiting the feel of him, hard and hot inside of her. She clutched his sweat-dampened back with both hands, urging him closer. But he pulled back and levered himself up, while keeping his hands bracketing her hips. Strands of blond hair lay plastered against his forehead, his shoulders and chest heaving from passionate exertion.

Widening her thighs for the coming pleasure, Amelia blinked in surprise when his hands, which had been on her hips, moved to her bottom, kneading the giving flesh briefly before carefully flipping her onto her stomach.

Startled, she shot a look over her shoulder, taking in the dark intensity of his expression as he slid a pillow beneath her hips to prop them up. A ragged groan emerged from his throat, and beads of sweat trickled down the sides of his face. His hands urged her thighs wider apart and then cupped, rubbed, and petted her buttocks. Her head dropped limply back onto the pillow. His fingers found her aching, wet sheath. Amelia wanted to wail and scream for more, but could only manage half-tortured sobs. Driving her hips back, her arms reached behind to bring him closer.

In one sharp jerk of his hips, he plunged into her. It was a tight fit, an excruciatingly good fit, a deeper fit than before. His pace increased with each sumptuous thrust. Before long he was pummeling her into oblivion, the peak so intense for a moment she was sure she lost consciousness. A grunt then a long hiss rent air humid with passion and lust signaled his release.

They remained like that, him still buried to the hilt inside her while her sex continued to contract around him, each catching their breaths as they floated down from the euphoria of their climax. When she found the strength, she rolled onto her back and reached for him. He came instantly, embracing her, kissing her as if he never wanted to let her go. Her sleep that night was the best she'd had in years.

Amelia was looking at the perfect tableau of Christmas morning: a family gathered around a beautifully decorated Christmas tree. The countess cradled her daughter in her arms while the earl held their son. Catherine was down on her knees, oohing and aahing over a flounced moss green velvet gown she pulled from a bulky box and held up against her torso. Charlotte, however, Amelia noted, sat perched on one of the nearby armchairs, plucking on the bow of a small box as she sent timorous glances at Lord Alex, who watched the festivities with the indulgence of Father Christmas himself.

"This is for you." Thomas had been digging about under the tree before retrieving a gaily decorated box. This he held out to her, his smile and piercing green eyes both tender and passionate all at once.

He had gotten her a gift. Her throat constricted and her eyes began to burn. *Don't you dare cry.* She wouldn't. She couldn't. Swallowing, she blinked the vaguest notion of tears away and accepted the round box with trembling hands. Their hands brushed. His eyes darkened, and Amelia had to fight to keep her mind in the moment and not think back to last night.

Focus. But her fingers lacked coordination and it took her much longer to open the box than it should have. When she finally did, nestled inside was a stunning sapphire necklace. She gasped and clamped her hand to her mouth. She turned wide eyes up at him. "It's beautiful, but I can't accept this," she whispered, her voice fraught with emotion.

"You most certainly shall." His voice was loving, but his tone indicated this wasn't a fight she would win.

"But everyone will think—"

"Who?" With an eyebrow raised, he briefly scanned the occupants in the room. "These are my family and friends, not strangers. And believe me, Missy and Rutherford wouldn't dare judge our relationship."

Amelia looked again at the necklace. What exactly did a gift like this mean? It wasn't a betrothal ring. Did he want them to continue as lovers? Could she live with that if that's all he was willing to offer?

"Thank you. It's beautiful," she choked. Despite being overwhelmed with emotion, she remained dry eyed, as tears of happiness were something her brain could not comprehend.

"Let me." He stood close, his scent an intoxicant to her senses. His warm breath disturbed the tendrils at her nape. With the ceremony of a formal marriage proposal, he removed the necklace from the box and secured it around her neck. The sapphire was a solid, cool weight against the exposed skin of her chest. The brush of his hands against her neck and shoulders felt more intimate than a kiss and had her heart bursting in restrained jubilation.

She may be many things, and perhaps once or twice he had caused her knees to buckle, and yes, there was the dizzying euphoria that happened all too frequently when he was near, but a female fit to swooning she was *not*. Today, however, she was at risk of doing exactly that if she dared meet his gaze, her composure around him now easier to shake than a dilapidated cabin during a high wind.

Had they been alone, she would have kissed him, but if she allowed herself even a chaste kiss, she'd want more. They'd both want more.

Amelia desperately looked everywhere but at him, feeling the burn of his gaze. Lord Alex's stare captured her attention. His teeth gleamed white against his dark complexion in a lazy smile. He inclined his head as if to acknowledge and approve the new status of her and Thomas's relationship. He then turned and sauntered to Missy's side and relieved her of her daughter.

"You may give me a more appropriate thank you tonight." Thomas's dark, smoky voice promised an evening of untold pleasures, his words conjuring up an image of tangled sheets, bare skin, and a hot furious coupling. A tide of heat washed over her from head to toe. Dear Lord, she really needed to control herself. They still had the entire day to get through before night fell.

"I also have something for you." Amelia left him to ferret out his present from the sea of gift-wrapped boxes under the tree. She returned to his side and handed him the box, only then permitting herself to meet his gaze. His look devoured her.

Thomas accepted the box and wasted no time in opening his gift. He stilled for a long second when he saw the model ship. His gaze flew to hers. The intimacy of that look turned her knees to the consistency of molasses.

"I hope you like it."

Missy, ever curious, had come to her brother's side. She peered into the box. "Oh, how lovely. Finally a ship more scaled to suit you."

Thomas ignored her quip as only a brother could and extricated it from the paper padding. Holding it up, he turned it around slowly several times, admiring the craftsmanship.

It was clear the ship had been carved by expert hands and with loving attention to every detail.

With his goddaughter still in his hands, Alex ventured toward them. "And here Father Christmas brought me only one fat lump of coal. Do tell, Armstrong, what did you do to earn such a jewel?"

Missy tried to muffle her laughter without success.

Thomas didn't so much as blink before replying, "I haven't earned her yet, but I'm hoping that's just a matter of time."

At that precise moment, Amelia conceded she might indeed be exactly the type of woman prone to swoons.

Following supper that evening, the women parted company with the men in the hall, proceeding upstairs to check on the babies. Thomas, Cartwright, and Rutherford filed into the drawing room.

"So, Armstrong, when can we plan for your upcoming nuptials? My calendar tends to become more crowded in the spring." Cartwright, with his unsinkable tact, did not prevaricate but got straight to the point.

Rutherford proceeded to the sideboard to pour the after-supper port without commenting but Thomas could tell by his expression he too awaited his response.

Thomas took a seat on the sofa and regarded Cartwright's arched-brow countenance. "Your schedule doesn't make the slightest difference to me. I'll marry her with or without you in attendance."

"You realize there will be talk. The ton is still abuzz from your infamous public encounter at Lady Stanton's ball."

"Let them talk. In any effect, our betrothal should put to rest any notion that there is any acrimony between us," Thomas replied with a short laugh.

Rutherford advanced toward them and paused by the sofa to hand him and Cartwright their glasses of port.

Thomas accepted his gladly, quickly tipping his head back for a swallow.

Rutherford took a seat in the nearby armchair while Cartwright remained standing, looking suddenly like a rudderless boat. "Bloody hell, it just occurred to me that both of you will be married." He made the final word sound more like some ghastly infection than the state of wedded bliss.

Thomas relished his friend's apparent disgruntlement. "What, afraid you're next?"

Cartwright waved his hand dismissively. "God, that's the last thing on my mind. My father thanks the saints every day he has Charles to carry on the name." And as with every reference to his father, his voice held an acerbic note.

"So when's the long-anticipated proposal to be made? Missy will, of course, insist on having a hand in the preparations."

Thomas regarded his brother-in-law. Rutherford was right. His sister would turn his plans for something simple and small into something worthy of royalty, which meant expeditiousness could only be considered a feeble ray of hope.

"I will speak to Harry once he returns from America."

"A mere formality," Cartwright said with another dismissive wave of his hand.

"Then I say we drink to your upcoming marriage." Rutherford lifted his glass in a toast.

"Hear, hear." Cartwright appeared resigned to the fact he'd now be the lone bachelor left standing.

"To your good fortune," Rutherford said.

"To my good fortune," Thomas echoed clinking his glass with that of his closest friends.

The visit came to a close much too quickly. If Amelia could have made the time in Berkshire stretch another month, she would have done so readily. But with the holidays over, reality crept in. Thomas had a business to attend to, as did Lord Alex and the earl.

In the two weeks of their visit, she and Missy had formed a very close bond. And it wasn't just Missy with whom she felt close, but the entire Rutherford family. That's what made their departure so painful. Having to say good-bye caught and pinched at her heart.

Their trip back to Stoneridge Hall proved as uneventful as crossing the French Riviera in a gondola draped in silken swaths of fabric and sipping the finest champagne in all of France—with a chaperone. Hélène sat quiet yet content beside her, seemingly oblivious to the fact both of the other members of her party wished her anywhere but there. For between she and Thomas existed a chemistry no words could describe. Their intimacy was familiar now and fraught with all the passion and lust between two new lovers. They needn't look at one another to light the spark that had them touching, kissing, and exploring one another. That had happened often enough over the last few weeks.

It was well past ten o'clock in the evening when they arrived at Stoneridge Hall. But despite the late hour, Lady Armstrong, attired in a pale yellow silk supper dress indicating she'd hadn't yet changed to retire for the evening, was there to greet them.

The viscountess's green eyes sparkled and her cheeks were the pink of a gleeful young girl fresh from her first time at the Crystal Palace. It was clear she'd benefitted greatly from her trip to America.

"The girls waited up as long as they could, but the poor dears started nodding off to sleep in the morning room."

Thomas dropped his hand from the small of Amelia's back and advanced toward his mother. They embraced warmly, the viscountess kissing both his cheeks.

"I suppose a 'Happy Christmas' is in order. I gather you enjoyed your trip," he said, drawing back, clasping both her arms in his hands. "I don't think I remember seeing you looking quite so happy. Good Lord, I'll go even so far as to say that I believe you're glowing." His eyes danced with merriment. "Perhaps you met a gentleman during your visit?"

A deep pink heightened the color suffusing his mother's cheeks. "You are even more impertinent than your sisters," the viscountess scolded with a smile. She evaded the teasing question by turning her attention to Amelia.

"Hello, dear, I hope my daughter made you feel at home."

How could one put into words the friendship that had developed between her and Missy? "Missy and James were the most gracious hosts. And the girls made me feel very much a part of the family. And as for your grandchildren, I could wax poetic about them for hours."

The countess took Amelia's gloved hand in hers and gave it several pats. "Well, you might be happy to hear you should be bound for home very soon. Your father returned with us. He's currently at his residence in town. He expects to come and collect you himself."

Amelia's gaze instantly flew to Thomas.

"Harry is in town?" Thomas asked before she could form an appropriate response. He appeared happily surprised.

"Yes, he managed to wrap up his business two days before our ship was due to depart."

Her father. For the first time in years, the thought of him didn't cause the clenching in her chest or anger to rush through her like blood pumps through veins. It was difficult to pinpoint exactly what she was feeling. "I must say I am indeed surprised," she said quite honestly.

"Well, you both must be weary from your travels. I will bid you good night. We will speak in the morning."

"Then I will see Amelia to her bedchambers. Good night, Mother."

"Good night, Lady Armstrong." Amelia was rather cognizant of the speculative look in the viscountess's eyes.

Thomas proceeded to escort her up the stairs, his hand

resting lightly on the small of her back and his eyes surveying her with a possessiveness that thrilled her. His whole manner screamed to the world theirs would be more than an affair. More than lovers meeting behind closed doors with curtained windows, brimming with heat and passion. He'd been treating her as if he was courting her. He'd graced her with flowers, chocolates, and books, many novels, since he'd learned how much she loved them. Amelia didn't think she had felt so near bursting with happiness in her entire life.

At her chamber door she faced him, her tongue sweeping her lips in sweet anticipation of the good-night kiss.

He drew a harsh breath and took a step back. "If I kiss you now, I won't stop. I simply don't know how to have you in doses anymore."

"I don't want you to stop." Her breath emerged a faint rasp. She promptly closed the distance between them, her hands lifting to encircle his neck.

"Amelia." He groaned and clamped her arms back down to her sides. "My mother and sisters are in residence."

"Then let's go to your room."

"We can't," Thomas said, but his eyes said he very much wanted to.

"Why not? You certainly displayed no such reticence at your sister's home," she whispered, reaching up to nuzzle his throat. She loved the feel of his bristled jaw against her flesh.

His eyes closed briefly as he let out another groan. "Believe me, I'm beyond tempted." Grasping her hips in his hands, he brought her hard against the ridge of his erection.

Liquid heat coiled low in her belly as a dampness formed between her thighs. It had been less than twenty-four hours since she had him last, yet here she was rubbing against his hardness like a female in heat.

"Missy was no innocent when she wed Rutherford, and as much as I care for Charlotte and Catherine, they're not *my* sisters. So out of respect for my mother and my innocent sisters, we truly should not." Thomas's voice wavered on the last four words.

Amelia knew she could press her advantage if she chose. It was clear he was just as vulnerable as she to what flared hot between them, but his reasons managed to do what a bucket of cold water could not—prick her conscience. His actions spoke of high integrity and morals while her lack of thought to his family indicated the true wanton she'd become.

Slowly, she stepped away from the solid warmth of his body. His hands lingered at her waist, as if reluctant to let her go, before dropping to his sides.

"Then I shall see you in the morning," she said softly.

His eyes darkened and he clenched his hands in a fist. For a moment it appeared he might change his mind. Instead, he stroked the crest of her cheek with his thumb. "Dream of me," he murmured darkly.

That was like directing a fish to swim or a bird to fly. Dreaming of him was inevitable, as if preordained before the beginning of time. All Amelia could do was nod. She cast him one final longing glance before entering her bedchamber and closing the door, leaving her greatest temptation standing silent and still on the other side.

Chapter 28

The day after their arrival back at Stoneridge Hall and only one month since the first occurrence, Thomas found himself in the unenviable situation of being forced to deal with Louisa once again. (He'd thank his mother for that later, as she could have turned the duchess's footman away at the door). Appearing at his home unannounced breached all levels of decency and respect. The woman's audacity knew no bounds.

They adjourned to the library, and he chose to remain standing, regarding her without the veil of societal politeness. Louisa, who appeared the picture of tranquility, took a seat in a blue balloon chair near the fireplace.

"You have precisely ten minutes of my time." He was in love and soon to be married. He could afford to be generous as Amelia was currently occupied in the morning room with his sisters, listening to Emily practice the piano.

"My, you have become so cold. Please don't tell me I am responsible for your lack of manners." She wore the smile of a woman who truly thought much too much of herself and her vaunted appeal to the opposite sex. Why hadn't he seen that tendency in her seven years ago?

"Don't flatter yourself as nothing could be further from the truth. Just be happy I granted you an audience." He turned and strode over to the sideboard. With a sharp tug, he uncorked the top from the crystal decanter, then snagged a glass and poured himself a drink. One it was apparent he would require to get through the next ten minutes.

Louisa rose gracefully to her feet and rounded the center table. "Does the forsaking of niceties mean I shan't be offered a drink?"

Thomas turned to face her and watched as she drew closer, a pout on her red lips. He preferred pink lips. Deep pink. Amelia's delicious mouth. "I don't expect you'll remain long enough to enjoy it."

"How cruel you are," she chided mildly. "God only knows why I made this journey. It's fortunate I have a house in Somerset as it appears I'll also find you lacking in hospitality." She halted in front of him, her full skirts brushing his trousers. A scent accosted his nostrils. Overbearingly florid and sweet, much like its owner.

"Yes, so I'm sure you don't want to keep me in suspense any longer," he responded dryly. Eager to put a distance between them, he stepped around her and made his way to the sitting area and took a seat in an armchair farthest from where she'd recently sat.

Undaunted and not to be outmaneuvered, Louisa followed and took up a spot on the adjacent sofa. "I thought of you often over the years, you know. I thought of what married life would have been like with you. I used to imagine that Jonathon was yours."

She had a son? That was the first he'd heard of him. A life with Louisa would have been a disaster, but a child to tie him to her for life would have been an unmitigated catastrophe. He gave a silent prayer of thanks to his father for mismanaging the estates and leaving him penniless. If not for that, his youthful folly might well be the albatross that was the Duchess of Bedford.

"Actually, your betrothal to your duke was the best thing that could have happened to me."

The duchess's brows furrowed, and her mouth became a tight line of displeasure. Finally, a glimpse of the real woman under all that burgundy and black velvet. "I see I'm not going to be able to reason with you." Her tone had adjusted accordingly, now carrying the tartness of lemons. "Which really is a shame given what I've learned. I'm certain it's information that would interest you greatly."

"I sincerely doubt you have anything to say that I want to hear—that is except good-bye, adieu, or adios. Any language will do fine as long as you mean it," he said dryly.

Her brown eyes glinted unpleasantly, giving her visage a hard, sinister look. "Oh, I do believe this will be of some interest to you. It has to do with your mother's houseguest, the Marquess of Bradford's daughter."

Although Thomas's senses instantly sprang into awareness at her mention of Amelia, he made certain he exhibited no outward reaction. "Then do tell." He issued the invitation easily before taking a swallow of his drink.

Louisa's smile instantly reappeared. "Somehow I sensed that particular subject matter would be of interest to you. Although I must warn you, you might not be pleased with what I'm about to divulge."

"I'm not naïve enough to imagine you've traveled all the way to Devon to bring me *good* tidings of Lady Amelia."

"Well, I feel it is my duty to warn you the young lady under your roof has a reputation. While it's not public knowledge, she's been quietly linked to several gentlemen. The first is—if you can believe this—the son of some tradesman in one of the shires. A tradesman, of all things!" She paused for his response. After it was apparent none would be forthcoming, she continued. "And ever so recently, Lord Clayborough. And by linked, I mean in the same manner we were once linked."

"Is that so?" Thomas drawled, hiking up an eyebrow.

Louisa appeared nonplussed by his reaction. For a moment, she sat utterly still, her brows furrowed and mouth pursed. But dogged in her purpose, she charged on. "Yes indeed. I'm told the marquess has managed to thwart her marriage efforts so far. Regardless, it's quite obvious her innocence is little more than an illusion, although I'm certain the marquess paid a princely sum to keep these incidents hushed up."

Thomas smiled wryly. A princely sum would have been required to settle Clayborough's debts, that was for certain. He knew in reference to Cromwell, Harry had threatened to sponsor a law that would greatly increase the taxes for companies doing business overseas, thus curtailing the senior Cromwell's profits from his factories.

"And just what should all of this information mean to me?" *You scheming wretch.* How low would she sink? he wondered idly.

Louisa shifted in her seat as if uncertain how exactly she should deal with his response—or more aptly, lack thereof. Several seconds passed in silence as she watched him intently. He in turn watched her with bored disinterest. And then quite abruptly, she tipped her chin.

"Well, I would imagine if such a thing were to become public . . ."

Thomas had never heard a voice so softly cunning or so ruthlessly self-serving. "Did you come here to make threats, Your Grace, or will that be the happy result of your call?"

"My dear Thomas, I can't think why you would think that of me," she said, sounding suitably aghast. "I was speaking of other people who might already have this information. You know how the ton loves a scandal."

Thomas drained the rest of his rum before pushing to his feet. "Your Grace, if this is the reason for your call, you've made it in vain. Now I'm going to bid you farewell and pray I will never see you at my residence again."

Louisa bolted to her feet in a violent clash of velvet and brocade, staring up at him through narrowed eyes. "Do you understand she'll be ruined?"

"The ton will have enough to gossip about when our engagement is announced."

Louisa blanched, splaying her hand against the base of her neck. "Good God, you actually intend to marry the girl?"

"Not only do I intend to wed her, but I will challenge anyone who dares question her innocence. I can assure you with 100 percent certainty that no man has laid a hand on her."

A savage glint of understanding lit her eyes. "If you think I'm going to believe—"

"I truly don't give a whit what you believe. Now I *believe* your ten minutes elapsed one minute ago." He turned and motioned for her to take her leave just as the library door opened.

"Thomas, I—" Amelia halted at the sight of the woman standing at Thomas's side. "Excuse me, I wasn't aware you had company." *Certainly not such beautiful* female *company*, she thought with a pang of jealousy as she turned to leave.

"No, Amelia, please stay. Her Grace was just leaving." There was a hardness in his tone that made the latter a command not a statement of fact.

Her Grace? This time, Amelia gave the woman a more probing look. She vaguely recalled mention that the Duchess of Bedford had returned from France. All reports claimed she was blond, young, and beautiful. That would be an apt description of the woman standing before her.

"Truly, Thomas, you have all the manners of a dock worker. Are you not going to introduce us?" The duchess chided him with a smile but surveyed Amelia with a coldness in her eyes that conveyed anything but congeniality toward her.

Amelia stiffened. Women had subjected her to those

kinds of looks before. However, this time was different. Thomas was hers. Duchess or not, this woman hadn't a right to regard her as one would assess an unwanted rival for a gentleman's affections.

"Yes, Thomas, I believe an introduction is in order," Amelia replied, walking toward them. She stopped at his side and curled her hand intimately around his forearm. *Mine.* The gesture couldn't be mistaken for anything but proprietorial.

"Lady Amelia, the Duchess of Bedford. Your Grace, Lady Amelia Bertram." Thomas's voice was filled with restrained laughter. She was glad he found this so amusing.

The duchess inclined her head but just barely. Without removing her hand from Thomas's, Amelia curtsied, also just barely.

"If you'll excuse me, love, I was just seeing Her Grace out." Taking Amelia's hand in his, he brought it up to his mouth and kissed the inside of her wrist. "I'll be but a moment."

The duchess inhaled an outraged breath. Amelia barely heard her, for the feel of his lips on her skin started her senses rioting.

Thomas then hustled the blond woman out of the room, his every move sharp and impatient as if he had much better things to do. The duchess bore the indignity with the regality of a queen in the process of losing her crown: in stalwart silence while she undoubtedly plotted her revenge.

"What was that all about?" Amelia asked the moment Thomas reappeared in the library several minutes later.

After firmly closing the door, he sauntered toward her wearing a wicked grin on his face. "I could ask the same. I got the distinct impression you just stamped me your private property."

Amelia didn't refute his claim as that had been her intention. "I want to know why the Duchess of Bedford looked as if she would like nothing better than to see me an ocean away on some frozen tundra or in a tropical rain forest."

Upon reaching her, Thomas slowly enveloped her in the warmth of his embrace. "I don't want to waste another moment on the subject of the duchess. Suffice it enough to say she is someone of no relevance to you or me. Hopefully, we have seen the last of her," he murmured as he nuzzled the ultra-sensitive spot behind her ear.

Weakly, Amelia twisted her head trying to dislodge his mouth. "Don't try to-to distract me, Thomas. . . ." His name ended on a moan when he nipped her neck with his teeth then proceeded to soothe the spot with his tongue.

Perhaps he took pity on her, reduced as she was to gasps and whimpers of pleasure, for he raised his head and regarded her somberly. "I swear to you, she is nothing to me. A folly of my youth, nothing more. Since her return to England, I hadn't seen her for seven years. God, Amelia, you must know by now I love you and only you."

Amelia's breath stilled, all thoughts of the duchess forgotten. Dazed, she wondered if she'd heard him correctly. Then he was kissing her, sucking her into a maelstrom of passion. *Oh, Thomas, I love you too,* she yearned to say but she found the words impossible to say aloud. She gave herself up to his kisses, his touch, and the promise of more to come. She'd confess her love to him later. Yes, very soon. Perhaps, after the kiss.

Chapter 29

"Mademoiselle, the baron is here!" Hélène's panicked voice penetrated Amelia's bemused thoughts.

As it was, Amelia didn't confess her feelings to Thomas after the kiss, which had quickly escalated to intimate touching and heavy fondling. Thomas had halted it before it had burned out of control. After they parted company at the bottom of the stairs, their bodies still throbbing with unfulfilled desire, she took herself off to her chamber to rest until the evening meal.

"The who?"

"Lord Clayborough. 'E is 'ere. Out there." Her hand gestured wildly at the window.

"But—" Amelia broke off. Lord Clayborough was at Stoneridge Hall? Good Lord, why? Then she recalled one of the last things she said to him when she was in town. *Next time don't require a written invitation. You know where I am.* Well, this was a fine time for him to start listening to her.

Lord, that time felt like eons ago, the events happening to a different woman at another time in her unhappy life. She wasn't that woman any longer, and she hadn't wanted to marry the baron for some time now. Blast, she should have written him the moment she'd realized. Now he was here—at Thomas's home. A wave of terror swept over her. Good

Lord, if Thomas were to discover . . . With ruthless calculation, she squashed further such thoughts. She had to think. She needed to find a way out of this miserable situation.

"And you saw him where?"

"I-I, um, well, Johns was showing me the grounds before it got too dark, and 'e saw us near the groundskeeper's house. 'E's zare now." A blush painted Hélène's face red as she lowered her gaze.

Another time Amelia would have found her maid's discomfiture at having to explain her tryst with one of the footmen amusing, but now wasn't that time.

Think, Amelia, think. Dare she risk meeting with him now? Or worse yet, dare she not? She thought of Thomas and knew her future happiness hinged on what she did now.

Everyone had turned in for the evening, and ten or fifteen minutes was all the time she needed to send Lord Clayborough on his way. No doubt, he would be disappointed, but it was not as though they were a love match.

"I'll need my cloak." The decision made, Amelia wanted nothing more than an expeditious ending to the entire affair with Lord Clayborough.

Thomas couldn't sleep, which came as no great surprise to him. After the kiss in the library, it was a small miracle he could walk upright. He'd existed in a state of semi-arousal for the remainder of the evening.

Supper had been an exercise in self-control. Food was necessary and food could be pleasurable, but never had he imagined it could be sensual as well. But then he'd never watched Amelia joyously consume a dish while imagining what it would be like to have her lips wrapped around him. The sight of her savoring the chocolate-dipped strawberry had made him harder than a poker iron. A veritable feast for the palate indeed.

They'd parted company at her bedchamber door, his

control too tenuous for even a chaste kiss on the cheek. To touch her would have been the height of foolishness, given his noble intention not to forsake his mother and sisters and screw her blind.

An hour later, however, as he lay in his bed nursing an unflagging erection, his bed linens in disarray, he was having second, third, and fourth thoughts about the hindrance that was his moral code, which was keeping him from her bed. After all, he was going to marry her. Theirs wasn't some torrid, illicit love affair. And, of course, they would be discreet. His mother and sisters would never know, for they occupied bedchambers in a different wing.

Decision reached and conscience sufficiently appeased, Thomas bolted from his bed. He snatched up his dressing robe from the footboard and exited the room.

Ten minutes later, Thomas paused at the library window to adjust his bearings. The anticipation that had coiled his insides to knots, now unfurled like tentacles of concern. Where was she? He'd gone to her room and found it empty. He'd then searched the study and library, morning and dining rooms, his worry increasing by the half minute. Even the billiards room—a space she'd rarely ever ventured into—received a thorough inspection. But again, that effort too proved fruitless.

He'd returned to the library on the off chance he'd crossed paths with her somewhere. She loved reading in the window seat overlooking the back. As he stared out that same window, his mind racing, his thoughts occupied, a movement outside caught his peripheral vision. A moment later, a figure emerged from a copse of dogwood to the left of the groundskeeper's lodgings.

From the light of the full moon Thomas could make out the form. *Amelia*. Air rushed from his lungs in relief. He'd recognize her dressed in burlap from a mile away. Since the groundskeeper's house was set back not far from the main house, his current position gave him an eagle's view of the area in play.

As quickly as relief had soothed his mounting concern, another figure—this one definitely male—joined her. The man's head was bent down close to hers, their conversation intimate. These certainly weren't two people exchanging polite pleasantries.

Thomas saw the kiss occur as if wrapped in a dream. None of it seemed real. The man moved in closer until his lips touched hers. One, two seconds passed before she jerked her head back, glanced hurriedly around, and then grabbed him by the sleeve and pulled him back behind the shelter of the dogwood.

"Sir."

Thomas turned with a start at his butler's voice, observing him through a mist of red-hot anger and the green tint of jealousy. Alfred stood tall and straight at the library threshold, his expression graver than usual.

"A problem, Alfred?" Thomas was frankly surprised by his calm tone when a voice inside him was raging out of control.

"Sir, one of the servants has discovered an empty carriage on the property. It is behind the trees near the pond. How would you like me to proceed? Should I alert the constable?"

Thomas processed the butler's words like a drowning man taking in mouthfuls of water, flailing about only now realizing he didn't know how to swim. But while his eyes might deny the scene he'd just witnessed, his mind couldn't deny the facts pointing to Amelia's obvious betrayal. The only question now was, who was he this time? *Treacherous, lying, witch.*

"The horses?"

"Yes, still there, sir, both tied to a tree."

Thomas nodded slowly. "I will deal with it."

His normally stoic butler appraised him with raised

brows and wide eyes. His look of bafflement was gone a moment later. "As you wish, sir." Alfred pivoted on his heel to go, then paused and turned back to him. "Sir, would you like the lamps lit?"

Both figuratively and literally, Thomas stood shrouded in darkness. He'd been too impatient to light the lamps when he'd thrown open the doors to find the room empty and silent.

"No, I'm on my way out," he said but didn't move except to stare out the window again.

Alfred exited as quietly as he'd appeared. She was planning to leave him. Tonight. There could be no other explanation for the scene he'd just witnessed, no other explanation for the presence of the coach on his property.

While the future he'd envisaged with Amelia crashed down around him in fitting apocalyptic fashion given their introduction the prior year, she emerged from behind the bush and began hurrying up the path leading to the servants' door at the back.

Thomas turned and strode from the room, intent on being there to greet her.

Chapter 30

The doorknob gave way beneath Amelia's grasp as the door opened with an abruptness that left her struggling to retain her balance. Her gloved hands found the frame of the door.

Her gaze flew to the opening. Thomas stood framed in the doorway, his eyes a Siberian winter and granite hard.

Amelia gasped. "Thomas." His name was all she could manage with her throat constricted and her mouth suddenly dry.

"Rather late to be out in the cold." His tone held no particular inflection, but his eyes could cut glass.

Amelia shivered, from both an icy gust of wind and his steady, deliberate regard. He, on the other hand, appeared impervious to the outside elements, his stance wide-legged and his hands at his side.

"Who is it this time? Someone new or are you reverting back to your old favorites, Cromwell or Clayborough?" He spoke as if they were exchanging pedestrian pleasantries.

Amelia opened her mouth, but nothing resembling speech emerged. The air prickled the flesh beneath her coat. Nervously, she stepped forward, half expecting him to bar her, but he moved aside to permit her entrance. Once in the drafty, dimly lit alcove, she pulled the door closed behind her.

"Who was it?" he asked again softer.

"I—it's not what you—"

"I saw you, so please don't insult my intelligence." A faint growl now threaded the accusation in his tone. "Or if you'd prefer, I can have one of my men stop him before he makes it off the premises. I believe trespassing is a crime."

Tell him the truth, a strident voice inside her commanded. *Please understand. Please understand.* "It was Lord Clayborough." She gulped. "But I sent him away," she hastened to add. "He still believed that we—well, that we would be married."

At the baron's name, Thomas remained motionless, his expression impenetrable. "And why would he believe such a thing?"

Because I was too stupid and too giddy in love with you to give him a second thought, much less write and inform him of my change of feelings. "We haven't corresponded since Lady Forsham's ball. He assumed nothing had changed."

"So you're telling me he snuck onto my grounds against your wishes and without an invitation?"

Tell him the truth, the voice continued to chant. Like an idiot, she blindly, desperately followed its directive. "Not precisely. What I—"

"Did you or did you not give him leave to trespass on these premises?"

One tiny little lie would settle the issue. But the last thing she wanted was to lie to him. "I may have done so, but not in the manner as it appears. I—"

Again, he didn't give her an opportunity to finish, a chance to mount her defense. "I'll expect you to be packed and gone by tomorrow."

It took a moment for Amelia to comprehend what he had said, what she had heard, before a crippling pain seared her heart, nearly sending her to her knees. "Thomas, please allow me to explain," she implored. Reaching out, she touched the sleeve of his dressing robe.

He jerked his arm from her as if he could scarcely bear her touch. "Tomorrow."

The single word sentenced her to a bleak and empty future. A life without him.

Her gaze slid helplessly over him, taking in his strong, tall frame, tousled golden hair, and shadowed jaw. Silently, she cursed Lord Clayborough for his less-than-impeccable timing, Thomas for his hard-nosed stubbornness, but mostly herself for thinking she could deal with the issue without involving Thomas.

"I don't love him. I never did. Since the ball, I knew I could not marry him. I want to be with you. Please don't make me leave," she said, sounding pitiable and dejected. What she yearned to say was, *I love you*, but the words were still too foreign to her tongue.

He didn't respond immediately. Instead, he perused her from her boot-shod feet up to her wind-rumpled coiffure. "You let him kiss you." His words were a searing accusation, brimming with checked vehemence.

"He did so against my wishes." And no one had been more surprised at his impassioned gesture than her. She'd put a halt to the kiss as soon as she'd gathered her scattered wits.

"Tomorrow I want you gone." His tone was unyielding.

"Thomas, you can't mean to—"

"Very well, then stay." Without further ado, he turned and walked away.

It was only as he rounded the corner to the main corridor that Amelia was wrenched from her state of dazed confusion. Had he in fact acquiesced?

Instinctively, she made a move to follow him but halted after the first step. She watched him disappear from sight. Tonight nothing she said could penetrate his anger. Even a verbal declaration of her love would be ill received.

Clutching her coat around her shivering form, she made her way up the servants' staircase directly ahead and finished the circuitous route to her bedchamber without hearing or seeing a soul.

Thomas would be of a calmer mindset tomorrow. And if not by tomorrow, the day after. Certainly by then he'd be willing to listen to her. It was that fervent prayer that finally lulled her into a fitful sleep.

Amelia found only the viscountess in the breakfast room the following morning. She sat at the head of the table, sipping from a porcelain cup. At her entrance, Lady Armstrong lowered the cup and set it on the table.

"Good morning, Lady Armstrong." Amelia greeted her politely. Too politely given their past closeness.

The viscountess watched her intently, a faint line marring her forehead. "Thomas has returned to London."

Amelia shuddered to a stop while everything shattered about her like glass hitting a marble floor. Her eyes began to burn and breathing became a chore.

"He's gone?" she choked, sounding like a half-wit lost in the maze of the Royal Gardens.

Lady Armstrong rose quickly from her chair and came to her side, her expression a mixture of pity and concern. "Did something occur between the two of you last evening?"

Amelia was too stupefied to respond. She had anticipated many things from him—silence, coldness, anger, and perhaps even scorn—but not this. Never this.

Because she had refused to leave, he had. Just like that. Without a hint of forewarning. She had convinced herself that his, *Very well, then stay*, had meant he would eventually give her a chance to explain. But now he was gone. He had finished with her not long after she'd discovered she couldn't imagine her life without him. The irony made her stomach roil.

"I no longer have an appetite. If you'll excuse me, Lady

Armstrong, I think I'll return to my chamber," Amelia whispered hoarsely.

The viscountess placed a restraining hand on her arm. "My dear, are you sure you don't want to tell me—"

Amelia pulled her arm away and shook her head vigorously and then violently. "No, no, I just need to lie down. If you'll excuse me." She then hurried from the room and back up to her bedchamber where she could mourn her loss, dry-eyed and in private.

Three days after Thomas left, and on the third day of Amelia's self-imposed imprisonment in her bedchamber, the viscountess personally informed her she had a caller awaiting her in the drawing room. She revealed nothing of the man's identity, telling Amelia the gentleman in question wanted it so.

Upon hearing the news, Amelia's heart nearly burst from her chest until reality doused her faint flicker of hope. The viscountess would not be coy with her if Thomas had returned home.

Her thoughts then flew to Lord Clayborough, but he too she dismissed swiftly. Their last encounter hadn't left any room for doubt as to her feelings, or in regard to him, the lack thereof. And after he'd bitterly bemoaned the amount of time he'd spent courting her with money he could ill afford, she very much doubted he'd make the trek to Devon again.

Amelia entered the drawing room not knowing who or what to expect. Perhaps Thomas had sent Lord Alex or James to speak with her. The sight of her father sitting in the leather armchair dashed all her hopes.

He came to his feet. "Amelia." He spoke her name softly, almost reverently, which was most unlike her father. He was normally all briskness and business.

"Hello, Father." She addressed him without feeling her

usual rancor or indifference. Somewhere, somehow, much of that was gone.

The marquess came forward, his arms reaching out to her before falling limply to his sides as if the incongruity of the gesture had just occurred to him.

In appearance, he was impeccable, his garments the finest money could buy, but his face looked drawn and older than his years.

"You look well."

He was lying. She knew she didn't look the closest thing to well. Lack of sleep had produced unbecoming circles under her eyes and she was pale. But she wouldn't argue the point.

"Have you come to take me home?" she asked casually, as she walked over to the fireplace.

"Do you want to come home?"

Amelia shot him a look over her shoulder. When had her father ever asked her . . . well anything really?

"Do I have a choice in the matter?"

"Lady Armstrong would very much like you to remain until after her winter ball."

Grateful, she nodded and said nothing. She wanted to remain until Thomas returned home.

"I saw Thomas yesterday," he said in an abrupt change of topics. The gravity of his tone indicated it hadn't been a happy encounter.

Amelia's pulse leapt at the mention of Thomas's name. She quickly schooled her expression and said, "Yes, I imagined you would."

"He seems to believe I have neglected you over the years."

This time Amelia whipped around to face him. "He told you that?"

Her father, the Marquess of Bradford, an aristocrat among aristocrats, briefly shifted his gaze as if he found it hard to look her directly in the eye.

"He insinuated something of the sort and then gave me a

dressing-down for neglecting to inform him you had scarlet fever as a child." He raised his gaze to hers, and she could see from the stern set of his jaw, he'd been offended by the charge. "That is why I am here. Why I *had* to come."

Amelia stood silently reeling over the notion that Thomas had dressed down the marquess because of her. But in the same time it took hope to flicker in her heart again, it was snuffed out just as quickly.

Over the course of the last few months, she had learned many things about Thomas Armstrong: he could be a formidable foe, was fiercely loyal to those lucky enough to have gained his affection, and possessed a streak of integrity the breadth, depth, and length of the Atlantic Ocean itself. Undoubtedly, the latter trait had prompted his outburst. He'd been advocating for the thirteen-year-old girl she'd been then, not the woman she had become. The woman he now despised.

". . . and it was only when I wrote to Reese did I learn the truth. He admitted he and Mrs. Smith kept your illness from me. Although I understand why they doubted that I could deal with it so soon after the loss of your mother, I should have been consulted."

He emitted a dark, harsh laugh and shook his head in bewilderment. "I would have only learned about it if they thought you were going to die. How could they imagine I wouldn't have suffered a thousand deaths to know you died alone . . . without me?" His voice was rife with emotion as the final two words caught in his throat.

With her ears now attuned to his every utterance, Amelia had long gone motionless. The seeds of everything she'd believed about her father had grown and flourished from that one incident. And over the years, she'd watered and tended them, creating roots so strong and entrenched, nothing short of a tornado would dislodge her mind from the fallacy.

"But—but . . ." Words as well as coherent thought failed her.

"I may be many things, that I will admit, but I pray you

don't believe me capable of leaving you to fight scarlet fever without me. I implore you to write to Reese if you're not convinced. He can substantiate everything I've said."

Amelia shook her head slowly. She didn't need to write to Reese. Her father had that desperate look in his eyes, as if her belief in him was the culmination of a year's dream. He wasn't lying.

"I believe you," she said softly.

His shoulders rose and fell as he heaved a long, ragged sigh of relief. For several seconds, he gazed upon her with a tenderness in his eyes she'd never seen. Reaching out, he placed his hand on her arm. She didn't pull away but received his touch like poultice on a long-festering sore.

"A girl needs her mother and you were no exception. When she died, I-I was a wholly inadequate substitute. Looking back now, I can see I acted selfishly, too locked in my own prison of misery. There was hardly enough room in there for me, much less you. You needed—deserved much better than me."

"I needed my one remaining parent, and that was you." For years she'd suppressed the truth, but now she wanted to stop hiding and pretending. She was tired of the fortress of stone she'd erected around herself.

A forlorn smile curved his mouth. "My greatest cross to bear was that you reminded me of her. Your mother. And those months after her death, I couldn't bear any reminders of her. I wanted to lose myself in a world that held no connection with our life together. Heavens, I remember you used to look up at me as if expecting me to make everything all right when I was barely holding onto my sanity."

For the first time in her life, Amelia felt the depth of her father's grief at the loss of his wife. All her young life she'd seen him as a father, infallible and indestructible. But he had also been a husband who had probably lost a piece of himself when the woman he loved had passed away. And his grief was compounded, not relieved, with a living, breathing reminder of that inconsolable loss. Her throat locked up, making speech impossible.

"But that is no excuse for how I handled your upbringing. After your illness, you became distant and cold. I should have known it was more than your mother's death. I should have pressed harder. However, I'm embarrassed to say, I was relieved that you were no longer looking to me for answers or for comfort. Thomas's problems—financial issues— I could solve. With you, as I said, I was ill-equipped, ill-prepared, and wholly inadequate."

Thomas. The sound of his name burned her ears; memories of him tore at her weak and battered heart. "I always believed you loved Thomas more than you did me."

Her father looked stricken in the ensuing silence. Slowly, he raised his hand to gently cup her cheek. "If you fail to believe anything else I say, believe me when I say I love you above all others." He then pulled her close, and she stood pliant as he enfolded her into his arms. It had been so long since he'd held her like this. Soon, she was returning his embrace, holding onto him tighter as time progressed.

A minute later, he drew back and held her at arm's length. "I will endeavor to make it up to you. All of it."

Amelia smiled tremulously. "I'd rather we start fresh."

Pulling her to him again in a brief hug, he said, "A fresh start it will be."

What Amelia wouldn't give to hear those same words from Thomas.

Chapter 31

Thomas should have breathed a sigh of relief when he crossed the threshold of Stoneridge Hall; instead he felt the emptiness of knowing Amelia was gone.

It had been three weeks and four days since he'd seen her. Midnight would add yet another day to the crawling total.

Harry had taken her home, back to Fountain Crest. His letter informing Thomas of this had arrived at his residence in London three days before. It was a timely departure as his mother's winter ball was set for this evening. At least he wouldn't have to see her.

"Thomas, you are late," his mother said as she coasted toward him, her chartreuse taffeta and tulle gown floating about her. She kissed his cheek in the manner of a mother affectionately admonishing her offspring.

"Good evening, Mother." He wanted to protest he wasn't that late. In fact—he glanced around—he appeared to be one of the first people there.

"I have so many little things to tend to before the guests begin to arrive and every one of the servants is occupied. Dear, would you mind terribly if I asked you to check about the place for the punch bowl. I've mislaid it somewhere, I simply cannot remember where. Oh, and you can store your coat in there. I have no idea where all the footmen could have gone."

Thomas glanced around, noting the frenzy of activity in the brightly lit Stoneridge Hall. It appeared his mother had emptied the biggest local candle shop of its inventory.

"You might want to start with the library. I believe I went in there earlier for some reason or another." She finished with a motherly pat on his hand, before turning and hurrying toward the ballroom.

With his great coat draped over his forearm, Thomas strode down the corridor to the library. It too was brightly lit although the curtains were closed. He walked over to the brown leather armchair. His coat fell to the floor at the same time his mouth fell open in dull surprise.

A wide-eyed Amelia stared at him from the sofa. She looked ravishing in a lavender gown, the neckline leaving an expansive amount of creamy skin on display. And that was all it took after over three long weeks to make him hard. And then angry with her, but more with himself for his lack of control.

"Thomas." She whispered his name like a prayer come true.

His heart slammed against his chest. "I was told you were gone," he said coldly, as he bent and scooped his coat from the floor.

The light in her eyes dimmed. "I can't imagine who would have told you such a thing," she said, coming to her feet.

"Your father." And idiot that he was, he'd believed him. He should have known. Damn, he should have known. Harry Bertram had proven to be a premier manipulator.

"By any chance, have you seen my mother's punch bowl?"

Amelia shook her head, giving him a blank-eyed stare.

You might want to start with the library. I believe I went in there earlier for some reason or another.

And it appeared his mother was in line to assume his mantle should Harry ever relinquish it.

"Then my business here is done." He bowed deeply and turned to go.

"Thomas, please. May I speak with you?" He'd heard Amelia plead but once. He discovered the second time made it all that harder to deny her.

He halted but kept his back to her. While his traitorous heart urged him to go to her, his pride willed him to continue on his way. He'd told her he loved her and she'd said nothing. His pride—as always—won the battle. At the door, he heard a muffled noise that sounded like a sob. But that was impossible because Amelia never cried. Never allowed herself to give in to the weakness of tears.

Once standing outside the library door, he saw he was still in possession of his coat.

"You will go back in there and speak with that girl."

The viscountess's presence several feet away startled him. The tone of her voice even more so. It had been a long time since she'd reprimanded him with such rank censure.

"I've spoken all I care to, to Amelia. And I beg you to keep out of my personal affairs. I manage them quite fine without either yours or her father's interference." Rarely was he forced to speak to his mother in this manner, but then rarely did she give him cause.

She approached him, her mouth set in a line of disapproval. "I don't know what crime Amelia has committed to cause you to treat her this way, nor do I really care to. What I do know is that for almost a month she's become a shadow of the girl who returned from your sister's home. She mopes about the place like a lost soul. She jumps every time someone comes to call because she believes it might be you returning home. She looks haunted every time your name is mentioned. If not for her sake or your own, then go back and talk to her for my sake. Listen to her. Perhaps you'll see sense enough to lower that pride of yours."

Thomas wasn't sure for whose sake he turned and reentered the room, but he did.

* * *

Amelia's throat locked up, and the corners of her eyes stung. She heaved in another painful sob. But her eyes remained dry.

After another minute of grieving the death of her hopes, Amelia rose to take her leave when the door opened and Thomas strode in, halting by the table of spirits. Without glancing at her, he poured himself a drink, downing it in one swallow. Only after he'd placed the empty glass back on the table, did he turn to regard her.

Amelia longed to sink back onto the stability of the chair, but as it was, he was peering down at her, his green eyes glacial and narrowed, his mouth a slash under his nose. So she remained standing, her hands clammy and cold.

"I returned at my mother's urging," he stated coldly.

"Thank you," she whispered hoarsely.

The room went silent.

"I'm waiting," he said, impatience and a trace of anger in his voice.

Lord, he was going to make her crawl—not that she believed it would do much good. "My father was here. We talked."

"And your point being? I am quite aware your father was here."

Amelia swallowed hard, and before her courage splintered into a train wreck at her feet, she whispered, "He told me that you might care to see me again. That perhaps you've been unhappy since you left . . . me."

A short, dark laugh rent the air. "And in your arrogance, you believed him? Well let me clarify my position. If I was at all unhappy, it was not due to our parting but due to my own gullibility. That for even one second I believed you to be anything than the utterly selfish and feckless woman I met the year before."

Amelia's head dropped as if her neck couldn't bear the

weight. She closed her eyes briefly and drew in a shaky breath. "Since Christmas, I've wished to apologize for my behavior toward you. I've long realized how truly abominable I'd been. But as I thought we had become close . . ."

At her words, Thomas abruptly turned from her. Amelia raised her head and viewed the black jacket covering the broad expanse of his back. Despair caused a tight knot to form in her throat. She should go. He was lost to her. Any affection he'd had toward her was obviously long gone. But she wouldn't leave until she'd said what she had to say. She refused to be her father, living his life with those kind of regrets. Regretting that he hadn't tried harder, hadn't pushed for explanations when she'd grown cold and distant, hadn't fought to keep her affections. He hadn't fought for her love.

"Once I believed you intended to ask my father for my hand."

Thomas slowly turned to face her. He regarded her in silence, his expression closed, his gaze hooded. A vein in his temple jumped. "Obviously a supreme lapse in judgment on my part."

His cool dismissal stabbed at her heart. "Mr. Cromwell, Lord Clayborough, neither truly meant anything to me. They were both just means of getting out from under my father's roof. Men who would demand little of me and I of them."

His expression did not shift. He did not blink. He merely regarded her with a cold, blank-eyed stare. "None of that matters now, as I said I will no longer be making that offer." He paused. "No doubt you'll soon find another marriage prospect." A hint of dry sarcasm fractured the coldness of his tone.

Amelia advanced closer, her gaze locked with his, willing him to show the barest hint of softening, anything to indicate he still cared—if only a little. He only stiffened, his jaw tight, drawing himself up to his full height.

"I couldn't marry Lord Clayborough. I can't marry any other man. Do you know why? Because I'm in love with you," she said quickly before her courage deserted her altogether. She halted in front of him, her head tipped to meet his gaze. "I love you, Thomas."

For a moment Thomas said nothing, did nothing, just stood fighting to control his emotions. She looked so beautiful, so vulnerable. He yearned to pull her into his arms. How he'd missed the taste and feel of her. He missed her indefatigable passion. But she'd let him walk away that night. Hadn't tried to stop him. He'd made a fool of himself over a woman once before, and damn if he'd do it again.

"Is that what you wanted to say?" He made his voice cold. "If so, you've wasted both our time."

"So what you felt for me is gone? In a month's time, it is gone?" her words emerged choked, raw with emotion.

The pain he'd buried inside him since he'd left exploded. Gone? What he wouldn't give that it was so. Unable to articulate his response, he inclined his head in a curt nod.

The light in her eyes went out like a snuffed candle. She turned her back to him, her arms wrapped tightly about her slender torso. He thought she was collecting herself, controlling her emotions, until her shoulders began to heave. Pitiful and desperate sobs shook her body as she stuffed fisted hands to her eyes. He knew what those tears had cost her. The last vestiges of seven years of control. She'd shed them only for him. Because she loved him, wanted him. Only him.

Thomas thought his head would burst and the ache in his heart would never subside. Watching her was more than any man could bear, never mind a man who loved her to his very soul.

"I love you, Thomas." She sobbed it. She chanted it. The sweet melody of the sound echoed throughout the room.

He couldn't stand anymore. Turning her around, he pulled her into his arms, absorbing her tears with his jacket.

"God, please don't cry, Amelia. Do you want to cripple me?" he asked, his voice hoarse with emotion.

Her response was to wrap her arms tightly around his neck, and pull his mouth to hers in a desperate kiss. He tasted her tears and tasted the sweetness of her lips, neither able to savor, their need frightening in its intensity. Tongues met, teeth clashed, hands grappled for the other.

His hands sought her hips and then moved to cup her buttocks, pulling her hard against his throbbing erection. He could think of nothing else but laying her out on the rug and losing himself in her slick warmth, taking her again and again.

Releasing her mouth, his lips trailed her cheek to feather the back of her ear. Amelia let out a whimper. "I want you now," he said on a groan. "Let's go upstairs."

Passion-drugged, glassy eyes stared up at him. "But the ball—"

He cut her off with a hard kiss. "I don't care about the ball. I've had to survive almost one month without you. Tonight, I'm going to make love to you until I've had my fill—at least for tonight." He would never get enough of her.

Without another word, he whisked her up to his chambers.

In short order he had them out of their clothes, black wool, lavender silk, and white muslin littering the floor. They came together in a burst of passion, desperate for the feel of their naked flesh in fiery contact. He kissed her deeply, plunging into her helplessly, his control long gone. She met every delectable stroke as her thighs encircled his hips. When Thomas felt the exquisite pressure of her contractions pulsing around him, he thrust into her one final time. Then he let himself go. His own peak catapulted him into unspeakable, unfathomable pleasure before he finally shuddered in completion. Limp and spent, he rested atop her, the brunt of his weight at her side, while he remained snug inside her.

* * *

Amelia never wanted to move from this position. Turning slightly on her side, she pulled him closer, her arms tight around his sweaty torso. "Does this mean you forgive me?"

Thomas made a sound between a groan and a laugh. "For that, I'd forgive you almost anything." His eyes grew serious as he gazed at her. "Will you marry me?"

Tears pricked the corners of her eyes. Amelia could only manage a nod as tears began to stream down her face.

"God, Princess, don't cry," he said in a pained voice. With his thumbs, he wiped the tears from her cheeks before pressing a long, tender kiss against her parted lips. "I love you. There will be no more running away for either of us."

Amelia wanted to laugh at his teasing tone, but tears continued unabated as if released from their prison of seven years. "Do you believe me when I say I never loved Mr. Cromwell or Lord Clayborough? Neither of them. Never."

"Yes, because you saved yourself for me."

Smiling through her tears, Amelia nodded. "And you were well worth it. If you want, I shall publicly attest to the supremacy of your sexual prowess," she teased, planting a kiss on the side of his smooth jaw.

"I'm content in the knowledge that the only woman who will judge my performance is more than satisfied." He smiled a wicked smile.

"I would say 'more than satisfied' is a vast understatement," Amelia whispered, her voice husky with desire. She then went on to demonstrate how an appreciative woman *showed* her appreciation.

More by Bestselling Author
Hannah Howell

Available Wherever Books Are Sold!

Check out our website at
http://www.kensingtonbooks.com

More by Bestselling Author

Janet Dailey

Available Wherever Books Are Sold!

Check out our website at **www.kensingtonbooks.com**

Books by Bestselling Author
Fern Michaels